TRUE
BELIEVERS

TRUE BELIEVERS

a mystery

MICHAEL BLAIR

Author's Note
The following is a work of fiction. Some of the locations in this book are real, although not necessarily as portrayed, but all events and characters are fictional and any resemblance to actual events or people, living, dead or extraterrestrial, is purely coincidental.

Cover design: Debbie Geltner
Cover photo: Matt Sutkoski
Author photo: Terence Byrnes
Book design: WildElement.ca

Printed and bound in Canada by Imprimerie Gauvin.

Library and Archives Canada Cataloguing in Publication

Blair, Michael, 1946-, author
True believers : a novel / by Michael Blair.

Issued in print and electronic formats.
ISBN 978-1-927535-64-6 (pbk.).--ISBN 978-1-927535-65-3 (epub).--
ISBN 978-1-927535-66-0 (mobi).--ISBN 978-1-927535-67-7 (pdf)

I. Title.
PS8553.L3354T78 2015   C813'.6   C2014-906288-5
                                                  C2014-906289-3

The publisher gratefully acknowledges the support of the Canada Council for the Arts and SODEC.

Linda Leith Publishing Inc.
P.O. Box 322, Victoria Station, Westmount QC H3Z 2V8 Canada
www.lindaleith.com

Audrey Ellen Blair

(1922 – 2011)

"Sir, there is a distinct difference between having an open mind and having a hole in your head from which your brain leaks out."
—James Randi

"What is it that compels a person, past all reason, to believe the unbelievable?"
—M. Lamar Keene

"Gullibility kills."
—Carl Sagan

Tuesday
DAY 1

1

At 7:15 on a blustery Tuesday morning in December, Myrtle Sanders, a retired school teacher and part-time "Grim & Bare It" greeting card writer, was walking her five-year-old rescued greyhound Spider along the bricked footpath on the edge of Burlington Bay, between the ECHO Lake Science Center and the Coast Guard station. A bitter northwest wind boomed in off Lake Champlain, an early Christmas present from Canada, whipping spume from the tops of the white caps beyond the breakwater. Overnight, the temperature had dropped to below freezing, and in the calm water inside the breakwater, a scum of ice had formed along the rocky shoreline. The little automated lighthouses at the north and south ends of the breakwater were still on, bright white lights surrounded by frosty nimbuses of morning mist. All in all, Myrtle thought, it was a typical Vermont December morning.

She wouldn't think so for long.

Spider, natty in his red tartan vest and booties, strained

at his leash, breath steaming, dim memories of mechanical rabbits urging him to run. Although the adoption agency frowned on letting greyhounds run free, Myrtle released Spider from his leash. With a doggish leap of joy, Spider galloped across the frost-rimed grass alongside the path, but after twenty yards or so he faltered and slowed, then stopped and looked about. Myrtle sighed and shook her head. Poor creature, she thought, and whistled. Spider bounded back to her, skidding to a halt and bumping his narrow head against her thighs.

"Stupid thing," she said fondly, rubbing his small silky ears with her bare hand.

She started to reattach his leash when Spider decided it would be fun to play on the ice and bounded down the rocky embankment to the edge of the bay.

"You fall through, you damned fool," Myrtle called, "don't expect me to come rescue you."

She clambered down after him. Spider ran out onto the ice, slipped, sprawled, tried to stand, and sprawled again. Finally, finding his ice legs, he walked gingerly across the slick surface, but stayed near the shore, where the ice was thicker. Then, spying something embedded in the ice, he angled toward the thinner ice farther from shore.

"Come back here, you idiot," Myrtle called. He ignored her. "Spidey. Come. Hot dog. Hot dog."

She took a frozen frankfurter out of her coat pocket and waved it at him, but as much as Spider liked franks, he'd found something much more interesting. He began pawing at an object partially embedded in the ice about

3

fifteen feet from shore. Oh, god, Myrtle thought, peering nearsightedly at the shape in the ice. He's found a dead dog or something; it was too big to be a fish or a seagull. She edged out for a closer look, but eased back toward shore when she felt the ice crack beneath her boots.

"Spider, get back here."

Spider whined and scrabbled at the object in the ice.

"Goddamnit," she shouted. "Get back here this minute."

The ice gave way, and Spider plunged into the icy water. Fortunately, it was not deep, barely halfway up Spider's deep chest. The thing Spider had been pawing at also broke free of the ice. Spider clamped his jaws onto a piece of it and began dragging it toward the shore, walking backward on his long, powerful legs, pulling desperately. It was quite a bit bigger than he was.

"Oh, shit," Myrtle said, when she saw what it was that Spider had brought ashore.

It was the body of a woman.

Myrtle dug into her pocket for her phone as Spider released the dead woman's arm and waited eagerly for his reward. He'd lost one of his red tartan booties.

When the police arrived later that morning at Hack Loomis's office on the fourth floor of the Bank Street Professional Building, he'd just hung up from a frustrating half-hour on the phone with his mother in Toronto. His ninety-two-year-old paternal grandfather Walter had had another small stroke, Helen Loomis had told him, and while his doctors said he would likely make a full recovery, they insisted that Walter stop going into the office. "All well and good," she'd said, "but I can't run the business by myself."

"You've been running it yourself for years," Loomis said. Ever since Loomis's father Christopher and older brother Denny had died in a road accident. Nearly twenty years. Had it really been that long?

"Nevertheless," she said, "it's long past time you accepted your responsibilities, came home, and took over the business."

Loomis Brewers was the third largest craft brewery in the Province of Ontario and while Loomis didn't mind a beer or two now and again, he had no interest in making the stuff. And besides, he'd reminded her, he'd built a life for himself in Burlington and nothing had changed since the last time she'd raised the subject. (Well, that wasn't entirely true: his relationship with Connie Noble had moved to a different level the night before last, when they'd slept together for the first time in the two years since she'd come to work for him.) So what was it that made him feel so guilty about not wanting to return home, make beer, and probably a vat-load of money to boot? Damned if he knew.

On the other hand, he grumbled to himself after saying goodbye and hanging up the phone, why not go home and make a vat-load of money? What would he really be giving up? Business was lousy, his ex-wife was driving him crazy, and Phil Jefferson, his former father-in-law and erstwhile employer, was constantly on his case about coming back to work for his security company. Maybe, Loomis thought, what he was feeling wasn't guilt at all. Maybe it was stupidity.

As for Connie, maybe she'd be willing to come with him. There wasn't much keeping her in Burlington, not since her husband Sam had died three years before of heart failure while running a marathon, leaving her with a mountain of debt and two kids. Her parents had retired to Florida the year before, and her sister lived in New York City. It was early days yet in their relationship, but—

He sat up with a start when someone banged on the outer door of the office.

Hauling himself to his feet, he went to Connie's desk in the outer office and pressed the button that released the door lock. The door swung open and the tallest man Loomis had ever known came into the office, ducking to get through the door without knocking his fedora off. He was Detective Alex Robillard of the Burlington Police Department major case squad. Loomis had known him from almost the first day he'd arrived in Burlington ten years before. He'd introduced Loomis to Phil Jefferson and, consequently, Jefferson's daughter Veejay, aka Valerie-Jean, Loomis's ex-wife. Once upon a time Loomis and Robillard had been friends. Maybe they still were, Loomis wasn't sure. Things had cooled off between them since he'd hung out his private investigator's shingle.

Following on Robillard's heels was a woman, also in civilian clothes and carrying a briefcase. Robillard's new partner, Loomis presumed. She was about Loomis's age, which was forty-four, fair-skinned, dark-eyed, compact and sturdy, her sandy hair cropped short. Loomis wondered if she'd last longer than Robillard's previous partner.

"What's up, Alex?" Loomis said. "Who's your friend?"

"Detective Vivian Scott. Viv, meet John Loomis, aka Hack. Don't ask him why."

"Mr. Loomis," Scott said. She didn't offer to shake hands.

"Would you like some coffee?" Loomis said. "It's relatively fresh."

"This isn't a social call," Robillard said.

"All right. No coffee. What can I do for you?"

"For a start," Robillard said, "can you account for your whereabouts between 6 p.m. Friday before last and 6 p.m. the following Monday?"

"Really?" Loomis said. "Probably. Why?"

"Just do it, all right," Robillard said. He sighed. "Don't give us a hard time, Hack. I know it's not something that comes naturally to you, but try. Please. This is serious."

Loomis went into his office, got his daily agenda from his desk, and returned to the outer office. He leafed back through half a dozen pages, then closed the agenda and put it down on Connie's desk.

"I don't really need this," he said. "Thursday till late Saturday afternoon I was working for Trevor Jefferson repairing the foundation of a house in Colchester. Sunday I did some work on my own house. Monday I was here."

"Business that good, eh?" Robillard said, as Scott scribbled in her notebook. "Maybe you should take up general contracting full time."

"Screw you, Alex," Loomis said, with a weary sigh. He looked at Scott. "You don't have to write that down."

"You should watch your mouth," she said with a scowl. It didn't look good on her.

"It's all right," Robillard said. "Mr. Loomis doesn't mean any disrespect."

"The hell I don't," Loomis said.

Robillard ignored the remark. "Can anyone verify that you were at home on Sunday and here on Monday?"

"Sunday," Loomis said. "No, I don't suppose so, unless some of my neighbours saw me. I did make a couple of calls, though. Monday, Connie was here till about three. That's Mrs. Connie Noble," he added for Scott's benefit. "She should be here soon."

He felt a sudden chill that had nothing to do with the weather. Connie was over an hour late. Despite the overnight deep-freeze, the roads were clear and dry, and Connie was a good driver, but the number of lunatics on the roads seemed to increase each year.

"Now would be a good time to tell me what this is all about," Loomis said.

Robillard nodded at Scott, who opened her briefcase on Connie's desk and took out a clear plastic evidence bag. She handed it to Robillard. He held it up for Loomis's inspection.

"You recognize this?"

"It looks like a business card," Loomis said, but one that had been through the wash cycle in someone's pocket.

"It's one of yours," Robillard said.

Loomis took the evidence bag from Robillard, turned on Connie's desk lamp and examined the front side of the card. It did indeed appear to be one of his. He turned the bag over to see if there was anything written on the back of the card. There wasn't. He handed the evidence bag back to Robillard.

"Okay, it's one of my business cards," he said. "Where'd you find it?"

"The body of a woman," Robillard said. "Twenty-five to thirty-five. Found early this morning partly frozen into the ice at the edge of the bay near the Coast Guard station. She'd been in the water a week at least, the ME says. We found your card in the pocket of her hiking pants. Have you got time to help us out with an ID?"

"Sure," Loomis said. "Just tell me where and when."

"The body's on its way to the ME's office." He looked at his watch. "Should be there now."

"All right," Loomis said.

"Thanks," Robillard said, sounding as if he meant it. Even Vivian Scott's expression thawed to a few degrees above absolute zero.

Loomis opened the door for them. Connie Noble was standing in the hallway, reaching for the door handle. Her cheeks were rosy from the cold, and her thick, dark-blonde hair was mussed from the wind.

"Good morning, Mrs. Noble," Robillard said, tugging the brim of his hat. Loomis was surprised by the rather old-fashioned gesture of deference.

"Detective," Connie said, glancing at Vivian Scott.

Robillard introduced Connie and Scott, then turned to Loomis. "Sorry for crack about your business," he said.

"Don't lose any sleep over it," Loomis said.

"Oh, I won't," Robillard said.

The two detectives went down the hall to the elevators, Robillard's Mutt to Scott's Jeff. Or was it the other way around? Connie and Loomis went into the office.

"What did they want?" she said, unwinding her six-foot-long scarf from around her neck. When Loomis told her, she rewound her scarf. "I'll come with you. I might know who it is."

"Really? Who?"

"I'll explain in the car."

2

"Sorry I was late," she said, as they got on to the elevator. He pressed the button for the ground floor. "My car wouldn't start, and I had to wait an hour for triple A." She drove a ten-year-old VW Jetta. Loomis had helped her buy it when she'd had to give up the lease on the BMW X3 her husband Sam had given her on her thirty-sixth birthday, the year before he died.

"You should have called," Loomis said. "I have jumper cables."

"What's the point in having a triple A membership then?"

"Is everything all right?" he asked, as the elevator door opened on the ground floor.

"Sure, of course."

He followed her out into the lobby. "I mean with us."

"I know what you mean."

When they were in Loomis's Outback, driving east on Pearl toward the Chief Medical Examiner's office on the

University of Vermont campus, Loomis said, "You don't have any regrets about the other night, do you?"

"No." Her expression became troubled. "Do you?"

"Hell, no," he said.

"Are you sure?"

"Yes, I'm sure. It's just I know from bitter experience that mixing business and romance isn't always a good idea. Look how well it worked out with Veejay."

"I'm not Veejay," Connie said, an edge in her voice. "And I don't appreciate being compared to her."

"Believe me," he said with feeling. "There's no comparison."

"But you're uncomfortable about our being lovers," she said.

"Is that what we are? Lovers?"

"I know it sounds pretentious," she said. "But I'm too old to call you my boyfriend. My daughter has boyfriends—I hope to god she doesn't have a lover yet." Connie's daughter Susan was fourteen.

"Does that mean I'm too old to have a girlfriend?" He grinned across the car at her.

"You can have all the girlfriends you want, as long as I'm your only lover."

"Fair enough," Loomis said. After a moment's silence, he said, "So who do you think Alex's floater might be?"

"I think it might be Belle Ryerson," Connie said.

Belle Ryerson was the office manager of Proctor, Proctor and McHenry, the law firm that occupied the top floor of the Bank Street Professional Building, in which

Loomis's office was located. She was plain and pleasant woman, about the same age as Connie, who had just turned forty, with a penchant for flower-print dresses and sensible shoes.

"When was the last time you saw her?" Loomis said.

"Friday afternoon."

"Then it's not her," Loomis said. "Alex's floater has been in the water a week or more, he said."

"A week," Connie said, relieved.

"That's the preliminary estimate," Loomis said. "They won't know for sure till they do the postmortem, but it was a week at least, according to the ME. You still want to come? Won't be pretty."

"I think I can handle it," she said. "Besides, if she had one of your business cards, I might know who she is."

"Why did you think it might have been Belle?"

"We were supposed to meet on Saturday afternoon, but she didn't turn up. There was something she wanted to talk about, she said, but she didn't want to say what it was until she'd spoken to someone else. It isn't like her to cancel an appointment without calling. She didn't come into work yesterday, either. I tried her at home, but all I got was her voice mail. Her cellphone goes straight to voice mail, too. I was going to go upstairs to see if she'd come into work today."

"Has she been reported missing?"

She shook her head. "I don't think so. I tried calling her sister, but got her voice mail, too. I left a message, but she hasn't called back."

"Maybe there was a family emergency," Loomis said.

"I'm sure she would have called me," she said.

"I didn't know you were close," he said.

"We've become friends in the last year or two. I don't think she has many friends. She's not very comfortable socially." She smiled at Loomis as they turned into the University of Vermont campus. "You're probably right. There was a family emergency and she didn't have time to call me. I'm worrying for nothing."

"Let's hope so," Loomis said.

Loomis didn't know the dead woman. Neither did Connie. Alex Robillard's disappointment was obvious.

"Take a good look," he said. "She might not look the same after spending a week in the water."

"No shit," Loomis said, earning a scowl from Scott.

The dead woman lay on a gurney in the refrigerated storage room the ME's office, where she awaited autopsy. Her clothing had been removed and a white sheet was draped over her, leaving only her head, shoulders and arms exposed. Once she might have been pretty, Loomis thought, but her face was bloated, skin stretched and unnaturally translucent, and her long dark hair looked like strings of lake weed. In fact, she looked just like you'd expect someone to look after spending a week or more in the water, nibbled by crawfish, pecked by gulls, and scoured by rocks. There were what appeared to be dog-bite marks on her left arm. Postmortem, Robillard had explained.

"Mrs. Noble?"

"I'm sure. I've never seen her before."

Robillard held up the evidence bag containing Loomis's business card. "What about this?"

"What about it?" Loomis said. "There are probably hundreds of them floating around—sorry, poor choice of words. She could have picked one up anywhere. I hand them out like candy, leave them in my dentist's office, laundromats, supermarkets, public washrooms—"

"Okay," Robillard said. "I get the idea. Has a woman contacted you recently about hiring you?"

"No," Loomis said. No one had.

Connie shook her head.

"All right, thanks," Robillard said. "If you think of anything …"

"We know how to reach you," Loomis said.

Robillard nodded to Scott, who smiled at Connie as she escorted her and Loomis to the door. She held the door for Connie, but let it swing shut on Loomis. He was hurt that she didn't seem to like him.

"So?" he said, as he zipped up the collar of his coat. The temperature had gone up slightly, to a degree or two above dangerous for brass monkeys, but a penetrating wind added a significant chill factor. "Any idea how that woman came to have our business card." He unlocked the car with the remote.

"As you said, there are plenty of them around."

"Yeah," Loomis said as he started the car and turned up the heater. "Too bad they don't seem to be generating any business."

Back at the office, Loomis put on a fresh pot of coffee. Connie had gone straight up to Proctor, Proctor and McHenry to see if Belle had come into work. The coffee had just finished brewing when Connie came into the office, a worried expression on her face.

"No luck?" he said.

"No," she said. "She hasn't called in, either."

She took off her scarf and coat and hung them on the tree by the door. She was wearing black jeans and a thick, off-white cable-knit sweater that suited her well. Hell, a gunnysack would have suited her well, Loomis thought, but he was biased. At a fraction of an inch under six feet in her socks, she was raw-boned and limber, with just the right amount of solid subcutaneous fat to soften the edges. Loomis felt a sudden rush of desire as he recalled how she'd felt in his arms the night before last, radiating heat, silken and slippery with arousal.

"What?" she said, looking at him as if she knew precisely what he was thinking.

"Nothing," he said. "Now what?"

"I'm going to try her sister again." Referring to a slip of paper, she keyed a number into her desk phone and a moment later said, "Hazel, it's Connie Noble again. It's 10:40 Tuesday morning. I'm sorry to be a nuisance, but I'm worried about Belle. Please call me." She reeled off a string of phone numbers—office, home, and cell—then added, "Thanks." She put down the phone.

"Her sister's name is Hazel?" Loomis said.

16

"Yes. Why?"

"It's not a name you hear much these days."

"I suppose not." She slumped into the old wood swivel chair at her desk. It creaked under her weight.

"What do you want to do?" Loomis asked, propping a buttock on the corner of her desk, looking down at her.

"About Belle?"

"All right. About Belle."

"I don't know. I thought maybe you'd …" She paused, looking up at him.

"What? Look for her? You're a detective too, you know," he said.

Probationary, anyway. She had her temporary licence and was working on completing the two thousand hours of on-the-job experience required for a permanent private investigator's licence. In the past year she'd submitted the requisite two sets of fingerprints, taken the forty hours of basic training, including firearms training, passed the state examinations with flying colours, and, most important, paid the state licensing fees.

"But you don't even know for sure she's missing," he said. "Did you talk to Dink?"

D. Lincoln "Dink" McHenry was the managing partner of Proctor, Proctor and McHenry, and Belle's boss. He had been Sam Noble's lawyer and had helped Connie sort out the mess she'd been left with after he'd died. When Loomis had first hung out his private investigator's shingle after leaving Jefferson Security, he'd worked regularly for McHenry's firm, but that had dried up to nothing in the past two years.

"No," she said, shaking her head. "He was with a client. I spoke to the receptionist. But, well, maybe you could talk to him."

"Me? I haven't spoken to him since he accused me of sleeping with his wife."

"What?" Her eyes widened. "You didn't ...?"

"No, of course not. Lizzie and I became friends, sort of, when I was doing some work for the mayor's office." Elizabeth Latimer McHenry, a former talking head on Channel Seven, was special assistant to the mayor. "It was a couple of years ago, just before I met you. We got together a few times for drinks or dinner. We didn't have much in common except unhappy marriages, but at least mine was behind me. She's a nice lady."

"Not to mention drop dead gorgeous," Connie said, with a dry smile.

"If you like 'em sleek and blonde and elegant," Loomis said.

"And you don't?"

Loomis sensed a trap. "Sure I do. Lizzie McHenry may be a nine on the sleek, blonde and elegant scale, but you're an eleven at least."

"Nice recovery."

"Thank you," Loomis said. "Anyway, I haven't seen her in two years. Or had any work from McHenry, for that matter. But why me? He's still your lawyer, isn't he?"

"I suppose," she said, colouring and looking at the floor. "But he tends to be very, well, hands-on. When

18

we were sorting things out after Sam died he was always touching my arm, putting his hand on my shoulder or on my back, patting my knee. It's meant to be reassuring, I suppose, but it creeps me out. Whenever I've had to speak to him recently I've tried to keep my distance, but …" Her smile was wry. "I think I offended him."

"You have to have some degree of sensitivity to take offense," Loomis said.

Something occurred to him. While Belle wasn't as attractive as Connie, in his opinion, anyway, she was far from ugly, and under her flowered dresses she appeared to have a decent figure.

"Could he and Belle be having an affair?"

"God, no," Connie said, shaking her head.

"It wouldn't be the first time he's wandered from the reservation," Loomis said. "And word on the street is Lizzie has left him again, for good this time. Maybe Belle's the reason."

Connie shook her head again. "She'd have told me if she were sleeping with him. Or let it slip—she isn't a very devious person. I don't think she even has a boyfriend." She smiled. "Or a lover. Anyway, even if she were sleeping with him, that doesn't explain why she didn't keep her appointment with me on Saturday."

"All right," Loomis said. "It's not like we've got anything better to do. Let's talk to her sister." Who knows? he thought. If Belle Ryerson really is missing, her sister might even hire them to look for her.

"Thanks, Hack," Connie said, standing and putting

her arms around his neck. She smelled nice. She felt nice, too. And she was one of the few women he knew who could look him nearly straight in the eye.

She kissed him quickly, stepped back and, crossing her arms, grasped the hem of her thick sweater and swept it off over her head, causing Loomis a moment of cardiac turbulence until he saw that under her sweater she was wearing a T-shirt.

"Whew," she said. "It's warm in here."

"You're right about that," he said.

3

Before they went out, Connie tried Belle's home and cell-phone numbers and Hazel Ryerson's home number, but in all cases got voice mail again.

"Where does Belle live?" Loomis asked, as they headed down to the car.

"They both live in their parents' old house in Winooski," Connie said. Winooski was a community of seven thousand or so, about half an hour northeast of Burlington.

In the car, Loomis said, "Okay, tell me everything you know about Belle and her sister. Mom, too."

"She died five years ago."

"Of what?" Loomis asked, more out of idle curiosity than suspicion.

"Natural causes, I suppose," Connie replied. "She was well into her seventies and had MS. Their father's been dead for twenty years or so."

"Belle's what, forty?"

"Thirty-nine. Hazel's two years older."

"Is Hazel married?"

"No. Belle and Hazel shared the care of their mother for the last fifteen years of her life, pretty much since their father died. Ted Proctor Junior was the family lawyer and the executor of their mother's estate. Since Mr. Proctor retired, Dink McHenry has been Belle and Hazel's lawyer, I suppose. I met Belle after Sam died, but didn't really get to know her till last fall when I ran into her at an exhibition of work by local artists. I've never met Hazel."

"When did Belle start working for McHenry?"

"Shortly after her mother died."

"Did she work during the years she and Hazel looked after Mom?"

"Yes. Some kind of part-time office work."

"What does Hazel do?"

"She's a freelance writer, apparently. Mainly scientific and technical. Belle told me she does a lot of work for the municipal and state governments. She works from home."

"Did Mom leave them anything else, besides the house?"

"There was some money. A fair amount, I think. Their father was a successful businessman. Transportation and warehousing. Oh." She paled. "Do you think she might have been kidnapped for ransom?"

"No, I don't," Loomis said. "If Hazel is waiting for a ransom call, don't you think she'd answer the phone?"

"Yes," Connie said, relieved. "I suppose she would."

Belle and Hazel Ryerson lived in a rambling old farmhouse set back from a wide, tree-lined street a stone's throw from the Winooski River. Loomis parked in the driveway behind an aging black Nissan Sentra that looked as if it hadn't moved in months. The yard was tidy behind a trimmed cedar hedge, lawn turning brown under a tall old spruce.

Loomis liked the Ryerson sisters' house. A deep, covered veranda ran the full width of the house, and a screen door at the south end led to a screened-in sleeping porch. There was an old wood glider on the veranda, painted green, seat cushions removed, and he could see wicker furniture stacked in the porch for the winter. The front door had a leaded stained-glass window, in a floral pattern, and the doorbell was a twist-knob centred beneath the window. It sounded like a bicycle bell when Loomis twisted it. Almost immediately a face appeared in the window, distorted by the old glass. The door opened to the extent the chain lock allowed, and a woman peered through the gap.

Loomis took of his hat. "Hazel Ryerson?"

"You're not the courier," she said.

"No," Loomis said. "My name's Hack Loomis. This—"

"Whatever you're selling, I'm not interested." She started to close the door.

"I'm a friend of your sister's," Connie said quickly, placing her hand against the door. "My name's Connie Noble."

"What do you want?"

23

Hazel Ryerson had interesting eyes, Loomis thought, well spaced and slate grey, but at that moment they were hard and narrow with suspicion.

"Do you know where she is?" Connie asked.

"At work I presume," Hazel Ryerson said. "Where else would she be?"

"She hasn't been at work since Friday," Connie said.

"When was the last time you saw her?" Loomis said.

"Are you the police?"

"No," Loomis said. He took out his wallet to show her his ID and investigator's licence. "We're private investigators."

She took the wallet, lifted a pair of reading glasses that hung on a cord around her neck, and examined his ID closely before handing the wallet back and lowering the glasses.

"Are you investigating my sister? What has she done?"

"She hasn't done anything," Loomis said. "May we come in? It's cold out here."

She studied them for a moment, grey eyes shifting from him to Connie and back. He waited patiently, hat in hand, trying to look his most benign. Then she released the chain lock and stepped back.

"Thank you," he said, stepping aside to let Connie precede him into the house. He followed, and Hazel Ryerson shut the door behind them.

About five and a half feet tall, Hazel Ryerson had the kind of features Loomis associated with aerialists and Russian ballerinas, attractive but too sculpted and angular to be called pretty. Her complexion was clear and pale, as though she didn't get out much, and her hair was streaky blonde, worn just a little longer than Connie's. She might have been slimmer than her sister, but it was hard to tell: she was wearing at least four layers of clothing. He realized then that it wasn't much warmer inside the house than outside. He wondered if the old house's heating system had broken down or, despite having inherited a sum of money, the Ryerson sisters were simply frugal. Loomis and Connie kept their coats on.

"Why are you inquiring about Belle?" Hazel Ryerson said.

"We were supposed to meet on Saturday," Connie said. "But she didn't turn up or call to cancel. I haven't spoken to her since Friday, and she hasn't been at work so far this week. I've been trying to reach you, but you haven't been answering your phone or returning calls."

"I'm on a deadline," Hazel Ryerson said, as if that explained everything.

"When was the last time you saw her?" Loomis said again.

"Last week. Or maybe the week before. I don't remember exactly."

"This is a big house," Loomis said. "But it's not that big."

"She has her own apartment," Hazel Ryerson said. "With a separate entrance. You're worrying for nothing, Ms. Noble. My sister's hobby is hiking and wildlife photography. She's most likely off in the woods taking pictures of some migratory bird."

Surely, Loomis thought, any bird with an iota of sense had already gone south. "Does she often go off for days at a time without telling you?" he said. "Or her employer?"

"No, not often," Hazel Ryerson said. "But it has happened. Now, I really must get back to work. Thank you for your concern, Ms. Noble, but I'm certain my sister is fine."

"Would you mind if we took a look at her apartment?"

"I'm not sure I can allow that," Hazel Ryerson said. "My sister is a very private person."

"Please," Connie said. "I'm very worried about her." The slight emphasis on "I'm" suggested that Connie thought Hazel should be, too. Loomis could see she was wavering.

"Oh, all right," she said, after a moment. She took a set of keys from a hook by the front door. "My sister's rooms are this way."

She led them to the back of the house, to a stout wood connecting door. It was not one of the cheap hollow-core interior doors used in the construction of more recent houses, such as Loomis's own, and it was equipped with a sturdy deadbolt lock. Hazel Ryerson sorted through the keys on the key ring, found the one she wanted, and unlocked the door. The hinges creaked, as though the door hadn't been opened for some time.

"Let me look around first," Loomis said. He was going to add, "Just in case," but before he could stop her, Hazel Ryerson went through into her sister's part of the house.

He and Connie followed.

He hadn't seen much of Hazel's living space, but what he had seen was spare, utilitarian verging on spartan. The living room of Belle's apartment contained enough furniture for two rooms. Most of it was old. Overstuffed easy chairs and sofas, dark wood end tables and chairs, lamps with shaggy shades, brooding cabinets, gaudy Persian carpets that had seen better days, Victorian throw-rugs on top of the carpets, perhaps to hide the worn spots. Loomis was afraid to move lest he knock over a lamp or trip over a hassock.

"After our father died," Hazel said, reading his mind, "my sister and I converted the back half of the house into an apartment for ourselves. After Mother died, I moved into the front. When I redecorated I wanted to get rid of Mother's furniture, but Belle wouldn't hear of it and moved it all back here."

Hazel opened heavy brocade draperies. Wintry sunlight filled the room.

Loomis breathed in a snout full of air, slowly, tasting it in the back of his sinuses. Belle's apartment was stuffy, and the old furniture gave off a dry musty smell, like mouldering hay. There was also a faint hint of some kind of room deodorizer, sweet and flowery. He didn't smell anything nasty—Belle kept her place warmer than Hazel did—but he didn't want to take any chances.

"Wait here," he said to Hazel.

"What are you doing? Oh." She put her hand to her mouth. "You don't think ..." She swallowed, turning even paler, which sharpened the angles of her face.

"Connie will stay with you," he said.

He checked the ground floor first—kitchen, half-bath, utility room/summer kitchen behind the main kitchen—then went upstairs and checked the master bedroom, spare room/home office, and main bathroom, which was equipped with fixtures from the 1930s at least, showing their age, but immaculately clean. Satisfied that Belle was not in the house, either dead, unconscious or hiding, he called down to Hazel and Connie.

"Okay, all clear."

Connie and Hazel came up the stairs.

"If she was going on a trip, even a short one," Loomis said, "she'd pack clothing. Would you know what was missing if she'd packed just the necessities?"

"I might," Hazel said.

Loomis and Connie followed her into Belle's bedroom. Like the rest of the house, the bedroom was furnished with too much massively dark furniture, Victorian and Edwardian, with the odd piece of Art Nouveau and Art Deco. Not your typical American homestead, Loomis thought, as Hazel checked Belle's dresser drawers. But she could not say for certain if they contained more or less than the usual amount of socks, underwear or bras. Then she looked in the closet.

"Her backpack is still here," she said, voice hollow.

She pulled a backpack out of the closet. Considerably larger than the small daypack Connie sometimes carried, Belle's backpack looked to Loomis like a serious piece of hiking gear, with padded shoulder straps, sturdy hip straps, lots of smaller straps for adjusting fit, mesh water bottle pockets, and a web of bungee cords on the back.

"If she'd gone on a trip she'd have taken her backpack," Hazel said. "Her boots and hiking poles are here, too."

Dropping the backpack, Hazel abruptly left Belle's bedroom. Loomis and Connie followed her down the hall to the other bedroom, which was Belle's home office. There was a closed MacBook Pro laptop on the drop-down panel of antique writing desk, with an inkjet printer on the top of the desk. The chair in front of the writing desk was a modern ergonomic office chair, equipped with half a dozen levers and knobs to adjust attitude, pitch and yaw.

Opposite the desk stood a rustic pine two-door wardrobe. Hazel tried the door, but it was locked. Loomis found a letter opener on Belle's desk and, with Hazel's permission, easily popped open the doors. One side of the wardrobe was a closet, in which hung an old raccoon coat and a long, yellowing wedding dress, both in dry cleaning bags. A pair of shoes that matched the dress, also wrapped in plastic, sat neatly on the floor of the wardrobe.

"Our mother's wedding dress," Hazel said.

Really? Loomis thought. *I'd never have guessed.*

The other side of the wardrobe contained three shelves above three drawers. The top shelf held books on geology, wildlife photography, birds of northeastern North America, and New England flora and fauna. On the middle shelf were Belle's cameras: two 35-mm SLR camera bodies, both professional-level Nikons and not particularly old, as film cameras go, but made virtually obsolete by the Nikon digital SLR that sat between them, likewise a top-of-the-line model. The bottom shelf held a selection of lenses of various focal lengths and a pair of big Bausch & Lomb binoculars.

"Does she have any other cameras?"

"Just a small one she carries in her purse," Hazel said.

Loomis checked the wardrobe drawers. The top two contained accessories for the cameras, more lenses, filters, flashes, and so forth. The bottom drawer contained miscellaneous bits and pieces, plus manuals and warranty cards for the cameras and accessories, as well as a couple of lead-lined film bags, also made obsolete by the digital age, intended to protect high-speed film from being fogged by airport security scanners.

He went to Belle's desk, lifted the lid of the computer, and pressed the power button. The computer chimed as it powered up. While it booted, he pulled open the drawers of a utilitarian steel filing cabinet beside the desk. All four drawers contained hanging files of hundreds—perhaps thousands—of photographic prints and pages of glassine sleeves containing negative strips, neatly organized by date, none more recent than 2007, which probably was when Belle had gone digital.

The computer screen displayed an astronomical photograph of a spiral galaxy and a login window with Belle's name and a password prompt. Loomis pressed the Return key and was rewarded with a cheerful bonk. He typed "password" and pressed Return. The computer bonked again. He tried a couple more popular combinations—"123456," "qwerty"—with the same results.

"Any idea what her password might be?" Loomis said.

"No," Hazel said.

"Where do you think she could have gone?" Connie said.

"I don't know," Hazel said. "While she doesn't always keep me apprised of her movements, I can't remember the last time she went away for more than a day or two without at least leaving me a note."

"Downstairs you implied that it wasn't that unusual," Loomis said.

"I may have exaggerated slightly," she admitted.

"But it has happened?"

"Yes, but not often." Her expression was bleak.

"When she goes away, she doesn't ask you to water her plants or feed her cat."

"She doesn't have a cat," Hazel said, "and she has a system for watering her plants."

She gestured to a tall potted plant under the window at the end of the hall. There was an upended plastic soda bottle stuck into the soil, half full of water. Loomis made a mental note to try Belle's system, if he ever got a plant.

He went into Belle's bathroom, but Hazel couldn't tell him if any of Belle's toiletries were missing. Her toothbrush was still in the holder by the basin, but that didn't mean much; many people, Loomis included, had spares for travelling.

They trooped downstairs to the kitchen, where Loomis looked in the refrigerator. There was a half-gallon jug of milk, a third full, on the door shelf. The sell-by date had expired that day, but the milk still smelled all right. The crisper drawer held a plastic container of salad greens that were starting to look a little wilted and blackened around the edges. Loomis knew from experience it didn't take long for that to happen. A re-purposed margarine tub contained a grey substance that turned out to be canned tuna and mayonnaise. It smelled as good as canned tuna and mayo ever did.

Loomis looked at Connie. She was looking worried. So was Hazel. "Now that you've had a chance to think about it," he said, "do you remember when you last saw your sister?"

"No, I'm afraid not. Not exactly, anyway. I'm sorry. I've been busy wrapping up a major project. Maybe it was early last week, Monday or Tuesday."

"Did you hear her coming and going on Friday or Saturday?" Loomis asked.

"Not that I recall," Hazel said.

Although it didn't look as though Belle had intended to be away from home for any length of time, it was possible that she had gone on a trip without telling anyone. It troubled him that she wasn't answering her cellphone or acknowledging Connie's messages, but that could easily be explained by a dead battery or a lack of coverage. Still, it had been three days since she'd missed her appointment with Connie.

"Oh, god," Hazel said. "What if she's been abducted

32

by a rapist or serial killer?"

"Don't let your imagination get the better of you," Loomis said, as they returned to Hazel's part of the house. She closed but did not lock the door to Belle's apartment. "That sort of thing is rare." He thought it better not to add that it did happen from time to time. "The most likely explanation is that she's taken a trip and just forgot to tell you. Shopping, maybe, or to visit a friend."

"She hates shopping," Hazel said. "And she rarely goes anywhere without her camera. But, yes, I'm sure you're right." She didn't sound sure at all.

"It wouldn't hurt to file a missing persons report," Loomis said.

"But what if she's just gone on a trip? She'd be angry if I reported her missing for no reason. She hates people making a fuss over her."

"It's up to you," Loomis said, glancing at Connie. He looked at Hazel again. "Could your sister be a danger to herself or others? She isn't suicidal, is she?" Or homicidal, he added to himself.

"No, of course not," Hazel said, as if affronted by the suggestion. "What are you saying?"

"If you file a report," he said, "the police would take her disappearance more seriously if there's a possibility she might harm herself or others."

"Well, there isn't," Hazel insisted.

"Okay," Loomis said. "But given that she has a history of going off without telling you, they might not take her disappearance very seriously at all. She's been missing the requisite forty-eight hours, so they'll issue an alert for her car and check with area hospital emergency rooms in the event she's had an accident and lost her ID. I assume you're her emergency contact."

"Yes, I suppose I am. She's mine."

"They'll interview you, her friends and co-workers, and alert her bank and credit card companies to let them know about any activity. But beyond that there's nothing much they can do."

"They won't look for her?"

"Where would you suggest they look?" Loomis said.

"What should I do?"

Before Loomis could reply that he'd already suggested she file a missing persons report, Connie said, "We can talk to the people she works with. And her friends, if you can give us some names."

"I'm not sure ..."

"Pro bono, of course," Connie said before Loomis could stop her.

"You'd do that?" Hazel said.

No, Loomis mentally shouted as Connie said, "We'll give you, um, the rest of the day at no charge. But if we don't turn up anything and she hasn't called or come home by tomorrow, you should definitely file a missing persons report."

"All right," Hazel said.

"What can you tell us about Belle's friends?"

"Very little, I'm afraid. Nothing, in fact. Excepting yourself, she hasn't any that I know of. And until today,

I didn't know you were her friend. She's never spoken of you to me."

"No boyfriend? Girlfriend?" Loomis said, resigned to giving Hazel a day of their time. "Ex or otherwise."

"Not that I'm aware of."

"The last time you spoke to her," Loomis said, "was there anything troubling her?"

"No, not really," Hazel said. She paused.

"What do you mean, not really?" Connie said.

"Well, I think there may have been someone at work she was having a problem with."

"Dink McHenry?" Loomis said.

"What? No, not Mr. McHenry. At least, I don't think so."

"Can you be more specific? Do you recall what she said?"

"No," Hazel said. "I'm sorry. I wasn't paying much attention."

"Does she like working for Mr. McHenry?" Connie asked.

"I think so," Hazel said. "Or at least for his firm."

"Outside of work," Loomis said, "does she have any other interests, besides nature photography?"

"She likes art and music, of course, but her interest isn't active."

"Meaning she doesn't paint or play a musical instrument?"

"That's right."

He went through the litany of usual questions. "Does

she gamble or use recreational drugs?"

"No."

"What about prescription drugs?"

"She required a prescription for an antibiotic last spring, but that isn't what you mean, is it?"

"No. Painkillers, antidepressants, sleeping pills, that sort of thing."

"No."

"Does she smoke?"

"No."

"Drink?"

"In moderation."

"Has she ever been arrested or convicted of a crime?"

"No," Hazel said. "Of course not."

"What kind of car does she drive?" he asked.

"A Toyota Yaris hatchback," Hazel said. "Blue. I don't know the licence number, I'm afraid."

"Easy enough to get," Loomis said. "All right, that should do for now." He gave her one of his business cards. "If you hear from her, give us a call."

"I will."

She escorted them to the door. When she opened it, a UPS courier was climbing the steps to the veranda, a thick envelope in his hands, boxy brown truck idling on the street, tailpipe smoking in the cold. Loomis told her they'd be in touch, which she acknowledged with a nod while scribbling her signature into the UPS man's hand-held device.

4

In the car Loomis said, "The next time you want to give our time away for nothing, warn me. A heads up would've at least saved me from looking like a complete idiot."

"I'm sorry," she said. "I was afraid you'd stop me."

"Damn right I'd've stopped you," he said. "Private investigators don't work pro bono. We're not lawyers. I should take it out of your salary."

"All right, fine," she said. "I'll pay for our time and cover any expenses myself."

"I'm kidding, Connie," he said. "Besides, what else have we got to do? But you know what they say about good deeds, don't you? They seldom go unpunished. I'm going to have to come up with a suitable punishment."

"As long as it doesn't involve whips and handcuffs," she said, smiling. "Well, whips, anyway."

"Speaking of which," he said. "I still think there's a good chance Belle and McHenry are playing house."

"Based on what? Anyway, what would Belle see in

him? He's so—so *smarmy*."

"Well, for one thing," Loomis said, "he's her boss."

She shook her head. "Belle may not be the most worldly person I know, but I doubt she'd tolerate sexual harassment. Or that Dink would risk it."

"Maybe you're right," Loomis said. "But we're still going to have to talk to him." *Unfortunately*.

"Of course," she said.

"And he doesn't have to know we're working for nothing. As far as he—or anyone else—is concerned, we've been retained by Hazel Ryerson. Okay?"

"Sure."

They picked up sandwiches at the deli across Bank from the Professional Building, ham and Swiss on rye for him, tuna on whole wheat for her, and took them up to the office. Connie called upstairs and made an appointment to see McHenry at 1:30 p.m. Loomis called the BPD and spoke to Lieutenant Bertha Trueness. No, she told him, after checking with her clerk, Hazel Ryerson had not filed a report about her sister. Lt. Trueness was able to confirm, however, that Belle Ryerson's car had not been ticketed or involved in an accident within the last seventy-two hours, nor had Belle or anyone else answering her description been involved in a crime within the same time period, either as victim or perpetrator.

Loomis and Connie had similar conversations with the Vermont State Police and the Chittenden Country sheriff's department, as well as the sheriffs' departments of the surrounding counties of Grand Isle, Lamoille, Franklin,

Washington, and Addison, with the same results. They spent a half hour calling hospital emergency rooms and clinics within a hundred mile radius of Burlington, likewise fruitless, then locked the office and took the stairs to the sixth floor.

As Loomis and Connie entered the reception area of Proctor, Proctor and McHenry, a tall, erect old man dressed like a funeral director emerged from the inner offices, followed by the dapper figure of D. Lincoln McHenry. McHenry gave Loomis and Connie a sidelong glance as he escorted the old man to the exit. He pulled the heavy glass door open.

"Don't hesitate to call if you have any further questions, Dr. Kilpatrick," McHenry said, almost shouting. "And please give my warmest regards to Mrs. Kilpatrick."

Holding the door, he shook hands with the old man, who bobbed his head and shuffled toward the elevators. With a pneumatic sigh, the massive plate-glass door swung shut behind him.

"Deaf as the proverbial post," McHenry said, as he joined Loomis and Connie by the reception desk. He smiled up at Connie—he was two inches shorter than she was—and placed his hand on her arm. "How are you, my dear? How are your children? Is Hack treating you all right? I hope so. If not, I'm sure I could find something for you here."

"I'm fine, Mr. McHenry," she said. "So are the kids, thank you." She removed her arm from his grasp.

Seemingly of its own volition, his hand reattached itself. "Please, call me Lincoln." Her discomfort was obvious, at least to Loomis.

McHenry released Connie's arm and turned to Loomis. In his mid-fifties, McHenry had added a pound or two since the last time Loomis had seen him. He'd shed a little more hair, too, that his comb-over could not disguise.

"Hack," he said. "It's been a while. How are you?"

"I'm okay," Loomis said. "All things considered."

"Sorry I haven't been able to send any work your way recently, but, well, you know how things are."

"Sure, Dink, I know how they are."

McHenry scowled at Loomis's use of his nickname. He minded his nickname more than Loomis minded his own, which was not at all. No one knew what the "D" in D. Lincoln stood for, although Loomis had his own theories, none of them polite. McHenry was always asking people to call him Lincoln. No one ever did for long: Dink just suited him too well.

"What can I do for you?" McHenry said, looking at his watch, a gold Rolex Daytona, all dials, knobs and pushbuttons, worn loose on his wrist. "I'm booked pretty solid this afternoon, but I'm sure I can spare a few minutes." He glanced around the empty reception area, then at the receptionist, who sat behind her L-shaped desk, studiously not listening. "Who's next, Glenna?"

"Sir." The receptionist was a prodigiously endowed woman whose helmet of glossy red hair, finely plucked eyebrows, artificial lashes, and liberally applied makeup made her look, from the neck up, anyway, like an animated department store mannequin. "You have a conference call with the nominating committee at 2:30."

McHenry glanced at his Rolex again. Loomis couldn't remember ever seeing it before. If it was new, the rumours that McHenry was in financial trouble must be wrong, he thought. That watch would have easily set him back $30,000. Assuming, of course, it was real. Loomis's own watch, a sixty-year-old Omega Seamaster that had belonged to his grandfather, read 1:40 p.m. They had plenty of time.

"What do you want to see me about?" McHenry said.

"Belle Ryerson," Loomis said.

"Belle? What about her?"

"Has she come into work yet?"

"I haven't seen her," McHenry said. "Glenna, is Belle in?"

The receptionist tapped a long fingernail on her computer keyboard and examined the screen. "No, sir. She wasn't in yesterday, either. Mrs. Noble was asking about her earlier."

"Has she called in?" Connie asked.

The receptionist almost clicked her tongue at Connie's impertinence. "No, she hasn't."

"What's the problem?" McHenry asked.

"We were supposed to meet on Saturday," Connie said. "But she didn't turn up, and I haven't been able to get in touch with her."

"Oh," McHenry said, with a dismissive shrug. "Well,

you know Belle."

"What does that mean?" Connie asked, voice sharp.

McHenry didn't like her tone, but before he could respond, the lobby door swung open with a glassy clang and Lizzie McHenry swept into the reception area. Sleek and blonde and elegant, she looked a decade younger than her forty-eight years.

"Lizzie," McHenry said. It was clear he had not been expecting her. "What are you doing here?"

"I need to speak to you," Lizzie McHenry said in her professionally modulated voice.

"I'm quite busy," McHenry said, a bit defensively, Loomis thought.

Ignoring her husband's protest, Lizzie McHenry smiled at Loomis. "Hack. How are you?"

"I'm well, Lizzie," he said, shaking her hand while McHenry scowled. "Thanks."

Before Loomis could perform introductions, Lizzie thrust her hand out to Connie. "Hi, I'm Lizzie McHenry."

"Yes, I know," Connie said, taking Lizzie's hand. "I'm Connie Noble."

"Oh," Lizzie McHenry said, smile warming. "I'm pleased to meet you, Mrs. Noble. I knew your husband. Please accept my belated condolences. His passing was a great loss to the community—oh, shit," she said. "That was incredibly insensitive of me. His death was an immeasurably greater loss to you and your family. I've been spending far too much time with politicians and speaking in sound bites. Please forgive me."

"No need," Connie said. "I appreciate your kindness."

"Thank you," Lizzie said. "Now, if you don't mind, I must borrow my husband."

"Of course," Connie said, as Lizzie went through the double doors to the inner offices, McHenry trailing after her.

"Would you like me to call you when Mr. McHenry is available?" the receptionist inquired, her tone suggesting she expected no for an answer: she took her responsibilities as McHenry's gatekeeper seriously.

"Thanks," Loomis said. "We'll wait."

"Very well," she said, dismissing them from her mind.

Loomis and Connie settled in the waiting area, in comfortable leather—or very good faux leather—chairs. Loomis riffled through the magazines on a coffee table that was formed from an apparently solid block of some darkly grained, reddish wood, but between *Architectural Digest*, *Business Week*, and *Law Today*, found nothing that struck his fancy. Connie leafed through an *Architectural Digest* while Loomis contented himself with resting on his spine and marvelling at the speed at which the receptionist typed. Perhaps she was more than mere decoration.

They'd been cooling their heels for fifteen minutes when Connie slapped her magazine closed. "How long are we going to wait?"

At that moment the door to the inner offices swung open and Lizzie McHenry strode into the reception area, telegenic features stormy. The receptionist stared wide-eyed as Lizzie marched toward the door, back rigid, boot-heels thudding, eyes straight ahead. She exited with a bang through the glass doors into the elevator lobby. Stabbing the elevator call button half a dozen times, she waited, arms folded and foot tapping impatiently. Loomis half expected to see steam vent from her ears.

Loomis stood and went to the reception desk. The receptionist looked up at him. "I'm sure Mr. McHenry will be with you as soon as he has a moment," she said.

"Perhaps you could remind him we're still here," Loomis said. "Otherwise, I'm sure we can find our own way."

"Oh, very well," she said. "Please be seated."

"We'll wait right here, if that's all right with you," Loomis said, as Connie joined him.

With a huff, the receptionist lifted the telephone and pressed a button. Speaking almost inaudibly into the mouthpiece, she said, "Sir, Mr. Loomis and Mrs. Noble are still waiting." She listened for what seemed to be an inordinately long time. Finally, as Loomis was beginning to wonder if McHenry was going to blow them off, she put down the phone. "Mr. McHenry will see you momentarily."

"Thank you," Loomis said.

After somewhat more than a moment, the inner doors opened again, admitting a whip-slim thirty-something woman into the reception area.

"Mr. Loomis," she said, regarding him through sleek, dark-rimmed eyeglasses. Her eyes were a deep, inky blue and slightly magnified by the lenses of her glasses. "I'm

Heather-Anne Allen, Mr. McHenry's executive assistant. Hi, Connie. How are you?"

"I'm fine, Heather-Anne, thank you," Connie said.

"Mr. McHenry will see you now. Come this way."

She held the door for them, then led them deep into the inner sanctum. The aisle between the enclosed offices and the partitioned workstations was too narrow to walk side-by-side without bumping shoulders, so Loomis and Connie followed in single file.

Ms. Heather-Anne Allen wore her fine dark hair up in an elaborate swirl, held in place by a big tortoise-shell clip. Her skirt ended two inches above her knees, the backs of which were prettily dimpled, and her long calves flexed nicely as she walked, balanced easily atop the three-inch heels of her black patent pumps. Ms. Allen rated high on Loomis's sleek, brunette and elegant scale. He wondered if she was the cause of Lizzie's stormy exit. He glanced over his shoulder at Connie, who smirked at him. He smirked back.

McHenry stood, glancing at this watch, as Ms. Allen ushered Loomis and Connie into his office.

"Thank you, Heather-Anne," he said, as he came around a desk the size of a billiard table, topped with a thick slab of black marble.

"Yes, sir," she said, waiting by the door.

"Sorry to have kept you waiting," he said. "Would you like something to drink? Coffee? Tea?"

Both declined. McHenry dismissed Heather-Anne Allen with a nod. She smiled and left, closing the door behind her.

"How can I help you?" McHenry waved toward a long leather sofa.

"Belle Ryerson?" Loomis said, as he lowered himself into the embrace of buttery leather next to Connie.

"Right. Sorry," McHenry said. "I'm a little distracted today."

"Her sister is worried about her," Loomis said.

"Hazel Ryerson has retained you?" McHenry said, his tone suggesting that he did not approve.

"She has," Loomis said.

"She's worrying for nothing," McHenry said. "I'm sure Belle's simply taken time off and neglected to tell anyone. I don't keep track of her comings and goings. As long as the work gets done. As office manager, her time isn't directly billable, and she's gotten the place to the point that it almost manages itself."

"Nevertheless," Loomis said, "we'd appreciate anything you can tell us that might help us find her."

"Assuming she's actually missing," McHenry said.

"Let's assume, for the moment, shall we," Loomis said.

"I don't know how I can help," McHenry said. "I've known Belle and Hazel Ryerson a long time. I was their mother's attorney. And still represent their interests. Belle is a highly competent office manager, but, well, somewhat eccentric. Hazel even more so. She hardly ever leaves that house, you know."

"Which is completely irrelevant," Connie said.

"I meant no disrespect to either Belle or Hazel,"

McHenry said. "I just want to be certain you are aware of the kinds of personalities you are dealing with."

"Unstable ones, you mean," Connie said.

"My dear …"

Connie started to say something, but Loomis cut her off. "Are you aware of any problems Belle might be having with someone at work?" he asked.

"No," McHenry said, shaking his head. "She gets along well with everyone. As I said, though, I don't micromanage."

"As long as the work gets done," Loomis said.

"That's right," McHenry said, smile tight.

"If Belle were taking time off," Loomis said, "who would she get to fill in for her? Does she have an assistant?"

"No," McHenry said. "We're not a large firm. Everyone wears a number of hats. Except the senior associates. And Ted and me, of course," he added.

Ted Proctor Junior was more or less retired. His father, Ted Senior, had founded the firm. Loomis had met Ted Junior precisely once. He spent his winters in Florida and his summers on his sailboat on Lake Champlain. Phil Jefferson claimed he cheated at golf.

"What about Heather-Anne?" Loomis asked.

"She works with Belle from time to time," McHenry said, "but I keep her pretty busy. Maybe Glenna. The receptionist. She often helps with administrative tasks."

"Do you mind if we speak with them?"

"As long as you don't take too much of their time. It's

year-end, you know. But Hazel is overreacting. Belle has done this before, taken time off without telling anyone. She calls them her 'jaunts.'"

"Any idea where she jaunts to?" Loomis asked.

"None at all."

"Do you mind if we look at her office?"

"She doesn't have an office. Just a workstation."

"Okay," Loomis said. "Do you mind if we look at her workstation?"

"As long as you limit your search to plain sight."

"No problem," Loomis said.

"Now, if you'll excuse me." McHenry stood. "I need to get ready for my conference call with the nominating committee."

"You running for dog catcher, Dink?"

"As a matter of fact," McHenry said, neck stiff, "I'm considering accepting the nomination to run for state attorney general."

God help us all, Loomis thought. "Well, thanks for taking the time to see us," he said.

"Not at all," McHenry said.

He walked them to the door and, perhaps practising for the hustings, shook hands with them both before handing them back to Heather-Anne Allen.

5

"Ms. Allen," Loomis said, as she escorted them to the front of the office. "Do you mind answering some questions?"

"What sort of questions?"

"How well do you know Belle Ryerson?" Loomis said.

"Well enough, I suppose," she said. She stopped by the exit to the reception area. "Why?"

"When did you last speak to her?"

"Friday afternoon. What's this all about?"

"When you spoke to her, did you get the impression that something was bothering her?"

"No. Look, what's going on? Why are you asking about Belle? Has something happened to her?"

"She didn't come into work today," Loomis said. "Or yesterday. And her sister hasn't seen her since last week. Did she say anything to you last week about taking time off or going on a trip?"

"No," she said. "We work together, but she doesn't

report to me."

"Does she get along well with her co-workers?"

"She tries hard to get along with everyone," Heather-Anne Allen said, inky blue eyes shifting a little behind the lenses of her glasses.

"You say that as though she isn't always successful."

"That's not what I meant at all." She opened the door to the reception area. "Now, if you'll excuse me."

"Ms. Allen," Loomis said. "Belle's sister is worried about her. If there's anything you can tell us that will help us find her, please, tell us."

"I wish there were," she said. "I don't really know her all that well. I like her, though. She's a very nice person, although quite shy, I think." She paused, regarding Loomis and Connie, expression thoughtful. "Perhaps I could speak to the other people she works with, see if she said anything to them about taking time off."

"That would be very helpful," Loomis said, suspecting that it probably wouldn't be. He handed her a business card. "Call us if you learn anything."

"I will." She went through into the reception area. "Glenna. Mr. Loomis and Mrs. Noble would like to speak to you about Belle. They would also like to look at her workstation."

"Of course, Heather-Anne," the receptionist said, baring teeth as white and perfect as her hair and makeup.

"Thank you," Heather-Anne said, baring her teeth back.

Loomis sensed a certain tension between the two

women. A dead man could have sensed it.

Ms. Allen bid Loomis and Connie a good day and disappeared back into the inner offices, letting the door swing shut behind her.

"Glenna," Loomis said to the receptionist. "You don't mind if I call you Glenna, do you? I'm afraid I don't know your last name."

"It's Campbell," she said, patting her glossy red coif, which looked as if it were made of vinyl.

"Glenna Campbell," Loomis said, barely able to keep a straight face.

"That's right," she said, as if daring them to launch into a rendition of "Wichita Lineman."

"Glenna," Loomis said. "Did Belle speak to you about covering for her this week?"

"No, she didn't."

"But she normally would?"

"I suppose so. To the best of my knowledge, though, she intended to come in this week. She's overseeing the implementation of a new system for tracking office expenses and billable hours, although I don't think there's much for her to do, really, except supervise the IT people. I keep the vacation schedules. She isn't due to take any vacation time till Christmas."

"And she would have called if something had come up?"

"You mean like an emergency? Yes. If she could. I mean, if she had time."

"How well do you know her?"

"As well as anyone here, I suppose. I do hope nothing has happened to her."

"As do we," Loomis said. "Can we look at her office now?"

"Certainly," she said.

She stood and came out from behind her desk. She wasn't as tall as Loomis thought she'd be, almost petite, and quite slim and graceful in spite of her generous endowment. Loomis wondered if anyone ever noticed the colour of her eyes, which were, he took pains to note, a very attractive sea-green.

"Belle doesn't have an actual office, of course," she said, as she led them once again into the inner sanctums of Proctor, Proctor and McHenry. "Those are in short supply and reserved for the partners and senior associates. She does have one of the larger and more advantageously placed workstations, though. Here it is."

If Belle Ryerson's workstation was larger or more advantageously placed than any of the others, it wasn't apparent to Loomis. Nor did it seem to be any differently equipped, with a multi-line telephone and a 21-inch Apple iMac computer. The computer's screensaver was engaged, displaying a series of woodsy photographs that slowly panned and zoomed in the style of a Ken Burns documentary. The desk and cabinets were modular, and the chair was ergonomic, identical to the chair in Belle's home office. The partitions surrounding the work area were covered with Post-it notes, spreadsheet printouts, schedules, charts, pages torn from travel and photography magazines, a Sierra Club calendar, plus a handful of four-by-six photographs. They were mostly group photos of other members of the firm in various venues, including one taken on a sailboat featuring Dink McHenry and Ted Proctor, vacuous smiles pasted on their faces, with Glenna Campbell in the background, barely contained by the top of her two-piece bathing suit.

"Does Belle always leave her computer on over the weekend?" Loomis asked.

"We all do," Glenna said. "It has something to do with the backup system."

"I see. Well, thanks. Don't let us keep you."

"Um ...? Oh, well, I do have to get back to the front," she said.

"Thanks for your help. We won't be long."

"I ... Well, all right."

With obvious reluctance, she left them.

Loomis lowered himself into Belle's fancy ergonomic chair. It settled under his weight with a pneumatic wheeze. He swivelled slowly, looking at the material posted on the partitions. The photographs included one of Belle standing on a rock ledge overlooking Lake Champlain, the Adirondack Mountains of New York State in the background. She was wearing hiking shorts and boots, with a backpack and a pair of trekking poles on the ground at her feet, the same backpack that they'd found in her bedroom closet. Slung around her neck was the Nikon DSLR they'd seen in the cabinet in her home office, equipped with a medium telephoto or zoom lens and scalloped sun shield.

"If these are her work," he said to Connie, indicating the photographs slowly panning across the computer screen, "she's good, isn't she?"

"She is," Connie agreed.

He tapped the keyboard spacebar and got what he expected, a bonk and a password prompt. Notwithstanding his promise to McHenry to limit his search to plain sight, he tried the desk drawers. Unsurprisingly, they were all locked.

Leaning back in the chair, he looked again at the material on the partitions, focusing on the personal items. The calendar and magazine pages reflected her liking of the outdoors and interest in photography. There was also a flyer, half hidden behind a spreadsheet printout, laser printed or photocopied on cheap blue copy paper. He took it down. It was a notice of a meeting of something called the Kentauran Foundation, dated two weeks earlier. It was decorated with clip-art graphics of shooting stars, ringed planets, and flying saucers. The "very special guest" was someone named Harriet Olsen, in bold face, and the event included a talk by James Maynard. Refreshments will be served. Bring a friend. The meeting place was at a church in the South End.

"What do you make of this?" he asked, handing it to Connie.

"The Kentauran Foundation? Never heard of it. But I bet it has something to do with UFOs."

"Brilliant deduction, Holmes. Is Belle interested in

UFOs?"

"I wouldn't think so," Connie said. Straight-faced, she added, "She seems pretty down to earth."

"You should be ashamed."

He took back the flyer. There was something familiar about the name James Maynard, but he couldn't place it. He folded the flyer and put it into his jacket pocket. He also took the photo of Belle in her hiking gear. They returned to the reception area.

"Did you find what you were looking for?" Glenna Campbell asked from behind her desk. Her eyes widened. "What *is* that sound?"

That sound was the fanfare to Richard Strauss's *Also Sprach Zarathustra*, popularized by Stanley Kubrick's *2001: A Space Odyssey*.

"Oh, sorry," Connie said, digging into her purse. "That's me. My son's been fooling with my phone again." She looked at the screen of her phone. "Excuse me," she said.

Loomis watched her go out into the elevator lobby to take the call, then turned back to Glenna Campbell. "Do you mind if I asked you more questions about Belle?"

"Not at all. But as I said, I don't really know her very well. Not personally."

"So you wouldn't know if she had a boyfriend."

"No."

"How about girlfriends?"

"I wouldn't know that, either," she said, her neck mottling.

Hmm, he thought. "So you don't hang out after work? Go for a drink. Talk girl talk."

"No, of course not."

"Why 'of course not'?" Loomis said. "Is it so unusual for co-workers to socialize outside of work?"

"What I meant was, if we socialized after work I'd know her better, wouldn't I?"

"Good point," Loomis said as Connie came back into the reception area. She smiled an apology at Loomis. He smiled back. "So there's nothing you can tell us about where she might be," he said to Glenna.

"I'm afraid not. As I said, I don't know anything about her personal life. I don't think she really has much of a personal life."

"Everyone has a personal life," Connie said.

"You know what I mean," Glenna said, bristling. "She isn't really much of a people person, is she?"

"Maybe she's just not your kind of people person," Connie said.

"I'm just trying to be helpful," Glenna Campbell said. "It's not my fault she's missing, is it? No, it's not. Will there be anything else? I do have work to do."

"Not for the moment," Loomis said. "Thanks for your time."

"Sorry about that," Connie said, as they took the stairs down to the fourth floor. "I really can't stand that woman."

"I could tell." He unlocked the door to the office. "What was the phone call about?"

"Oh, nothing important," she said, a little too casually.

"Is there a problem?"

"No, no problem," Connie said, refusing to meet his eyes. "What now?"

He took the Kentauran Foundation flyer out of his pocket and unfolded it. "You're sure she isn't into this UFO stuff?"

"She's never said anything that would suggest she is," Connie said. "Maybe her sister can tell us." She took her coat from the tree by the door.

"Going somewhere?" Loomis said.

"There's something I need to take care of," she said. "I shouldn't be more than an hour or so."

"Okay," Loomis said, as Connie put on her coat and wound her scarf around her neck. "See you in an hour?"

"Or so," Connie said. She pecked him on the cheek and left.

Loomis stood in the middle of the office for a moment after she had gone. Something was happening, he knew, but like Mr. Jones in the old Bob Dylan song, he didn't know what it was. Perhaps he was imagining things. Or being paranoid. Or both. It was probably something to do with one of her kids. She had two, Susan and Billy, fourteen and twelve. They were good kids, as kids went, Loomis supposed; he did not relate well to children. Susie wasn't exactly a child, though. An exquisitely perfect scale model of her mother, she professed to actually like Loomis and treated him with polite deference and infinite patience, but she made him feel stupid and old. Billy, on the other hand, was the kind of kid W.C. Fields had been talking about when he'd said that boys should be raised in barrels. When he wasn't playing video games featuring characters so fearsome and hideously ugly they made Loomis's skin crawl, he followed his sister and her friends around with a digital camera, recording them in shops and malls and restaurants and uploading selected segments— the more embarrassing the better—to YouTube or Facebook. If he survived puberty it would be a testament to his sister's self-restraint.

Shoving his adolescent insecurities about Connie's evasiveness to the bottom of his mind, he picked up the phone and keyed in Hazel Ryerson's number.

"Mr. Loomis," she said. "Have you news of my sister?"

"Not yet, I'm afraid," he said. "I have a question, though. Is your sister interested in UFOs?"

"UFOs? No. She thinks unidentified flying objects, not to mention alien abductions, crop circles and cattle mutilations, are a lot of nonsense. As do I. Why do you ask?" Loomis told her about the Kentauran Foundation flyer. "I'm certain my sister would never go to a UFO meeting."

"Has she ever mentioned the Kentauran Foundation?"

"No."

"Perhaps she has a friend who's interested in UFOs," Loomis said. "Do the names Harriet Olsen or James Maynard mean anything to you?"

"No. Sorry," she said.

Loomis told her he'd be in touch as soon as he had anything and hung up. He made a copy of the flyer on the multi-function inkjet printer, which had started printing in a putrid yellowy green, making everything look like a 3D movie viewed without the special glasses. Leaving the copy on Connie's desk, he folded the original into his pocket, put on his coat and hat, and went out for a walk. He usually thought better when he walked, but all he could think about as he walked down to the waterfront and along the boardwalk between the ECHO science centre and the Coast Guard station, past the spot where Alex Robillard's floater had been found, was why Connie was being so evasive.

6

Connie's car was parked out front when he got back, so before going up to the office, he picked up two coffees and a couple of chocolate-glazed doughnuts at Debbie's Donut Shoppe. As he left the shop and crossed Bank Street, the afternoon sun broke through a gap in the clouds, but it started to snow, big fat flakes, some almost as big as his nose, upon which he tried to catch a couple. They tickled as they melted on his cheeks. Upstairs, Connie was hunched over her laptop, stroking and tapping the trackpad, an expression of intense concentration on her face.

"I don't pay you to play around on Facebook," he said, placing the flimsy cardboard tray on the corner of her desk and hanging up his coat.

"Come look at this," she said, beckoning to him. She shifted to one side so he could see the screen.

"What is it?" he asked, peering over her shoulder. He breathed in the sweet, herbal scent of her hair.

"It's the Kentauran Foundation web site," she said,

adding, "Thanks," as she peered under the lid of one of the coffee cups, then selected the other, which contained milk. "Have you ever seen anything so cheesy and amateurish?"

To describe the Kentauran Foundation's web site as cheesy and amateurish, Loomis thought, was an insult to cheese and amateurs everywhere. It was a dog's upchucked breakfast of clashing colours, unreadable fonts, grainy photographs, and misaligned frames.

"Maybe whoever built it was colour blind," he said.

"Or just blind," Connie suggested.

"I'll go blind trying to read it," he said, squinting at the screen.

"Don't bother. I've printed out the important bits." She gestured toward the laser printer next to the door to his office.

"How about just giving me the condensed version?" he said.

He bit into his doughnut and washed it down with a sip of coffee as Connie tapped the trackpad, opening a grainy headshot of an unsmiling, middle-aged man with a shaved bullet head and a neatly trimmed salt-and-pepper beard. He had a small loop earring in his ear, which also sported a thick tuft of dark hair in the outer canal. He wore a plain collarless shirt, buttoned to the throat. He had no neck to speak of.

"This is the guy who runs it," she said, nibbling her doughnut. "Dr. Thaddeus Kellerman."

"Doctor of what?" Loomis asked.

"He's a psychiatrist."

"Figures," Loomis said. "Is he still practising?"

"He is. He has an office in the Burlington Medical Arts Building on Main." She handed him a piece of note paper with Kellerman's name, office address, and phone number written in her neat, square hand.

"What's his story?" Loomis said.

"About thirty years ago he was practising in California—he treats people who've 'lost time' due to alien abduction—when he claims he was contacted by a group of dissident aliens calling themselves Rigilians."

"Contacted how? Through his dental fillings?"

"Telepathically, apparently, in a sort of self-induced hypnotic trance. Anyway, to make a long story short, these Rigilians warned him that the earth was headed towards ecological and social collapse and told him to move to Vermont and build a giant radio transmitter to send messages to Alpha Centauri, also known as Rigil Kentaurus."

"Hence the Kentauran Foundation," Loomis said. "You said 'dissident aliens.' Dissenting from what?"

"I'm not sure. We can download an electronic copy of his book, if you like."

"Some other time," Loomis said. "What sort of messages were they supposed to send?"

"Examples of our art and music, literature and philosophy, apparently. Ours meaning the earth's, not just America's."

"And they're building this radio transmitter here in

Vermont?"

"If they did," Connie said, "it wouldn't do them much good."

"Why not?"

"If I remember from helping Susie with her home-work a couple of years ago, Alpha Centauri isn't visible from Vermont."

"Okay," Loomis said. "So where are they building it?"

"Costa Rica, apparently. Is it important?" Connie asked.

"Absolutely not," Loomis said. "How many people belong to his foundation?"

"About three hundred."

"Is there a membership list?"

"No."

"Anything else? What about the names on the flyer? James Maynard and Harriet Olsen?"

"Nothing much on Harriet Olsen," she said, "except that she's supposed to be in contact with the same aliens who contacted Dr. Kellerman, but ..." She tapped, and another browser window opened. It displayed a Wikipe-dia page.

Loomis leaned closer and read: *James Curtis Maynard, also known as Jimmy Maynard (April 6, 1939), was an Ameri-can astronaut who flew only one shuttle mission in 1984 ...*

"Hah," Loomis said, straightening. "That's why the name seemed familiar."

"I haven't read the article," Connie said. "As an astro-naut he'd be famous, I suppose, but I've never heard of him."

"He was an astronaut, all right," Loomis said. "But that's not all he was famous for." He pulled over a chair, sat, and scanned the article, refreshing his memory.

In 1984, Colonel James "Jimmy" Maynard, an aeronautical engineer and USAF test pilot, was a payload specialist aboard the space shuttle *Challenger* on one of the early classified Department of Defense missions to orbit a military communications satellite. On December 9, as the crew was preparing for re-entry, *Challenger* suffered a complete power failure. All communications with the ground were lost. The flight crew tried everything to restore power, but nothing worked. Thirty minutes after the power failed, it just as mysteriously came back on. All systems checked out, and on the next orbit re-entry commenced and *Challenger* safely touched down at Edwards Air Force Base in California without further incident.

Although NASA technicians were never able to conclusively identify the cause of the power failure, during debriefing Maynard reported that the failure had been caused by a UFO. He further reported that while the power had been out and his fellow crew members had been in a state of suspended animation, he'd been taken aboard an alien spacecraft, where a bio-electronic tracking device had been implanted in his right sinus cavity. NASA and the Air Force were skeptical, to say the least. After numerous physical examinations, which failed to reveal the existence of the implanted tracking device, and exhaustive psychological testing, the consensus was that Maynard had experienced a vivid hallucination brought on by the sudden stress of the power failure, exacerbated by the effects of micro-gravity.

Being a hard-headed military man without much in the way of imagination, Maynard accepted the diagnosis with a profound sense of relief. However, in the months that followed, he began to experience severe headaches, periods of deep depression, sleeplessness, and blackouts. Air Force and NASA psychiatrists diagnosed clinical depression and prescribed anti-depressants, but they only made matters worse. Maynard became increasingly paranoid. His behaviour became erratic, and his temper became violently unpredictable. He began drinking heavily. His marriage broke down and, slightly more than a year after his flight, his wife filed for divorce. Two months later Maynard had a complete psychotic break. He spent a decade in a psychiatric hospital before being released in 1997.

He'd never spoken publicly about his experience, but after his release he became active in the UFO movement, and the story came out. NASA and the Air Force refused to comment. In 1998, Maynard joined one of the loonier of the lunatic fringe of UFO cults called the Invader Network, whose membership believed that UFO sightings, abductions, cattle mutilations, and crop circles were a prelude to full-scale alien invasion. Two years later, however, Maynard denounced the Invader Network and its leader as a fraud, after which he dropped out of sight. He resurfaced in 2007, having reinvented himself as a motivational and inspirational speaker. He spoke of his career as fighter pilot, aeronautical engineer, air force test pilot, astronaut, and his single journey into space, as well as his breakdown. He did not speak of his supposed alien abduction, refusing to answer questions about it, apparently having put that part of his life behind him.

Until now, Loomis thought.

"Oh, boy," Connie said, who'd been reading along with him. "What has Belle gotten herself mixed up with? She seems so level-headed."

"We don't know that she's gotten herself mixed up with these people at all," Loomis said. "There may be some other explanation."

"Such as?" Connie said.

"I don't know, but Hazel doesn't think Belle is interested in UFOs. Still," he said, "I suppose we should check out this Kentauran Foundation."

"As a matter of fact," Connie said, switching back to the Kentauran Foundation website and pointing out the meeting schedule, "there's a meeting tonight."

"Speaking of meetings," Loomis said, "how did yours go?"

"Eh? Oh, fine," she said. "Better than I thought it would."

He waited, but that seemed to be all she had to say on the matter.

"That's good," he said, and went into his office, picking up the material Connie had printed out on his way past the printer.

Loomis's father had been a space buff. Loomis had been

born not long after Neil Armstrong had planted the first boot prints on the moon—the first human boot prints, anyway. One of his earliest memories was of watching an Apollo launch on television with his father and older brother Denny, presumably one of the last, if not *the* last, Apollo 17 in December 1972. Ten years later there were shuttle launches and landings. For all he knew, he'd watched Maynard's flight. He vividly remembered the destruction of *Challenger*, though, on January 28, 1986, less that two minutes after launch, due to the failure of a solid booster rocket—the same ship on which Maynard had flown two years before.

Loomis recalled a conversation he'd had with his father about the possibility of extraterrestrial intelligence. He didn't recall the circumstances, but it had been a year or so before the *Challenger* disaster. Although Maynard's purported abduction hadn't been made public by NASA or the Air Force, there were always rumours circulating through the broad community of space enthusiasts. Perhaps the topic had come up while they'd been watching a launch: Loomis had asked his father if he believed in UFOs and aliens.

Christopher Loomis had chuckled. "When your grandparents got their first television," he'd said, "every afternoon after school your Aunt Katie and I would watch the *Mickey Mouse Club* on a station from Buffalo. Or maybe Rochester. In any case, every spring the station would run public service announcements reminding resident aliens that they had to register by April 15. I imagined little green men and women with eyestalks lined up with their little green kids, waiting to register. I was disappointed when your grandfather explained to me that in the U.S. 'resident aliens' were what we called 'landed immigrants,' just people from other countries, not other planets."

"So you don't believe in UFOs?"

"I don't deny the possibility that ships from other worlds have visited the earth, but I think it's highly unlikely. What I do believe, however, is that given the two hundred billion stars in the Milky Way galaxy alone, and the umpteen billion planets circling those stars, it's improbable to the point of absurdity that the earth is the only planet that sustains intelligent life. It's yet to be conclusively proved, though, that even the earth supports truly intelligent life."

Christ, he missed his father, Loomis thought, smiling at the memory. He wondered what his father would think of the Kentauran Foundation. Probably as further proof that if there was intelligent life in the universe, it wasn't on earth.

Loomis clicked his mouse and scrolled through the address book on his computer. While his father wouldn't have known much about UFO cults, Loomis knew someone who might. He found the number he was looking for, picked up the phone, and dialled.

"Barrett," a gruff voice barked.

"Rog, Hack Loomis. Are you busy?"

"Always," Barrett said.

Roger Barrett was the expat British building manager who lived in an apartment in the basement of the Professional Building. He divided his spare time between writing lurid science fiction short stories for various male-oriented magazines and working on an epic alternate history novel. The premise, he'd explained, was that the Colonies had lost the War of Independence and had been absorbed into Canada, wherein resided the Royal Family since the Nazis had nuked Great Britain before being nuked in return by the Allies. Loomis couldn't wait to read it.

"Have you got a minute to answer a couple of questions?" Loomis said.

"Sure. Shoot."

"Can you tell me anything about the Kentauran Foundation?"

"Never heard of it." Loomis heard the clatter of a keyboard. "But Kentauran likely refers to Rigil Kentaurus, or Rigil Kent, otherwise known as Alpha Centauri. It's the closest star system to the Sun, only about 4.3 light years away. It's actually three stars: Alpha Centauri A, which is almost identical to the Sun, but slightly larger and brighter; Alpha Centauri B, which is slightly smaller and dimmer; and Alpha Centauri C, also known as Proxima Centauri because it's actually the star that's closest to ours, only 4.2 light years away. It's a red dwarf, though, quite small and dim, not visible to the naked eye."

Loomis took a breath to speak, but Barrett rattled on.

"Alpha Centauri A and B form a binary system. They're relatively close to each other, about the same distance as the planet Uranus"—he pronounced it *your anus*—"is to the Sun, and rotate around each other every eighty years or so. Alpha Centauri C—Proxima Centauri—is twelve to thirteen thousand AUs from AB—an AU, or Astronomical Unit, is the mean distance between the centre of the Sun and the centre of the earth—with an orbital period of 100,000 to 500,000 years. They—"

"Okay," Loomis said, interrupting Barrett's lecture. "Thanks for the astronomy lesson."

"Sorry. I do have a tendency to prattle on."

"So Alpha Centauri is where the flying saucers are from."

"What flying saucers?"

"Well, flying saucers in general."

"Alpha Cen A is the most likely to have planets in the habitable zone, also known as the goldilocks zone, where liquid water can exist. None have been conclusively identified so far, but they're working on it."

"You believe in UFOs then?"

"Me? No, probably not. I refuse to believe we're the only intelligent life in the universe, though."

"I refuse to believe in the IRS," Loomis said. "Fat lot of good it does me."

"Ha. Good one, Hack. In the event, I don't believe we've been visited or, if we have, that the visitors abduct people and perform experiments on them. Cattle mutilations and crop circles are pure bunk, ninety-nine point nine percent of UFO sightings are hoaxes, swamp gas, weather balloons or conventional aircraft, and abduction fantasies are probably due to something called sleep paralysis. That's—"

"Never mind," Loomis said. "I'm not really interested in UFOs or alien abductions."

"I didn't think you were," Barrett said. "Does this Kentauran Foundation figure in an investigation?"

"It might," Loomis said.

"I googled it while we were talking," Barrett said. "Let's see …" He paused for half a minute or so, then said, "Hmm, reminds me of the Raëlian movement, with a pinch of apocalypticism thrown in to add spice."

"Rileyan?" Loomis said. "As in 'living the life of …'?"

"Eh? Oh. No. Raël. Spelled *r, a, e* umlaut, *l*. Raël is a former French journalist and race car driver named Claude Vorilhon. He claims to have been contacted by race of little humanoid aliens called the Elohim, who told him that they were the ones who designed all life on earth and created us their image. The Raëlians call it intelligent design for atheists."

"Elohim," Loomis said. The word tasted familiar. "Isn't that a Hebrew word for God?"

"Good lad. Yes, it is, but Raël claims that it was wrongly interpreted as a singular noun, and that it literally means 'those who come from the sky.'"

"So the Kentaurans believe these Elohim are from Alpha Centauri?"

"Well, their version of the Elohim, anyway."

"They call them Rigilians," Loomis said

"Naturally," Barrett said. "The Raëlians believe that

Moses, Buddha, Mohammed, Jesus, Joseph Smith—and Raël, of course—were all contactees, selected and trained by the Elohim to spread their message."

"Which is what? Get ready, we're coming back."

"In a nutshell."

"Are they legit?" Loomis asked.

"In what sense do you mean 'legit'?"

"Do they really believe in UFOs and alien abductions? Or is it just an elaborate con job?"

"Well, speaking for myself I think all organized religions are con jobs, but to answer your questions, yes, I'd say Raël believes. Presumably so does, um, Dr. Thaddeus Kellerman. But, as you said, believing, or not believing, doesn't make it so."

"No, it doesn't," Loomis said, smiling up at Connie as she came into the office. "Thanks, Rog."

"Anytime," Barrett said, and disconnected.

Loomis hung up the phone. "What's up?" he said to Connie.

"I'm heading home," she said. "Do you want to meet at the church where the Kentauran Foundation is meeting?"

"No, I'll pick you up," Loomis said.

"Okay," she said, and left.

Loomis hung around the office awhile longer, trying to work out ways to drum up business, then gave up and headed home to get ready for their foray into the world of UFO cultists and alien abductees. He wondered what to wear.

7

Home for Loomis was an old, thirty-two-foot Airstream trailer, winterized (after a fashion), installed on a cinderblock foundation, and hooked up to city water and sewage. The trailer shared a thickly treed double lot overlooking the Winooski River with the unfinished shell of what was supposed to have been his and Veejay's dream house, but which had turned into a nightmare, a principal source of the irreconcilable differences she had cited in her divorce petition. He heated up and ate leftover supermarket pizza, then changed into his only suit and tie and called Connie to tell her he was on his way. Fifteen minutes later, he parked on the street in front of her little wood frame house in a neighbourhood of little wood frame houses in the Old North End. Resisting the adolescent urge to honk the car horn for her to come out, he went to the door. It opened before he could knock.

"A tie, no less," she said as they walked to the car.

"Pretend we're on a date," he said.

"You really know how to treat a girl," she said, as he opened the car door for her and she got in.

They arrived a half-hour early at the South End church where the Kentauran Foundation held their meetings. A sign by the front entrance proclaimed it to be *The First Congregational Church of Jesus Christ the Wanderer*, the congregation of which was ministered by the Rev. Hector Brossard. Services held every Wednesday and Sunday at 11 a.m. and 7 p.m. Despite the stylized steeple, equipped with a loudspeaker in lieu of a bell, it looked to Loomis more like a fast food restaurant than a house of worship. But what did he know?

He found a place to park where they could watch both the front and side entrances, as well as the parking lot, which already held some cars: a silver Lexus; an old, bilious green Chrysler Neon; a beige Ford Focus with Florida plates; and a hulking Mercedes military-style G-Wagen with a camouflage paint job. More people soon began arriving: on foot, by cab and private car, singly, in pairs, and in groups of three or four. Everyone seemed to be in good spirits, laughing, chatting, greeting one another with handshakes, hugs, backslaps, and air-kisses.

"Cheerful bunch, considering they believe the end of the world is nigh," Loomis said.

"Mmm," Connie said.

The parking lot filled up quickly. A significant percentage of the vehicles were not-quite-new pickups and sport utility vehicles, mostly full-sized American models, but with a sprinkling of Japanese and Korean makes, not to mention the G-Wagen. If the planet were indeed headed for ecological hell in a handbasket, the members of the Kentauran Foundation were not exactly helping to stave off the disaster.

After a while, the flow of arrivals slowed to a trickle. They hadn't seen Belle Ryerson, but they had a nice collection of licence plate numbers.

"Before we go in," Loomis said, "let's get our story straight. We don't need to mention we're PIs. We're curious about UFOs and we've come to the meeting on the recommendation of a friend. We thought she'd be there. Just keep your eyes and ears open. Okay?"

"I think I can handle it," Connie said.

"Is something wrong?" Loomis asked. "You've been awfully quiet."

"Everything's fine," she said. "Let's go in."

They got out of the car, Loomis locked it with the remote, and they crossed to the side door of the church. Inside, they found themselves in a narrow hallway that ran parallel to the church nave. The hallway was empty save for a pair of crowded rolling coat racks and a card table covered with neat stacks of paperback books and pamphlets.

"Where'd they all go?" Connie said.

Loomis opened a door and peered through into the nave. "Nope." He let the door swing shut. There was a double door at the far end of the hallway. "That way," he said.

But no sooner had they set out down the hallway than

a middle-aged couple came into the church, accompanied by a rush of cold air.

"Howdy, folks," the man said, smiling broadly as he helped the woman with her coat.

She was a cheerful, roly-poly redhead in her fifties, carrying a purse that looked large enough to hold a Vespa. He was the classic jolly fat man, except that for a fat man on the downside of sixty he looked fit and solid and carried himself well. He was an inch or two shorter than Loomis's six-two and bald as an egg, not even eyebrows, although he did have pale, nearly invisible eyelashes that gave his eyes a vulnerable look.

"You folks here for the meeting?" He made room on one of the racks for his and the woman's coats.

"Yes," Loomis said.

"I don't recognize you. Have you been to one before?"

"No," Loomis and Connie said simultaneously.

"Dave Ledbetter," the man said, thrusting out a hand the size of a stewing chicken. His handshake was firm, warm, and friendly.

"As in Ledbetter's Furniture Emporiums?" Loomis said, recognizing Ledbetter from the television commercials and print ads for his chain of big-box furniture stores.

"That's me," Dave Ledbetter said, pleased to be recognized. "Retired now, though. This little lady is my wife Betsy," he added.

"How you doin'?" Betsy Ledbetter said, shaking hands with Connie then Loomis.

"Pleased to meet you both. I'm Hack Loomis, and this

is my wife Connie."

"Here's some of our literature," Betsy said, handing them each a slick brochure and a slim, paperbound book with a headshot of Dr. Thaddeus Kellerman on the cover. It was a higher resolution version of the same photo on the foundation's web site, except that on the book cover Dr. Kellerman's head was surrounded by a subtly glowing nimbus of pearly light. "What kind of name is Hack?" Betsy asked.

"It's sort of Spanish for Jack," Loomis said.

Loomis's given name was John, but his parents, despite being Canadian—or perhaps because—had been great admirers of JFK and had called him Jack, which their Spanish-speaking housekeeper had pronounced as Hack, as in *Jorge*—hoar-hay—or *Jesús*—hay-seuss. His older brother Denny and younger sister Annie had started calling him Hack, too, then the kids at school. It had stuck.

"It's different, anyway," Dave Ledbetter said. "So what brings you to our little get-together?"

"A friend said we might find it interesting," Loomis said.

"Well, we'll try not to scare you off before you've had a chance to see that we're just ordinary folks, not a bunch of fruitcakes. Eh, Bets?"

"Ordinary as old socks," Bets said. "C'mon along," she added, taking Connie's arm. "We'll introduce you around. What did you say your name was?"

Loomis and Connie accompanied Dave and Betsy Ledbetter downstairs to a small auditorium in the basement of the church. There were forty or so stacking chairs arranged before a low stage. From left to right the stage held a lectern, equipped with a microphone and a reading lamp, a green faux-leather easy chair, and a long cafeteria table, behind which were five more stacking chairs. At the back of the stage stood a large flat-screen TV and DVD player on a rolling stand.

About thirty people milled about by a pair of long tables against the wall, under small clerestory windows that ran the length of the room. One of the tables held three big Green Mountain Coffee pump thermoses and a two-gallon plastic pail hopefully labelled "Donations." Next to the thermoses was a stack of trays of plain white mugs, a basket of plastic spoons, a two-pound margarine tub of sugar, and a two-quart jug of low-fat milk. The other table was loaded with platters of cookies, squares, muffins, and sliced pound cake, mostly, it appeared, homemade. Betsy Ledbetter placed her gigantic purse on the table and removed another platter of cookies, sealed with about eight yards of plastic wrap, which she carefully removed, neatly folded, and tucked away in her voluminous purse.

Dave Ledbetter's idea of "introducing them around" was to clamp a hand on to Loomis's shoulder and boom: "Folks! Meet Hack and Connie Loomis."

"Hello, Hack and Connie," a chorus of voices responded.

"They're newbies, so be on your best behaviour," Ledbetter added, eliciting laughter.

After Ledbetter's introduction, Loomis and Connie were left to their own devices.

"Do you want a cup of coffee?" Loomis asked.

"No, thanks," Connie said.

"Let's split up, then," Loomis said. "Eavesdrop a little."

"Okay," Connie said, and moved toward a small group standing by the stage. A plump, prematurely balding man in his thirties, wearing what looked like an African safari outfit, followed her with his eyes as she crossed the room. His gaze seemed to be focused somewhat south of the equator. Loomis had to admire his taste, at least.

Loomis pumped a mug of coffee from a thermos, added a few grains of sugar, and grabbed a couple of Betsy Ledbetter's chocolate-chip cookies. A schoolmarmish young woman in bookish glasses, dark hair pinned up in a tight bun, smiled at him as she dropped a dollar into the donations pail, then slipped away into the crowd. Loomis deposited a dollar in the pail, then carried his coffee and cookies to the far side of the room and stationed himself by a table of Kentauran Foundation literature—and another donations pail. Sipping and munching, he casually surveyed the crowd.

They were a pretty ordinary bunch, although an alarming number looked as though they'd dressed in the dark out of a laundry hamper. Nor did many of them look as though they'd missed many meals. There were somewhat more women than men. The oldest appeared to be a spry, chicken-legged woman of about eighty, while the pretty schoolmarm was among the youngest. The distribution between extremes tended toward the high side.

He didn't see Dr. Thaddeus Kellerman or James Maynard.

Or Belle Ryerson.

The bespectacled schoolmarm was staring at him past the shoulder of a grey-haired woman in a fuzzy pink sweater. He wondered if the schoolmarm might be Harriet Olsen, who communed with aliens. He smiled at her, but her expression did not change. Perhaps she was nearsighted, he consoled himself. Popping the last bite of cookie into his mouth, he picked up his coffee mug and headed in her direction. His inquiries had to begin somewhere, after all. However, as he made his way across the room, she smiled at the woman in pink and moved away to join a group at the far side of the room. Loomis changed course, angling toward the refreshments table to recharge his coffee mug, then began to mingle, smiling and eavesdropping. He asked a handful of people if they knew Belle Ryerson, but no one did—or admitted they did.

Half an hour or so later, he intercepted Connie at the refreshments table.

"Learn anything interesting?" he asked.

"Aluminum foil in your hat will prevent aliens from tracking you by blocking the transmissions from your implant," she said. "You?"

"Nothing even remotely that useful."

She started to say something, but was cut off by a screech of feedback from the PA system.

"Oops, sorry," Betsy Ledbetter said from behind the

lectern. "Is this better? Okay, why don't we all take our seats so we can get started."

There was much noisy shuffling and quiet banter as people found their seats. Loomis and Connie sat near the back of the room. On Loomis's right was a scruffy man who hadn't had a close encounter with soap and water in some time. On Connie's left sat a man wearing long, baggy shorts and elaborate sandals and woolly socks. The pretty schoolmarm was in the row ahead of Loomis, three seats to his right. She had a pleasing profile, despite the unfashionable glasses. He glanced at Connie, but she was looking the other way.

"Now that we're all comfy," Bets said, producing another screech of feedback, "without further to-do let me introduce the man we've all come to see. Dr. Thaddeus Kellerman."

She stepped away from the lectern, clapping and urging the audience to join in, as a door opened stage left. Thaddeus Kellerman stepped onto the stage, smiling and trying without much success to look humble as he acknowledged the applause. In the flesh, he looked even more like a biker-turned-Buddhist-monk than he did in the photograph. However, a good thirty years had elapsed since the photograph had been taken, putting him in his late seventies or early eighties. He'd shed the goatee and had his ear hair trimmed, although he still wore the earring. About five-foot-six, he was barrel-shaped and bandy-legged. He wore a pale blue, collarless shirt with the sleeves rolled up, revealing long, muscular forearms that ended in small, delicate hands, almost feminine except for the dark patches of hair on the backs of his fingers. There was a tattoo on his right forearm that resembled a caduceus, but with only one snake and no wings. Loomis couldn't remember what it was called—the *Rod of Something*—but it was the symbol of the American Medical Association.

"Good evening," Kellerman said. His voice was deep and strong. "And welcome. It's gratifying to see so many of you here tonight, despite the inclemency of the weather. Unfortunately, it's probably going to get worse before it gets better."

The audience laughed with more enthusiasm than the joke deserved.

"I understand from Dave and Bets," he said, scanning the audience, "that we have some newcomers here tonight. I'm certain you will find the evening informative and enlightening. Please don't hesitate to introduce yourselves later on."

He took a sheet of paper from his shirt pocket, unfolded it, and smoothed it on the lectern.

"Before proceeding with tonight's agenda, I'm pleased to report that the final design specifications for the transmitter are nearing completion. The site survey is also progressing, as is the environmental impact study, and we have received assurances from our contacts in the Costa Rican government that there will be no difficulty in obtaining the necessary permits. That's great news, of course, but if we are to stay on track we also need to keep on with our fundraising efforts. Construction of the transmitter remains our top priority, despite recent developments. It is critical to the success of our mission, not to mention our survival as a species, that the transmitter be completed by the end of the year after next. As you know, it will take four years for the first signals to reach Rigil Kent. As it is, we're cutting it fine. The earth's ecological collapse is imminent. Once it begins, we will have very little time."

A hubbub arose as audience members exchanged worried remarks. A man toward the front stood, arm raised.

"Yes, Ed," Kellerman said. "What is it?"

Ed wanted to know why they had to build the radio transmitter if there already was a Rigilian mother ship in orbit. Good question, Loomis thought, as Dave Ledbetter stood up.

"Ed, if you'd—"

"Now, Dave," Dr. Kellerman said. "I understand Ed's point. I wish there was more I could tell you, Ed. As you know, the group we're in contact with is operating outside the aegis of the Rigilian authorities. The official position of the Rigilians is hands off, like the old Star Trek prime directive of non-interference. Don't forget, they've been studying us covertly for centuries and, frankly, we haven't given them much reason to think we're worth saving. That's why the transmitter is so important. With it we will be able to send examples of our art and music, literature and philosophy, everything that's good about us as a species."

Kellerman turned his wrist over and looked at his watch.

"Before moving on, Harriet has been in touch with her Rigilian contact, who has some important news she needs to share with us."

A buzz ran through the room. Kellerman held up a hand, calling for quiet.

"I needn't remind our regulars to remain quiet and please turn off your phones and pagers. To the newcomers here tonight, you may find what you are about to see difficult to accept, but I can assure you, Miss Olsen's experiences are absolutely genuine. However, if you are unable to overcome your skepticism, I must insist that you show respect and consideration for others and refrain from interrupting the session. Now, would someone please get the lights."

The houselights dimmed.

"Thank you, Dave," Kellerman said.

He nodded to Bets, who opened the door to the left of the stage. The audience began to murmur as a trim, lantern-jawed man wearing a blue suit as if it were a uniform stepped onto the platform. Loomis recognized James Maynard from the photograph on his Wikipedia page. He looked younger than his seventy-plus years as he offered his arm to the young woman who'd followed him through the door. The murmuring increased in volume as the former astronaut escorted the young woman to centre stage.

8

Harriet Olsen was thirty, give or take a year or two, and modestly dressed in a silky green blouse, a knee-length black skirt, and low-heeled black pumps. In her pumps, she was as tall as Maynard—astronauts tended toward compactness—and two inches taller than Kellerman. Her face was heart-shaped, and her oblique, blue eyes were distinctly almond-shaped. Glossy wings of jet-black hair hung to just below her earlobes. She acknowledged the audience with a sweet, beguiling smile.

Connie leaned close and whispered into Loomis's ear. "Not exactly the kind of person you'd expect to be in contact with aliens from another planet."

"Who says only homely women can be delusional?" he whispered back. "Besides, if I were an alien looking for an earth girl to date, I'd pick someone like her before, say, that lady in the pink sweater."

"Or the woman in the owlish glasses you've been admiring?"

Oops. Busted. "Her too," he said.

"Shush," hissed the aromatic fellow on Loomis's right.

Maynard seated Harriet Olsen in the green easy chair, then took up a position toward the rear of the stage, standing rigidly at ease. Dr. Kellerman moved a stacking chair close to Harriet's chair and sat down.

"Are you ready, my dear?" he asked.

"Yes, doctor. As ready as I ever am."

"I understand. Let's get started." He began speaking softly in his rich, velvety voice as she stared into the space above the audience. "Now, Harriet, I want you to relax and listen to the sound of my voice. Are you comfortable?"

"Yes, doctor, thank you." Her voice was light and melodic, almost childlike, but not at all difficult to hear: the room was so quiet Loomis could have heard a hint drop.

"Good. Now close your eyes. Very good. Listen only to the sound of my voice. You will hear nothing but my voice. You are very relaxed. Calm. It is warm. You smell something sweet. What do you smell, Harriet?"

"Lilacs," she said, eyes still closed, her smile Mona-Lisa-like. "I love the smell of lilacs." Her voice took on an even more childlike quality.

"Does the scent of lilacs remind you of something?" Kellerman asked.

"Yes," she replied.

"What does it remind you of, Harriet?"

She didn't answer. She looked as though she was asleep, but her head did not loll.

"Harriet?" Kellerman said. "Can you hear me?"

"Yes, doctor. I can hear you." Her voice had become firmer, more confident.

"Where are you now?"

"I'm in—" Loomis winced as she made a sound in her throat like a cat coughing up a hairball. "I'm in *Cat-cough*'s spaceship."

"Where is this spaceship, Harriet?"

"Orbiting the dark side of the moon."

"How did you get there?"

"I don't know."

"Are you afraid?"

"No." She made the cat-coughing sound again. "*Cat-cough* is very nice. He gave me tea."

The audience was on the edge of its collective seat. It was all Loomis could do to keep from laughing out loud.

"Why has—" The sound Kellerman made was only vaguely similar to the one Harriet had made. "—taken you to his spaceship, Harriet?"

She giggled, childlike. "You didn't pronounce it properly," she said. "It's—" She made the cat-coughing sound again. Loomis wished she'd cut it out: it made his throat hurt just to hear it. "But he says we can call him *Charley*."

Loomis put his hand to his mouth as if stifling a cough and chewed the inside of his cheek.

"Why has, uh, Charley taken you to his spaceship, Harriet?" Kellerman asked again.

"He has some bad news for us."

That elicited a querulous grumble from the audience, which Kellerman silenced with a sharp look and a gesture.

"What sort of bad news, Harriet?"

"He's afraid that the Rigilian government is close to discovering his group's plans to convey the first wave of refugees to—" And she made another sound that Loomis wouldn't have believed the human throat could produce without spitting up a tonsil.

"That is indeed bad news," Kellerman said, ignoring the muttering from the audience. "Does that mean they won't be coming?"

"Oh, no," Harriet said. "Charley says it just means they'll have to move up the schedule."

"Did he tell you when they will be coming?"

"No. Only that it would be soon. We need to be ready. We …" She paused.

"What is it, Harriet? Is something wrong?"

"He says I have to leave." Her eyes closed, and her head drooped.

"All right," Kellerman said. "I understand. Harriet, I'm going to wake you up in a moment. When I do, you'll remember everything we've just talked about. Now, wake up Harriet."

Her eyes fluttered opened, and she raised her head. Kellerman looked at Maynard, who stepped forward, took Harriet's hand, and helped her to her feet. Someone started to clap, but no one else joined in. The clapping stopped.

"Sorry," someone said from one of the front rows.

Loomis's ribs were aching from the effort to keep from laughing as Connie leaned close again. "If that had gone on much longer," she whispered, "I was going to have to leave the room before I wet my pants."

Maynard moved the easy chair to the back of the stage, and Harriet Olsen sat down again. Kellerman stepped up to the lectern.

"I'm not sure what to make of Charley's news," he said. "After Harriet has had a few minutes to rest, she will try to answer any questions we may have. First, though, I'd like to reassure the newcomers with us tonight that what you've just witnessed is not some parlour trick or stage fakery. I know many people are skeptical of testimony given under hypnosis, but my methods are especially designed to avoid eliciting the so-called false memories that have given hypnotic regression therapy a bad name. You surely observed that I asked Miss Olsen no leading questions. For example, I asked her where she was, not if she was on a spaceship. Nevertheless, it is entirely up to the individual to decide whether he or she believes in the existence of the Rigilians. I ask only that you keep an open mind." He turned to Harriet. "Are you sufficiently rested, my dear?"

She nodded and stood. She took her place at the lectern and looked out over the audience. She did not seem happy to be there. In fact, she looked as though she were about to bolt at any second. Reassuringly, Kellerman held her arm for a moment, before sitting down at the table.

"Can everyone hear me?" she said, barely audible.

"No," a number of people at the back responded.

Kellerman wasn't quite as quick to jump to Harriet's

aid as Colonel Maynard, who adjusted the lectern micro-phone.

"Is this better?" Harriet asked.

"Yes," the people at the back chorused.

She looked at Kellerman for a moment, then turned back to the audience. "I've said this before, I know, but I can't say often enough how grateful I am for the friend-ship and guidance of Dr. Kellerman. If it weren't for him, and all of you, of course, I think I would have gone out of my mind." She looked at Kellerman again. "I'm not exag-gerating when I say you saved my life, doctor."

He bowed his head in humble acknowledgement.

"As for Colonel Maynard," she added, rewarding him with a warm smile, "he truly is a hero, in every sense of the word."

Maynard glowed with pride, and there was no mistak-ing the look of adoration in his eye.

Loomis was in awe. Harriet Olsen's understated beau-ty, her vulnerability, and the intimacy of her melodic voice had everyone in the room hanging on her every word. She was either completely delusional or a con-summate professional. Either way, she'd cast a spell over the audience. Of course, she was preaching to the choir: nearly everyone in the room was predisposed to believe her, to believe *in* her. And in Charley.

A man near the front raised his hand. Just like in school, Loomis thought, the eager beavers and brown-noses sat at the front of the room. Harriet Olsen looked at the man with trepidation. Kellerman stood up, grimacing as if his knees hurt, and moved to her side.

"It's all right, my dear. George doesn't bite. What is it, George? Do you have a question?"

A tweedy, professorial type stood up. There were even patches on the elbows of his jacket. "Miss Olsen, you said that, um, Charley's spaceship was orbiting on the 'dark side of the moon.'"

"Yes," she said, expression wary. "I believe that's what I said."

"You realize, don't you," George said, "that the moon doesn't really have a dark side?"

"I don't understand," Harriet said.

"From earth we only ever see one face of the moon, but the face we never see, the so-called 'far side,' receives the same amount of sunlight as the near side as the earth-moon system revolves around the sun."

Harriet looked to Dr. Kellerman for help, but it was Jimmy Maynard who came to her rescue.

"You are correct, sir," Maynard said. "The moon does indeed have a four-week day-night cycle and therefore does not have a 'dark side.' However, perhaps you will allow Miss Olsen a certain poetic latitude. After all," he added with a smile, "it was good enough for Pink Floyd." Loomis laughed along with the rest of the audience.

There were a few more questions, all as silly, in Loomis's opinion, before Kellerman called a break and everyone headed to the refreshments table.

"So, Hack, Connie, what do you think?"

"Honestly, Dave?" Loomis said. "I'm having a hard time getting my head around the idea that an alien named Charley is going to fly a bunch of you to another planet."

"Charley's not his real name," Ledbetter said.

"I think you know what I mean."

Ledbetter smiled and nodded his big, shiny head. "Yeah, I guess I do," he said. "But before you go writing us off as a bunch of crazy people, you should talk to Thaddeus—Dr. Kellerman. Would you like me to introduce you?"

"That'd be great," Loomis said, thinking that it was too late; he already thought they were a bunch of crazy people. Harmless, he hoped, but nonetheless delusional. "How long have you and Bets been members of the Kentauran Foundation, Dave?"

"Must be going on twenty years now," Ledbetter said.

"You must know most of the other members pretty well, then."

"I suppose. Why're you asking?"

"Well, like I said earlier, we came tonight at the suggestion of a friend. She said we'd find it interesting, and she was right. We were expecting to see her, though."

"What's your friend's name?"

"Belle Ryerson."

Ledbetter's expression grew wary. "Um, you folks wouldn't be reporters, would you?"

"No, Dave," Loomis said. "We're not reporters."

"That's good," Ledbetter said, smiling. "'Cause I was just getting to like you."

"Do you know Belle?" Connie said.

"She's been to a couple of meetings," Ledbetter said, "but I don't really know her, except to say hello to."

"When was the last time you saw her?" Loomis asked.

"A couple of weeks ago, I guess."

"Is she a member?"

"You're asking a lot of questions about someone who's supposed to be your friend," Ledbetter said, suspicions aroused. Dave Ledbetter might be crazy, Loomis reminded himself, but he'd built a successful home furnishing business and was far from stupid.

"I can tell you she lives in Winooski with her sister Hazel," Loomis said, "drives a blue Toyota Yaris, and is the office manager at the law firm of Procter, Procter and McHenry." Loomis pretended not to notice that Ledbetter had recognized McHenry's name. It probably didn't mean anything, though: Dink McHenry was well known in Burlington business circles.

"I don't mean to give offence or anything," Ledbetter said, "but we get a little sensitive about reporters coming around, asking questions about flying saucers and little green men from Mars."

"I suppose you do," Loomis said.

"It's just that we haven't seen Belle recently," Connie said. "Is there anyone else she spoke with?"

"I think Bets was talking to her the last time she was here."

Ledbetter led them over to the refreshments table, where Betsy Ledbetter was talking to the bespectacled schoolmarm. He reached out a long arm and tapped his wife on the shoulder.

"Bets."

She turned, smiling. "Yes, hon."

"The Loomises here are friends of Belle Ryerson's."

"Oh," she said, looking around. "Is she here?"

"Haven't seen her," her husband said.

"When was the last time you saw her?" Loomis asked, glancing at the younger woman, who stood nearby, expression curious behind her bookish glasses.

"Two weeks ago, I guess. I introduced her to Thaddeus. Have you talked to him?"

"Not yet," Loomis said. He turned to the schoolmarm. "Do you know Belle Ryerson?" He took the photograph of Belle Ryerson in her hiking gear out of his pocket and showed it to her.

She peered at it. "No," she said. She shook her head, smiling. "Sorry."

Her smile revealed a slight gap between her front teeth. Loomis thought it was kind of cute. But she really should let her hair down.

"You should talk to Thaddeus," Betsy Ledbetter said.

9

Before they could speak with Kellerman, however, Loomis and Connie had to sit through an unintentionally hilarious—in Loomis's opinion, anyway—1980s documentary, in which people who believed they'd been abducted by aliens described their experiences. The film was followed by a panel discussion, which degenerated into an argument about whether or not the Rigilians had been responsible for all "confirmed" abductions since Betty and Barney Hill in the early 1960s. One of the panellists even trotted out the classic oversimplification of Occam's Razor, that the simplest explanation was most likely the correct one. It was, Loomis thought, the only semi-intelligent anyone on the panel said, the simplest explanation being that they were all completely deranged.

Afterwards, Dave Ledbetter guided Loomis and Connie through the crowd gathered around Kellerman, Harriet Olsen and James Maynard. A woman with unruly tendrils of hennaed hair was holding forth about how something called "ear-candling" was an effective method of removing alien implants. Loomis had no idea what ear-candling entailed, but it did not sound pleasant. When the woman paused to take a breath, Ledbetter jumped in.

"Thaddeus, do you have a minute?"

"Certainly, Dave," Kellerman said, beaming at Loomis and Connie.

"This is Hack Loomis and his wife," Ledbetter said.

"Mr. and Mrs. Loomis, a pleasure to meet you," Kellerman said, shaking hands with each of them. "May I introduce Miss Harriet Olsen?" Harriet Olsen smiled her Mona Lisa smile, but did not offer to shake hands. "And Colonel James Maynard." Maynard's handshake was firm and quick, but he avoided eye contact, focusing instead on Loomis's chin. The pudgy, balding guy in the safari suit hovered nearby, but Kellerman ignored him. Rather pointedly, Loomis thought.

"Mr. and Mrs. Loomis are friends of Belle Ryerson's," Ledbetter said.

"I'm sorry, who?" Kellerman said, looking nervous as he glanced at Harriet Olsen, who seemed to have gone somewhere else. Charley's spaceship, perhaps.

For a shrink, Loomis thought, Kellerman did not dissemble well at all. He knew exactly who Belle Ryerson was. Loomis couldn't say whether Harriet Olsen did or not, but if Kellerman did, it was a good bet she did, too. He wasn't sure about Maynard, who was as expressionless as a statue.

"You remember," Betsy Ledbetter said. "I introduced

her to you at the meeting two weeks ago. She was asking about how you use hypnosis to get Harriet to remember her visits with Charley."

"Oh, yes, of course," Kellerman said, recovering his memory. He glanced at Harriet again, but she was still lost in space. "Delightful woman, highly intelligent, very interested in what we're doing."

"Do you know where she is?" Loomis said.

"I don't understand," Kellerman said. "How would I know where she was?"

"How about you, Miss Olsen?"

She blinked and came back to earth. "Pardon me?"

"Do you know where Belle Ryerson might be?" he said.

She shook her head, looking at Kellerman, as if flustered by Loomis's question.

Kellerman regarded Loomis warily. "Are you with the media, sir?"

"I already asked him if they were reporters," Dave Ledbetter said. "He told me they weren't."

"Nevertheless," Kellerman said, "I wonder if you are being completely honest about your reasons for being here, Mr. Loomis. I don't believe you're here out of interest in our movement, are you, sir?"

"You're right," Loomis said. "We came hoping someone would be able to help us find Belle Ryerson."

"Find her?" Kellerman asked.

"She hasn't been seen since Friday," Loomis said.

"Are you with the police?" Kellerman said.

"No," Loomis said. "We're private investigators." He glanced at Ledbetter, whose expression had turned sour. "Sorry, Dave."

"Don't the police usually handle missing person cases?" Kellerman asked.

"Depends on the circumstances," Loomis said.

"I see," Kellerman said. "Well, I'm sorry we can't be more help."

Harriet Olsen placed her hand on Kellerman's arm. Loomis remembered the name of the device tattooed thereon: the *Rod of Asclepius*.

"Thaddeus," she said.

"Ah, yes," Kellerman said, as if remembering an appointment. "Please, excuse us. If we can be of any further assistance ..." His voice trailed off.

Loomis reached into his pocket for his card case, but Kellerman had already taken Harriet by the arm and was leading her—or was being led by her—toward the door by the stage. Jimmy Maynard and the chubby guy in the safari suit trailed after them.

"You could've told me you were private dicks," Dave Ledbetter said. He looked at Connie. "If you'll pardon the expression."

"We prefer to be called private investigators," Loomis told him.

"I'll try to remember that," Ledbetter said. He looked past Loomis's shoulder. "Oh, shit."

Loomis turned to see what he was looking at. The guy in the safari suit was talking to a man in his forties, squat and powerful, wearing a baseball cap, brim so curved the edges nearly touched. His companion was a hard-faced, awesomely-muscled blonde, taller than he was, and dressed to emphasize her physical development in stretch jeans and a thin leather jacket. They kept glancing toward Loomis, Connie and Ledbetter.

"Who's the dude in the safari suit?" Loomis asked Ledbetter, returning the man's stare as he strode in their direction, walking with a lot of up-and-down motion in what looked like new hiking boots. The other two followed, like a pair of trained guard dogs.

"Quentin Parker?" Ledbetter said. "He's supposed to be some kind of famous adventure writer. Never heard of him myself."

"And the other two?"

Ledbetter snorted, but didn't have time to answer.

"Dave," Quentin Parker said. "I'm going to have to insist that these two leave right now."

Parker's voice had an unpleasant nasal quality, which was not ameliorated by the sneer of contempt on his fleshy face. Loomis normally didn't take instant dislikes to people, but for Parker he made an exception.

"Perhaps you know where our friend is," Loomis said, hiding his feelings. He showed Parker the photograph of Belle in her hiking gear.

"No, I don't know where she is," Parker said, barely glancing at the photo. "Now, please leave. The rest of the meeting is for inner circle members only."

"How about you two?" Loomis said to the hard-bodied

blonde and her mesomorphic partner. They glared at him with undisguised hostility, not even bothering to look at the photograph.

"They don't know her either," Parker said, batting the photograph out of Loomis's hand. "Dave, escort these people from the premises."

Ledbetter's expression darkened. "Since when did you give orders around here?"

Loomis retrieved the photograph from the floor, then stepped inside Parker's personal space. "Mr. Parker," he said, as Parker backpedalled into his companions. "Consider yourself fortunate I'm an easy-going guy and abhor unnecessary violence, otherwise you'd be on your ass on the floor, minus a couple of teeth."

Parker paled and swallowed.

"And you really should do something about your breath," Loomis added. He turned his back on Parker and his pit bulls. "Thanks for your help, Dave." He gave Ledbetter some business cards. "Just in case anyone remembers something that might help us find Belle."

"Sure." Ledbetter slipped the cards into his shirt pocket.

"Dave," Loomis said, as Ledbetter walked him and Connie up to the vestibule. "All this stuff about interstellar radios, ecological disaster, and aliens from Alpha Centauri taking people to another planet ..."

"Rigil Kent, you mean."

"Don't take this the wrong way, but it seems pretty, um, farfetched."

"Sure, it might seem farfetched, but like I said, if you spent some time with Thaddeus you might see it differently. You can't tell me, can you, that out of the billions and billions of stars in the galaxy, ours is the only one with a planet capable of supporting intelligent life?"

"No, I don't suppose I could tell you that," Loomis admitted.

Loomis didn't think his father would have, either. However, Loomis was sure his father would have found it too much to swallow that an advanced civilization occupied a planet circling one of the closest stars to earth, if only because SETI—Search for Extraterrestrial Intelligence—hadn't detected their versions of *How I Met Your Mother* or *Survivor*. Loomis didn't say that to Dave Ledbetter, though: he'd probably just tell him that by the time earth had the technological capability to detect the Rigilian's radio and television signals, they'd upgraded to cable.

"How much is this interstellar radio going to cost?" Loomis asked instead. "A million? Two?"

"More like five million."

"How much have you collected so far?"

"Not enough. Care to make a contribution?"

"No, thanks," Loomis said. "Tell me, have you and Bets signed up to be in the first wave of refugees to, well, whatever your new planet is called?"

"That's not really any of your business."

Loomis smiled. He'd take that as a yes. "Nice meeting you, Dave. Say goodbye to Bets for us."

He went to the coat rack and retrieved his and Connie's coats. A number of other people were also collecting their coats, among them the pretty schoolmarm and the ear-candling lady, apparently also not members of the inner circle.

"Mr. Loomis," Ledbetter said as Loomis helped Connie with her coat.

"Yes, Dave?"

"Much as I hope you and Mrs. Loomis find your friend, and much as I enjoyed seeing Parker taken down a peg, I think maybe it might be a good idea if you didn't come around here again."

"I'm sorry you feel that way, Dave," Loomis said. "I was just getting to like you."

"Well, that was weird," Connie said when they were in the car with the engine running and the heater on high. People were trickling out of the church, and the parking lot was slowly emptying. A light wind was whipping a fine, thin snow through the headlight beams of the departing vehicles.

"Most of them seem like nice enough folks," Loomis said. "Even if they are completely delusional."

"Do you think they have anything to do with Belle's disappearance?" Connie asked.

"Sure," Loomis said. "Quentin Parker abducted her and is going to take her with him to the new planet to be the mother of his children. Or maybe she's going voluntarily. She's into the outdoors, as it were, and he's a famous adventure writer, after all, even if he dresses like an escapee from a Tarzan movie."

"Be serious," Connie said.

"Sorry," Loomis said. "Whether they do or not, when I first mentioned her name, Kellerman tried to pretend he didn't know who she was. I think Parker also recognized her name. Possibly Maynard, too. I don't know about Harriet: I had a hard time reading her."

"She's very attractive."

"Okay," Loomis said warily. "Your point being?"

"Maybe your hormones were clouding your judgment."

"Leave my hormones out of it," he said. Connie was a very attractive woman, too, but he could usually read her like a book, hormones notwithstanding. Not this time, though. Something was going on with her. He was damned if he could figure out what it was, though. "Harriet Olsen is a very good looking woman," he agreed, watching for a reaction. Connie's expression remained, well, unreadable. "But I'm not sure that's why I couldn't read her."

"So," Connie said. "Why is it?"

"Maybe I'm guilty of egregious stereotyping but, like you said, she doesn't seem the type to believe she has tea with an alien from Alpha Centauri who calls himself Charley."

"As *you* said, being beautiful doesn't preclude being delusional."

"I'm not sure Harriet Olsen is delusional."

"You don't think she's really in contact with aliens, do you?"

"Of course not," Loomis said. "It's got to be a con. I'm just not sure who's conning who. Dave Ledbetter said they needed five million dollars to build their space radio. And who knows how much they've bilked from the people who signed up for their cockamamie refugee scam. If Kellerman can attract that kind of money, he can also attract the kind of sharks that would like to bite off pieces of the action."

"And you think Harriet might be one of the sharks?"

"I'm not sure what to think," he said. "Maybe it's hormones, but she doesn't strike me as the predatory type. You never know, though. Quentin Parker might fit the bill if he weren't so bloody stupid."

"What about Dave Ledbetter?"

"I doubt it," Loomis said. "He and Bets have been with Kellerman for twenty years. They're true believers."

"Do you think that, despite his, ah, disclaimer, Dr. Kellerman might be implanting false memories in her?"

"Could be," Loomis said.

The trickle of people from the church had dried up. There were still five vehicles in the parking lot, though, four of which had been there when they'd arrived: the Lexus, the Neon, the Focus with the Florida plates, and the G-Wagen. The fifth was a half-ton crew-cab pickup with a Leer cap on the back. It was the only vehicle they didn't have a plate number for. Loomis reckoned it belonged to Dave Ledbetter, but he ducked across the road and wrote the plate number down, anyway.

"I know you want to get home to the kids," he said,

when he got back into the car. "But I want to stake these people out for a bit. See who's in the inner circle. Do you mind taking a cab home?" Maybe Hazel Ryerson would cover expenses.

"No problem." Connie took out her cellphone and called for a cab. "Can I ask you a question?" she asked Loomis.

"Okay."

"About your conversation with your mother this morning."

"Yeah …?"

"Have you ever thought about moving back to Toronto?"

"Not seriously," he said. "No."

"Why not? It's not like business is so great here."

"There are other things here besides business," he said. "My life is here." He looked at her. "You're here."

"I like that." Her voice was soft.

"Where's this coming from?"

"Oh, nowhere in particular," she said. "You know, that was the first time you ever really told me anything about your family. I knew your father was dead, but I didn't even know you had a brother."

"Dennis. Denny. A year and a half older than me. I have a sister, too. Annie. Lives in British Columbia. Works for the provincial department of natural resources. Drives a Land Rover. A year and a half younger than me. Mum wanted three kids, but wanted to get it over with in a hurry."

"If you don't mind me asking," Connie said, "how did your father and brother die?"

"They were killed in a car crash twenty years ago. Denny was driving under the influence. Lost control and hit a concrete abutment."

"I'm sorry," Connie said.

"It was a long time ago," he said.

"Not that long."

"I guess not. I still miss them,"

A cab pulled up behind the Outback and flashed its lights. Connie leaned across the centre console and kissed him. "G'night," she said. "Don't stay out too late."

"See you in the morning," he said.

"Um …"

"Yeah?"

"Why don't you come by for breakfast?"

"Sounds good to me."

10

It was after 10 p.m. and his feet were nearly frozen. He was just about to call it quits when the side door of the church opened and five people emerged: Kellerman, Harriet Olsen, Jimmy Maynard, and Dave and Betsy Ledbetter. Kellerman and Harriet got into the silver Lexus, Maynard got into the grey Ford Focus with Florida plates, and Dave and Bets got into the pickup with the Leer cap.

After a moment's hesitation—there were still two vehicles in the lot: the rusting, bilious green Neon and the camouflage-painted G-Wagen that Loomis would have bet belonged to Quentin Parker—Loomis followed the Lexus. Kellerman was an erratic driver, driving 5 or 10 mph under the speed limit one minute, then 5 or 10 mph over it the next. Twice he sat at a light so long after it had changed that the driver behind him had to honk. Nor did he use his turn signals, catching Loomis off guard when he turned onto Queen City Parkway. Loomis hung back as the Lexus meandered along the dark, tree-lined residential streets toward the lakeshore, before finally turning on to a short cul-de-sac off South Cove Road and pulling into the driveway of a modest two-story house.

Loomis watched from the corner as Kellerman and Harriet Olsen walked to the front door of the house. The porch lights blinked on as they approached. Kellerman unlocked and opened the door, then stood aside as Harriet went inside. He followed, closed the door, and a few seconds later the porch lights went out and the house lights went on, first in what was probably the living room, then in another room, likely the kitchen.

There were only three houses on the street, one on either side and Kellerman's at the end, perpendicular to the others. Kellerman's house sat on a lakefront lot, surrounded by an acre or so of lawn and some wind-whipped shrubbery, much of it wrapped in burlap for the winter. The shoreline was rugged and rocky. Except for a couple of hardy old cottonwood poplars and a struggling oak, all the trees had been cut down, or had blown down, exposing the house to the full brunt of the wind.

Loomis waited a few minutes, then started the Outback and drove into Kellerman's driveway, parking beside the Lexus. Zipping up his jacket, he went to the door. The porch lights went on. He pressed the doorbell button and heard chimes loud enough to startle the dead.

"Yes, who is it?" a tinny, disembodied voice answered.

"Dr. Kellerman?" Loomis said.

"Yes. Who is this?"

"It's Hack Loomis, sir," he said. "Forgive the intrusion, but I would like to talk to you and Miss Olsen for a minute, if you don't mind."

"This is not a good time, Mr. Loomis. Good night."

"Just a couple of questions, sir?" No answer. "Hello? Dr. Kellerman?" Loomis pressed the doorbell button, but didn't hear the chimes: Kellerman had turned the doorbell off. Then the porch lights went out, and no amount of waving or jumping up and down would activate them again.

Loomis drove back to the corner and parked across from the entrance to the cul-de-sac. He killed the engine and the lights and settled in to wait. For what, he wasn't sure. Perhaps Harriet Olsen would leave once they'd finished doing whatever they were doing that made it "not a good time." He'd give it an hour. No point in wasting Hazel Ryerson's money. That is, if she were paying them.

An hour later nothing had happened, except that Loomis's feet had gotten colder and his bladder had started to complain. He was about the start the engine, figuring he could make it home before the situation became urgent, when another Subaru Outback pulled up beside his, pointed in the opposite direction. It was identical to his own, save for the magnetic Jefferson Security sign on the door and the flashing blue strobe light on the dashboard. One of Phil Jefferson's security goons was behind the wheel.

While Loomis's car looked like an ordinary Subaru Outback, it wasn't. During the security boom following 9/11, Phil Jefferson had had six identical models modified with run-flat tires, bullet-resistant glass, ballistic material in the doors, roof, and side panels, and a central dead-bolt locking system. They weren't exactly armoured cars, but you'd need the jaws of life to break into one. Phil had sold one to Loomis when he'd left Jefferson Security to go into business for himself. It was getting on in years, the run-flat tires long gone, but was still tough and reliable.

The window of the other Outback rolled down. The driver was a dark-featured man whose thick eyebrows merged over the bridge of his nose. In the ghastly electric-blue light of the strobe, his jaw was dark with stubble.

Loomis turned the key and powered his window down. "How can I help you?" he asked with a benign smile.

"You can tell me what y're doin' sittin' here?"

"Freezing my ass off," Loomis said.

"What?"

Loomis sighed. "I'm working," he said.

"Working?"

Loomis showed the man his ID. "I'm a private investigator. My name is Loomis."

"Loomis? Like, any relation to Mrs. Loomis?"

Even though they'd been divorced for five years, Veejay had kept her married name, only her therapist knew why. "She's my mother," Loomis said.

"What?"

Phil Jefferson was definitely hiring a lower grade of gorilla these days. "Never mind," he said. "You've done your duty. Run along now. Give my regards to Veejay."

He powered the window up.

The man reached across the gap and rapped his knuckles against Loomis's window. Loomis powered the window down again. "Now what?"

"I ain't gonna axe you again. Move along or I call the cops."

"What's your name?" Loomis asked him.

"Uh?"

"Your name. Surely that's an easy enough question."

"It's Fisker. Agent Gene Fisker. Look, just move on, okay?"

Loomis took out his phone, found Phil Jefferson's cellphone number in the directory, and called it. It rang twice.

"What do you want, Hack? I'm kinda occupied, if you get my drift."

"So you're on the can," Loomis said. "I'm on the job. There's a gentleman here who wants a word with you." Loomis held the phone out the window.

Fisker took the phone as if it were a hand grenade with the pin pulled. "This is Agent Eugene Fisker of Jefferson Security. To who am I speaking to?" He listened, his swarthy complexion acquiring a deeper unearthly tinge in the light of the blue strobe. "No, sir," he said at last and held the phone out. "He wants to talk to you."

Loomis took the phone. Fisker rolled up his window and drove away.

"Phil?"

"Yeah. I'm here. 'To who am I speaking to.' Jesus God,

where does Veejay find them? Assholes 'R' Us? What'll it take for you to come back to work for me?"

"Hell freezing over."

"Yeah, yeah. I know. Why won't you be reasonable?"

"Why won't you?" Loomis said.

"Why can't you two just bury the hatchet and get along? Get counselling or something. Maybe if you had a k—"

"*Don't say it!*"

"Yeah, yeah," Jefferson grumbled.

A cab turned into the cul-de-sac and pulled into Kellerman's driveway.

"Gotta go," Loomis said. He flipped the phone closed.

The front door of Kellerman's house opened, spilling a fan of warm yellow light on to the frozen lawn, and Harriet Olsen came out and got into the cab. Thaddeus Kellerman's beer-barrel shape was silhouetted in the doorway, watching as the cab reversed out of the driveway and swung about in the turnaround. Loomis slouched in the seat as the cab went by, then started the engine and followed.

Twenty minutes later, Loomis slowed as the cab turned right into the main entrance of the Green Mountain Motel on Williston Road near Burlington International Airport. Loomis continued fifty yards farther along Williston, past the motel office, then turned into the motel's south entrance. He parked on the far side of the empty swimming pool, from where he watched Harriet get out of the cab, unlock the door to Unit 42, and go inside. As the cab left, the lights in the unit went on. Harriet Olsen, still wearing her coat and hat, pulled the drapes across the windows. A few minutes later, the lights in the unit went out. It was nearly midnight.

Loomis sat for a moment, then drove across the court, parked where the cab had let her off, and knocked on the door of her room. He waited a moment, then knocked again. He heard movement on the other side of the door, and the drapes twitched, but the room lights did not go on.

"Who is it?" Harriet Olsen asked from the other side of the door.

He took a step back so she could see him through the peephole. "It's Hack Loomis."

After a few seconds of silence, she said, "You followed me from Dr. Kellerman's house, didn't you? I saw the same beige car near his house. That was you, wasn't it?"

"You're very observant," Loomis said.

"What do you want?" she said.

"I know it's late," he said, "but I'd like to ask you some questions."

"If it's about the woman you're looking for, I told you at the meeting, I don't know anything about her."

"Her name is Belle Ryerson," Loomis said. "And you didn't answer when I asked you if you knew where she was."

"I'm telling you now, I don't know where she is."

"You do know her, though, don't you?"

"No, I don't know her. Now, please. It's late and I'm very tired. My sessions with Dr. Kellerman are quite exhausting."

"I'm sure they are," Loomis said. "I really could use your help."

She didn't answer.

"Miss Olsen?"

"Please go away."

"Just a few minutes of your time," he said. "Maybe you could tell me more about your experiences with, um, Charley."

"You're not interested in my experiences," she said.

"Where are you from, Miss Olsen?" he said. "You're not from around here, obviously."

"Please, leave me alone."

"Look, I'm going to leave you one of my cards." He slipped one under the door. "Why don't you give me a call tomorrow, and we can talk."

"I've got nothing to say to you."

"Call anyway. You never know." He tipped his hat toward the lens of the peephole. "Good night, Miss Olsen. Sleep well."

Wednesday
DAY 2

11

When Loomis got home, the message light on his phone was blinking, but his eyes were grainy with fatigue, his stomach was sour from too much coffee, and his teeth were scummy from Betsy Ledbetter's chocolate chip cookies. He spooned some Eno into half a glass of cold water and drank it down. He urinated, brushed, flossed and rinsed, then undressed and got into the cold bed he had shared with Veejay until she'd gotten fed up living with him in a trailer. Or maybe just with him.

At least he wasn't paying alimony. Then again, neither was she.

Picking up the bedside phone, he dialled into his voice mail. He had one message. It was from Veejay. He erased it without listening to it, then turned off the lights and drifted to sleep to the sound of the wind rattling in the trees. Some unknown time later he was wakened from a dream about Harriet Olsen, Hazel Ryerson and an ironing board—a dream he wouldn't be telling Connie about—

by the ringing of the telephone. Groping for the handset, he peered at the glowing characters on the call display. Veejay. Shit. He burrowed under the covers until the call went to voice mail—only to have it ring again a minute later. With a growl, he jabbed the talk button.

"For Christ's sake, Veejay, it's two o'clock in the morning."

"Is it really? Golly, so it is. Well, since you're awake, how'd you like some company?"

"Thanks," he said, with a rising sense of panic. The summer before she'd showed up in the middle of the night with a bottle of wine and a pizza, wearing nothing but a suntan under her coat. Getting rid of her had been like trying to catch smoke in a butterfly net. "But no thanks. It's been a long day."

"You're such a prick, Hack, you know that?"

"I should," he said. "You've told me often enough."

"What were you doing hanging around South Cove tonight?" she said.

"G'bye, Veejay."

Before she could call back he turned the handset off, then got up, went into the galley—you couldn't call it a kitchen—and turned off the base station phone. He went back to bed, hoping he'd remember to turn the phones on again in the morning. He thought about writing himself a sticky note, and drifted off still thinking about it. He'd forgotten his cellphone, though, and was startled awake by its insistent buzz. Cursing, he found it and turned it off, then got back into bed and lay staring into the darkness, waiting for the knock on the door that mercifully never came.

He managed to get a few hours sleep, but it was fraught with dreams he couldn't quite remember, and when his alarm went off at 7 a.m., he felt as though he hadn't slept at all. His body was achy and sluggish, and his head felt lose on his neck. Was he getting a cold? he wondered, as he rolled over and tried to go back to sleep. He must have succeeded, because when he opened his eyes again and looked at his alarm clock, it was nearly 8 a.m. He didn't feel any more rested, but by the time he climbed out of the shower, he felt almost human. He was spooning coffee into the filter basket of the coffee maker when the indicator light on the galley telephone begin to flash—he'd forgotten to turn the phones back on. The call display showed Connie's name and number. Oh, crap. He'd also forgotten about her breakfast invitation.

"I overslept," he said. "Is it too late for breakfast?"

"No," she said. "The kids will have left for school by the time you get here. But that was probably part of your evil plan anyway."

"Why would you think that?" he said. "Little Lisa and Bart are great kids."

"Would you mind picking up some orange juice on your way?"

"No problem," he said. He had a relatively fresh carton in the fridge, opened only two days before.

"Oh, and some low-fat milk."

"Okay," he said. He was going to have to stop at the grocery store after all. "Anything else?"

"Not unless you want sausages or Canadian bacon

118

with your pancakes."

"Good old American bacon will do just fine."

"Then you'd better get some of that, too."

"How are you fixed for pancake mix?"

"I make 'em from scratch," she said.

"See you anon."

Thirty minutes later, he rang Connie's doorbell, a five-cent plastic bag of groceries in each hand, containing milk, a carton of orange juice with extra pulp, half a dozen farm eggs, maple smoked bacon, multigrain bread, and a cantaloupe, fresh off the truck from Mexico.

"I invited you for breakfast," Connie said, as he emptied the groceries on to the kitchen counter. "Not to move in."

"Are the pancakes made?" he asked, telling himself it was silly to be stung by her remark, but he was, mildly.

"I was waiting for the milk," she said.

"Then I'll make my famous scrambled eggs," he said.

"Be my guest," she said. "Do you want coffee?"

"Yes, please," he said, with feeling.

She poured him a mug of coffee and he set about making breakfast. She sat at the kitchen table, sipping orange juice as he told her about following Kellerman and Harriet Olsen to the house in South Cove, his encounter with Agent Gene Fisker, and his conversation with Harriet at the motel. She seemed to only half listen, though, barely reacting to his recounting of Veejay's nocturnal call.

"Is everything all right?" he asked, placing a plate of scrambled eggs, bacon and toast in front of her. He was asking her that a lot lately.

"Yeah, everything's fine."

"Try the eggs. They're pretty good, if I do say so myself."

"I don't have much of an appetite this morning," she said, but she ate a forkful of egg. She looked surprised. "You're right. They are good." She ate some more.

"You're sure everything's okay?"

"Yes, Hack, everything's fine. It's just that I'm—"

The buzz of Loomis's phone cut her off. Hazel Ryerson's name and number were displayed on the screen.

"Hello, Ms. Ryerson," Loomis said.

"Mr. Loomis," she said.

"I was going to call you," he said, holding the phone away from his ear so Connie could listen in. "Has your—"

Hazel wasn't listening. She rushed on in a spill of words. "There was a report on the news this morning about the body of a woman found in—"

"It wasn't your sister," Loomis said, before she could go any further.

"How can you be sure?"

"Because the police asked us to identify the body. It wasn't Belle."

"Who was it?" she said.

"We couldn't identify her," he said, wondering what difference it made. "I take it Belle hasn't come home or called."

"I would hardly be asking about the dead woman if she had, would I?"

120

"No," Loomis agreed, looking at Connie and rolling his eyes. "You wouldn't."

Connie's expression was stern, a look she'd likely perfected during her time as an elementary school teacher, before she'd married Sam and had kids of her own to use it on.

"What have you been doing to find her?" Hazel Ryerson asked.

He was tempted to say "As little as possible," since she wasn't paying them, but that would have earned him another look from Connie. "We've spoken to her employer and some of her co-workers," he said. "Last evening we attended a meeting of the UFO group whose flyer we found in her office."

"I thought I told you she wasn't interested in that sort of thing."

"You did," Loomis said. "But, frankly, it was the only lead we had. And, as it happens, she'd been to a couple of meetings."

"I find that difficult to believe."

"So do we," Loomis said. "They're a pretty eccentric bunch. The leader is a psychiatrist named Thaddeus Kellerman. Does the name mean anything to you?"

"No," she said. "Is it a cult? Could they be holding my sister against her will?"

"I suppose you could call it a cult," Loomis said. "But I don't think they've recruited her to sell flowers on street corners. I don't know why she attended the meetings, but I'm pretty sure it wasn't because she believes aliens are going to take her to Alpha Centauri."

"Pardon me?"

"It isn't important. Has Belle ever mentioned a Quentin Parker? He's supposed to be some kind of adventure writer."

"I don't recall her ever mentioning anyone by that name. What about hospitals, Mr. Loomis? Have you contacted the police? Have you located her car? Perhaps she's had an accident. Have you checked ..." Her voice caught. "Have you checked the city morgue?"

"We've contacted all the hospitals within a hundred mile radius of Burlington, Ms. Ryerson. As well as the state police and sheriffs' departments of all the surrounding counties. It's standard operating procedure. I'm afraid we've nothing to report, although in some ways that's a good thing. Have you filed a missing person's report?"

"Not yet," she said. "I was hoping you'd find her."

"You should file a police report," he said.

"Are you giving up?"

Before Loomis could reply, Connie took the phone, pressing the speakerphone button that he could never find.

"Ms. Ryerson. Hazel. It's Connie Noble. I told you we'd give you a day of our time. We've done that. And more. Hack was working till after midnight last night. As much as we'd like to keep looking for Belle"—Loomis was sure Connie would continue looking for her, no matter what—"we can't afford to do it for nothing. This is our livelihood, after all. The time we spend working for you for free is time taken away from paying clients."

If we had any paying clients, Loomis thought.

"If I paid you," Hazel said, "would you continue looking for her?"

"Of course," Connie said. "But are you sure you want to do that? It can get quite expensive."

What are you saying? Loomis silently mouthed. But she wasn't telling Hazel Ryerson anything he wouldn't have told a prospective client himself. In novels and on TV the intrepid detective often charged a daily rate, but in real life the majority of private investigators charged by the hour, like any consultant, anywhere from $75 to $150 dollars, plus expenses. Loomis and Connie were nearer the lower end of the scale, but it added up. Fast.

"I'm sure," Hazel said.

"You should still file a missing persons report," Connie told her.

"I'll do that."

Connie handed the phone back to Loomis. "Connie's right, Ms. Ryerson. It can get expensive, especially for something as opened-ended as a missing persons case Our usual rate is $90 an hour."

"That's fine."

"Plus expenses."

"I understand …"

Loomis sensed some uncertainty in Hazel Ryerson's voice. He'd heard it before, with other clients. It made people uncomfortable, placing a dollar value on the lives of their loved ones.

"We'll take it a day at a time," he said. "And there probably won't be much in the way of expenses, beyond mileage, but we'll clear any unusual expenses with you first."

"Thank you," she said. "Of course, I don't expect to pay for the time you've already spent, nor for any expenses you may have incurred before ..." She paused, probably checking the time. "Before 9 a.m. today."

"No, of course not," he said. "One of us will come by later with the contract. If that's all right."

"I'll be here."

12

When Loomis and Connie got to the office, Loomis called McHenry and was told he wasn't in. He asked to be connected to Heather-Anne Allen.

"I spoke to some people here about Belle," Heather-Anne said, when she came on the line. "I'm afraid no one was able to shed any light on where she might be. Sorry."

"I appreciate the effort," he said.

"Please let me know if there's anything else I can do," she said.

"There is one thing. Do you know if Belle is interested in UFOs or alien abductions?"

"The topic never came up, but I'd be surprised if she did. Why do you ask?"

He told her about the flyer and asked her if she'd ever heard of the Kentauran Foundation. She hadn't. Nor did the names Thaddeus Kellerman, Harriet Olsen, or James Maynard mean anything to her.

Leaving Connie to prepare their standard contract and

releases and to run the plate numbers they'd collected the night before, Loomis went out with Belle's photograph and talked to people in the building and in nearby stores and coffee shops who might know her. The only person who told him anything even remotely interesting was Mrs. Khorasani, the diminutive, elderly Iranian lady in the black hijab who, with her grandson Amal, minded the convenience store and newsstand in the lobby.

"One day I see Miss Belle and Mister Mac Henry," she said, in her heavily accented but grammatically precise, present-tense English. "It is last week on Wednesday in the early morning. They are arriving together. They are arguing. I am not hearing what they are saying, but Miss Belle is very angry, I think. Mister Mac Henry, he is upset."

"But not angry?" Loomis said.

"Not angry. Afraid, I think."

"Afraid?"

"Yes, I think he is afraid."

"And you didn't hear what they were arguing about?"

"I am hearing voices only, not words," she told him. "The only word I am hearing is Miss Belle saying the name of Mister Mac Henry's wife. Miss Lizzie."

Upstairs, he told Connie about his conversation with Mrs. Khorasani. "She thinks they were arguing about Lizzie."

"Just because her name came up?" Connie said.

"I still think there's a good chance that McHenry and Belle are—or were—having an affair," Loomis said. "It's the simplest explanation."

She followed him into his office with a notepad in her hand. "Then why are we bothering with these?" she said, gesturing with the notepad.

"Are those the plate numbers from last night?"

"Most of them," she said, sitting down across from him.

"Well, the simplest explanation isn't always the right one. What have you got?"

"The Lexus is registered to the Kentauran Foundation at an address on Cove Lane."

"Kellerman's home address."

"The Ford Focus with Florida plates is a National rental. I haven't called National yet, though."

"Jimmy Maynard was driving it, Loomis said. "What about the G-Wagen?"

"It's registered to a Hubert N. Gasche, 847 Willow Lane in North Burlington, not far from where you live. The others include a 1994 Neon registered to a Jane Smiley of North Hero, and a 2001 Dodge Ram pickup registered to Ledbetter Enterprises, and a 2012 Ford Fiesta registered to a Katherine Wernicky."

"What about our intrepid adventurer, Quentin Parker?"

She shook her head. "Nothing registered to anyone named Parker."

"That it?"

"I've got another dozen or so to run," she said.

"Okay," he said. "When you're done, we'll divide up the list and start talking to them. We'll get more from them, anyway, out of range of Kellerman's reality distortion field, apologies to Steve Jobs. In the meantime, one of us should take the contract and releases to Hazel for her signature."

"Would you mind doing it?" Connie said. "There's something I need to take care of."

"Okay," he said. "I need to dig a little deeper into Belle's life, anyway."

He suppressed the almost irresistible urge to ask her what it was she needed to take care of.

Hazel Ryerson took her time answering the doorbell. He was about to twist it a third time when her face appeared in the stained glass window. She stared at him for a moment before opening the door.

"Come in," she said.

"Thank you." Loomis wiped his feet on the mat in the entrance hall.

Hazel was wearing jeans faded almost white by washing and a pale green sweatshirt at least two sizes too large for her. Her feet were shod in soft moccasins with tassels and beadwork, and her streaky blonde hair was cinched back with a hank of pewter-grey yarn the same colour as her eyes. It was noticeably warmer in the house than the day before. Hence, he supposed, the fewer layers of clothing.

"I'm sorry I took so long to answer," she said. "I was upstairs trying to get into my sister's computer. Without success, I'm afraid. Have you brought the contract?"

He took the contract and the releases out of his brief-case and handed them to her. He explained the purpose of the releases. They gave Loomis Investigations permission to ask Belle's bank and telephone, cellphone, Internet, and credit card service providers for information about her account activity.

"Pretty standard stuff," he added. "You should read them carefully, though."

"I intend to," she said. "I can courier them to your office later today, if you like. Or would you rather wait?"

"Are you very busy?" he said. "I was hoping I could ask you a few more questions."

"I'm not too busy," she said. "Would you like some tea?"

"No, thanks," he said. "I'd also like to look around Belle's apartment a little more thoroughly, if you don't mind."

"Not at all."

He followed her through to Belle's apartment and up to her home office. Belle's laptop was open on the desk, a foolscap writing pad beside it. Half a dozen or so pages were turned back, the fresh page two-thirds filled with neatly written notes documenting Hazel's attempts to guess Belle's password. She'd been busy.

"Most people use easy-to-remember passwords," he said. "That doesn't necessarily make them any easier to guess. My mother uses anagrams of the names of her cats and changes them every week or so. The passwords, not the cats."

"I doubt my sister would go to the trouble of making up anagrams, even if she had a cat. I have a program that generates passwords, but they are so complex and non-intuitive they're impossible to remember. I know you're not supposed to write them down, but ..." She shrugged.

"I write my passwords on sticky notes and leave them stuck to the front of my computer, on the principle that no one would believe anyone was that stupid."

She smiled. It was like the sun coming out and made her look almost pretty, but it was quickly gone. "I don't believe you," she said.

"Really? I'm told I'm a pretty fair liar. It's a useful talent in my line of work."

"I'm sure it is," she said, the smile flickering back for a moment. "But I've been told I have a pretty fair bullshit detector."

She typed a string of characters into the computer, an inhumanly fast blur of key clicks. The computer bonked and the login window shimmied. She crossed out an entry on the pad.

"Birthdays are always worth trying," Loomis said, as he started looking through the books, magazines and photo albums in Belle's bookcase.

Hazel typed, pressed enter, and the computer bonked again.

"I've tried all the birthdays I could think of," Hazel said. "In every form I could think of." She made three more attempts. The bonking was starting to get on his nerves.

"There's someone I could take it to," Loomis said. "But if she's used a program like yours to generate a secure password, the chances aren't good that he'd be able to crack it any time soon."

"I never thought of my sister as particularly security conscious," Hazel said.

"She works for lawyers," Loomis said.

Hazel smiled again. A tentative smile, a bit sad, but better than nothing. It faded when he asked if she could think of any reason why, if Belle didn't believe in UFOs and extraterrestrial visitations, she would have gone to a meeting of the Kentauran Foundation.

"I don't know. She's never indicated that she'd changed her views on the subject. But we haven't spoken much recently."

"According to an acquaintance who knows about such things," Loomis said, "the Kentauran Foundation is what's known as an apocalyptic or doomsday cult. They believe the planet is hell-bent for ecological disaster. Given her interest in the outdoors, I imagine Belle is an environmentalist or a conservationist."

"She is," Hazel said. "I wouldn't call her radical, though. I'm probably more militant than she is, but neither of us has made a religion out of it."

He ran more names past her. She recognized Dave Ledbetter's name, not from his television commercials, but from having purchased a bedroom suite from one of his stores when she'd redecorated her part of the house. However, none of the other names they'd gleaned from the plate numbers—Hubert Gasche, Jane Smiley, or Katherine Wernicky—meant anything to her.

"Does she belong to any social clubs or special interest groups?" Connie had already checked to see if Belle was on Facebook, LinkedIn or another social media site. She wasn't. "A photography club or a hiking group, say."

"She belongs to a photography club, but I don't know where or when it meets."

"Have you met any of the other members?"

"No," she said. "Did the people you spoke to at the meeting know Belle?"

"Some did, but they claimed to know nothing of her whereabouts."

"Are they lying?"

"I'm not sure. It's possible. My bullshit detector isn't as good as yours."

She smiled again. He took a chance. "You have a nice smile," he said. "You should use it more often."

"If that's an attempt to test my bullshit detector," she said, colour rising on her cheeks, "it's pretty pathetic."

"I wasn't testing you, Ms. Ryerson. I was trying to pay you a compliment."

"Why?"

"Why does anyone pay someone a compliment? All I meant was that you have a nice smile and I wouldn't mind seeing more of it. I wasn't trying to bullshit you. I was simply trying to be friendly. Full stop."

She shook her head. "I'm sorry. I'm not good with people, I'm afraid. I never have been. I don't make friends easily. Perhaps that's why I chose the kind of career I did. I— What's the matter? Why are you smiling?"

"A simple 'thank you' would have sufficed."

"Yes, of course. Thank you."

"You're welcome."

"It's almost lunchtime," she said. "Would you care for something to eat?"

"It's kind of you to offer," Loomis said. "But I had a larger breakfast than usual this morning. Later than usual, too. Don't let me keep you from anything."

"All right," she said. "I'll be downstairs if you need anything."

13

Loomis spent an hour going through the drawers and cupboards, closets and cartons of Belle Ryerson's life. He learned a lot about her, but nothing that provided a clue about where she had gone or whom she might have gone with. Unsurprisingly, she was orderly and organized, everything in its place and a place for everything. Not quite obsessive, but close, at least by Loomis's less-than-rigorous standards. He wondered how she was ever able to find anything.

Her taste in reading material ran from how-to books on photography and wilderness survival through pop-psyche self-help and personal discovery to American history and bodice ripper historical romances, with a smattering of sword-and-sorcery sci-fi and a pinch of chick-lit of the Bridget Jones variety to add spice. She had an old, leather-bound *King James Bible*, her mother's name inscribed on the flyleaf, paperback translations of the *Qur'an*, the *Rig Veda*, and the *Tibetan Book of the Dead*, as well as an old, well-thumbed paperback of Huston Smith's *The Religions of Man*. Nothing on UFOs or extraterrestrial life, intelligent or otherwise—unless one considered God to be an extraterrestrial.

With the exception of photographs and books, she did not appear to collect things, stamps or coins or carvings of owls. Nor, apparently, did she save old Christmas or birthday cards, postcards, personal letters. If she kept a journal or diary, it was well hidden, but more likely it was on her computer. If she corresponded with anyone, her correspondence was probably also on the computer. She contributed to the Sierra Club, Doctors Without Borders, the Chittenden County Humane Society, and a couple of local women's shelters. She paid her credit cards, phone and utility bills on time and online, judging from the notations on the bills. That she did her banking on her computer perhaps explained why it was password protected.

He found a fireproof steel lockbox on the top shelf of her bedroom closet. He didn't bother searching for the key, easily picking the lock with his handy-dandy, six-in-one pocket lock picking kit, although a straightened paper clip would have sufficed. The lockbox contained her passport (at least she hadn't left the country), her birth certificate, a copy of the deed to the house (it was in both her and her sister's names), her will (prepared by Ted Proctor Junior) leaving everything to Hazel, and other personal documents. There were some old family photos and a thin packet of yellowing letters between Belle and a man named Robert Abbot, written when Belle was in her mid twenties. He read two of them. They were love letters, but they were stilted and restrained, neither Belle nor Robert Abbot being especially good at expressing their emotions. Loomis could identify.

Her bedroom held one small surprise. While her shoes were universally sensible, and her wardrobe tended toward dowdiness, her underwear was remarkably frilly and sexy—although far from kinky—and, if Loomis was any judge, expensive. He wondered if she had any other secrets. If she did, he didn't find them in her bedroom.

Belle's bathroom medicine cabinet contained nothing out of the ordinary, no prescription drugs and very little in the way of over-the-counter medication. She had the biggest bottle of generic acetaminophen Loomis had ever seen.

She had a Bose Wave music system in her living room, but there was nary a CD in sight. There was an empty iPod dock connected to the stereo, though, suggesting that her music collection was also on her laptop. The tuner was set to Vermont Public Radio.

She purchased household supplies such as laundry soap and toilet paper in bulk. She had an expensive Italian coffee mill, a Braun four-cup coffee maker, and a two-pound bag of Arabica dark roast fair-trade coffee beans in the freezer compartment of her refrigerator. The freezer also contained a half a bottle of Smirnoff, a half-empty carton of Ben and Jerry's Cherry Garcia ice cream, and two frozen pizzas. There were two bottles of Otter Creek Copper Ale in the back of her refrigerator, next to a mason jar of fresh-ground peanut butter, and some cooking sherry and two bottles of

Rufino chianti in the pantry. She was one of the few people he knew, besides himself, who did not own a dishwasher.

He found Hazel in her office at the front of her part of the house. It had formerly been the dining room, as evidenced by the plate rails high on the walls, which were lined not with plates, but with hundreds of paperback books. It was disaster area compared to Belle's work spaces. There wasn't a flat surface, including the floor, that wasn't piled high with books and magazines and newspapers, maps and technical drawings and spiral-bound notebooks, file folders and stacks of printer or photocopy paper, some of which had toppled over. There was a Dell computer tower on the floor by her desk and a flat-screen monitor on her desk, surrounded by paper. An open HP laptop perched precariously on a stack of files. An older computer tower and CRT monitor had been retired to a corner. An industrial-strength shredder stood against a wall, bin overflowing with shredded paper, two bulging orange leaf bags next to it.

"*G'nu*," Loomis said, awestruck. "For a moderately militant environmentalist, you're death on trees."

"Disgusting, isn't it?" she said, surveying the mess. "Every six months or so I take a week and sort through it all, shred anything sensitive, and call the recycling company, but it never seems to make much difference."

"You don't smoke, I hope."

"No." A smile tugged at the corners of her eyes.

"Thank the *Great G'nu* for that."

"The great g'nu?" she said.

"My personal deity," he said. "A wildebeest by any other name."

"Ah," she said. "Is that the Canadian pronunciation of gnu?" She pronounced it "nu."

"I don't think so," he said. "I grew up pronouncing it *g'nu* from a song called 'I'm a Gnu' that my father liked to sing in the shower. How did you know I was Canadian? I didn't think it showed."

"I've got a good ear for regional accents," she said. To go with her bullshit detector, he thought. "Did you find anything helpful in Belle's rooms?"

"Not really," he said. "I think she keeps a lot of her life on her computer."

"I've been doing some research," Hazel said. "I may have found a way to reset her master password. Did you come across the operating system disks when you were searching her office?"

"No. Why?"

"If I can find them, I may be able to reset her password."

"It would help a lot," he said.

She picked up the contract and waivers from her desk and handed them to him. "I've signed these. Do you require an advance?"

"No," he said, putting the documents into his briefcase. "Do you have time to answer some questions?"

"Of course. Let's go into the kitchen. Would you like something to drink?"

"I wouldn't turn down a cup of coffee," he said, remembering the dark roast Arabica in Belle's freezer and hoping Hazel at least shared her sister's taste in coffee.

He followed Hazel into her kitchen. In contrast to her workroom, her kitchen was neat as a pin. Almost as neat as Belle's. It had all the modern conveniences, including a dishwasher, but he didn't see a coffee maker. She filled an electric kettle and plugged it in, then took a mug from the cupboard over the sink and a jar of Nescafe from the freezer compartment of her refrigerator. She spooned some freeze-dried crystals into the mug.

"I don't drink coffee," she said. It was a simple statement of fact, with none of the holier-than-thou overtones of recovering caffeine addicts or health-food fascists. "I keep this for emergencies," she added. "I hope it's all right."

He hoped so, too.

"I found some old letters between your sister and someone named Robert Abbot."

"Robert Abbot," Hazel said. "God, I haven't heard that name in years. My sister and he were high school sweethearts. After they graduated from university they got engaged, but he died of some form of cancer when he was only twenty-seven. I don't think Belle ever quite got over it. Is it relevant to your investigation?"

"Anything that helps me get to know her better is relevant," Loomis said. "Could something have happened recently that brought back painful memories?"

"I'm not aware of anything," she said. "I'm saying that a lot, aren't I? Too much of my sister's life is a total mystery to me. We may as well be strangers."

"How did you and Belle become estranged?" he asked, as the kettle began to growl.

"I think 'estranged' is too strong a word," Hazel said. "Or maybe not," she added. "We spent so much time together in the final years of our mother's life that when she was gone Belle and I just went our separate ways."

Emotionally if not physically, Loomis thought, but he didn't interrupt.

"Our mother was the binding force between us, I suppose, but once that force was gone we simply spun apart." She unfocused momentarily, acquiring the faraway look of someone who has turned inward. "Perhaps too much so. I haven't been much help, have I?"

"No better or worse than the families of other missing persons cases I've had," he said. "It's not easy when a loved one goes missing for no apparent reason. It's never something we anticipate. Your sister's disappearance is not your fault, Ms. Ryerson."

The kettle began to rumble. She unplugged it and poured water into the coffee mug. "Do you want milk or sugar?"

"No, thank you."

She handed Loomis the mug. He set it on the kitchen table, where it steamed and smelled like wet cardboard.

"Mr. Loomis?" She paused, as if uncertain she wanted to ask the question she'd been going to ask, afraid perhaps of the answer.

"Call me Hack," Loomis said.

"Hack," she said. "It's an unusual name."

He explained the origin.

"You may call me Hazel, if you like. It's a silly, old-fashioned name, I know, but I'm something of a silly, old-fashioned person."

"Look," he said, anticipating her question, "it's possible that Belle just forgot about her date with Connie, or tried to get in touch with her but wasn't able to—maybe her phone died—and went on a trip somewhere without telling anyone."

"She can be a bit impulsive," Hazel said.

"She may think that no one really gives much of a damn about her. You have more in common than you think. She doesn't make friends easily, either. Pretty much everyone I've talked to who knows her likes her, but no one has managed to get very close to her. Is she afraid of letting anyone get close? Could it have something to do with Robert Abbot's death?"

"She was very close to our mother," Hazel said.

"Closer than you were?"

"A little, perhaps. She's younger and was our mother's favourite, I think, although Mother would never have admitted that, even to herself. Are you telling me to be patient? That she may come home at any moment and wonder why everyone is making such a fuss?"

"It's a possibility," he said.

She hesitated for a moment, then said, "Do you really believe that?"

"Honestly? No, I don't. She may be impulsive, but I don't get the impression she's irresponsible. It is a possibility, though. Dink McHenry is convinced that she's just gone off on a jaunt without telling anyone."

Her expression soured at the mention of McHenry's name. "You say that as though you don't think he really believes that's what she's done," she said, a sharp edge in her voice. "Could he be involved in her disappearance?"

"He could be," Loomis said. "But so could you. Or your postman. But I doubt that he, you, or your postman have anything to do with it. How well do you know him?"

"Mr. McHenry or the postman?" she said, smiling.

He returned her smile. She had a sense of humour after all. He'd wondered.

"I know him well enough to know I don't like him," she said. "After our mother died, when my sister told me he'd offered her a job at his firm, I tried to persuade her to turn it down. In addition to my personal dislike of him, I never felt he did an adequate job of managing Mother's affairs; however, Mr. Proctor Senior was Father's lawyer, and Ted Junior was Mother's until he retired. I would have changed firms, but Mother was ill and it would have caused her too much distress. He still manages Belle's affairs."

"Not yours?"

"No. I have my own financial advisor; however, Mr. McHenry is still my legal representative."

"Do you doubt his honesty?"

"Perhaps I do," she said. "It's a purely subjective judgment, however. Perhaps I'm impugning him simply because I don't like him."

As good a reason as any to impugn someone, Loomis thought. "Do you have any objective reason to believe he mishandled your or your mother's affairs?"

"Had I," she said, "I would have reported him to the police."

"Do you know Lizzie McHenry?"

"I've spoken to her a couple of times at charity events, but I doubt she'd remember me. Why?"

"A few days before your sister went missing she and Dink were overheard talking about Lizzie. They may have been arguing. Do you think it's possible your sister and McHenry are having an affair?"

Hazel Ryerson gave a short, sharp snort of derisive laughter. "I think it's highly improbable. But if she were having an intimate relationship with him, it speaks volumes about her taste in men, doesn't it? Of course," she added after a moment's thought, "I may be wrong. I've been wrong about many things."

"May I ask why you dislike him so much?" Loomis said.

Her pale cheeks blazed. "No, you may not."

Why not? Loomis wondered. Could it be that her dislike of McHenry was because she'd had an "intimate relationship" with him that hadn't ended well? It seemed unlikely, but then, Loomis thought, he was frequently wrong about things, too.

"When was the last time you spoke to him?"

"I haven't spoken to him since Mother died."

He picked up the coffee cup and risked a sip. It tasted as though it had been brewed from sawdust.

"It's that bad, is it?" Hazel said.

"I'm afraid so," he said. "It's been in your freezer too long, I think."

"Only a year or so," she said, straight-faced. She took the mug and dumped the contents down the sink. "I have some herbal tea."

"I'll pass, thanks." He stood. "I should be going. Let you get back to work. And get to work myself."

"Yes," she said, standing with him and walking him to the front door. "This may sound odd, under the circumstances," she said. "But I—I enjoyed your company, Mr. Loomis."

"I thought you were going to call me Hack," Loomis said, putting on his coat.

"Sorry," she said. "Hack." She thrust out her hand. "Thank you."

"You're welcome." Her hand was small and warm and slightly rough, unusual in a "knowledge worker." Perhaps she did carpentry in her spare time.

As he drove away from the house, it occurred to him that it wasn't impossible that Hazel had done away with her sister and had buried her in the cellar of the old house. Based on what? That Hazel and Belle weren't close? Maybe she wanted the house or their mother's money all to herself. Or maybe Belle played her music too loud or had killed all of Hazel's goldfish. Maybe she was jealous of Belle's "intimate relationship" with McHenry, if it existed. No, he thought, it was ridiculous. Not impossible, but ridiculous. Again, based on what? That he liked her?

He wasn't that good a judge of character.

14

The Burlington Medical Arts Building was on Main, two blocks east of City Hall. It was a square and unprepossessing four-story structure of dark red brick and small windows. According to Connie's notes, Thaddeus Kellerman's office was suite 309, confirmed by the list of tenants in the lobby. Loomis took an elevator to the third floor. There was no name on the frosted glass door of suite 309. A small sign above a button beside the door read "Ring and Enter." Loomis pressed the button, but did not hear a bell or a buzzer, and when he tried to enter he found that the door was locked. He pressed the button again and waited. The office lights were on but there was no response. Perhaps Kellerman was with a patient. He pressed the button a third time and waited some more. Still no response.

The door of the office directly across the hall stood open. A plaque beside the door identified it as the office of Dr. Donald Dan, DC. Loomis went in. The small waiting room was crowded with uncomfortable looking moulded plastic chairs and magazine-strewn tables, but no patients. From the garish posters of spinal columns on the walls Loomis concluded that Dr. Dan was a chiropractor.

An attractive, fit-looking brunette smiled at him from behind the counter. About forty, Loomis guessed, she had dark brown, rectangular eyes and braces on her teeth. Her pale green uniform was tailored to her trim figure, a couple too many top buttons unfastened.

Her name tag read "Tracy."

"Can I help you?" she said.

"I hope so," he said.

"Oh, dear, it's not an emergency, is it? Dr. Dan isn't in today. His back is bothering him," she added, with an impish metallic grin.

"I was just wondering if you could tell me anything about Dr. Kellerman," Loomis said.

"Sorry, who?"

"Dr. Thaddeus Kellerman. He has an office across the hall."

She leaned over the counter and peered through the door toward Kellerman's office. Loomis caught a whiff of a warm, musky scent.

"I never knew his name," Tracy said, straightening, regarding Loomis with wide-eyed innocence. Had he missed something? he wondered. "What kind of doctor is he? Wait, don't tell me. He's a shrink, right?"

"That's right."

"Figures."

"Why do you say that?"

"Oh, shit. You're not one of his patients, are you?"

"No."

"Whew." She leaned forward again, gesturing him closer, giving him a second opportunity to enjoy the view, in case he missed it the first time. "You wouldn't believe some of the weirdos I've seen going into that office."

Wouldn't I? Loomis said to himself. Kellerman's specialty was treating people who believed they'd been abducted by aliens.

"And none of them ever comes out again," Tracy said, with a conspiratorial wink.

He showed her the photograph of Belle. "Have you ever seen this woman?"

Tracy cocked her head as she looked at the photo. "I don't think so. Anyway, she doesn't look halfway weird enough."

He put the photo away. "In what way are Kellerman's visitors weird?"

"Well, there's this one guy who dresses like a guide at that African safari park in Quebec I took my kids to when they were little."

Quentin Parker, Loomis thought.

"Then there's this woman and her husband," Tracy said. "You should see her. She's this tough looking blonde with implants like melons and muscles like a video game superhero. Dresses to show it all off, too. I dunno, do men find that sort of thing attractive?"

"I suppose some do," Loomis said, recalling the hard-bodied blonde in leather at the meeting.

147

"I mean, I believe in keeping in shape …" She took a step back from the counter and pirouetted to give him a better look.

"I can see," Loomis said.

She smiled her bright metallic smile. "Women who do that to themselves must suffer from some kind of weird neurosis or something. Maybe that's why she sees a shrink."

"Could be," Loomis said. "What did her husband look like?"

"Sort of, well, like a bulldog," she said. "They even brought two actual bulldogs with them once. Ugly things, but still kinda cute. The dogs, not him. He was just ugly. Shorter than her and very thick through the chest and shoulders. Wore a baseball cap with a really curved bill. Y'know, I think—what did you say the shrink's name was?"

"Kellerman."

"I think maybe he was scared of them. I don't blame him. They were pretty scary. Especially her, with all those muscles and her nasty mouth. Did I mention that?"

"No," Loomis said. "What makes you think he's afraid of them?"

"Well, a couple of weeks ago he was just opening up when they snuck up behind him—they must've come up the stairs—and shouted 'Hiya, doc!' He almost jumped out of his shoes. Old guy like that could've had a heart attack, but they thought it was hilarious. 'Specially her. Anyway, as they went into the office he seemed real nervous, and I heard him tell them that he didn't want them coming around anymore."

"How long did they stay?"

"I only ever see people going in. His patients leave by a door into the stairwell. A lot of them take the stairs down, I suppose."

"How often had you seen them before that time?"

"A couple of times, I think."

"Do you know their names?"

"I heard him call then something like Nash or Cash. No. It was Gash. Mr. and Mrs. Gash."

The Mercedes G-Wagen parked outside the Kentauran Foundation meeting was registered to a Hubert Gasche.

"Do any of Kellerman's other visitors stand out?"

"Not really. Most of them are pretty ordinary, actually. One of them, a big bald-headed guy, did look kind of familiar, though."

Dave Ledbetter, Loomis thought. "What about a woman about thirty, medium-length dark hair, slim and pretty, good cheekbones, about five-seven?"

"I dunno," she said, shaking her head. "Maybe. Are you a cop or something?"

"Or something. I'm a private investigator."

"No kidding. I never met a private eye before."

"I hope I've lived up to your expectations," he said, handing her a card. "Thanks for your help."

"Anytime," she said, her mischievous metallic smile full of invitation.

"How'd it go with Hazel?" Connie asked, when Loomis went into the office. "She didn't change her mind, did she?"

"No," Loomis said, hanging up his coat and hat. "We're on the payroll."

"Then what's wrong?"

"Nothing, really. Just tired, I guess, thanks to Veejay."

"She needs professional help," Connie said.

"You think?" Loomis said. "How did your research go?"

"Belle doesn't seem to have any kind of Internet presence that I can find."

"I don't either, probably," Loomis said.

He opened his briefcase and took out the signed letter of agreement and waivers, as well as Belle's most recent landline and cellphone bills, and handed them to Connie. Pouring himself coffee, he told her about his visit to Kellerman's office. She smiled as he recounted his conversation with the flirty Tracy.

"According to Dorothy Parker," Connie said, "men don't make passes at girls who wear glasses. What about girls who have braces?"

"She was hardly a girl," Loomis said. "But I did get the impression she liked kicking over the traces once in a while."

"Huh?" Connie said. "I don't get it."

"I guess it's a Canadian expression," he said. "Kicking over the traces means to be wild, reckless, devil-may-care. My father used to say it."

"I still don't get it. What are traces?"

"In this context, they're the straps used to secure a horse to a wagon."

"Oh, well, that explains it." She grew serious. "Could it be a coincidence Belle went to those meetings?" she said. "Maybe she really has just gone walkabout."

"I don't like coincidences," he said. "And they aren't statistically meaningful. But they do happen, don't they? Otherwise why invent a name for them. But you're right. Except for attending a couple of meetings there's nothing substantive to connect Belle's disappearance to the Kentauran Foundation or anyone associated with it. Do you have any idea what she wanted to talk to you about? Or who she wanted to talk to before she talked to you?"

"No."

"Where were you supposed to meet?"

"She was going to call me."

"Do you think she might have wanted to hire you? Or us?"

"To do what?"

"If we knew that, we might have some idea where to start looking for her."

"Do you want me to do backgrounds on Kellerman and the people in the inner circle?"

"Can't hurt," he said. "But don't dig too deep till we get a stronger connection between Belle and Kellerman's foundation. See what you can find on Hubert Gasche, though. He and his wife were Parker's pit bulls last night. What have you managed to dig up on him?"

"On Parker? For a supposedly famous adventure writer, he isn't very famous. As far as Google is concerned, there is no such person, at least no one named Quentin Parker that matches our guy. Maybe he's an alien, and I don't mean the extraterrestrial kind. One of your former countrymen, maybe."

"Or he writes under a pseudonym. What about Harriet Olsen?"

"There was an actress in the forties named Harriet Olsen. There was also a Harriet Olsen in her seventies who went missing in 2000 from Franklin, New York. The only hit I got on our gal was the Kentauran Foundation website. Speaking of which, for what it's worth, Kellerman's foundation is legit, or as legit as it can be. It's registered as a not-for-profit corporation called the Meta-Philosophical Research Institute of Vermont, whatever that means. Dave Ledbetter is on the board of directors. So is Bets. It probably won't surprise you that Dave and Bets are worth a moderate fortune, were loaded even before they sold out to Mega Stores PLC two years ago. They've been married for thirty-five years. No kids. Until recently she raised prize dachshunds. Gave it up around the same time they sold the stores."

"Couldn't take them to Alpha Centauri, I suppose." Loomis wondered how much of their moderate fortune Dave and Bets had handed over to Kellerman. He stood. "I need to gird my loins," he said.

"For what?"

"I'm going to make a copy of this," Loomis said, picking up the waiver giving them permission to obtain Belle's bank records. "Then talk to Dink. He looks after Belle's financial affairs. If she's made any unusual withdrawals lately, he'll know about it." He looked down at her.

She looked up at him. "What?"

"How does one gird one's loins, anyway?"

"I think it involves a sword."

15

"Good afternoon, Ms. Campbell," Loomis said cheerily, as he walked into the reception area of Proctor, Proctor and McHenry and headed toward the doors to the inner offices. "How are you today?"

"I'm well, thank you," she said. "Wait, please. You can't just ..."

But he did. He pulled open the doors and strode past the startled occupants of the workstations toward McHenry's office, Glenna Campbell trailing after him like an anxious nanny.

"Please, Mr. Loomis."

At her workstation outside McHenry's office, Heather-Anne Allen stood. Her dark hair was loose on her shoulders and she wasn't wearing her glasses, the combined effect of which was to make her look about sixteen. McHenry's office door was closed.

"Can I help you, Mr. Loomis?" She interposed herself between Loomis and the door to McHenry's office.

"I need to speak with your boss," Loomis said.

"I'm sorry," Glenna Campbell said. "He just barged through. Shall I call security?"

"I don't think that'll be necessary," Heather-Anne Allen said. She looked at Loomis. "Will it?"

"Heck, no," Loomis said. "I'm certifiably harmless. I just wanted a word with your boss and didn't want to give him the chance to duck out on me."

"I'm afraid he's occupied at the moment," Ms. Allen said. "It's all right, Glenna."

Glenna gave him a withering look, then turned on her heel and marched toward the doors to the reception area.

He nodded toward the door to McHenry's office. "Is he alone?"

"No," Heather-Anne said. "He's with a client."

"You're not a very good liar, Ms. Allen."

A blush bloomed on her cheeks. "I'm not lying."

"Yes, you are, because if he was with a client, you'd have said so."

"All right, fine," she said, a bit petulantly, Loomis thought. "He's alone. But he is busy."

"I won't take much of his time." Loomis reached past her and rapped hard on McHenry's office door. "Wake up, Dink." He rapped again. "Nap time's over."

The door snapped open. "Goddamnit," Dink McHenry barked. "I told you ..." He saw Loomis. "Hack. What do you want? I'm in the middle of something." He glanced back toward his desk, as if afraid he'd left whatever he was in the middle of in plain sight.

"All I need is a minute or two of your time," Loomis said.

"Would it make any difference if I told you I was busy?" McHenry said.

"To whom?" Loomis said.

McHenry sighed and gestured Loomis into the office. "All right, what is it?"

"Has there been any unusual activity on Belle Ryerson's bank accounts recently?" Loomis said.

"How would I know?" McHenry said.

"You handle her financial affairs, don't you?"

"I manage her trust," McHenry said. "She handles her own day-to-day banking."

"I'm not sure this falls under the category of day-to-day banking," Loomis said. "What about from her trust? Has she asked for an unusually large amount recently?"

"If she had," McHenry said, "it would be privileged information, wouldn't it?"

"You're saying she hasn't?"

McHenry sighed. "I'm saying it's privileged."

"I have Hazel Ryerson's signed permission to look at Belle's recent financial activity." He waved the waiver in McHenry's face.

"Hazel is Belle's sister, not her legal guardian," McHenry said.

Loomis wasn't sure McHenry was quite right about that. One of the documents in Belle's lockbox had been a power of attorney, prepared by Ted Proctor Junior, giving Hazel the authority to make decisions in the event that Belle became incapacitated due to illness or injury. Did being missing count?

"I'm confused, Dink," he said, eliciting a smirk from McHenry, which he ignored. "Why are you being difficult about this? Don't you want us to find Belle?"

"You haven't given me any compelling reason to believe she needs to be found," McHenry said.

"Perhaps not," Loomis said. "But Hazel hired us to find her. She's also filed a missing persons report. The police could be asking you these same questions."

"When they do," McHenry said, "I'll tell them whatever I can without violating privilege. Perhaps, unlike you, they will appreciate that my responsibility is to protect my clients' interests. And privacy."

"Even if by doing so you could be putting Belle's life at risk?"

"What evidence do you have that she's in danger?" McHenry said. "As I've already told you, and Hazel has probably confirmed, this isn't the first time she's gone off without telling anyone. I wonder if you aren't taking advantage of Hazel Ryerson's naiveté for your own benefit. Business hasn't been very good for you lately, has it?"

"No thanks to you," Loomis said, keeping a tight grip on his temper. He stepped closer to McHenry and glared down at him. "I'm going to ignore for the moment that you just accused me of attempting to swindle Hazel Ryerson. I'm not going to forget it, though, so you'd better tread carefully. The next time you impugn my honesty or integrity, I might not let you off so easily. As it is, I'm having a hard time resisting the temptation to bust your nose."

"Even you're not that stupid," McHenry said, with more bluster than bravado.

"Don't count on it."

"Your threats don't scare me."

"I'm not threatening you, Dink. I'm just giving you fair warning. Watch yourself."

"I think you should leave."

"Soon enough," Loomis said. He took a breath, let it out, calming himself. "Look, I get you don't like me, Dink. You may even still believe there was something going on between Lizzie and me. But don't let your dislike of me put Belle's life at risk. Maybe you really do believe she's just gone off on one of her jaunts without telling anyone, but what if you're wrong? What if she is in trouble?" Loomis paused for a moment, looking at McHenry. "Unless there's something else going on."

McHenry's face clouded. "What are you implying?"

"I'm not implying anything. I'm asking you straight out if you know where she is."

"No, I don't know where she is," McHenry said. "And I resent the implication."

"Resent it all you want," Loomis said. "I'm just trying to understand why you're so sure I'm wasting my time and Hazel Ryerson's money. And don't give me that crap about protecting your clients' interests. Hazel is your client too, isn't she? Shouldn't you be taking her concerns about Belle seriously?"

"Yes, Hazel is my client and whether you like it or not

it's my duty to safeguard her interests as well. If you are taking advantage of her, I will see to it that you are prosecuted to the fullest extent of the law."

"Do you *want* me to punch you in the nose?" Loomis said.

"Do you *want* to be sued for everything you're worth?" McHenry said, opening the office door.

"You wouldn't get much," Loomis said. "Might even be worth it. Consider yourself on notice."

McHenry slammed the door shut as Loomis left the office. Heather-Anne Allen emerged from her workstation, expression troubled.

"Walk me out," Loomis said. Without waiting for her reply, he started toward the doors to reception.

"What is it?" she said, catching up.

"What are the chances that McHenry and Belle are having an affair?"

"What?" Heather-Anne said, taken by surprise. "I'd say slim to none, but …Do you think they are?"

"You know his wife has left him …"

"She has? No, I didn't know that."

They exited into the reception area, where Glenna Campbell glowered at him. Loomis took Heather-Anne Allen's arm and walked her out the heavy glass doors into the elevator lobby.

"Do Lizzie and Belle know one another?"

"I suppose they do," Heather-Anne said. "Not well, I don't think, but they do know each other."

"How well do *you* know Lizzie?"

"Obviously not well enough to know she'd left her husband," she said. "What's this about?"

He followed her glance through the glass doors into the reception area, where Glenna Campbell sat behind her desk. Was she watching them?

"I'm just trying to get a feel for the social dynamic around here," he said. "How about I buy you a cup of coffee?" He looked at his watch. "Or lunch?"

"I'm afraid not, Mr. Loomis."

"I'm not asking for a date, Ms. Allen." Her smile was thin. "Try to control your disappointment. Anyway, I'm spoken for. But I do want to pump you for information and you're obviously not comfortable talking to me in the office."

"There's nothing I can tell you," she said.

"I'm not as sure of that as you seem to be," he said. "Fifteen minutes. Max. Bring your phone in case he needs you."

"I'm sorry, Mr. Loomis," she said. "It could cost me my job." And with that she turned and went back into the reception area.

Loomis watched her cross the reception area and disappear into the inner offices, then took the stairs down to the fourth floor. Alex Robillard and his partner were getting off the elevator.

"This is indeed serendipitous," Robillard said.

"What do you want, Alex?"

"Testy today, aren't we?" he said.

"Sorry," Loomis said. "What can I do for you?"

"We need to talk about the Lady of the Lake."

"Do I look like Raymond Chandler?" Loomis said.

"You misconstrue my literary allusion," Robillard said. "The Lady *of* the Lake refers to the woman who raised Sir Lancelot and presented King Arthur with *Excalibur*."

Viv Scott shook her head, eyes half closed, looking as though her stomach hurt. "Jesus save me," she said.

"What?" Loomis said.

"Her name was Viviane," she said.

"Ah," Loomis said. "What about Connie? Do you want her to sit in?"

"You can fill her in later," Robillard said.

"All right," Loomis said. "Just let me get my coat and tell her where I'll be if she needs me." He cocked an eye at Robillard. "Where will I be?"

"The café on the corner will be satisfactory, I think," Robillard said.

"Fine with me. I haven't had lunch."

Leaving Robillard and Scott waiting in the hall, Loomis went into the office. Connie was at her desk, staring intently at the screen of her laptop.

"I've got some interesting stuff on Hubert Gasche and his wife," she said.

"Can it wait?"

"Sure. Why? What's up?"

Loomis told her where he'd be and with whom.

She waved toward the door. "Okay. Go. Don't keep them waiting."

16

Loomis and the two detectives crossed Bank Street to the café, where they lined up at the counter to place their orders. Loomis ordered a chicken salad sandwich and a coffee, and Robillard and Scott both ordered coffee. Loomis offered to pay for their coffees, but Robillard insisted on paying for everything.

"Thanks," Loomis said, as they found at a table by the window.

"Yeah, thanks, boss," Viv Scott said, placing her briefcase upright on the floor beside her chair.

"My pleasure," Robillard said. He tore open a sachet of artificial sweetener, poured the contents into his coffee mug, and stirred thoroughly with the long plastic stir-stick. He removed the stirrer from the mug and placed it on the table. He picked up his coffee, took a long noisy sip, then smacked his lips and put the mug down.

"Good, huh?" Loomis said, around a mouthful of sandwich.

"My doctor says I should cut back on caffeine," Robillard said. He picked up the mug and drank again. "Shoot me now, I told him." He sipped again and put the mug down. "I tried decaf. I really did. I'd rather drink ditch water." He took another sip of his coffee, then said, "Does the name Maya Thomas resonate with you?"

"Doesn't ring a bell," Loomis said, making Robillard smile and Scott groan. "Am I to surmise from major case's continuing interest that her death wasn't accidental?"

"You surmise correctly," Robillard said. He slurped some more coffee. "Have you given any thought to how she might have come to have your business card on her person."

"Not much, I'm afraid," Loomis said. "We've been busy on a case."

"Someone missing a cat?" Robillard said.

"Beggars can't be choosers," Loomis said. "I take it the COD wasn't drowning."

"No, indeed," Robillard said. He hesitated, then went on: "Preliminary finding is classic blunt force trauma to the right occipital region. COD acute subdural hematoma. The ME opines she was struck a single blow from behind. Probably a fist. No signs of struggle or defensive wounds. In other words, she was sucker punched by a very powerful, right-handed attacker, most likely male. Not a frenzied attack, so not likely to be a crime of passion, as in boyfriend or husband. She didn't die immediately, the ME says. She bled into her brain for a while. But she was dead when she went into the water. There's a remote possibility that her attacker didn't intend to kill her, but the ME says the blow was extremely violent."

"Where'd she go into the water?" Loomis asked.

"As near as we can determine she was dumped out beyond the north breakwater and the current or wind carried her into the bay. Whoever dumped her doesn't appear to have made an effort to weigh the body down. Because she was dead when she went into the water, her lungs didn't fill with water right away, so she floated for a while, then started to sink. Once decomposition began, she came back up and drifted ashore."

Loomis wondered what Robillard was holding back. The police usually held something back in homicide cases, if there was something to hold back. He knew better than to ask.

"Do you know anything else about her, besides her name?"

Robillard looked at Scott, who shrugged, as if to say, "It's your call." Robillard looked at Loomis.

"If I knew something about her," Loomis said, "it might shed some light on how she happened to have my business card on her when she was killed."

"True," Robillard said. He took out a notebook and flipped through a couple of pages before closing it and never referring to it again. "Okay, here's what we know. Maya Thomas was twenty-nine years of age and single. She was from St. Lambert, Quebec, a suburb southeast of Montreal. She worked in Montreal as a graphic designer for a software developer. She crossed into New York State from Quebec at the Champlain border crossing on Saturday, November 21st at 2:52 in the afternoon. She was traveling alone, driving a 2009 Kia Rio, which hasn't been located. She was supposed to return home on November 28th. On November 30th she was reported missing by her mother, Christine Gervais, also of St. Lambert, Quebec. We didn't get the alert because, according to her mother, Thomas was supposed to be in Toronto attending a week-long computer graphics workshop. The mother says she has no idea why her daughter was in the States. We're heading up there first thing in the morning to talk to the mother, as well as Thomas's employer, co-workers, and friends. You know the drill." He put his notebook away. "So?"

"Well," Loomis said, "besides the fact that Maya Thomas was Canadian, I can't think of any connection between me and her. I was in Montreal on business in September, but if I met her, I don't remember. I was there for only a few hours and spent the whole time in a very dull meeting downtown. A Canadian transportation engineering firm with offices in Burlington, nothing to do with software development or graphic design. I did hand out a number of business cards at the meeting. Which was all men, as it happens. As to why Maya Thomas had one of my cards, perhaps she needed the services of a security company or a private investigator in Burlington. Have you spoken to anyone at Jefferson or New England Security to see if she'd contacted them?"

"We had the pleasure just this morning of speaking to Mrs. Loomis," Robillard said. "Or should I say the former Mrs. Loomis?"

"Please," Loomis implored.

Robillard's grin was wolfish. "Charming woman, wouldn't you say, Viv?"

"Oh, indeed," Viv Scott said. "Except for a slight tendency to grind her teeth at the mere mention of Mr. Loomis's name."

"Yes, well," Robillard said. "Be that as it may, she didn't recognize Maya Thomas from either the morgue photograph we showed her or the ones we received from the Quebec police. Neither did the receptionist or anyone else. Nor have they any record of receiving a recent inquiry from anyone named Maya Thomas. Likewise NES and the other private security agencies in Vermont, New Hampshire and upstate New York. Let it not be said that we've left any stone unturned."

"Can I see the photograph you got from the Quebec police?" Loomis asked.

Robillard nodded to Scott, who lifted her briefcase on to the table, opened it, and took out a kraft envelope closed with a loop of red twine. She unwound the twine, removed two five-by-seven colour photographs and handed them to Loomis. One was a group shot of nine people in a room full of big flat-screen computer monitors. A young woman in the middle of the group had been digitally highlighted, as if by a spotlight. The other photograph was a slightly pixelated blow-up of the woman highlighted in the group photo. In life Maya Thomas had been an attractive young woman, with dark curly hair, large dark eyes and a bright, guileless smile. Loomis studied her face for a moment, trying to match it to the memory of the dead woman he'd seen the day before, lying on the slab at the morgue, then handed the photos back to Scott.

"I think I'd remember meeting her," Loomis said. "She was very pretty. But I've never seen this woman before yesterday at the ME's office." She wasn't so pretty then.

Robillard took the photos from Scott and looked at them for a moment before handing them back. Scott slipped them into the envelope and returned the envelope to her briefcase. Robillard took out a business card and handed it to Loomis. "If you think of anything, anything at all, give us a call."

"Of course," Loomis said.

Robillard stood up. The top of his head seemed to brush the ceiling. When Viv Scott stood up, he seemed even taller. She could have tucked her head into his armpit, although it would have been unseemly. Loomis stood, shook hands with them both, then they put on their coats and went out into the cold. Loomis sat down to finish his sandwich.

17

Connie was on the phone when Loomis went into the office. "All right, thanks for your help," he heard her say as he passed her desk on his way into his office. She hung up and followed him.

"So? I'm guessing they wanted to talk to you about the body in the lake. Who was she?"

"Her name was Maya Thomas." He quickly filled her in on what Robillard had told him. "Did Belle ever mention someone by that name?"

"Not that I recall," she said. "You don't think there's a connection, do you?"

"Probably not," Loomis said. "But you know how I feel about coincidences." He picked up the phone and called Hazel Ryerson. She picked up on the first ring.

"Mr. Loomis. Do you have news about Belle?"

"Not yet," he said. "Did your sister ever mention someone named Maya Thomas?"

"I don't believe so. Who is she?"

"Maya Thomas is name of the dead woman found yesterday in Burlington Bay," Loomis said.

"Oh," Hazel said.

"There's no reason to believe there's a connection," he said, "but has your sister been to Montreal recently? Say within the last two years." It wouldn't hurt to cast a wide net.

"No, I don't think so. Why?"

"Maya Thomas is from St. Lambert, a suburb of Montreal," he said. "Does your sister have any interest in computer graphic design?"

"I don't think so."

"All right, thanks," Loomis said. "Any luck resetting Belle's computer password?"

"Not yet," she said. "But I found the operating system disks."

"Okay," Loomis said. "But if takes much longer, I think we're going to have to give my expert a crack at it."

"All right," Hazel said, and hung up without saying goodbye.

Loomis put down the phone.

"What now?" Connie said. "Do you want to see if we can find a connection between Belle and Maya Thomas."

"Where would we start?" Loomis said. "I still think the Kentauran Foundation is our strongest lead so far, although Dink McHenry is a running close second."

"For god's sake, Hack," she said, temper flaring. "Why do you insist on believing Belle and Dink McHenry are having an affair?"

"Why are you so adamant they're not?" he said, keeping a rein on his own temper. "I don't *want* McHenry and Belle to be having an affair any more than you do, but we wouldn't be doing our best for our client if we ignored the possibility, would we?"

"There are other possibilities."

"There are unlimited possibilities, especially if we throw Maya Thomas into the mix. We can't chase them all. We have to focus on those that have a higher likelihood of leading somewhere. Do you want to consider the possibility that Hazel killed her sister and buried her in the cellar?"

"What? No. That's ridiculous."

"I agree, but you know as well as I do that in most murder investigations the police look at family first. That a member of the family is involved is the hypothesis that generally makes the least assumptions?"

She sighed. "Oh, for heaven's sake, Hack. Occam's Razor. Really?"

"Occam's Razor is getting dull. Let's try a corollary. Woodward's Law."

"Which is …?"

"If you hear hoof beats, think horses, not zebras."

"It's zee-bras," Connie said, with an edge to her voice. "Not zeh-bras, you beaver-eating Canuck."

Loomis gaped at her, then broke up.

"Why are you laughing?" Connie said indignantly. "Goddamnit, what's so funny?"

"Okay," Loomis said, after drinking a glass of water backwards in an attempt to cure the hiccups. All he'd accomplished was getting water up his nose. "Tell me what you found out about the Gasches." He hiccuped. "Shit."

"Serves you right," Connie said, without sympathy.

"I can't believe you didn't know that 'eating beaver' is a euphemism for cunnilingus," he said. He hiccuped. "Especially considering how much—hic—you appeared to enjoy it."

"Oh, shut up," she said, cheeks blazing. "Is it my fault I had a sheltered upbringing? Goddamnit, will you please stop grinning."

"Sorry," he said, controlling himself with an effort. He felt another hiccup coming, which usually meant he was over them. "All right, tell me about the Gasches."

Connie tapped the trackpad of her computer. The screen displayed a photograph of a woman dressed—so to speak—in a skimpy sci-fi warrior princess outfit that left little to the imagination.

"Holy cats," Loomis said.

Connie smirked. "I thought you might like that."

"I'm not sure I do. What does she do, bench-press cars?"

"No amount of pumping iron will produce boobs like that," Connie said. "The rest is real, I suppose. Don't you recognize her?"

He looked more closely. "Oh," he said.

"The Gasches are former movie people," Connie said. "Hubert Gasche was a special effects technician and his wife Virginia, aka Ginny, was a stuntwoman. Her specialty was being hit by a car and flipping up over the hood. She also worked as a stunt double for various actresses, including Yancy Butler and Tia Carrere."

Whoever Yancy Butler was, Loomis thought

"The last production he worked on was a 2005 low-budget sci-fi horror film called *Alien Predators*. She worked more recently on a film called *Princess of Mars,* starring former porn star Traci Lords as Deja Thoris. They both have police records. The Gasches, not Traci and Deja."

"Do tell," Loomis said.

"A five-year-old New York state conviction for extortion. They ran a variation of the badger game. They'd stake out a bar with a parking lot and pick men coming out alone. Ginny would step in front of the mark's car and get herself knocked down while Hubert recorded Ginny's performance on his video camera. The victims, usually over the limit, would rather pay off than have them call the cops. It blew up on them when they had the bad luck to try it on a stone-cold-sober off-duty cop who was the designated driver just bringing the car around for his friends. Ginny did two years, and Hubert did eighteen months."

"I wonder if Kellerman has much success treating the terminally stupid," Loomis said. "Good work, though."

"Thanks," Connie said, as he stood. "Where are you going?"

"To see if I can get a better idea of Belle's movements after she left the office on Friday. Want to come along?"

172

"I've got a few more names to run."

"Okay. See you later."

He went down to his car and drove to Winooski, where he began knocking on doors, starting with the Ryerson sisters' southern neighbour. Two old Ford pickups of seemingly identical vintage sat in the driveway, both without wheels and up on steel work stands. One had been stripped of its bodywork from the doors forward, cannibalized for parts for the other, Loomis supposed.

"Do you know Belle and Hazel Ryerson?" he asked a long-haired, thirty-something man wearing a muscle shirt that revealed colourful tattoos from wrists to neck on both arms.

"To say hello to, is all," the illustrated man said. "One of them, anyway. The younger one. Don't think I've ever seen the other one, except when she opens the door for deliveries."

"Do you remember seeing Belle Ryerson on the weekend?"

"That'd be the younger one? Belle?"

"Yes. What day did you see her?"

"Didn't see her either day," the man said. "Not sure when was the last time I saw her. Sorry."

Loomis thanked him for his time and crossed the road to the house directly opposite the Ryerson house. A late middle-aged woman with huge plastic curlers in her hair answered his knock.

"Of course I know Belle and Hazel," she told him. "Since they were little girls. They're a bit peculiar now, though. No surprise, considering."

"Considering what?" Loomis asked.

"That they spent nearly half their lives looking after their mother. She was an invalid the better part of twenty years. Maybe the better parts of Belle and Hazel's lives, too. It's no wonder neither of them is married."

"How do they get along?"

"Hard to say, you hardly ever see them together anymore. I don't think Hazel ever leaves the house. Gets everything delivered. My husband says she must be, um, angora-phobic."

Angora-phobia. A pathological fear of fuzzy sweaters.

"When was the last time you saw Belle?"

"Must've been weekend before last. Or maybe the weekend before that. Cal—that's my husband—him and me were collecting donations for the Christmas food bank at our church. Hazel wouldn't even answer the door, but Belle, God bless her, gave us two shopping bags full of groceries and fifty dollars."

"And you haven't seen her since."

"What did I just tell you, young man? I'm not senile, you know?"

"I didn't mean to suggest that you were," Loomis said. "It's just that in my line of work you often have to come at things from different directions. It's amazing what people remember if you can get them to think about it."

"Maybe so," the woman said tartly. "But if I thought about it till Christmas it wouldn't change nothing."

"That's all right," Loomis said. "Thanks—"

The door banged shut.

Loomis crossed the road again and knocked on the door of Hazel and Belle's northern neighbour. The yard had been completely dug up and turned into a vegetable garden, put to bed for the winter. A towering old man wearing a flour-dusted apron answered the door.

"What can I do for you, young fella?" he said.

Loomis introduced himself and asked the man if he knew Belle and Hazel. Before the man could answer a woman shouted from inside the house.

"Who is it, Rufus? If it's those goddamned Jehovah witnesses again …"

"It's not, dear. It's a detective asking about Belle and Hazel Ryerson."

"Why? Who have they murdered this time?" A woman waddled into the foyer. She was half the height of her husband and twice the girth.

"They haven't murdered anyone, dear," Rufus said patiently, rolling his eyes at Loomis.

"I can hear you rolling your eyes, you old bastard," the woman said. She fixed a single, milky eye on Loomis, the other eye swivelling off in another direction entirely. "They murdered their mother, you know."

"Agnes," Rufus said. "They did nothing of the sort." To Loomis: "Don't pay her any mind. Belle and Hazel are good people."

"He just says that because he wants to have sex with them. Don't you, you old bastard? I've seen the way you stare at that one's chest whenever she works in the yard.

Why do you think he has that big garden?" she said to Loomis. "So he can spend all his time staring at bosoms. Isn't that right, you old bastard?"

"If you say so, dear," the old bastard said in a long-suffering voice.

"When was the last time you saw Belle?" Loomis asked.

"Don't lie, you old bastard," Agnes said. "Tell him you were staring at her on Saturday morning. I saw you. Yes, I did."

"Is that right?" Loomis said. "You saw her on Saturday?"

"Yes, I did," Rufus said.

"I knew it," Agnes crowed. "You old bastard." Her husband ignored her. Loomis admired his fortitude.

"At what time?" Loomis asked.

"It must have been around ten in the morning. She was getting into her car."

"Did you speak to her?"

"He wouldn't dare," his wife said.

"No, I didn't," he said.

"Just stares, he does, with his tongue hanging out like a dog."

"Excuse me for a moment," Rufus said. "Agnes, come with me, please, dear. It's time for your medication."

He took his wife by the arm and gently led her into the house. He was back a few minutes later. He'd removed his apron.

"Now, where were we? Yes, I was telling you that I

saw Belle Ryerson on Saturday morning as she was getting into her car, but I didn't speak to her."

"Was she alone?"

"Yes, she was," Rufus said.

"Did you see Hazel?"

"No. One seldom sees Hazel anymore," Rufus said. "Not since the old lady died. When she was alive I'd often see Belle and Hazel sitting in the glider on the veranda. Now Hazel rarely leaves the house. It's sad, really. I hope she's all right."

"When was the last time you spoke to her?"

"Oh, it's been some time since I've spoken to Hazel. Couple of years, at least."

"What about Belle?"

"Let's see. It was a week or so ago. At the farmers' market. I should have asked after Hazel, I suppose," he added with a shrug, "but she was with someone."

"A man or a woman?"

"It was a woman," Rufus said.

"Do you know her name?"

"No, I'm afraid not."

"Can you describe her?"

"She was younger than Belle. Maybe around thirty, although it's harder and harder for me to guess young peoples' ages anymore. At my age anyone under sixty looks young. She was very pretty, though. Dark hair. Nicely proportioned," he added as an afterthought.

"What colour were her eyes?"

"I couldn't say."

"Was she taller than Belle or shorter?"

"Shorter, I think. Yes, shorter."

"How was she dressed?"

"I didn't really notice."

Too busy evaluating her proportions, Loomis thought. "How was Belle's mood or demeanour? Did she appear upset or worried at all? Anxious? Afraid."

"Now that you mention it," Rufus said, stroking his chin.

"What?"

"I may have interrupted something. I didn't notice until after I joined them, but Belle's friend may have been crying." He shrugged. "My wife says—well, used to say, before she got the old timer's—that I have the sensitivity of a truck. Belle was trying to comfort her, I think. When I realized I was intruding, I excused myself."

"So you really didn't speak to Belle?"

"No, I don't suppose I did."

There was a panicky cry from inside the house. "Ruuufffuus!"

"Coming, dear," Rufus called to his wife. "Sorry, gotta go."

"Thanks for your time," Loomis said, as the door swung shut.

18

Connie was out when Loomis got back to the office. It was a few minutes before 5 p.m. According to the sticky note on his computer screen, she was checking out some of the people who were at the Kentauran Foundation meeting. He heated up what was left of that morning's coffee in the microwave. It tasted bitter and burned, but he drank it anyway as he called Connie's cellphone.

"Where are you?" he asked.

"Just got home."

"Any luck?"

"Not much. I interviewed three people who were at the meeting. They remembered Belle but had no idea where she might be. It's very strange. They all seem so ordinary. A bit, well, spacey, but otherwise pretty normal, even though they were all convinced they'd been abducted by aliens."

"I read somewhere," Loomis said, "that something like sixty percent of Americans believe in angels, astrology, and that reality TV is real, but you could walk right past any one of them on the street without realizing it. Except for the ones carrying signs, of course. Anything else?"

"I wasn't able to get hold of Jane Smiley, owner of the green Neon. How about you?"

"I spoke to half a dozen of Belle and Hazel's neighbours. Hazel is 'angora-phobic,' according to one of them."

"Helpful," Connie said.

"Another neighbour, though, name of Rufus, told me he saw Belle at the market the Saturday before last, apparently comforting a young woman."

"Did Rufus get a name?"

"No. Or much of a description. Just young, pretty, dark-haired, and nicely proportioned."

"What are you thinking?"

"The description fits Maya Thomas. And the timing fits, too. It would have been around a week ago Saturday that Maya Thomas was killed and thrown into the lake."

"You're not thinking that Belle killed her, are you?"

"No, but Belle may have been one of the last people to see her alive."

"The description fits a lot of women," Connie said. "Except for the dark hair, it fits me. I'm attractive and nicely proportioned. Or so you say."

"And so you are," Loomis said. "But Rufus thought the woman he saw was younger than Belle and not as tall."

"Okay, but it's still a stretch. Maybe it was Heather-Anne Allen that Rufus saw. She and Belle are friends, aren't they? She's younger, not quite as tall, as well as pretty, dark-haired and nicely proportioned."

"It's possible" Loomis said. "But I didn't get the impression that Heather-Anne and Belle hung out."

"The description also fits Harriet Olsen," Connie said.

"So it does," Loomis said, thinking that he needed some photographs to show to Rufus.

"All right, so now what?" Connie said.

"Who have you not spoken to on our list?"

"I was leaving Dr. Kellerman and Dave Ledbetter for you. There's also a Dr. William Spender. He's a dentist with an office in the Medical Arts Building, on the same floor as Dr. Kellerman."

"Have the police turned up Belle's car?"

"No," Connie said. "Nor has there been any activity on her credit cards or bank cards. I'm still waiting on her landline and cellphone history."

"What kind of phone does she have?"

"An iPhone, I think. A smartphone anyway."

"So there may be email and texting histories as well."

"I'm on it."

"Good," he said. He paused.

"Is there something else?" she said.

"No, not really."

"Look, why don't you come for dinner?"

"I'd love to," he said. "But it's the first Wednesday of the month." His monthly night out with "the boys," pizza, beer and darts at the Spotted Pig with Phil Jefferson, his brother Trevor, the general contractor for whom Loomis occasionally worked, and Bob Barnstable, publisher of the *Burlington Free Press*.

"Oh, so it is. Well, come by later, if you like."

"I like," he said. "But I might fall asleep on you. Well, maybe not literally 'on you,' but you never can tell."

"You can teach me more of your cunning Canadian lingo. Maybe that'll keep you awake."

"Not to mention your kids and your neighbours."

"Enjoy yourself," she said. "Save some room for dessert." She hung up.

Loomis squirmed in his chair to ease the tightness in his jeans as he dialled the number for Dr. William Spender, DDS. An automated messaging system answered. He listened to the entire message, in case there was a number to call in the event of an emergency. There was, but when he called it, all he got was a series of annoying tones followed by a voice message telling him the number was not in service.

According to Connie's list, and the printout of the Google map she'd left on his desk, Spender lived in Williston, southeast of Burlington. Loomis looked at his watch. He had time to drive to Williston and back and still make it to the pub on time, but it wouldn't leave much time in between to talk to Spender, if he found him. Tomorrow would be soon enough, he told himself. He had one more call to make first, though. He dialled.

"Hello?"

"Dave? It's Hack Loomis."

"Mr. Loomis. How'd you get this number?"

"You're in the book, Dave."

"Not at this number I'm not," Dave Ledbetter said.

"Depends on the book," Loomis said. The Internet was a wonderful thing, if you knew what you were doing—which Connie did.

"What do you want?"

"I was wondering if I could buy you a beer."

"I don't drink alcohol."

"Coffee then."

"Why? We ain't gonna be friends. We got nothing to talk about."

"I'm sorry we got off on the wrong foot last night, Dave. We just want to be sure we're doing everything we can to find Belle Ryerson and bring her home safely. Thing is, I'm not sure Dr. Kellerman was being entirely truthful with us last night and I have a feeling you know why."

"Thaddeus wouldn't lie to you about something like that," Ledbetter said.

"You think a lot of him, don't you?"

"I've known him a long time," Ledbetter said. "He's a good friend and helped Bets when she ... He's a good man."

"I'm sure he is," Loomis said. It was easy to guess what kind of help Bets had needed from a psychiatrist who treated people who believed they'd been kidnapped by aliens. "But you don't last long in my business without being able to read people."

"Maybe you don't read people as good as you think," Ledbetter said. "You're wrong about Thaddeus. If he knew where your friend was, he'd tell you."

"Maybe he doesn't know where she is," Loomis said. "But he knows something. You seem like a pretty good guy, Dave."

"Gee, Mr. Loomis," Ledbetter said.

"No need to be sarcastic. I mean it. I'm pretty sure you want to help us find Belle."

"Sure, but what can I do?"

"Dr. Kellerman might feel more like talking to me if you were there."

"That's not something I'd feel comfortable with," Ledbetter said. "Anyway, he's pretty busy these days."

Right, Loomis thought. Moving to another planet must take a lot of planning, not to mention careful packing.

"Okay, then maybe you can tell me how to get hold of Maya Thomas?"

"Who?" No hesitation, flat affect: he didn't recognize the name.

"A friend of Belle's," Loomis said. "I think she may be a member of your group?"

"I never heard of anyone by that name. Look, the wife's calling. I gotta go."

"Give my regards to Bets," Loomis said, but Ledbetter had already hung up.

He put on his coat and hat, locked up, and set out on foot for the Spotted Pig.

The temperature had climbed to a degree or two above

freezing, and as Loomis walked back to his office after his evening out, it began to snow. Huge fat flakes fell out of the dark December sky, accumulating on the shoulders and lapels of his coat. They melted soon after they hit the ground, though, leaving wet marks on the pavement like tiny Rorschach blobs. It wasn't long before the blobs merged into a uniform wetness. He picked up a coffee at Debbie's and took it up to the office. It was a little past 9 p.m.

He called Connie. "I'll be over in half an hour or so," he said. "If it's still all right with you."

"Of course. How was your evening?"

"It was okay," he said. "It would've been better if Phil hadn't kept trying to get me to come back to work for him."

Loomis called his mother in Toronto for an update on his grandfather, who was doing much better. They chatted for a few minutes, and she extracted a promise from him to make an extra special effort to get home for Christmas.

He called Hazel Ryerson.

"Your neighbour Rufus told me he saw Belle comforting a woman at the Winooski farmers' market a week ago Saturday. Did your sister ever mention a friend, a woman a few years younger than her, who was in some kind of trouble?"

"Not that I recall. Which neighbour was it?"

"The older man who lives next door. The gardener. His wife has Alzheimer's."

"I know who you mean. I didn't know his name."

"How are you doing with Belle's computer?"

"I'm ready to try resetting the password," she said. "I just needed to be sure it won't wipe everything on the hard drive."

"All right," he said. "Let me know how it goes."

"Of course."

"Have a good evening, Hazel."

"Thank you, uh, Hack." She paused, then said, "I can't say I really like your nickname. Would it be all right if I called you John?"

"Why not?" Loomis said. "Almost no one else does."

"Goodnight, John."

"Goodnight, Hazel."

He put on his coat and hat, locked up and went down to his car. Fifteen minutes later, he rang Connie's doorbell. She let him in and took his coat and hat. The house smelled wonderful.

"I hope you saved room for dessert," she said as she hung his coat in the hall closet.

"Geez, lady, at least give me time to take my boots off."

"Not that," she said, blushing. "I mean real dessert. I've been domestic."

She led him into the kitchen. The delicious aroma was almost overwhelming.

"It's an almond paste and berry tort."

"It smells fantastic. Where's yours?"

"You'll have to share," she said. She cut him a healthy slice and poured him a glass of wine. "It's a dessert wine.

I know you're not a wine drinker, but wait till you taste it with the tort."

Both tasted fabulous.

"Where are the kids?" he asked.

"Susie's on an overnight school trip to Montpelier for her civics class and Billy is chained up in the basement." She giggled and poured more wine for them both. "Not really."

"I thought you'd finally decided to take W.C. Fields' advice about how to raise boys."

"Actually, he's next door slaughtering aliens with Xavier Ducharme's new X-Box." She looked at him and blushed even more deeply. "He's staying over."

"On a school night?"

"His school had to close. They discovered some old asbestos insulation when they were doing some work on the heating system. It'll be a day or two before they can find a temporary location."

"I see. So we have the place to ourselves."

"Yes, indeed," she said. "Eat up, big fella."

Some time later they lay in a tangle of sheets, damp with exertion and limp—at least in Loomis's case—with near exhaustion. Connie's breath was warm and sweet on his neck.

"Can I tell you something?" she said.

"Sure."

"Promise you won't get angry."

"I promise I won't get angry."

"Sam didn't like doing that."

"Who?"

She nipped his earlobe.

"Ouch."

"Sorry. Did I hurt you?"

"No. I was just being dramatic. Can I tell you something, with the same caveat attached?"

"Sure."

"Veejay didn't share your enthusiasm for my cunning linguistic abilities, either."

"You mean she didn't like it at all?"

"She never indicated that she enjoyed the experience. She just endured until I lost interest."

"Maybe you weren't doing it right."

Loomis laughed. "Maybe not."

"Am I …? Do I …? I mean, Sam didn't like me doing it to him, either."

"His loss."

"He liked fucking, though."

"So did Veejay, as long as she was in charge."

"You mean on top?"

"Not necessarily."

"Sam was pretty much the straight missionary type, although when he was feeling adventurous we'd do it doggie style, which—Hey! What's this?"

"Talking dirty will do it every time."

Connie wriggled under the covers just as Loomis's cellphone began to buzz. He reached for it. "It's Hazel," he said.

Connie surfaced. "Invite her over." She blushed furiously. "Oh, god, I didn't really say that, did I?"

"Must be the endorphins. Shush now." He opened the phone and held it so Connie could listen in. "Hello, Hazel?"

"Oh, thank god. Can you come right away?"

Connie choked back a laugh.

"What's wrong?" Loomis said.

"I've apprehended an intruder."

"An intruder? Are you all right?"

"Yes, I'm fine."

"Have you called the police?"

"No, I—. He insisted I call you."

"Me? Who is it?"

He heard a scuffing sound then a muffled, "What's your name?" He did not hear the reply, but there was more scuffing, then: "He says his name is Quentin Parker and that you will vouch for him."

"He's got that part wrong." Why on earth would a supposedly famous adventure writer try to break into Belle's house? Loomis wondered. Nevertheless, his curiosity could wait. He had more pressing needs to satisfy. He said, "Call the police, let them handle it."

"Please, John," Hazel said. "He says he has information about my sister that he will only divulge to you."

"All right," Loomis said, stifling a sigh. "I'll see you in twenty minutes."

He closed the phone. Connie was already getting dressed. "She called you John."

"I'll explain in the car," Loomis said, stuffing himself

into his trousers.

"You're a good man, Hack Loomis," Connie said. She kissed him. "Jesus. You stink of me." She chuckled. "I stink of you, too, I bet. What will Hazel think when she gets a whiff of us?"

"Maybe she'll pay us a bonus," Loomis said.

19

When Hazel Ryerson opened her door, she was holding a flat spade.

"Come in. Don't bother with those," she said, as Loomis and Connie began to remove their footwear.

She led them into Belle's part of the house, through the main kitchen into the summer kitchen. Quentin Parker sat on the floor, his left wrist shackled to the leg of an ancient cast iron wood stove with a pair of handcuffs that were decorated with scrollwork. He held a hand towel to his head with his right hand. There was blood on the towel, but not a lot. He wasn't wearing his African safari outfit, just jeans and a ratty leather jacket.

"Loomis. Christ. Get me out of here. She's crazy. She hit me with a fucking shovel. She could've killed me."

Ignoring him, Loomis said to Hazel, "Where'd you get those handcuffs? They look like they belong in a museum."

"They belonged to my great-grandfather," Hazel said, with a bemused look. "He was a policeman in Boston."

She handed Loomis the key, which resembled an old-fashioned roller skate key. He squatted beside Parker, while Hazel stood guard with her spade.

"You want to tell me what the hell you're doing breaking into Belle Ryerson's house?"

"Unlock me," Quentin Parker demanded.

"Ask him where Belle is," Hazel said, brandishing the spade.

Parker cringed. "Keep her away from me."

Loomis stood and said to Hazel, "I think we should let the police sort him out."

"Hold on," Parker said. "We don't need the police. Just let me go and I won't press charges for assault with a deadly weapon."

Hazel snorted. "Tell me what you know about my sister's disappearance," she said, "and I won't press charges for trespassing and attempted rape."

"I didn't try to rape you, you crazy bitch."

Loomis prodded Parker's thigh with the toe of his boot. "Be polite."

"She's a fucking lunatic."

Loomis prodded Parker's thigh again, harder. "What did I tell you?"

"Yeah, yeah, okay."

"This man is associated with the UFO cult I told you about," Loomis said. "He claims to be an adventure writer, but when we googled him we didn't find anything. He may know something about Belle's disappearance and he may not. Personally, I suspect it's the latter. He just told you he did to keep you from calling the police."

"Then what's he doing here?" Hazel said. "Why did he try to break into Belle's house?"

Loomis squatted beside the chubby, self-proclaimed writer. "Well?"

"Well what?"

Loomis sighed. "Listen, you moron. You've got two choices. Either answer our questions or face charges of trespassing, assault, attempted rape and whatever else we can think of."

"Come *on*."

"Your choice. Do you need a doctor?"

"No, I don't need a fucking doctor. Just unlock me and get me the hell out of here."

"In good time," Loomis said. "What do you know about Belle Ryerson's disappearance?"

"Nothing," Parker said. "Like you said, I just told the crazy bitch that so she wouldn't call the cops."

Parker winced as Loomis jabbed stiffened fingers into flab of his chest. "I told you to watch your mouth. Don't make me remind you again."

"Yeah. All right." Parker rattled the cuff attached to the stove leg. "Unlock this thing."

"Not until you tell us why you tried to break into Belle's house."

"I was going to take her computer, if she had one."

"What were you hoping to find?"

"Information about Kellerman's foundation for an article I'm writing."

Loomis shook his head. "You're still insisting you're a writer," he said.

"Yeah, well, I am a writer."

"If you're a writer, I'm an alien from Alpha Centauri. Name a publication you've been published in."

"The *National Enquirer*?"

"Right," Loomis said, standing.

"Look, Kellerman's people are a bunch of nuts," Parker said. "I only ingratiated myself with them to write a tongue-in-cheek travel story, like to another planet."

"Ingratiate," Connie said. "Golly, he must be a writer after all."

"Are either of you buying this?" Loomis said.

Connie shook her head. "Not for a minute."

"I don't know," Hazel said. "Are you certain he doesn't know where Belle is?"

"No," Loomis said. "All I know for certain is that we shouldn't believe a word that comes out of his mouth."

"What are we going to do?" Hazel said.

"Well, if I thought beating on him with that shovel would get the truth out of him, I'd say go for it."

"Hey!"

"Shut up!" Connie and Hazel said simultaneously.

"Enhanced interrogation has its attractions," Loomis said, "particularly in this case, but it's not really an effective technique. Subjects will tell the interrogators whatever they think the interrogators want to hear."

"Maybe just a little whack," Hazel said.

"Why not?" Loomis said with a shrug.

"I abhor senseless violence," Connie said. "However, under the circumstances ..."

Hazel raised her shovel and took a step toward Parker.

"Oh, come on!" Parker yelped, raising his free arm. "You're not serious."

Hazel rapped him on the shoulder with the flat of the shovel blade.

"Ow! Jesus!"

"So, what do we do with him?" Connie said.

"It's up to you," Loomis said to Hazel.

"What do you think I should do?" she asked him.

"Turn him over to the police," Loomis said.

"C'mon," Parker said. "We're on the same side here."

"How do you figure that?" Loomis said.

"We both want something from Kellerman's bunch, don't we? You want to find out where the Ryerson broad is. I want a story. Maybe we can help each other."

"How do you figure that? Do you know where Belle is?"

"Me? No. But maybe Kellerman does. Or maybe not. All I'm saying is I can help you find out if he does or not, and if he does, where he's got her stashed."

"Right," Loomis said. "You've *ingratiated* yourself into his organization." Loomis unlocked the bracelet from the stove leg. "We're going to make ourselves more comfortable then you're going to tell us everything you know about the Kentauran Foundation." While Hazel raised her spade lest he make a break for it, Loomis pulled Parker to his feet by the bracelet still attached to his wrist.

"C'mon, take this thing off."

"Not yet."

Loomis led him into Hazel's living room. The old house was heated by hot water circulated through cast-iron radiators. Loomis dragged a chair next to a radiator. "Sit."

"This isn't funny," Parker protested, as Loomis cuffed him to the radiator. "I could have you charged with kidnapping or forcible confinement or something."

"Comfy?" Loomis said, ignoring his threat. "Good. What kind of car are you driving?"

"What? A green Neon. Why?"

"Give me the keys," Loomis said, holding out his hand.

Parker reached into his jacket pocket and produced a set of car keys with a big, plastic daisy key fob. He handed them to Loomis.

"Be right back," Loomis said to Connie and Hazel. "You won't give them any trouble, will you?" he said to Parker.

"Right. Handcuffed to fucking radiator."

The blade of the shovel rang as Hazel rapped Parker's kneecap.

"Ow! Fuck. What was that for?"

"Language," Hazel said.

Loomis went out and found the green Neon two doors down the street. He returned to the house carrying Parker's khaki computer satchel. He placed it on a table.

"Who's Jane Smiley?" he asked Parker.

"What?"

"The car you're driving is registered to Jane Smiley of North Hero. Who is she?"

"My aunt," he said.

Loomis opened Parker's satchel. In addition to a dog-eared paperback entitled *Abduction: Human Encounters with Aliens*, by John E. Mack, M.D., the satchel contained an eight-by-ten spiral-bound notebook and a Dell laptop at least five years behind state-of-the-art. Loomis opened the notebook.

"Hey, man," Parker said, trying to snatch the notebook away with his free hand. "That's private."

With Connie and Hazel peering over his shoulder, Loomis turned the pages of the notebook.

"Oh, for heaven's sake," Hazel said.

The notebook was largely blank but for a dozen or so pages of random schoolboy scribbling and crude doodles. There were numerous elaborate variations of the letter "D"; half a dozen renderings of the words *Alpha Centauri* and *Rigil Kent* in a variety of primitive font styles; amateurish drawings of spaceships and flying saucers and pointy-eared alien women with huge breasts being ravaged by male aliens with gigantic phalluses; and a few somewhat more realistic but poorly rendered semi-pornographic drawings of naked women in what Loomis presumed were intended to be provocative poses.

"I don't know what kind of writer you are, Mr. Parker," Connie said, "but you're certainly no artist. My son draws better naked women than you do and he's only twelve."

"Mr. Parker's mental age obviously isn't much higher," Hazel said.

A number of pages contained a series of crude caricatures: a barrel-shaped man with no neck and stubby legs that bore a vague resemblance to Dr. Thaddeus Kellerman; an immensely fat, bald-headed man that Loomis presumed was intended to represent Dave Ledbetter; an ape-like man with a protruding jaw and dragging knuckles; a woman with bulging, anatomically fanciful muscles and gigantic balloon-like breasts; and, finally, a man in a spacesuit with a huge helmet and rabbit-ear antennae. Loomis turned the page to a list of names: D. & A. Thomas, Randy Booth, and Oscar Schuh. Notably absent from the gallery of caricatures or the list of names was Harriet Olsen.

"These names," Loomis said, tapping the notebook page under Parker's nose. "Are they all members of the Kentauran Foundation?"

"Yeah," Parker said. "They're people I interviewed for my story."

"What about Harriet Olsen?"

"I haven't had a chance to talk to her. Kellerman keeps her on a pretty short leash."

"What do you know about her?"

"Nothing, really, except that she's a total nut job. I'm not sure who's crazier, her or Kellerman, but neither of them's firing on all cylinders, that's for sure. You saw their stupid hypnosis routine last night. Crazy or what?"

"They both seem to sincerely believe she's in contact

with aliens. And, judging from the audience's reaction, so do a lot of other people."

"Yeah, well, what can I tell you?" Parker said. "Bunch o' losers, you ask me."

"You're not a believer yourself then?"

"Hell, no."

Loomis riffled the pages of the notebook. There were no story notes, outlines, quotes from interviews, or observations. "Where are your interview notes?"

"I've got a good memory."

Loomis put the notebook aside and lifted the lid of the laptop. The screen brightened as the computer woke up and demanded a password.

"What's your password?" Loomis said.

"Get serious," Parker replied.

Loomis closed the laptop with a hard snap. "For someone who claims to be on the same side as us, you aren't being very cooperative. I don't know what kind of game you're playing, Quentin. Maybe you are just a pathetic clown with delusions of grammar, but if you know anything about Belle Ryerson's disappearance tell us now or there's going to be serious hell to pay. Trust me on that."

"I told you, I don't know anything."

Loomis looked at Hazel. "How's your bullshit detector working today?"

"Not very well, I'm afraid. I *want* him to be lying."

"I don't think we can take anything he says at face value," Connie said.

"We might as well turn him over to the police,"

Loomis said. "We've probably learned everything we're going to learn from him."

"Which, so far, is nothing," Connie said.

Loomis gripped Parker's nose between thumb and forefinger, squeezed hard and twisted.

"Ow-ow-ow-ow," Parker wailed, clinging to Loomis's wrist with his free hand.

"John," Hazel Ryerson said.

"Don't worry," Loomis said. "I won't hurt him— much." He released Parker's nose. "So? Quentin? What'll it be?"

"All right, fine," Parker said, massaging his nose.

"Darn," Loomis said, feigning disappointment. "That was too easy. So, what's your game, really?"

"Same as yours," Parker said. "Just trying to make a living."

"Doing what?" Loomis said.

"Anything I can."

"I'm sure you can be a little more specific than that," Loomis said. "Or do you need a little more encouragement."

"I'm trying to cut myself a piece of Kellerman's action, all right?"

"You aren't part of their space colony scam, then?"

"Who says it's a scam? Kellerman and the others really believe in UFOs and aliens and all that shit." He glanced at Loomis. "Don't they?"

"What about Belle Ryerson? How is she involved?"

"I don't know, man," Parker said. "Really. I only ever

saw her at a couple of meetings."

Parker had to be lying, but there wasn't much Loomis could do about it. Physical intimidation would just result in more lies and obfuscations. Loomis considered turning him over to the police to teach him a lesson, but Parker might be more useful on the loose.

Loomis unlocked the handcuffs. Parker mumbled his thanks and massaged his wrist. Loomis picked up Parker's computer satchel and tossed it at him. Surprised, Parker fumbled it. It fell to the floor with a thump.

"We'll talk again, Mr. Parker," Loomis said. He handed Parker the car keys with the plastic daisy fob. "Your car's out front."

Hugging his satchel to his chest, Parker beetled to the front door and out into the night.

"We'll be in touch," Loomis said to Hazel. "Let's go," he said to Connie.

"Um …" Hazel said, looking flustered.

"We're going to follow him," Connie explained.

"Oh."

Hazel waited by the front door with Loomis and Connie until Parker's aunt's little green car pulled away from the house. "That's ingenious," she said.

The sky had cleared, and the glowing X of reflective tape Loomis had applied above the Neon's rear licence plate was clearly visible in the light of the nearly full moon.

"Just a little trick of the trade," Loomis said.

20

"Hazel was a bit spooked, you know," Connie said. "Me, too, I guess. A little, anyway."

"By a nose tweak?" Loomis said, keeping his eyes on the glowing X thirty yards ahead in the southbound lane of I-89. "Christ, it's not like I was torturing the poor bastard. You almost sound like you feel sorry for him."

"Hardly," she said. "But he is one of the more pathetic representatives of the male half of the species."

"That he is—oops." Parker had taken the exit to Williston Road. "Here we go."

"Is he going to the airport?"

"I don't think so," Loomis said. "I think I know where he is going, though." Parker turned left off the ramp on to Williston Road and continued south.

"The Green Mountain Motel isn't far from here."

"Give the lady a kewpie doll."

Sure enough, Parker turned into the court of the Green Mountain Motel. As on his previous visit, Loomis continued along Williston, turned into the south entrance, and parked by the empty swimming pool. The Neon was in front of Unit 42, Harriet Olsen's room. Parker went to the door of the unit and knocked. No lights showed.

The door remained closed, and the unit remained dark. Parker knocked again. Still no answer. He gave up and got back into the car, where he sat for a moment before starting the engine and driving a few yards, parking in front of Unit 48. He let himself into the unit, turned the lights on, and closed the drapes. A few minutes later the lights went out, but the eerie glow of a television flickered through the gap in the drapes.

"What do you want to bet he's watching porn?" Connie said.

"Let's find out," Loomis said.

"Must we?" Connie said as Loomis put the car in gear and drove across the court to Parker's unit.

"It's a long shot," Loomis said, as he and Connie got out of the car. "But who knows? If he's involved in Belle's disappearance, he just might be stupid enough to have her stashed in his room."

He knocked on the door of Parker's unit, then placed his thumb over the lens of the peephole. The flickering light of the television died, the room lights went on, and the door opened. Parker's face fell when he saw Loomis and Connie. Clearly, he'd been expecting someone else. Harriet Olsen, perhaps.

"Shit," he said.

"Is that any way to greet your friends, Quentin?"

Loomis said.

"What do you—?" Loomis pushed past him into the room. "Hey!"

"Mind if we take a look around?" Loomis said. "No? Good." Connie followed Loomis into the room and shut the door behind her.

"Knock yourselves out," Parker said, standing by the king-sized bed, which looked as though it hadn't been made in a month.

Connie stood with her back to the door. Her nose wrinkled. "It smells like the inside of my son's gym bag in here," she said. "When was the last time you did your laundry?"

"Very funny," Parker said, picking up a sock from the floor by the bed and dropping it into a drawer of the dresser.

Loomis went into the bathroom. The toilet seat was up and judging from the stains on the rim of the bowl and the floor, Parker's aim was shaky. The towel rack was empty, and used towels hung over the shower rod and the rim of the tub. The complimentary bottles of shampoo and conditioner were empty. There were whiskers and hairs in the basin, and on the vanity top. A cheap shaving kit held a stick deodorant, a can of aerosol shaving cream, and a disposable razor. The bristles of his toothbrush were badly splayed, as if it had been used to scrub floors, and his toothpaste tube was crumpled almost flat. He did not appear to use floss or mouthwash. Loomis returned to the main room.

"How long have you been staying here?" he asked, as he began going through the dresser drawers.

"None of your business," Parker said.

"What about Harriet?"

"Eh? She's not staying here."

"We saw you knock on her door, Quentin."

"Oh."

The dresser contained nothing but dirty laundry. Likewise Parker's carry-all, which was his only item of luggage, besides his computer satchel. His safari jacket, a pair of khaki cargo pants, and his leather jacket were hanging in the closet. He had three sets of footwear: his new-looking hiking boots, a pair of broken-down Boulet cowboy boots, handmade in the Province of Quebec, and the sneakers he was wearing. His taste in reading material was confined to soft-core porn magazines and violent, semi-pornographic graphic novels. There was nothing tying him to Belle Ryerson.

"Well, we'll let you get back to your TV program," Loomis said.

"Thanks," Parker said sourly. "Drop by any time— not."

Loomis and Connie left Parker's unit and walked to Unit 42. While Parker watched from the door of his unit, Loomis knocked on Harriet's door. And knocked again. Either Harriet wasn't in or she wasn't answering, afraid, perhaps, that it was Parker again.

"Miss Olsen," Loomis said, knocking again. "It's Hack Loomis."

Still no sign of life. They crossed the court to the motel office.

"Can I help you?" the night clerk said from behind the desk. He set aside his book. *Great Expectations*. He looked young enough to be a high school senior.

Loomis displayed his ID and licence. "Maybe you can," he said. He showed the clerk the photograph of Belle Ryerson in her hiking outfit. "Have you seen this woman recently?"

The clerk studied the photograph for a few seconds, then said, "No, sir, but I'm only on nights." He looked at Connie and smiled. She smiled back.

"What can you tell us about the guests in Units 42 and 48?" Loomis said.

The clerk tapped a key on the keyboard of a computer. "That would be Ms. Olsen." Another tap. "And Mr. Parker. Nothing much I can tell you, except that he doesn't like housekeeping going into his room."

"How long have they been staying?"

The clerk squinted at the computer screen. "Since November 1st." More than a month.

"Both of them?"

"Yep."

"Has either of them had any visitors?"

"I haven't seen anyone, but, like I said, I'm only on nights."

"Has either of them made any phone calls through your switchboard?" Since the advent of the cellular telephone few people used hotel room telephones anymore, but it was worth a shot.

The clerk tapped at his keyboard. "Nope. Hardly anyone does nowadays."

"Did they pay by credit card?"

"Cash in advance. Got our special long-term corporate rate, looks like."

"For how long?"

"Till December 10th." A week away.

"Is there a billing address of any kind?"

The clerk looked at the screen again. "Something called the Kentauran Foundation, number five Cove Lane, Burlington." Kellerman's home address.

"Has either Mr. Parker or Ms. Olsen indicated they'll be staying on after December 10th?"

"Not according to the register," the clerk said.

"Well, thanks," Loomis said. "You've been very helpful."

"No problem," the clerk said. He looked at Connie. "Are you a detective, too?"

"Yep," she said, favouring him with a heart-stopping smile. "I'm his beautiful assistant."

"I'll say."

"There is one more thing you might be able to do for us," Loomis said. "Could you let us into Unit 42? Just for a quick look, to make sure this woman"—he held up Belle's photo—"isn't there."

"I dunno," the kid said. "I'm on alone. Who'd watch the desk?"

"I could watch it for you," Connie said.

"It'll only take a minute," Loomis said. "In fact, I don't even have to go in. You could check the room for me."

"It could get me fired, you know," the clerk said. He looked from Loomis to Connie and back. "All right, screw it. It's a crummy job, anyway."

He took a key from a cabinet, and he and Loomis crossed the lot to Unit 42. The clerk knocked on the door. Connie watched from the door of the office.

"Ms. Olsen," the clerk called. "It's the night manager. Are you here?" No answer.

Quentin Parker emerged from his room as the clerk unlocked the door to Unit 42. "Hey, you can't do that," he said.

The clerk looked at Loomis.

"Stay out of the way, Quentin," Loomis said. "It sounded like someone was calling for help."

"Bullshit," Parker said. "I should call the cops."

"You do that," Loomis said.

Muttering under his breath, Parker returned to his room.

"Don't worry," Loomis said to the clerk. "He won't involve the police."

While Loomis waited, the clerk leaned into Harriet Olsen's room. "Hello, anyone here?" No answer. He went into the unit. He left the door open.

Loomis peered into Harriet's room. It was identical to Parker's, but neater. And it smelled better. Turning on the lights, the clerk looked in the closet, under the bed, and into the bathroom. He turned off the lights.

"No one," he said, closing the door, making sure it was locked.

Loomis thanked him again, and Connie rewarded him with another smile as he went back into the office.

"Nice kid," Connie said, as they got into the car. "A real charmer."

Loomis started the engine. "I was going to give him twenty bucks," he said, turning right on to Williston Road, heading south, "but I think he appreciated a smile from my beautiful assistant more."

"He probably wouldn't have turned down the money, though," she said. "You're going the wrong way."

"There's something I want to check out while we're in the neighbourhood." He took a sheet of paper from his coat pocket and handed it to her. It was the Google map to Dr. William Spender's home address.

They drove south on Williston, past the junction with Route 2A and the Williston Fire Department, then turned right into a small housing development. Spender lived on a short crescent called Abbey Road, which looped off Rita Road; the developer had obviously been a Beatles' fan. There wasn't a meter maid in sight, though, as Loomis parked in the driveway of a nice split level ranch secluded behind tall honeysuckle hedges and a six-foot cedar fence. The house was dark, except for a single yellow porch light, and there was a *For Sale* sign at the end of the driveway, a *Sold* banner pasted across it.

"Be right back," Loomis said.

Taking a Maglite flashlight from the glove compartment, Loomis went to the front door and rang the doorbell. He heard the classic ding-dong made famous by Avon TV commercials, but no one came to the door. He played the beam of the flashlight through the living room window. The room was as bare as the day the house had been built. He returned to the car and wrote down the real estate agent's name and telephone number.

"Can we go home now?" Connie said. "We've got some unfinished business to take care of."

"You're insatiable."

"No, I'm not. You just haven't sated me yet. I'm almost ashamed to admit it, but I'm horny as hell. My panties are soaking."

"We can see if there's a vacancy at the motel, if you like."

"Don't tempt me," she said. "Just take me home."

"These seats recline," Loomis said.

Thursday
DAY 3

21

Loomis woke up to the aroma of coffee and for a moment couldn't remember where he was. When he did, he grinned. The clock on the bedside table read 7:36. Time to get up, he thought, but he was just too damned comfortable, despite the pressure in his bladder and a full-blown erection. Where was Connie when he needed her? His grin widened as he recalled making love with her in the Outback.

"Well, sir," she'd said afterward. "I am well and truly sated."

"Thank god," Loomis said. "I was near to cardiac arrest."

"Good thing I came prepared," she said.

"Yes, indeed."

She giggled. "You know, this is the first time I've ever done it in a car."

"You're joking," Loomis said. "I thought making out in a car was a requisite coming of age experience for every

North American teenager. Canadian and American, anyway. I can't speak for Mexico."

"If that's true," Connie said, "then I have finally come
of age. How old were you the first time you did it in a
car?"

"Too young," Loomis said.

After they'd gotten back to her place, they'd discovered they still had some reserves left—sufficient to get
started, at least—but they'd fallen asleep still joined. It
was a nice way to fall asleep.

He got up and, bobbing ridiculously, went into the
en suite bathroom. He urinated—eventually—showered
quickly, dressed in clothes that still smelled of Connie,
and went into the kitchen. Connie sat at the table, talking
on the phone.

"Yes, that would be fine," she said into the phone. She
waved toward the coffee pot as he leaned over and kissed
the top of her head. "I'll see you next Monday then.
Goodbye." She poked a button on the handset and put it
down. "Hi!"

"Hi, yourself," he said. "Who were you talking to?"

She looked at him.

"Sorry," he said, feeling a vague uneasiness. "I didn't
mean to pry. I thought it might be work related."

"No. Just a personal matter." She went around the table and dropped into his lap, nearly upsetting his chair. She
wrapped her arms around his neck. "Last night was fun."

"Which part?" She bit his neck. "Ouch!"

"Serves you right," she said, with a savage smile.

She kissed him, long and humidly, then stood, her face flushed.

"God, I'm actually *sore*. It's been a long time since I've been made love to so often and so enthusiastically in so short a period of time. Actually, I don't think I've ever been made love to so often and enthusiastically in so short a period of time. And I'll shut up now, okay."

"Please," he said, standing, adjusting himself. "This isn't a zucchini in my pocket."

She grinned. "I'll start breakfast."

"I'll grab something at home," he said. "Have you arranged for someone to watch Billy today?"

"Xavier Ducharme's mother is going to take him for the day."

"Good, because you're going to be staking out the Green Mountain Motel."

"Ah. Who am I watching, Quentin Parker or Harriet Olsen?"

"Both. Either. Tail whichever one leaves first. If they both leave at the same time, but go in different directions, follow Harriet."

"And what are you going to be doing while I'm sitting in my car freezing my can off and peeing in a bottle?"

"Having a heart-to-heart with Heather-Anne Allen."

"Poor you."

"I think she knows more than she's telling. Dress warm."

"Oh, god," she said, dismayed. "I'm going to have to wear a skirt."

"I suppose you are, unless you can figure out some other way to pee in a bottle. And be careful. We shouldn't underestimate these people. As silly as Kellerman's group seems to be, there's a lot of money involved, and greed makes people unpredictable. Particularly people who aren't that firmly attached to reality in the first place."

Loomis kissed her, slipping his hand up inside her T-shirt, cupping a warm, bare breast.

"Hey, watch it, pal."

"Just a little something for the road," he said.

When Loomis arrived home he discovered he'd forgotten to leave the heat on, and the interior of the trailer was like a deep freeze. Just what he needed, he thought as he lit the small propane space heater, was burst pipes. The message light on the phone was blinking. Jefferson Security's number. Loomis logged into his voice mail.

"Hack," Veejay's voice said. "It's—"

He skipped to the end of the message, erased it, and hung up, wondering what the hell to do about her. "Like mother like daughter," Phil Jefferson had said, around the time Veejay had filed for divorce. "Just be thankful she hasn't gone completely off the rails like her mother did before she ran away with the circus." After a moment of blissful nostalgia, he'd added, "She was a damned good sword swallower. It's the only thing I miss about her."

Loomis changed, went out to his car, and drove to the office, taking the elevator to the sixth floor. Glenna Campbell smiled coolly at him from behind her desk.

"Can I help you, Mr. Loomis?"

"Is Dink in?"

"*Mr. McHenry* is in Montpelier today."

"How about Ms. Allen?" he said.

"She's taken a vacation day."

While the cat's away, Loomis thought. "Can you tell me where she lives or give me her home or cellphone number?"

"It's not our policy to give out that information," she said, as if nothing could be more obvious, even to someone as dim-witted as Loomis.

"Here's the thing, Ms. Campbell," Loomis said. "She has some information pertinent to Belle Ryerson's disappearance, and it's imperative I speak with her at once. Perhaps you would be kind enough to call her and ask her if it would be all right for you to give me her address or phone numbers. Could you do that? Belle's life may well hang in the balance."

Glenna Campbell eyelashes fluttered, and for a second Loomis thought he'd laid it on a bit too thick. To his relief, however, she said, "Yes, I could do that. Please have a seat."

Not wanting to push his luck, he stood in the waiting area while Glenna made the call.

"Mr. Loomis."

He went to her desk and she handed him a yellow sticky note. Written on it in a swooping flowery hand were two telephone numbers, landline and cellphone.

"She said it would be all right to call her."

"Thank you, Miss Campbell. You've been very helpful."

"You're welcome. I pray that Belle is all right."

Loomis went downstairs, woke his computer, and in a few keystrokes had Heather-Anne Allen's home address, courtesy of the reverse directory. Fifteen minutes later he was parked on Lake Street, in front of the townhouse development at the foot of the bluff below Battery Park. A bitter northwest wind off Lake Champlain buffeted the Outback as he called Heather-Anne Allen's landline.

"Mr. Loomis," she said. "Glenna said I could expect to hear from you. How can I help you?"

"Are you decent?" he said, as he got out of the car. It had started to rain.

"Pardon me?"

"I'd like to speak to you in person, if you don't mind."

"Yes, I'm decent, but—"

"That'll be me ringing your doorbell," he said, pressing the doorbell button.

"I've half a mind to leave you standing out in the cold," she said.

"That wouldn't be very nice," he said. "Besides, you don't want me camped out on your doorstep, do you? Your neighbours might talk."

"They do already," she said. His phone chirped as she disconnected. Her door opened. "Come in," she said.

"Thank you," he said, meaning it. His backside was growing numb and the wind-driven, icy rain stung his face.

She closed the door against the wind and rain. "Would

217

you mind taking your boots off?"

"Not at all," he said. He hung his coat on a hook, then unlaced his boots and toed them off.

"My house is upside down," she said. "The kitchen and living room are upstairs and the bedrooms are on the ground floor. Please." She gestured for him to precede her up the stairs.

"Nice," he said as he emerged into a spacious, open-concept living room, dining room, and kitchen. "Are you going to furnish it soon?"

"It is a bit minimalistic, isn't it?"

"Is that a chair?"

"Yes, but if I'd known how difficult it was to get out of I'd never have bought it. The sofa is quite safe. Would you like coffee?"

"Don't go to any trouble."

"No trouble," she said.

He stood at the broad living room window that overlooked Waterfront Park. A hundred and fifty yards away, through the curtains of rain blowing in off the lake, he could just make out the shoreline of the bay, where Maya Thomas's body had been found partly frozen into the ice three days before.

"So," Heather-Anne said, as Loomis perched on a tall stool at the kitchen island. "How can I help you?" She placed a cup of coffee in front of him.

"Let's start with why you're holding out on me," he said. "And, more important, *what* you're holding out."

"I'm not holding out anything," she said.

"With respect, Ms. Allen, I don't believe you. You aren't a very good liar, you know: you blush too easily." Loomis was bluffing, but from the look in her eyes knew he was right. "I'm not just another pretty face, you know."

"God, I hate this. It's so fucking *messy*. Shit."

"So she was having problems with someone in the office. Was it Dink?"

She shook her head. "Despite being a complete asshole sometimes, he's okay to work for. Not great, but okay. Nor are they having an affair."

"You're sure?"

"Yes, I am."

"You weren't so sure yesterday."

"I've had a chance to think about it, I suppose."

"All right," he said. "What about Glenna Campbell? How do she and Belle get along?"

"Belle is one of the few people in the office who actually seems to like Glenna."

"Okay then, who?" Loomis said.

She looked at him, eyes misty behind her glasses.

Oh, shit, he thought.

Voice barely audible, she said, "I think there's a possibility her disappearance might have something to do with me."

"What makes you think that?"

She took a shaky breath. "She may have been afraid that I was, well, going to try to seduce her. I mean, I like her—quite a lot, as a matter of fact—and if she was inclined in that direction, I might let her know I was interested."

"But you haven't."

"No. I'm certain she knows, though. She's quite sensitive to other people's feelings." She slumped on to a stool. "God."

"Relax, Heather-Anne," Loomis said. "I don't think Belle's disappearance has anything to do with your feelings for her. Besides, how can you be sure she isn't 'inclined in that direction' if you haven't told her how you feel?"

"It's not quite that simple," she said, voice bleak.

It seldom is, he thought. "Were you with her at the Winooski farmers' market the Saturday before last?"

"No," she said. "We've never socialized outside of work hours." She smiled, rallying, but it was a smile tinged with regret. "Life's a bitch, isn't it?"

"It can be a bugger sometimes, that's for sure," he said.

Her smile broadened at his use of a non-American idiom. "Connie told me you tended to lapse into Canadianisms from time to time." He felt the blood rise in his face. "Oh," she said. "I've embarrassed you. I'm sorry. But why would you find that embarrassing?"

"No reason," he said, avoiding her eyes.

"Hmm," Heather-Anne said. "I'm looking forward to our next girls' night out."

Swell, Loomis thought, as his phone began to vibrate in his pocket.

22

Loomis dug out his phone and looked at the screen. Hazel Ryerson.

"I need to take this," Loomis said.

"Go ahead," Heather-Anne said.

"Yes, Hazel," Loomis said

"John," Hazel Ryerson said. "I've reset my sister's password. What should I look for?"

"Look through her recent emails and her calendar for anything relating to her activities over the last couple of weeks. Who she might have met, where and when. You'll probably know what's relevant when you see it."

There was a pause, accompanied by the staccato clatter of a keyboard. "Where did Quentin Parker go after he left here last night?"

"We followed him to the Green Mountain Motel," Loomis said, exchanging a look with Heather-Anne. "That's where he's staying."

"I suppose it was too much to expect that he'd lead

you to her."

"It was a long shot," Loomis said. "I'll talk to you later."

"All right," she said, and hung up.

Loomis closed his phone. "Belle's sister has been trying to unlock Belle's home computer," he explained to Heather-Anne.

"Have you checked her work computer?"

"Not yet. I was going to ask you about that, but I doubt Dink would allow it."

"Have you spoken to him about it?"

"No."

"Why not?"

"I have my reasons," Loomis said.

"You still think he knows something about Belle's disappearance?"

"No comment. So, how about Belle's computer? Do you think I could take a look at it?"

"I don't know," she said. "I'm not sure I should let you poke through her computer without Mr. McHenry's permission."

"You could make sure I didn't see anything I shouldn't. As I told Hazel, I'm only interested in Belle's movements a week or ten days prior to her disappearance."

"I'm not sure I should do it, but I do want to help. I'd feel awful if something happened to Belle that I could have prevented." She stood. "All right, let me get changed."

She went down the stairs. A few minutes later, she called up to him, "All set."

She waited for him at the foot of the stairs, dressed in a long black parka from *The North Face* and a bright red wool hat with earflaps. He laced up his boots and put on his coat and presently they were in the Outback, grinding through the rain.

When they got to the offices of Proctor, Proctor and McHenry, she led him to Belle's workstation and sat down at Belle's computer. As Loomis watched over her shoulder, she tapped the spacebar. The screen saver prompted her for a password. She picked up the phone and dialled a four-digit number.

"Greg, it's Heather-Anne …I'm good, thanks. Look, could you give me the admin password for Belle Ryerson's computer?" She held the phone between her jaw and shoulder as she typed a password and tapped the Return key. The screensaver disappeared. "Got it, thanks," she said, and hung up. "Okay," she said to Loomis. "What are we looking for?"

"I'm not sure," Loomis said. "How about her agenda?"

She moved the mouse pointer to the dock at the bottom of the screen and clicked on a calendar icon. The icon bounced a couple of times as Belle's calendar application launched and displayed the month of December in a standard calendar format, with the current date highlighted in light grey. Most of the weekdays, up to, including and beyond the current date, contained a half a dozen or more entries showing the time of each appointment, as well as a name, topic or location. All the entries in the first week of

December were highlighted in red, indicating they were work-related. She'd missed a lot of appointments since Monday.

"Can you go back to November?"

Heather-Anne clicked and the screen displayed the month of November. Again, most entries were highlighted in red. Except for two blue ones ...

"Oh, shit," he said.

"What?"

He pointed to a blue entry for the previous Saturday, November 28, the last day anyone had seen her. It read "2 p.m. Maya." Just Maya, no last name or location. Directly beneath it was another blue entry: "4 p.m. Connie."

"Maya," Heather-Anne said. "What's wrong? Who is she?"

"Did you hear about the body of a woman found in the bay the other day?"

"Yes," she said. "It was one of my neighbours who found her. Her dog, actually."

"Her name was Maya Thomas," Loomis said. He summarized what the police had told him.

"My god."

He started to ask her to check Belle's address book, but she'd already clicked the dock icon. When Belle's contacts program opened, Heather-Anne typed "Maya" into the search field, but there was no entry for a Maya, Thomas or otherwise. She then opened Belle's email program and typed "Maya" into the search field there, but if Belle had exchanged emails with or about anyone named Maya, she'd deleted them.

"May I ask what you think you're doing?"

Loomis straightened with a guilty start. Glenna Campbell stood in the entrance to Belle's workstation, hands on hips, glaring from beneath her gleaming red bangs.

"Certainly," Heather-Anne replied, as she quit the email program and slid the mouse pointer to the bottom corner of the screen, activating the screensaver. She stood up.

"Well?" Glenna Campbell said.

"Oh," Heather-Anne said, with mock surprise. "You actually expected an answer?"

"I certainly did."

"Ah," Heather-Anne said, picking up her coat and walking away without another word.

Glenna Campbell huffed with indignation. Loomis gave her a sympathetic smile, then followed Heather-Anne back to her own workstation by McHenry's office. Draping her coat over a partition, she down at her desk, picked up her phone and punched in the same four-digit number she'd called a few minutes earlier.

"Greg, me again. I need another favour. Can you pull Belle Ryerson's deleted emails from the server going back to, oh, say the beginning of November? Search for Maya." She spelled it. "Possible last name Thomas. Forward any you find to me ASAP. Great. Thanks." She hung up. "He says it shouldn't take him more than a few minutes."

"Even if there are no emails between Belle and Maya," Loomis said, "a look at her emails might help me figure out where she might have gone."

"You'd have to clear that with Mr. McHenry," Heather-Anne said. "Client confidentiality and all that."

"How often would Belle communicate with clients?"

"Not often, but her emails could contain information about clients. If Mr. McHenry okays it, maybe I could look through Belle's emails for you. I have a pretty good idea what to look for."

"I might take you up on that," Loomis said. "But for now, don't mention it to him."

Her desk phone rang. She peered at the call display as she picked it up.

"Greg?" She listened for a moment, then said, "Thanks anyway. I owe you one." She hung up and looked at Loomis. "Nothing. He searched subject lines, to and from fields, and body text. No references to anyone named Maya or Maya Thomas."

Loomis looked at the telephone. "Does your phone system keep a log of incoming and outgoing calls?"

"I haven't any idea." She picked up the phone, called Greg again, apologized for being a pest, and asked him the same question. "It does?" she said. "Hang on." She put her hand over the mouthpiece. "Now what?"

"Can he pull up a listing of the calls to and from Belle's extension?"

He could.

"Ask him if there are any calls to or from Montreal. The area code is 514. The 450 area code, too." That was the area code for the communities surrounding the island of Montreal, such as St. Lambert, where Maya Thomas had lived.

She made the request, then hung up. "He'll call back in a minute."

"This isn't going to get you into trouble, is it?" he said.

"I don't know. But the cat's out of the bag. As you may have gathered, Glenna and I don't get on. If you've gotten me fired, maybe you could hire me as your second string assistant."

"Sure," he said. "If you're willing to work for next to nothing."

The phone rang. She answered, listened for a moment, then said, "Thanks. I owe you another one." She hung up. "Nothing to or from either area code." He hadn't really expected anything, but it had been worth a shot. "What will you do now?"

"Maybe there's something on her home computer. We're also waiting on her landline and cellphone usage details. Can I give you a ride home?"

"Thanks," she said. "But since I'm here, I might as well stay for a bit."

23

Downstairs in his office, he heated up leftover coffee in the microwave and called Connie. "How's it going?"

"Oh, very exciting," she said. "Neither Quentin or Harriet has budged an inch and neither of them has had any visitors. I can't feel my feet. I'd kill for a hot cup of coffee, but it'd only make me need to pee worse than I do. I'm afraid that if I try to use the juice bottle, I'll pee all over my feet."

"That would warm them up," Loomis said.

"How about you? Did you have a nice chat with Heather-Anne?"

"It was interesting. Did you know she was gay?"

"I did. But what's that got to do with anything?"

"Nothing, really, but it might be why Hazel had the impression that Belle was having problems at work."

"C'mon, Belle's not the least bit homophobic. Glenna Campbell, maybe, but not Belle."

"I wasn't suggesting she was," Loomis said. "But how

would she feel if someone had feelings for her that she could not reciprocate?"

"She'd feel bad for that person, of course, but she'd expect them to deal with it. Does Heather-Anne have feelings for her?"

"Pretty strong ones," Loomis said. "And I'm not sure how well she's dealing with them. Listen, I know I asked you this already, but are you sure Belle never mentioned anyone named Maya?"

"I'm sure."

"It might have slipped your mind."

"It didn't."

"Relax, Connie. You don't know Belle all that well. She might have mentioned the name in passing and you simply took no note of it."

"You're right," Connie said. "I'm sorry. I shouldn't be so sensitive. Does she?"

"Heather-Anne and I found the name Maya in Belle's work computer calendar. No last name, though. She was apparently supposed to meet this Maya a couple of hours before she was supposed to meet you."

"If it's the woman whose body was found in the bay," Connie said, "she'd already been dead a week or more by then."

"Yeah," Loomis said.

After a moment's silence, Connie said, "Oh-oh. Parker's on the move. He's knocking on Harriet's door. She doesn't looked pleased to see him. My lip reading is rusty, but it looks like she told him to 'fuck the hell off.' He's getting into his car … Just sitting there … Maybe I've got time to pee in my bottle. Oops. Nope. Should I follow him or stay on her?"

"Follow him," Loomis said.

"Call you later."

He got up and stood with his coffee at the grimy window staring at the grimy wall of the building across the alley. One of the symptoms of insanity was doing the same thing over and over again, expecting different results. No matter how many times he looked out his window, the view never changed. Occasionally, a rainstorm washed some of the grime from the window and the narrow strip of sky he could see changed with the time of day and the weather, but the view was basically always the same. Fortunately, he didn't expect it to change, so by that particular parameter, at least, he wasn't insane. Just a little crazy. He had plenty of company, at least.

His cellphone began to buzz. He picked it up from the desk and peered at the call display before flipping it open.

"Yes, Hazel."

"I've been through Belle's email," she said. "I didn't find much, I'm afraid. Most of it's work-related. I recognized the names of people she works with. Heather-Anne Allen. Glenna Campbell. Mr. McHenry, of course. She's also exchanged a number of emails with your Ms. Noble."

"Anything to or from someone named Maya?" Loomis asked. "As in the peoples of the Yucatan." He started to spell it, but she interrupted.

"I know how to spell, John."

He was beginning to regret telling her his given name.

He heard the rattle of the keyboard.

"The only reference to a Maya is in her calendar," Hazel said. "She had an appointment to meet someone named Maya on Saturday, November 28th at 2 p.m."

"That much I already know," Loomis said. "Can you check her mail program or browser to see if she has a Gmail or Yahoo account?"

"I can," Hazel said. "Maya? That was the name of the dead woman the police found in Burlington Bay."

"That's right. Maya Thomas."

"Is that who my sister was supposed to meet?"

"Possibly," Loomis said.

"Does this mean that my sister is dead, too?"

"No," Loomis said. "It doesn't."

"All right," Hazel said. "Should I search Belle's computer for other references?"

"Yes, please."

Loomis sat at his desk in the gloomy office. Hazel hadn't found any references on Belle's computer to any of the other names associated with the Kentauran Foundation. Or to the Kentauran Foundation itself. She had found a link in Belle's Internet browser to a Gmail account, but she wasn't able get into it: unsurprisingly, Belle hadn't saved her Google password. Belle also had a Skype account, which she may have used for long distance calls, but she hadn't saved the password for that, either. She had a password manager, which probably contained all her passwords, but of course it was also password protected.

Perhaps, despite everything, Belle's apparent interest in Kellerman's organization was purely coincidental. Maybe the foundation had nothing to do with Belle's disappearance, and he and Connie were barking up the wrong tree entirely. That word again. Coincidence. No matter how hard Loomis tried to convince himself that the Kentauran Foundation was not involved, he just couldn't manage it. Nor did he believe that it was a coincidence that Belle knew someone named Maya. He knew in his bones that there had to be a link between Belle Ryerson, the Kentauran Foundation, and Maya Thomas. He hoped his bones were more reliable than his bullshit detector.

He turned on lights to dispel the afternoon gloom. The empty office seemed even emptier and gloomier without Connie. He wondered where Parker was leading her. Had they made a mistake letting Parker go, rather than turning him over to the police? The possible connection between Belle Ryerson and Maya Thomas had given the case a frightening new dimension.

He thought about calling her. He did not want her to think he was checking up on her, she was a big girl, but he was worried about her. Despite what he'd told Hazel, there was a chance Belle was dead too, killed by the same person or persons who'd killed Maya Thomas. He'd give a lot to know if Maya Thomas was a member of the Kentauran Foundation. He wondered how he could lay his hands on a membership list. He was pretty sure Kellerman wouldn't just hand it over. It couldn't hurt to ask, though.

He tried to think of a reason why he shouldn't tell

Alex Robillard about the possible link between Belle Ryerson and Maya Thomas. He couldn't. In fact, there were a number of very good reasons why he should tell him, not the least of which was that it would ensure that the police took Belle's disappearance seriously. The police couldn't cut him completely out of the investigation, but they didn't like civilians meddling in their investigations. Nevertheless, his responsibility to his client came before his personal like and dislikes. If telling the police about the entry in Belle's calendar would improve the chances of finding Belle alive, he had to tell them.

Loomis took out Alex Robillard's business card and reached for the phone. It rang as he touched it. He snatched his hand back, as if he'd gotten an electric shock. He peered at the call display. No name and an unfamiliar cellphone number.

"Loomis," he said.

"It's me," a familiar nasal voice said.

"Me who?" Loomis said, letting his annoyance show.

"Quentin."

"Parker. What do you want?"

"I'm being followed," Parker said. "You wouldn't know anything about that, would you?"

"No," Loomis said. *Shit*. Had he underestimated Parker? Was he smarter than Loomis had thought?

"'Cause it sure looks like that dyke bitch partner of yours, driving a blue VW."

"Must be your imagination," Loomis said. "She wouldn't let you make her. If she were following you.

Which she isn't." *Don't overdo it*, he told himself. "While I've got you on the phone, you wouldn't have a copy of the Kentauran Foundation's membership list, would you?"

"Eh? No. Why?"

"My middle name is Diligence," Loomis said.

"Uh, right. Are you looking for anyone in particular? Maybe I've spoken to them?"

"That's all right." He wanted to be able to see Parker's face when he ran Maya Thomas's name past him. "Keep in touch," he said.

He disconnected and dialled Connie's number.

"What's up?" she said.

"You've been made," he said.

"Shit. He was being tricky, but I kept at least three cars back. Are you sure?"

"Whether he made you or not, as long as he thinks he's being followed, he won't lead you anywhere. Don't worry about it. It happens. Might as well head back to the motel. Maybe Harriet's still there. If she is, sit on her for a while. You can grab some lunch while you're at it."

"And a pee." She disconnected.

Loomis dialled Robillard's office number. Robillard's BPD voice mail picked up.

"Alex," he said. "It's Hack. I've got something for you. A possible connection between my mis-per and your Lady of the Lake. Belle Ryerson was supposed to meet someone named Maya at 2 p.m. Saturday, November 28th. No last name and no indication of where. And do you think I could get copies of the photographs of Thomas the Quebec police gave you? Thanks. Talk to you later."

He hung up, wondering if he should also try Robillard's cellphone. To heck with it. He'd done his due diligence, and Robillard checked his voice mail regularly.

The phone rang.

"Loomis."

"You called?" Alex Robillard said.

"That was fast. Did you listen to my message?"

"No. If anyone leaves a message I get paged. We're still in Quebec. What's up?"

Loomis repeated what he'd told Robillard's voice mail.

"Where'd you get this?" Robillard said.

"The name Maya was in Belle's calendar on her computer." He saw no reason to involve Heather-Anne Allen or McHenry's firm.

"No last name, though."

"Just Maya."

"And no indication of where this meeting was to take place."

"No," Loomis said.

"Why do you want copies of the photos?"

"To show to people who may have seen Belle and Maya together."

"All right," Robillard said. "I'll see what I can do. If you turn up anything else, you'll let me know."

"Of course," Loomis said. "Have you turned up anything to connect your victim to Belle Ryerson?"

"No. We weren't looking. We will now."

"Or an apocalyptic UFO cult called the Kentauran

Foundation?"

"No again. What's that about?"

"They believe the world is racing toward ecological and social collapse and claim they're in contact with a group of aliens from Alpha Centauri who have agreed to transport them to another planet. It's run by a local psychiatrist named Thaddeus Kellerman."

"Nothing surprises me anymore," Robillard said. "But we haven't come across mention of either the Kentauran Foundation or a Thaddeus Kellerman. Any other names we should be on the lookout for?"

"A former astronaut named James Maynard and a woman named Harriet Olsen."

"James Maynard? Wasn't he that astronaut back in the seventies who thought he'd been abducted from an Apollo or something?"

"It was from a shuttle in the eighties, but, yes, that's him."

"And Harriet Olsen. What's her story?"

"She claims she's in contact with an alien named Charley. Not his real name, of course. His real name sounds like a cat spitting up a hairball."

"You private sector fellows have all the fun."

"Don't we, though? Your turn."

"Who said this was a fair exchange? Sorry, Hack. You know how it is. I'll see what I can do about the photographs, though."

"Thanks for that, anyway," Loomis said sourly.

"What are friends for?" Robillard said, and hung up.

24

Loomis went down to the deli next to Debbie's Donut Shoppe, scarfed down a pastrami on rye, then hiked over to the Burlington Medical Arts Building to check Dr. William Spender's dental office. The office was locked, and the lights were off. Likewise, the lights were off in Dr. Kellerman's office. Back at his own office he opened his notebook and called the real estate agent whose name had been on the sign at Spender's house. Dan Bumgarner was a big-voiced man whose speech was punctuated with nervous laughter. Loomis introduced himself and explained his problem.

"I don't know how I can help you," Bumgarner said. "I mean, heh-heh, we can't go giving out clients' telephone numbers to just anyone, can we? Privacy issues, you understand. Confidentiality, heh-heh."

"Mr. Bumgarner," Loomis said. "This is a matter of some urgency. A woman is missing, and Dr. Spender may be able to help me locate her. If you're worried about your or your firm's reputation, he doesn't need to know where I got the information."

"So you say, heh-heh. If you want to come to my office and show me some proof you are who you say you are, well, maybe I can help you. Of course, I'd need references, heh-heh."

"If you insist," Loomis said. "However, if my missing person should come to harm as a result of the delay, I will advise her family to include you and your firm in any lawsuit they file. You may know their lawyer. Mr. D. Lincoln McHenry. His wife is special assistant to the mayor." Heh-heh.

Mr. Bumgarner was silent for a moment. Loomis could hear the soft hissing of his breath through the phone line. Finally, Bumgarner said, "Can you guarantee Dr. Spender won't find out I gave you his number?"

"I can guarantee he won't learn it from me," Loomis said.

"Somehow, that doesn't make me feel a whole lot better. But, all right ..." He gave Loomis a cellphone number, then said, "Dr. Spender isn't in some kind of trouble, is he?"

"Why would you ask that?"

"He was in an almighty big hurry to sell his house. Listed it for considerably less than market value, even these days, and accepted the first offer that came along. Against my advice, too. Heh-heh."

Loomis thanked him and hung up, then dialled the number Bumgarner had given him. A man answered on the fourth ring.

"Bill Spender."

"Dr. Spender, my name is Loomis."

"How can I help you, Mr. Loomis?" Spender said. "I'm not taking any new patients, though. In fact, I've closed my practice. However, I'd be happy to provide you with a recommendation."

"I don't need mental work," Loomis said. "Sorry. Slip of the tongue. I meant dental, of course." He could probably use some mental work. "I'm a private investigator. I'm working on a case I think you may be able to help me with. Could we meet?"

"What sort of case?"

"Missing persons," Loomis said. "Do you know a Belle Ryerson?"

"I ...don't think so," Spender said. His hesitation suggested otherwise.

"It would be easier to do this face to face," Loomis said. "Where are you?"

"This isn't a good time," Spender said. Where had Loomis heard that before? "How did you get this number, anyway?"

"We have our resources," Loomis said. "Please, Dr. Spender, I need your help. Belle Ryerson needs your help. Her family is very worried about her."

"I don't know how I can help, but I suppose I could make some time later this week."

"Could you make it today?" Loomis said.

"I don't have time today, I'm afraid."

"Dr. Spender," Loomis said, tone hardening. "You'll

either make time or I will track you down wherever you are. If I found this phone number, I can find you. And when I do, I will not be in a good mood. Do you understand me?"

After a lengthy silence, Spender said, "All right. Can you meet me at my office in, say, an hour? Would that be satisfactory?"

"Yes, it would," Loomis said.

"Do you know where it is?"

"Yes," Loomis said. "I'll see you in an hour."

He toggled the switch hook to get a dial tone and called Connie.

"Where are you?"

"I'm at the motel," she said.

"Anything happening?"

"Nothing at all. No sign of life in Harriet's room, and Quentin hasn't come back. I'm parked on the other side of the court so he won't see my car."

"You might as well come back here. I've got an appointment to see William Spender in an hour. He's sold his house and closed his practice. What do you want to bet he's bought a ticket on Charley's spaceship? It might be more productive putting a tail on him. The suckers must be lining up somewhere. Maybe Spender will lead us to them."

"Okay," Connie said. "Do I have time to stop at home to change?"

"If you make it quick," Loomis said.

Loomis waited by the pharmacy in the lobby of the Medical Arts Building, reflecting on the conversation he'd had with Connie in the car on the way from the office.

"You know I've got enough hours to get my permanent licence," she'd said.

"I thought you did," he'd replied. "Congratulations. How should we celebrate?" He glanced at her. Her expression was woebegone. "What's wrong?"

"I don't think I'm going to apply for it."

"Eh? Why not?"

"I'm thinking of going back to teaching," she said. "I've been taking night classes to bring my certification up to date."

She'd been doing more than just thinking about it, he thought glumly.

"I won't abandon you, Hack. I'll stay on till you find someone to replace me—assuming you need to replace me."

"I thought you liked being a private investigator," he said, already feeling abandoned.

"It has its moments," she said. "And I like working with you. But let's face it, you don't really need a partner. Or a beautiful assistant," she added with a rueful smile. "There's barely enough work to keep you busy, let alone the two of us."

"Things have been a bit slow lately, but they'll pick up."

"I hope so," she said. "For your sake. But I haven't really been pulling my weight, have I? Be honest. You've been carrying me from the beginning, even though you couldn't really afford it."

"I don't pay you that much," he said. "Besides, when you're a fully-fledged PI I expect you to start bringing in work yourself."

"And where am I supposed to find this work?" she said. "Anyway, I'm not sure I'm really cut out to be a PI." She looked at him for a moment. "Why did you hire me in the first place?"

"To get into your pants," he said.

She smiled. "And it only took you two years," she said. "Seriously."

"You needed a job, and I needed someone to do the paperwork I'm too lazy and disorganized to do myself. I didn't think you'd be happy being just a secretary so I encouraged you to get your licence. Okay, you don't want to do fieldwork. There are still security needs analyses and background checks. It often pays better anyway."

"Not that much better," she said. "I do the books, Hack, and I know for a fact that there have been times you haven't paid yourself in order to cover my salary."

"I'm doing all right," he said. "I don't need much."

"That's crap and you know it. How much time have you spent this year doing general contracting work for Trevor Jefferson? And, even if it were true, it's not fair to you, is it? But it's not just the money. I need to be home for the kids. Susie's going to be ready for college soon, Billy not long after. I need something with more regular hours."

"We can work something out," Loomis said, not sure they could. PI work wasn't nine-to-five.

He'd parked across the street from the Medical Arts Building, and sat for a moment, staring straight ahead, hands at ten and two on the wheel.

"I'm sorry," Connie had said.

"What about us?"

"I'm not moving to Alpha Centauri," she'd said, and had leaned over and kissed his cheek.

In the lobby of the Medical Arts Building, Loomis's phone buzzed, Connie's name on the screen.

"Heads up," she said from the car across the street. "This might be our guy. Mid-forties. Heavy-set. Camel-hair coat. Thinning dark hair."

"Got him," Loomis said, closing his phone as the man Connie had described came through the revolving doors. "Dr. Spender?"

The man nodded, smile thin. "Mr. Loomis, I presume."

"I appreciate you meeting me," Loomis said, as they shook hands.

"You didn't give me much choice, did you?" Spender said. "Shall we go up to my office?"

They took an elevator to the third floor. Spender's office was at the opposite end of the hallway from Kellerman's. Spender unlocked the door, stood aside as Loomis went through, then locked the door behind them.

The windowless reception area was small, with a half a dozen moulded plastic chairs and a chrome and glass coffee table littered with magazines, some of which looked as though they'd been around since the Bush II administration. Many of the surfaces were covered in a thin patina of dust. Loomis wondered how long it had been since Spender had started shutting down his practice.

"My office is in the back," Spender said, taking off his coat.

Loomis followed him to a small, cluttered office, past two treatment rooms from which most of the equipment had been removed. Spender indicated a chair facing a small desk almost hidden beneath stacks of files.

"Let me move some of those," Spender said, shifting files to a table against the wall. Much of the wall space in Spender's office was taken up by tall bookcases, the shelves largely empty. The space left over was covered with framed diplomas and certificates. Spender had obtained his degree at McGill University in Montreal.

"Are you Canadian?" Loomis asked.

"No," Spender said. "Born and bred in Vermont. I grew up in St. Albans. I studied at McGill because it was close to home, in addition to being a world-class school." He paused. "So, how I can help you, Mr. Loomis? This woman you're looking for …"

"Belle Ryerson," Loomis said.

"Yes. As I said, I don't know her, though."

"But her name, well, rings a bell, doesn't it?"

"I may have heard it somewhere," Spender said.

"Do you know Dr. Thaddeus Kellerman? He has an office down the hall."

"Yes," Spender said, guardedness increasing.

"Are you a member of his foundation?" Loomis asked.

Spender regarded Loomis for a long moment, then said, "You're not working for him, are you?"

"No," Loomis said.

Spender seemed relieved, which piqued Loomis's curiosity. Why would Spender think Loomis might be working for Kellerman? Perhaps Kellerman ran background checks on prospective colonists, Loomis thought. He would.

"We've been retained by Belle Ryerson's family. You're a member of the Kentauran Foundation, aren't you?"

"Well, yes, I am," Spender said.

Loomis took the photograph of Belle Ryerson out of his inside pocket and handed it to Spender.

"Have you ever seen this woman?"

"This is Belle Ryerson?" he said, a look of surprise on his face.

"Yes, it is. Do you know her?"

"Not exactly."

"But you've seen her."

"Yes."

Loomis took the photograph back and waited, hoping Spender would fill the silence with an explanation. "Don't screw with me, Dr. Spender," Loomis said, when he'd waited long enough. "This woman's life may be in danger. When and where did you see her?"

"Two weeks ago," Spender said. "At a Kentauran Foundation meeting."

"Why were you surprised when I showed you her photograph?"

"Well ..." Spender said.

Getting Spender to open up was like pulling teeth. "Well *what*?" Loomis said.

"I saw her two weeks ago outside the meeting hall, talking with Dr. Kellerman and a woman named Harriet Olsen. She's ..." He paused.

"I know who she is," Loomis said. "What were they talking about?"

"I couldn't hear what they were saying—I was in my car talking to my realtor on the phone—but from their body language it was obvious they were arguing. Dr. Kellerman seemed particularly agitated, although it was hard to tell who he was upset with, your missing person or Miss Olsen. I hoped things would calm down when another man joined them, but he only made the situation worse."

"Who was this other man?"

"A fellow named Quentin Parker," Spender said. "He's supposed to be some kind of writer, but, well, he doesn't seem all that bright."

"I know him," Loomis said. "How did he makes things worse?"

"He was almost jumping up and down in anger, waving his arms and shouting. And he was quite physically aggressive with Miss Olsen. I thought he was going to actually strike her. So did Miss Olsen, I think."

"What was he so upset about?"

"I've no idea."

"And you have no idea what Belle, Olsen and Kellerman were arguing about?"

"I'm afraid not. My car is virtually sound-proof and I was on the phone."

"What happened then?"

"Nothing, really. Miss Olsen left with Mr. Parker. I'm don't think it was entirely voluntary. He practically threw her into his car."

"What about Belle?"

"She and Dr. Kellerman spoke for a few minutes. It looked like she may have been trying to calm him down. Then she got into her car, and he went back into the meeting hall."

"The next time you saw Kellerman, did you ask him about it?"

"No, I didn't."

"I was at a meeting Tuesday night," Loomis said. "I don't recall seeing you."

"My wife and I were with our real estate agent."

"Your car was there."

"A friend was using it. He's buying it."

Spender wouldn't need a car where he was going, Loomis supposed. "How long have you been a member of the Kentauran Foundation?"

"Seven years or so," Spender said.

"How long has Harriet Olsen been on the scene?"

"Dr. Kellerman introduced her to the group about six weeks ago," Spender said.

"And Parker?"

"Around the same length of time, I think."

"Outside of their association with Kellerman, did Parker and Harriet Olsen appear to know one another?"

"I wouldn't have said so. I don't recall them exchanging more than a casual word or two. To be honest, I got the impression she didn't like him much."

"Do you believe she's in contact with an alien spaceship?"

"Are you suggesting that she's not? That she's delusional? Or lying?"

"It's not everyday you come across someone who claims to commune with extraterrestrial beings."

"No," Spender agreed. "But Dr. Kellerman is convinced her experiences are genuine."

He would, Loomis thought, since he believes he's had similar experiences. "So you do believe her?"

"I guess I do," Spender said. "Can you imagine what it would mean to make contact with an extraterrestrial spacefaring race? Why, the potential for medical and technological advancement alone is mind-boggling."

"I shouldn't be in a hurry to upgrade my iPod then," Loomis said, struggling to maintain his composure.

"Perhaps not," Spender said, with a tolerant smile. "What does this have to do with your investigation?"

"Perhaps nothing, but if Belle Ryerson is a member of your, um, group …"

"You were going to say 'cult,' weren't you? Whether she's a member or not, I'm sure the fact that she's missing has nothing to do with Dr. Kellerman's foundation."

"I'm not," Loomis said. "Could she be a member of the first wave of refugees Dr. Kellerman was talking about the other night? I'm going to have a hell of a time finding her if she moves to another planet."

Spender shook his head. "I don't believe she is."

"Are you?"

"No. No, I'm not."

The needle of Loomis's bullshit detector jumped into the red.

"Why are you closing your practice?"

"I'm retiring," Spender said.

"Young to retire, aren't you?"

"We have no children." He gestured with a wave of his hand to his offices. "I've done well. I might as well retire while my wife and I are young enough to enjoy it."

"Planning to travel?" Loomis said.

"Yes, we are."

"Not by car, though."

"Pardon me?"

"Never mind. How well to you know Dr. Kellerman? I mean, do you know him personally, or simply as head of the foundation?"

"I suppose you could say I know him personally? Since I joined the foundation, he's become a friend. He's also a patient."

Loomis wondered if the professional relationship was mutual. "How would you characterize Dr. Kellerman's relationship with Harriet Olsen?"

"Characterize?"

"Are they intimate?"

"That would be a violation of Dr. Kellerman's professional ethics."

"Which profession? Psychiatry or ufology?"

"Psychiatry, of course."

"She's his patient?"

"That's my understanding." Spender looked at his watch, then stood. "I'm afraid that's all the time I can give you, Mr. Loomis."

"You've been very helpful," he said.

"I'm pleased to hear it," Spender said. He escorted Loomis into the reception area and unlocked the door.

"Oh, by the way, Dr. Spender, does the name Maya Thomas mean anything to you?"

"No. Nothing. Sorry." No hesitation.

"All right, thanks for your time."

"You're welcome," Spender said.

Loomis took an elevator down and went out to where Connie waited in the Outback. She'd moved into the driver's seat. He got into the passenger side.

"Well?" she said.

"Spender is seriously cracked," Loomis said. "It wasn't a complete waste of time, though." He summarised his conversation with William Spender.

"I wonder what the argument was about," Connie said, when he'd finished.

"Maybe it was over who got the window seat."

"So, do we stake out Spender or stick with Parker and

Harriet Olsen?"

"Since we haven't had much luck with Parker, let's see if we can shake Kellerman or Olsen out of their trees, find out what that argument was about."

Connie started to open the door.

"You might as well drive," Loomis said, fastening his seat belt.

Connie settled back and reached for the ignition. Loomis caught her wrist as a cab pulled up in front of the Medical Arts Building.

"What?"

"Our girl just got out of that cab."

They watched as Harriet Olsen went into the Medical Arts Building.

25

"Are you going to need a chaperone?" Connie asked, with a coy smile.

"I might," Loomis said. "Besides, she might relate better to a woman."

"Actually, I think she'll relate better to a big strong alpha male."

"Too bad there isn't one available," Loomis said.

"Do you want me to come with you? Or wait here and follow Spender?"

"Forget it," Loomis said. "Go home to your kids."

"You sure?" she said.

"Yeah. Go home."

"All right," she said.

She got out of the car and he clambered over the console to the driver's seat. He lowered the window.

"Call me later?" she said, looking down at him. "If you want to talk."

"Okay," he said.

She leaned down and kissed him through the open window, gave him a reassuring smile, then headed back to the office. He watched in the rear-view mirror as she crossed Main and cut through City Hall Park. He felt like throwing up.

Shit.

He sat in the Outback, watching the entrance of the Medical Arts Building. All right, so Connie didn't want to be a private investigator. Don't take it personally, he told himself. It wasn't him she was rejecting, but the uncertainty of the job. She wanted more stability, regular hours, and a reliable paycheque. Hell, so did he. She was right, though, there usually wasn't enough work to keep them both busy, let alone bring in enough money to pay them both a decent wage. Besides, in the long run, not working together might be a good thing. Look how it had worked out with Veejay.

He locked up the car and crossed Main to the Medical Arts Building, taking the elevator to the third floor. No sign of Harriet Olsen, but the lights were on in Kellerman's office. Ignoring the invitation to "Ring and Enter," Loomis tried the door. It was unlocked. He opened it carefully and poked his head through, into a small waiting room. He heard a woman's voice coming through an open door to another room, but he couldn't make out what she was saying. He stepped into the waiting room and eased the door shut behind him.

Kellerman's waiting room was plushly carpeted and decorated in cool pastels. There were two wingback chairs, a side table and a lamp between them. A small bookcase held a couple dozen paperbacks and a neat stack of magazines. Half a dozen small framed prints hung on the walls, pastoral scenes in soothing blues and greens.

Loomis crept noiselessly across the carpet to the other door and peered through into what appeared to be Kellerman's consulting room. It wasn't much bigger than the waiting room, but contained a blond wood wall unit, a matching desk, and two more wingback chairs. No couch. There were two more doors, one closed, one partly open. Harriet Olsen's voice was coming from the other side of the partly open door.

" ...don't like it," she was saying. "You said it would be easy. A piece of cake, you said."

She paused, listening. To whom? Loomis wondered. He glanced at Kellerman's desk, but there was no extension. He didn't think she was talking to Charley, though.

"You keep saying that," she said. "It's not my fault it's taking so long. We've got to be careful. He's not stupid, you know, despite what you think." A pause, then: "Fine, but I don't know how much longer I can keep him under control. Those two steroid-addled morons aren't helping, either." She listened for a moment. "Yes, yes, I know," she said wearily, "but you weren't there, were you? She's a fucking psychopath. She scares the shit out of me."

Loomis smiled. He imagined the members of the Kentauran Foundation would be shocked by Harriet Olsen's out-of-character language. The "steroid-addled morons" worried him, though. Hubert and Ginny Gasche fit the profile.

"No, goddamnit," Harriet Olsen said. "I told you before, I won't do that. I'm not a whore. Anyway, he hasn't shown any interest in me in that way."

She paused. She must have been holding the phone slightly away from her ear, because Loomis could hear the tiny insect buzz of the voice at the other end of the line. He couldn't tell if it belonged to a man or a woman.

"Well, he's your problem, isn't he?" she said. "I'm sure you can handle him. It had better be soon, though, because if this goddamned thing goes any more sideways, I'm getting the hell out of Dodge, screw the money." Loomis heard the sound of the phone banging down. "Shit," she said, sounding discouraged.

He retreated silently across the thick carpet to the door and opened it, rattling the handle.

"Hello," he called. "Anyone home?" He let the door swing shut.

He thought he heard her swear again, then she called, "One moment, please."

A few seconds later Harriet Olsen came into the waiting room. She looked pale and drawn, Loomis thought, but she was still a lovely woman, disarmingly so. He'd have to be careful that he wasn't disarmed.

"Oh, hello," she said, with a tentative smile. "You're the detective. Mister ...?"

"Loomis," he said. "Hack Loomis."

"Dr. Kellerman isn't here," she said.

It was warm in the office, and she was wearing a pale

green cardigan with sleeves that extended almost to her fingertips, but she stood with her shoulders slightly hunched and her arms folded, hugging herself as if she were cold.

"That's all right," he said. "I wanted to speak with you."

"Me? What about? Oh, of course. Your missing person. What was her name? Bess Myerson?" She shook her head. "No, she was an actress in the fifties or sixties, wasn't she?"

"My missing person's name is Belle Ryerson," Loomis said, concealing his annoyance at her disingenuousness.

"Yes, of course," she said. "I'm sorry. I'm not very good with names. I told you the other night that I didn't know where she was. Nothing has changed since then. I still don't know where she is."

The needle of Loomis's bullshit detector did not quiver. If she was dissembling, he couldn't tell. She might actually be telling the truth.

"You, Dr. Kellerman and Belle Ryerson had an argument outside the church a couple of weeks ago. What was it about?"

She blinked. "Who told you that?"

"A reliable source," Loomis said. "What were you arguing about?"

"Your source may not be as reliable as you think."

"Then you weren't talking with Kellerman and Belle Ryerson outside the church hall."

"Thaddeus and I have spoken outside the church a

number of times. He's an occasional smoker. Other people join us from time to time as well, perhaps even your Ms. Ryerson. I don't recall. I certainly didn't quarrel with her. Or Thaddeus. Except perhaps about his smoking."

"What's your relationship to Quentin Parker?"

"I'm acquainted with him, of course."

"He didn't manhandle you and throw you into his car the night of your non-argument with Belle Ryerson?"

"Certainly not," she said, blue gaze steady.

Loomis didn't need his bullshit detector to tell him she was lying. He didn't know how to call her on it, though, other than to say it straight out. He suspected, however, that it wouldn't make any difference: she was in complete control. He considered asking her about the telephone conversation he'd overheard. It might shake her up, but it might also shut her down completely. He decided to keep it in reserve.

"Perhaps you need better informants, Mr. Loomis," she said.

"You're right," he said, feigning defeat. "Eyewitnesses are notoriously unreliable. It's a major headache in my line of work. Yours, too, I suppose."

"I'm not sure I know what you mean."

"According to an acquaintance who knows about such things, most UFO sightings are hoaxes or the result of witnesses mistaking conventional aircraft or weather balloons for unidentified flying objects."

"Many are," she said. "Perhaps even the majority. But some sightings can't be explained away so easily. I know

very little about the phenomenon. Until my own encounter with—" she made the cat-coughing sound in her
throat "—I would have said UFOs and extraterrestrials
didn't exist."

"I wish you wouldn't do that," Loomis said. "Just call
him Charley, please. For my sake, if nothing else."

"It does hurt a little," she admitted.

"How does that work?" he said. "I mean, how do you
get to Charley's spaceship? Do you fly somehow? Does he
beam you up? Or do you just wake up and you're there?"

"Don't mock me, Mr. Loomis. You're not really interested in my experiences. You think I'm delusional or perhaps confabulating. Perhaps I am. How would I know? A
memory is a memory, is it not? But I am not deranged.
God, if I had such an obsessive need for attention, I'd have
been a stripper or a contestant on American Idol." Her
eyes glistened and a single tear made a track down her
cheek to the corner of her mouth.

Christ, Loomis thought. One little tear and he practically turned to marshmallow. If she could sing and dance
as well as she could act, she'd burn up the American Idol
phone lines.

"It must be difficult," he said. "You're lucky to found
have Dr. Kellerman."

"Yes, I am."

"How did you learn about him?"

"Dr. Kellerman is well known in the field of alien abduction. I contacted him when I began having very vivid
and disturbing recurring dreams of being with a human-

like alien aboard a spacecraft of some kind." She smiled bravely. "Until Thaddeus hypnotizes me and tells me it's all right to remember, I have no memory of what transpires during my time aboard the ship or the details of my conversations with—Charley." She was silent for a moment, eyes unfocused. Then she looked Loomis in the eye and said, "Despite Charley's apparent benevolence, it's not always a very pleasant experience."

"I imagine it can be a bit disconcerting," he said.

"But you still think I'm mentally ill, don't you?"

"No," he said. "I don't think you're mentally ill at all. However, as much as I'm enjoying our chat, it's time to come back down to earth."

Her mouth stretched in a wintry smile.

He returned her smile. "It doesn't matter to me one way or another whether you believe in aliens from Alpha Centauri or you're running one of the most bizarre confidence games I've ever heard of. All I care about is finding Belle Ryerson and bringing her home safe and sound. Maybe I'm not the best judge of character, but you seem to be an otherwise decent person. Under other circumstances, I might even come to like you. But don't think for one second I won't come down on you like a gang of rabid Wookies if you or your pals are responsible for Belle Ryerson coming to harm."

She glared at him as he stepped around her into Kellerman's consulting room. Just the desk, chairs, and wall unit. No filing cabinets or computer or phone. His patient records must have been in the other room. The shelves of the wall unit were empty but for a small video camera mounted on a bracket and aimed at the wingback chairs. The cables disappeared through a hole the back of the unit.

"This is Dr. Kellerman's psychiatric consulting room," she said. "You shouldn't be in here."

He tried the door, now closed, to the back room. It was locked. The other door opened into the stairwell. There was no handle on the stairwell side. The patient exit, he presumed. He let it swing shut.

"Please," she said. "Dr. Kellerman would be very upset if he knew you were in here."

"So let's not tell him," Loomis said, causing her to frown disapprovingly. "What's in the back room?"

"Dr. Kellerman's private office," she said.

He held out his hand. "Give me the key?"

"I don't have a key."

"No?" Loomis said. "I—"

"Harriet," a gruff voice called from the waiting room. "Harriet, are you here?"

"Oh, shit," Harriet Olsen said, half under her breath.

26

"Harriet," Dr. Thaddeus Kellerman said, as he came into the consulting room. "Why is the front door unlocked?" His eyes widened when he saw Loomis.

"Thaddeus," Harriet Olsen said. "You remember Mr. Loomis, don't you? The private investigator? He was at the meeting the other night, asking about Belle Ryerson."

"Yes, yes, of course, of course," Kellerman said, disconcerted by Loomis's presence. "Have you been successful in your efforts to locate Miss Ryerson? No? I wish there was something we could do to help, but I'm afraid I have no idea where she could be."

"Perhaps," Loomis said, "you could tell me what you, Harriet, and Belle Ryerson were arguing about outside the meeting hall two weeks ago."

"I beg your pardon," Kellerman said. "I can assure you I have not *argued* with Miss Ryerson at any time."

"Don't bullshit me, doctor. I'm not in the mood."

Kellerman flushed, mouth twitching with agitation.

261

Harriet placed her hand on his arm. The gesture caused the sleeve of her sweater to slip back from her wrist. She quickly removed her hand from Kellerman's arm and pulled her sleeve over her wrist again, but not before Loomis saw a vivid ring of discolouration around her wrist. She looked at Loomis, clearly worried that he had seen the bruising.

"My source couldn't hear what you were saying," Loomis said, watching Harriet, seeing the relief in her eyes: perhaps he hadn't seen the bruises, after all. "However, from your body language and raised voices he was certain you were having, well, let's call it a 'heated discussion.' You were interrupted by Quentin Parker, who subsequently hustled Miss Olsen into his car and drove off. You and Belle spoke for a minute or two more, then you went back into the church, and Belle left in her car. Any of this sound familiar to you?"

"Who is this source of yours?" Kellerman demanded.

"All you need to know is that he's a member of your organization who has no reason to lie. I'll ask you again, what were you arguing about?"

"And I'll tell you again, we were not arguing."

"All right," Loomis said, close to the limit of his patience. "You weren't arguing. What were you not arguing about?"

"It was a private matter," Kellerman said. "Not relevant to your investigation."

"Forgive me if I don't take your word for that," Loomis said.

"Thaddeus," Harriet Olsen said. "Perhaps we should

let Mr. Loomis decide what's relevant to his investigation and what's not. His only interest, after all, is returning Ms. Ryerson safely to her family."

"Yes, of course," Kellerman said. Although he was full of blustery confidence, his eyes shifted uneasily from Loomis to Harriet Olsen and back. She put her hand on his arm again, careful not to reveal the bruising on her wrist. He calmed down.

"I recall the conversation now," Harriet said, looking Loomis in the eye, dissembling shamelessly. "Belle was concerned about what she'd seen at the meeting that evening. Frankly, she accused Thaddeus of being a charlatan. She believed he was using hypnosis to create false memories of my visits to—to Charley's spaceship."

"She was mistaken, of course," Kellerman said. "The techniques I employ are especially designed to prevent the creation of false memories in my subjects. I do not ask leading questions. For example, I ask Harriet where she is, not if she is on, ah, Charley's spaceship."

"Yes, yes," Loomis said. "You explained all that at the meeting the other night." He also recalled Betsy Ledbetter commenting that Belle had been asking about Kellerman's use of hypnosis to help Harriet remember her visits with Charley. "That's what you were arguing about? Your methodology?"

Kellerman's eyes sought Harriet.

"Arguing is perhaps too strong a word," she said. "But I suppose we were having, as you put it, a somewhat heated discussion."

"My source seemed to think Dr. Kellerman was upset with you, too."

"Well, to be honest, I thought Thaddeus was too dismissive of Belle's concerns. She was only concerned for my welfare, after all. And Thaddeus's credibility."

An answer for everything, Loomis thought. "What was Parker's problem then?" he said. "My source told me it looked like he was going to hit you."

"What? Oh, no," Harriet said, the cuffs of her sweater sleeves bunched in her hands. "Quentin wouldn't. He's—well, Quentin has a tendency to overreact at times."

"Is that how you came by those bruises?"

Her cheeks coloured and she glared daggers at Loomis, folding her arms across her breasts, tucking her hands into her armpits.

Loomis glanced at Kellerman. The old man's mouth was twisted, as though he had just tasted something foul. Loomis sympathized: Parker left a bad taste in his mouth, too.

"How long has he been a member of your group?" Loomis asked.

"He isn't," Kellerman said, spitting the words out. "He claims to be a writer doing research for an article or a book about our work."

"Did you know he tried to break into Belle Ryerson's house last night?"

Kellerman's mouth fell open. Harriet Olsen just shook her head slowly, a look of disgust on her face.

"No, I didn't," Kellerman said. "Was he apprehended?"

"In a manner of speaking," Loomis said. "Belle's sister Hazel brained him with a shovel and called me." He looked at Harriet Olsen. "You don't seem surprised."

"I suppose I'm not," she said. "I was skeptical from the very beginning of his claim to a writer. Frankly, he doesn't seem intelligent enough."

"Where is he now?" Kellerman asked. "Did you turn him over to the police?"

"No," Loomis said. "We turned him loose, hoping he would lead us to Belle Ryerson. He led us to you."

"Me?"

"He's staying at the Green Mountain Motel."

"Yes," she said. "Unfortunately."

"If you don't like him, why did you leave with him the night of your non-argument with Belle Ryerson?" Kellerman's expression soured.

"He was quite upset about—well, I'm not sure what," Harriet said. "I was worried he might do something rash. With some justification, as it happens."

"When I first came in," Loomis said, playing his hole card, "I overheard you in Dr. Kellerman's back office talking to someone on the phone. Who were you talking to?"

Harriet Olsen's steely self-control wavered, but for so brief an instant that if Loomis hadn't been watching carefully he would have missed it. As it was, he wasn't absolutely certain he'd seen anything at all.

"I don't know what you're talking about," she said, her mask clamped back into place. "I wasn't talking to anyone."

"Whoever it was," Loomis said, "you told him you were having a hard time controlling someone. I suspect she was talking about you, Dr. Kellerman."

"Control me? Don't be ridiculous," Kellerman said, but there was a momentary flicker of something in his eyes. Doubt? Fear?

"She isn't in contact with aliens from outer space any more than I am," Loomis said. "You and the members of your foundation are being fleeced like so many sheep."

"Don't listen to him, Thaddeus. I don't know why, but he's"—her voice caught convincingly—"he's lying."

"I know he is, my dear," Kellerman said, patting her shoulder.

Tired of playing their game, Loomis pressed on, hoping to rattle them into making another slip. "He also wanted you to do something you didn't want to do. You said, and I quote, 'I'm not a whore.' That was probably also about you, Dr. Kellerman. Whoever is pulling Harriet's strings figures she could control you more easily by sleeping with you."

"Why are you doing this?" she said, eyes filling with tears. "Thaddeus, please make him stop. Make him go away."

"Dr. Kellerman," Loomis said. "Who is Maya Thomas?"

"Pardon me?" Kellerman said, disconcerted by the abrupt change of direction. "I don't know anyone by that name."

"How about you, Harriet? Does the name Maya

Thomas mean anything to you?"

"No," she said. "Who is she?"

"Her body was found in Burlington Bay on Tuesday morning."

"Oh," she said.

"Belle was supposed to meet someone named Maya the day she disappeared," Loomis said. "Except by then Maya Thomas had been dead for at least a week. She'd been struck on the head—punched, actually—and thrown into the lake just a few days after you and Belle had your non-argument."

"What are you insinuating, sir?" Kellerman said. "That someone in my organization is responsible for this woman's death or Miss Ryan's disappearance?"

"Her name is Ryerson," Loomis said. "And, yes, that's exactly what I think. I think Harriet here ordered Belle's abduction—and not by aliens—because she was afraid Belle was going to screw up her con. Where have you got her stashed? Or did you kill her, too, and dump her body in the lake?"

"That's preposterous" Kellerman said.

"Mr. Loomis," Harriet Olsen said, gripping Kellerman's arm, her distress seeming genuine. "You must believe me. We had nothing to do with this Maya Thomas's death or Belle Ryerson's disappearance."

"Who were you talking to on the phone?"

She shook her head. "I'm not answering any more of your questions."

"Would you rather answer the police's questions?"

Loomis said. "I can arrange that."

"Mr. Loomis," Kellerman said. "Please. There's no need to involve the police. There's nothing we can tell them about that woman's death or Miss Ryerson's disappearance. Would that there were. Perhaps if you knew more about the Rigilians and what we are striving to achieve, well, I wouldn't expect you to join us, but you would realize that the idea of harming another person is abhorrent to us, anathema to everything we and the Rigilians believe."

"You're wasting your time, Thaddeus," Harriet Olsen said. "Mr. Loomis has made up his mind. He thinks we're all either delusional or perpetrating a fraud, and nothing you say will convince him otherwise. He has no evidence to support either theory." She turned to Loomis. "And you don't have any evidence connecting us to the death of Maya Thomas or Belle Ryerson's disappearance, do you? No. Because none exists and none exists because we aren't involved. Goodbye, Mr. Loomis."

Loomis looked into her eyes. He expected her to smirk or look triumphant, but all he saw was fear.

"Mr. Loomis," Kellerman said from the door.

"All right, I'll go," Loomis said, suspecting he wouldn't get anything more out of them. "I'll give you this, Harriet," he added, looking into her eyes. "You stay in character. But if things start to go too far *sideways* and you need help getting out of *Dodge*, give me a call. You still have my card, don't you?"

She blinked.

27

Loomis went down to his car and sat, waiting for Kellerman and Harriet Olsen to leave. In spite of himself, he found that he did almost like Harriet Olsen. Or whoever the hell she was. She was a grifter, sure, and likely more than a little amoral and lazy. And, yes, she was conspiring to perpetrate a bizarre con on Kellerman and his followers. But he was beginning to wonder if, in fact, she really knew anything about Belle Ryerson's disappearance or Maya Thomas's death. Connie would attribute it to hormones, but she'd be wrong. Well, not entirely. Harriet Olsen was a very attractive woman, no denying that. There was more to it than that, however. He couldn't shake the feeling that she was just a frightened young woman, involved in something way over her head that was rapidly spinning out of her control.

Notwithstanding his sympathy for her, though, he should have pushed her harder about who she'd been talking to on the phone. It hadn't been Kellerman, obviously.

Could it have been Quentin Parker? Possibly, but Loomis doubted it. Whoever it was, he—or she—was calling the shots and Loomis didn't think Parker was man enough. Or smart enough. Could it have been Dave Ledbetter? Loomis didn't think so. Ledbetter was a true believer, like Kellerman, a long-standing member of the Kentauran Foundation. Besides, even though Ledbetter was an order of magnitude smarter than Parker, Loomis didn't figure him for the evil genius type, lurking in the background, sending out his minions to do his dirty work. Whoever Harriet had been talking to, she was more afraid of him and his "steroid-addled morons" than she was of Loomis.

Loomis jumped when someone rapped on the passenger door window.

"Shit, Quentin," he said, turning the key and lowering the window an inch or two.

"Hey, sorry, man," Parker said. He tried the door. "How about letting me in? I'm freezing my ass off out here."

Loomis stared at Parker for a moment, thinking he could afford to lose some of his ass. Then he raised the window and pressed the lock release.

"What are you doing hanging around here?" Loomis said as Parker got into the car.

"Probably the same as you," Parker said.

"And what do you think that is?"

"I figure you must be staking out Kellerman and Olsen."

"That's what you're doing? Still looking for a story?"

"Yeah, well," Parker said with a shrug. "I also figured maybe I could find out something that would help you find the Ryerson broad."

"I've got it covered," Loomis said. "But since you're here you can tell me what Kellerman, Olsen and Belle Ryerson were arguing about outside the church hall two weeks ago."

Parker tried to mask his surprise, but he didn't to a very good job of it, and he knew it. "That was your missing person?" he said.

"So you know the night I'm talking about?"

"Yeah, but I didn't know it was her they were talking to. If I'd known, man, I'd've said something."

"I showed you her photograph."

"You showed me a photo of a chick on a mountain decked out in hiking gear," he said. "The woman they were talking to looked different. Older, like."

"What were they talking about?"

"I dunno. The usual shit, I suppose. Flying saucers and aliens from outer space. They clammed up when I got there."

"Why did you hustle Harriet Olsen into your car?"

"Huh? Who says I hustled her into my car?" Parker said. "She asked me to take her back to the motel."

"When you got to the motel, did she invite you into her room for a drink?"

Parker looked at Loomis for a long moment, trying to work out if Loomis was joking. "She just went into her room and I went into mine."

"Too bad. She's very attractive."

"Don't let those looks fool you, man. She may look hot, but she's ice cold. Not to mention crazy as a tree full of squirrels. Gotta be, believing the shit she does. I wouldn't kick her out of my bed, though," he added with a shrug.

You should be so lucky to have the chance, Loomis thought. "She's not very happy with you right now," he said. "Neither is Kellerman."

"Huh? Why not?"

"I told them about your attempt to burgle Belle Ryerson's house last night."

"Aw, shit, man. I'm gonna be totally *persona non gratis* with them now."

"*Grata*," Loomis said.

"Eh?"

"The expression is *persona non grata*."

"Oh." He shrugged. "Whatever."

"Tell me about Maya Thomas," Loomis said.

"Who?"

Loomis sighed. "Where are you from, Quentin?"

"Huh? What do you mean?"

"Where's home? The place the IRS thinks you live. And I don't mean the Green Mountain Motel."

"Oh. Well, I kind of moved around a lot, growing up. I was born in Portland, though. Maine, not Oregon. Haven't been back there in a long time."

"I'll make it easier for you," Loomis said. "What's the address on your driver's licence?"

"What's this about, man? What do you care where I live?"

"So I can tell them where to send flowers in the event something happens to you."

"Tell who? What are you talking about? What's going to happen to me?"

"Keep lying to me and you'll find out."

"C'mon, man, why would I lie to you?"

"Same reason the scorpion stung the fox: it's in your nature."

"That's funny. Haw. Look, what have I lied to you about?"

"Everything, I imagine. Frankly, if you told me you lied all the time I'd still think you were lying, despite the logical conundrum."

"The logical what?"

"Conundrum. Paradox. Inconsistency. If you lie all the time, telling me so would be the truth, in which case you don't lie all the time. See where I'm going?"

"Uh, no."

"Forget it," Loomis said. "Why don't you run along. Slither back under whatever rock you call home."

"C'mon, man. Gimme a break. Anyway, I thought I'd hang out with you a while, see if I could pick up some pointers from a pro."

"Maybe some other time," Loomis said. He was beginning to wonder what Kellerman and Harriet Olsen were up to that was taking so long.

"I been thinking," Parker said.

"Don't pull a muscle," Loomis said.

"Funny. Anyway, I'm thinking we should check out Dave Ledbetter. He's, like, Kellerman's second-in-command. I bet he knows where the Ryerson broad is."

"You know," Loomis said. "You might be right. Why don't you do that?"

"I thought we could do it together, like."

"First rule of detective work," Loomis said. "Don't waste resources. Think of it as your initiation into the brotherhood. Just don't expect me to split my fee with you. You're strictly unpaid help. An intern, so to speak, without the fringe benefits."

"Okay, I get it," Parker said. "It was a dumb idea."

"Not at all," Loomis said. "It was a great idea. Best I've heard all day. Hop to it, old son. You've got my number. Let me know if you come up with something. Don't dawdle. Time's a-wasting."

"Nah," Parker said. "It was a stupid idea."

Loomis laughed. "You're not keeping an eye on Kellerman or Olsen, are you? You're keeping an eye on me. What are you playing at? And don't give me any crap about helping me or picking up pointers."

"Like I told you last night, I'm just trying to pick up a few bucks. There's a story here, man, I can smell it. The tabloids love stories about aliens and shit. Throw in some sex, a murder or a missing broad, and they eat it up."

"There you go again," Loomis said.

"What?"

"Lying. I know Harriet is scamming Kellerman and

the members of his foundation, and I figure you're part of it." He held up his hand as Parker opened his mouth to deny the allegation. "You're obviously no criminal mastermind, Quentin. Someone else is running the show. I'm probably wasting my breath asking, but I've got nothing to lose, do I? Who is it?"

"I don't know what you're talking about, man."

Loomis reached across the car and opened the passenger door. "Out you get, Quentin."

"Hey, man—"

He put his hand on Parker's shoulder and pushed. Parker yawped and fell out of the car on to the sidewalk. Loomis pulled the door shut, started the engine, and drove away.

He didn't drive far, though. Turning left on to Union, he parked illegally, locked up the Outback, and ran back to Main in time to see Parker go into the Medical Arts Building. He was talking on his cellphone. Loomis jogged down the block and peered through the glass doors into the lobby. He didn't see Parker, but an elevator door was sliding shut. He went inside and took the stairs. When he reached the third floor landing he waited a few seconds before opening the door and taking a quick look up and down the hall. He was on the far side of the elevators from Kellerman's office. There was no sign of Parker.

He waited a few seconds more, then stepped into the hall and walked quickly to Kellerman's office. The lights were on, but he couldn't see anything through the frosted glass. He carefully tried the door handle. The door was locked. He pressed his ear to the glass, but heard nothing. Going into the stairwell next to Kellerman's office, he pressed his ear to Kellerman's patient exit door. He heard muffled sounds that might have been voices, but could not distinguish words. A psychiatrist's office would be well sound-proofed. Too bad he didn't have a stethoscope.

He returned to the hall. The door to the chiropractor's office across from Kellerman's was closed, but the lights were on. Loomis wondered if Tracy, Dr. Dan's flirty receptionist, would lend him a stethoscope. Did chiropractors even use them? He tried the door, but it was locked. He knocked softly. A moment later the door opened.

"Well, hello," Tracy said, smiling her bright, metallic smile. Her hair was cinched back and she was wearing a fitted shirt with the top buttons unfastened, stretch jeans, and calf-high boots with fur trim. Another type of uniform. "What can I do for you?"

"This is going to sound strange," Loomis said, "but could I borrow a stethoscope?"

"A stethoscope?" she said, eyes widening with amusement. "You're right. It is strange. I suppose there's one around here someplace. Come in while I look for it. What do you need a stethoscope for?"

"To eavesdrop on Dr. Kellerman," Loomis said, as Tracy went into Dr. Dan's examining room. She returned a moment later with a stethoscope.

"I should've known better," she said, handing him the shiny chrome and rubber device. "Seriously? Is that ethical?"

"You're not going to turn me in, are you?"

"Me? Heck, no. Hey, wait. I should tag along, make sure you don't run off with Dr. Dan's 'scope. Afterwards, I'll let you buy me a drink. Just let me lock up." She lifted a faux fur coat from a hook behind the reception desk.

Loomis didn't wait for her. He crossed the hall and went into the stairwell. Fitting the earpieces into his ears—they weren't very comfortable—he placed the amplifying disk against Kellerman's patient exit door. The stethoscope helped, but not a lot. The voices were still muffled, but he was able to make out most of the words.

" ...already at the staging area." Harriet Olsen's voice. "The rest are heading up there tonight. I wish I could tell you how long you'll have to wait, but I can't." She started to make the cat-coughing sound, but changed her mind. "Charley couldn't tell me precisely when they will come. I'm sure it won't be long ..."

"Can you hear anything?" Tracy asked, joining him in the stairwell.

Loomis put his finger to his lips.

"Oh, sorry," she whispered, hunkering down beside him.

" ...wasn't supposed to go." Kellerman's voice. "I'm far too old. And what will happen to the foundation when I'm gone? Who will organize the next wave of refugees? Who will complete construction of the transmitter?"

"I don't know," Harriet said. "But Charley says it's imperative that you're in the first wave."

"But why aren't you coming?" Kellerman said.

"*I wish I could,*" Harriet Olsen said. "*But my work here isn't finished. I don't know what else Charley needs me to do, but I have to trust him.*"

"*In the meantime,*" Quentin Parker said, "*what do we do about Loomis? He could really fuck things up if he keeps poking around. He's already got Ledbetter spooked.*"

"*What do you suggest we do?*" Harriet Olsen said. Even though her voice was muffled, Loomis could hear the edge in it. "*His only concern is Belle Ryerson.*"

"*What are you really doing here, Mr. Parker?*" Kellerman said. "*Who are you? You're obviously not a writer. What are you?*"

"*Thaddeus,*" Harriet Olsen said. "*Please. You're not supposed to become agitated. If it hadn't been for Quentin I would never have found you.*"

"*That may be so, my dear, and for that I'm grateful, but he's also the reason Mr. Loomis believes we're responsible for Belle Ryerson's disappearance. I very much regret that you wouldn't allow me to invite her to join us. She would have made a valuable addition to the colony.*"

"*You're far too trusting, Thaddeus,*" Harriet said. "*She didn't really believe in our cause, did she? She thinks Charley is a figment of my imagination, created by you.*"

"*I still think we need to do something about Loomis,*" Parker said. "*Uh, Charley's people have other agents on the ground, don't they? What if Loomis gets the police involved? If, ah, word gets back to Charley that the police think we had anything to do with Ryerson's disappearance or that other woman's death, all bets are off. It could wreck everything.*"

Loomis was astounded—gobsmacked, to use his favourite British colloquialism—that Kellerman, an otherwise seemingly intelligent man, could swallow such utter nonsense. No matter how delusional he was. Parker wasn't even a particularly convincing actor. He certainly couldn't hold a candle to Harriet Olsen.

"As much as it pains me to say this," Kellerman said, *"he's right, my dear. The Rigilian authorities monitor our media closely. If there is even the slightest suggestion that the dissidents have made contact, Charley will have no choice but to abandon us."*

"Thaddeus," Harriet Olsen said. *"It would be a grave mistake. If we leave Mr. Loomis alone, he'll focus his energies on finding Belle Ryerson, not on us. The farther we stay away from him, the better. Besides, what can we do that won't make matters worse?"*

"I have an idea or two," Parker said.

"Leave him alone," Harriet said. *"Do you hear me, Quentin? Don't do anything stupid. You've already done enough damage. What were you thinking, breaking into Belle Ryerson's house? All you did was raise Loomis's suspicions. You're lucky you're not in jail. In a few days it will all be over and we won't have to worry about Loomis at all."*

"We should be going," Kellerman said. *"Dave and Colonel Maynard will be at the house at seven. We need to prepare."*

"Quentin?" Harriet said.

"Yeah, yeah," Parker said. *"I hear you."*

"I hope so, because ..."

Her voice faded, presumably as they left Kellerman's consulting room. Loomis listened for a moment longer, but heard nothing more. He straightened.

"Did it work?" Tracy asked. He'd forgotten all about her.

"Keep your voice down," he said. He heard Kellerman and the others through the stairwell door as they headed to the elevators. Harriet was still berating Parker. "Yes, it did. Thanks."

He handed her the stethoscope. She rolled it up and shoved it into her bag. He started down the stairs.

"How about that drink?" she said, following him. "I know a nice little place not far from here. Do you like jazz?"

"I owe you," Loomis said. "But I'm afraid you're going to have to take a rain check."

"I don't do rain checks," she said. "It's now or never, buster."

"Regretfully, then," Loomis said, "it will have to be never."

"Well," she said, with a coy smile, "you do owe me. And like the man said, never say never."

28

There was no sign of Kellerman, Olsen, or Parker when Loomis and Tracy reached the street. He thanked her again and went around the corner to his car, unlocked it with the remote and got in. The dashboard clock read 5:18 p.m. According to the digital readout next to the time, the temperature was just a couple of degrees above freezing, and the glow of the city lights reflected off the underside of low clouds. He drove to Bank Street, parked in front of the Professional Building and went into the café across the street. He ordered a blueberry muffin and bottle of orange juice and took it to a table by the window. He glanced around as he called Connie. Half the people in the café were also on their cellphones. A third had laptops open in front of them, taking advantage of the café's free Wi-Fi service. Half a dozen or so had tablets of one sort or another. He could almost feel the electromagnetic radiation sleeting through him.

"I was just about to call you," she said.

"What's up?"

"I'm at the motel," Connie said.

"What are you doing there? I thought you were going home."

"I had to go to the office for a minute. Then I went back to see if you were still sitting outside the Medical Arts Building. I don't like the way we left things ..."

"So you thought you'd make it up to me by renting the honeymoon suite. I'll be right there."

"Keep it in your shorts, big fella," Connie said. "When I got to the Medical Arts Building I saw Dr. Spender getting into a cab. I wrote down the cab number, called the cab company, and sweet-talked the dispatcher into telling me where the cab dropped him off."

"The Green Mountain Motel. Popular spot."

He wondered if the motel could be the "staging area" Harriet had mentioned. There was plenty of room in the parking lot to land a flying saucer, as long as it was an older model, not one of the gigantic things from *Close Encounters of the Third Kind* or *Independence Day*. It would give the air traffic controllers at Burlington International Airport screaming fits, though.

"Good work," he said. "You should be a detective."

"Should I hang in here?"

"I overheard Harriet say everyone was heading to what she called the 'staging area.' It could be the motel."

"I'll stick around awhile, then. What about the argument between Kellerman and Belle?"

"Apparently Belle suspected Kellerman of creating false

memories in Harriet that she was in contact with aliens. Parker says they were just arguing about the 'usual shit' but that they stopped when he arrived. I'm not sure we can believe much of anything any of them says, with the possible exception of Kellerman. I think he's a true believer."

"True believers can be dangerous," Connie said.

"Yeah," Loomis said. "Are you sure you're okay to hang out there for a while?"

"I've arranged for Mrs. Ducharme to keep an eye on the kids. I can't be too late, though."

"All right. I'm going to head over to Kellerman's place. They're meeting Ledbetter and Maynard there at seven, perhaps before heading to this staging area. If nothing comes of it, I'll come out there and take over, let you get home."

"Okay," she said. "I'll give you a call if anything interesting happens here."

"To what do I owe this pleasure?" Phil Jefferson said when he answered Loomis's call. "You haven't changed your mind about coming back to work for me, have you?"

"Nope. I'm on a stakeout in South Cove and I don't want to get hassled by your gorilla."

"All right, I'll let that idiot Fisker know you're on the job. You driving the Outback?"

"Yes. Thanks."

"Anytime." The line went dead with a click.

Loomis settled back to wait, the compact Canon eight-power binoculars on the dash. At least the Outback had comfortable seats. Too bad they weren't heated.

It was almost 7 p.m. Kellerman's Lexus was in the driveway, but his other guests hadn't arrived. The lights were on in the house, upstairs and downstairs, and through the binoculars Loomis saw the slim figure of Harriet Olsen standing with her back to the living room window. He snacked on the dried fruit and chocolate he'd brought with him, washing it down with hummingbird sips of orange juice. Even though he was better equipped for it, he didn't like peeing in a bottle any more than Connie did. Ten minutes after he'd called Phil Jefferson, an Outback identical to his own cruised slowly past, but the driver ignored him. Twenty minutes after that his phone buzzed, Connie's name displayed on the screen.

"I hope you're having more fun than I am," he said.

"I don't know about fun," she said. "But something's going on. A half-size school bus with the Kentauran Foundation's name on the side pulled into the motel a couple of minutes ago. Ginny Gasche is driving. There are maybe six or eight other people on the bus, but room for twenty or thirty. The roof rack is piled high with gear. It looks like camping gear. Ginny—Christ, she must be freezing in that thin leather jacket—and Hubert are helping Spender pile more stuff on. Who goes camping in December, for god's sake?"

"Maybe the climate's better on their new planet," Loomis said.

"Should I follow the bus?"

"I'd rather you didn't," Loomis said.

"C'mon, Hack," Connie said. "I'm a big girl. I can take care of myself."

"You didn't let me finish," Loomis said. "I'd rather you didn't follow them on your own, but I doubt I can make it there in time. I know you can take care of yourself, but that's not the point. We've no idea where this staging area is. Most likely it's out in the boonies somewhere. I'm not sure I'd feel all that comfortable myself, following them on my own without some preparation. You don't have a gun with you, do you?"

"No, of course not."

"I know you have basic survival gear in your car—I put it there—but how are you dressed?"

"Boots, lined khakis, a parka. We don't have time for this, Hack. They've finished loading. They're going to leave any minute."

"All right," he said. "But be careful. Keep back and keep in touch."

"Do you want to stay connected?"

"No," he said. "But call me as soon as you have some idea where they're headed."

"Roger. Over and out."

"Don't call me Roger," he grumbled, as she disconnected.

Shit. Maybe they should have stayed connected so he could follow her. He was pretty sure he could catch up before they got where they were going. The old artillery range out near Jericho, for example. That would be the perfect place to land a flying saucer, even a big one. On the other hand, the staging area could be farther south. The area southwest of Chittenden was pretty sparsely populated. Hell, half of Upstate New York, Vermont and New Hampshire was damned near wilderness. The staging area could be anywhere. Best to sit tight until they had a better idea where the bus was headed.

Headlights washed over the Outback as a pickup with a Leer cap turned on to the cul-de-sac and pulled into Kellerman's driveway. Dave Ledbetter lumbered to Kellerman's front door. The motion-activated porch lights went on as Ledbetter climbed the front steps and pressed the bell button. A moment later, Kellerman let him in.

Where was Bets? Loomis wondered. Maybe she was already at the staging area. Or taking the bus.

The porch lights went out.

A few minutes later, another car arrived and parked behind the pickup. A grey or beige Ford Focus with Florida plates. James Maynard got out and walked to the house. The porch lights went on again. Maynard rang the bell and was admitted by Harriet Olsen. A moment later, the porch lights went out again.

Loomis was getting antsy, anxious for Connie's call. He tried calling her, but got her voice mail. Maybe she was trying to reach him, he thought, and disconnected without leaving a message.

Kellerman's porch lights went on again and Dave Ledbetter stepped out on to the stoop. He wasn't wearing a coat. He stood on the stoop, looking up the short street. The porch lights went out. Ledbetter waved his arms and they

286

went on again. He looked toward the Outback. Although it was unlikely Ledbetter could see him in the car, Loomis slid down in the seat. Ledbetter continued to stare in Loomis's direction. Then he waved and began walking toward the car.

Shit.

Keeping his phone low and out of sight, he keyed in Connie's speed-dial number.

"Hi, this is Connie Noble's mobile voice mail—"

He swore again as he closed the phone and shoved it between the passenger seat backrest and seat cushion. Maybe he should just get the hell out, he thought, but he was curious about what Ledbetter wanted. He reached under the dash and flipped a hidden rocker switch. The central deadbolt locking system engaged with a solid clunk.

Smiling, Ledbetter tapped on the bullet-resistant glass of Loomis's window. Turning the ignition to the accessory position, Loomis powered the window down a couple of inches.

"Hey, Dave."

"What are you going here, Mr. Loomis?" Ledbetter asked in a friendly tone of voice.

"It's called a stakeout, Dave," Loomis said.

"You're watching us?"

"That's right. I'm watching you."

"Why?" Ledbetter said. "You still think we know where Belle Ryerson is? Is that it?"

"No," Loomis said. "I want to join the space pioneers."

Ledbetter shook his head. "You're wasting your time," he said. "We don't know where she is."

"You're all I've got," Loomis said.

"Look, if you won't believe me, maybe you'll believe Thaddeus. Why don't you come into the house so we can talk properly. It's cold out here."

"No, thanks. Don't worry about me. Go back inside if you're cold."

He tried to raise the window, but before it had fully closed Ledbetter stuck the muzzle of an old Colt forty-five automatic through the gap.

"Shit, Dave," Loomis said.

"Yeah. Sorry. Are you armed?"

"No, unfortunately."

"I don't know if I believe you, but it doesn't matter. Unlock the door and put your hands on the wheel."

Although Loomis figured he could probably get away without having his brains spattered all over the inside of the car, he rocked the hidden switch and released the deadbolts, then put his hands on the top of the steering wheel. Ledbetter opened the door a couple of inches, swivelling the muzzle of the forty-five so that it was still aimed at Loomis's head.

"Now lower the window a bit, if you don't mind. Reach across with your right hand."

Loomis lowered the window with his right hand, then put it back on wheel. Ledbetter withdrew the pistol and opened the door.

"Keys," Ledbetter said. "Keep your left hand on the wheel."

Loomis took the key out of the ignition.

"Put them on the roof," Ledbetter said. "Keep your

right hand on the wheel."

Loomis transferred the key and remote to his left hand, reached up and placed them on the edge of the roof. Ledbetter stepped forward, snatched the key off the roof, then stepped back.

"Okay," he said. "Now get out. Slow."

Loomis got out of the car. "Harriet made me, didn't she?"

"Got eyes like an eagle, that little gal," Ledbetter said. "Close the door."

Loomis closed the door. "You didn't used to be a cop, did you?"

"MP," Ledbetter said. "Marine Corps. Long time ago, but you don't forget. Turn around and lean against the car. Step back. A little farther, please. Farther. Good. Thanks."

Ledbetter patted him down and stepped back again.

"Don't you think you're overdoing it a bit, Dave?" Loomis said.

"Better to err on the side of caution," Ledbetter said.

The regular door locks thudded as Ledbetter used the remote to lock the car. The remote panic button engaged the deadbolt locking system.

"The lights don't flash," Ledbetter said.

"The horn doesn't honk, either," Loomis said. "What about the window?" It was still open a couple of inches.

"Leave it. Let's go?"

"I don't think so," Loomis said. Ledbetter stepped farther back, his pistol aimed at Loomis's chest. "You're not going to shoot me, Dave. You're smarter than that. You're going to give me my car keys and I'm going to get into my car and drive away."

"I don't want to shoot you, but if you want your car keys, you're going to have to take them away from me. I may look like a fat old man, but I'm still pretty quick, and I've kept up with my training. Just come into the house. I don't know how you got it into your head we have anything to do with Belle Ryerson's disappearance, but we can't let you mess up our plans, can we?"

"C'mon, Dave. You don't really believe aliens are coming to take you to another planet, do you?"

"It doesn't matter what I believe. Let's go."

"I guess we're going to have to do this the hard way," Loomis said, taking another step away from the car.

Ledbetter stood his ground. "The hammer's back and the safety's off, so if you make any sudden moves, it might go off. I'd really hate for that to happen. You probably would, too."

"You're right about that."

Ledbetter gestured toward the house. "Let's go. I'm getting cold."

"No," Loomis said.

Loomis heard movement behind him as Ledbetter's eyes shifted and widened slightly and his mouth formed an "O" of surprise. As Loomis started to duck and turn, someone said, "Fuck this shit."

A bolt of lightning hit the back of Loomis's neck and all his fuses blew out in a flash of pain and blinding light.

Friday
DAY 4

29

Loomis woke up slowly—and wished he hadn't. His head throbbed horribly, as if his brain had swelled to twice its normal size and threatened to burst his skull with every beat of his heart. He remained as still as possible, afraid to open his eyes lest his eyeballs pop out from the pressure. Just breathing hurt.

He gradually became aware that he was sitting on a hard, unyielding surface, his backbone against a narrow steel post. He wasn't wearing his coat. His wrists were secured behind his back. He tried to shift his position, relieve the strain on his shoulders ...

Big mistake.

He fell back against the post, waves of pain and nausea washing over him. Bile rose in his throat. He swallowed convulsively, lips parched, tongue glued to his palate. He carefully cracked his eyes open. They felt as though they'd been packed with sand. He closed them and concentrated on not being sick. He dimly suspected he'd been drugged, as well as shocked with some kind of stun gun. He felt like an idiot. He could have handled Dave Ledbetter, but letting Quentin Parker—he was sure he'd recognized Parker's voice—get the drop on him, that really pissed him off.

A while later he opened his eyes again. It was dark. Not stygian, but the only illumination was the dim light shining through a pair of small, high windows. He looked around carefully, pleased that his head did not explode or fall off. He was in an unfinished basement, with a painted concrete floor and studded walls, lined with bats of Styrofoam insulation and covered with clear poly vapour barrier. Exposed copper plumbing and armoured electrical cabling ran through the studding. It was too gloomy to see how big the room was, but he assumed it was the basement of Kellerman's house.

Ignoring the pain, Loomis strained against his bonds. There were a number of turns of tape around his wrists, duct tape by the feel of it. He explored the bottom of the steel post with his fingertips. The post had a square steel baseplate, fixed to bolts embedded in the concrete floor. He squirmed around until he could drag the edges of the duct tape across the sharp threads of a bolt-end. It wouldn't be impossible to get loose, but it would take time.

He winced as the burr of the bolt-end cut into his wrist. He was doing as much damage to himself as the tape. He continued to scrape the tape—and his wrists—against the end of the anchor bolt. After a while, he strained against his restraints in the hope that his efforts had weakened the tape. The tape held. He went back to work, the pain in his shoulder joints excruciating, head throbbing, drenched with perspiration.

Finally, he felt the tape tear a little. Twisting, almost dislocating his shoulders, he gritted his teeth and strained at the tape. It parted with a rip and his arms were suddenly free. Shoulders protesting, he unwound the remains of the tape and massaged his wrists, feeling the slickness of blood and sweat. More sweat than blood, he hoped, as he wiped his palms on the thighs of his jeans. Knees cracking, he stood. Wobbly and fighting nausea and an almost debilitating headache, he climbed the basement stairs to a door on a narrow landing, making as little noise as possible. He listened at the door for a moment, but heard nothing. There hadn't been a sound from the house while he'd been working to free himself, but he wasn't taking any chances.

He grasped the doorknob, hoping the door wasn't locked. It wasn't.

Opening the door, he stepped silently into a dark kitchen, lit only by moonlight through patio doors that overlooked the yard and the lake beyond, its grey, wintry expanse ruffled by a northerly wind. Crossing the kitchen, he turned on the cold water tap, bent over the sink, and drank from the spout. He then went down the short hall, past a dining room to the living room. No lights were on, and the house was steeped in gloomy silence. He looked out the front window, relieved to see that the Outback was still parked where he'd left it.

His coat was on the floor of the hall closet, his wallet still zipped into the inside pocket. No sign of his car keys, though, and replacing the specialized remotes was expensive. He turned on the vestibule light and found the key and remote in a crystal vase on a table by the door.

He went out—he didn't bother locking up behind him—and hurried to the Outback. He zapped the car with the remote and got in. According to the dashboard clock it was a few minutes after midnight. He started the engine, then retrieved his phone. He flipped it open. The screen showed a missed call from Connie. He dialled into his voice mail.

"Hack, where are you? It's almost nine o'clock. I haven't a clue where I am, really. I followed the bus to a farmhouse on something called Bingham Line, about two miles from the turnoff from Bingham Road, maybe forty minutes north of Essex Junction. The bus picked up some more people, then Ginny dropped Hubert off at home. At the farm they loaded more stuff on to the bus then went into the house. Cellphone coverage is lousy. Nonexistent, really. I had to drive back to Bingham Road to get a signal. What should I do, Hack? Call me, please."

The message ended. She'd left it three hours earlier. Loomis keyed in her speed-dial number, but the call went straight to her voice mail. Her phone was either off or out of range.

"Connie. Don't do anything. Stay where you are. Don't try to follow if the bus leaves the farmhouse. I'll get there as soon as I can. It's ten past twelve now. Call me as soon as you get this message."

Loomis jammed his phone into his coat pocket and yanked the gearshift lever into drive.

30

When he went into the office, there was a kraft envelope on the floor beneath the mail slot in the door. There was a note attached, on BPD letterhead.

"Hack," it read. "Here are the photos of Maya Thomas you asked for. Also, the ME finished the post. He found some burn marks on her neck from a Taser or stun gun. He didn't see them during the preliminary exam because they were above the hairline. He also found a puncture mark on her thigh. She was injected with something. It will be a while for the toxicology results to come back, though. Alex."

Dropping the envelope on to Connie's desk, Loomis began throwing things into a backpack: a couple of spring water bottles refilled with tap water, half a dozen energy bars, a compact but powerful Maglite LED flashlight, a small roll of duct tape, and the fancy Leatherman Super-Tool Connie had given him on his birthday—seventeen tools in one, complete with instruction manual and a genuine leather belt sheath. As an afterthought, because you never knew, he added four sets of wire-tie plastic handcuffs.

He changed into thermal long johns and a long-sleeved T-shirt, dark trousers, shirt, dark pullover, and black lace-up boots. He tucked gloves and a dark wool tuque into the pocket of his Columbia jacket. Finally, he unlocked the gun-safe bolted to the wall in the back of the closet and took out the Glock 19, a slightly smaller and lighter variation of the original Glock 17.

Loomis wasn't keen on guns. From his years as a security consultant and private investigator, he was thoroughly trained and familiar with their use and operation, but he didn't really like them. Blame it on his Canadian upbringing. The gun control laws in Canada, while not as strict as in Britain, were considerably tougher than in the United States, where gun ownership seemed almost mandatory—and where the per capita rate of firearms-related homicides was ten times that of Canada. But he didn't trust the largely false sense of security a gun afforded. A gun could make you careless, make you take chances you wouldn't normally take, even get you killed. However, Dave Ledbetter had a forty-five and if the bad guys had guns, it was generally a good idea to have one yourself. As the old saying went, you didn't take a knife, even a Leatherman, to a gunfight.

Removing the trigger guard, he went through the ritual: insert magazine, check action, eject magazine, eject round in chamber, dry fire, replace round in magazine, and re-insert magazine. He then slipped the Glock into a nylon belt-clip holster and put it into the backpack along with an extra 15-round magazine. Finally, he found Alex Robillard's card and dialled his cellphone number. He got Robillard's mobile voice mail. *Shit.* He didn't know Robillard's home number, though.

"Alex," Loomis said after the tone. "Hack. It's 12:40 a.m. Friday. I think I may know who killed Maya Thomas. A couple of hustlers named Harriet Olsen and Quentin Parker are running a long con on the Kentauran Foundation, the UFO outfit I told you about. Parker zapped me with a stun gun outside Dr. Thaddeus Kellerman's house in South Cove about 7:30 p.m. and taped me up in Kellerman's basement. I may have also been injected with something. Whatever it was, it wasn't a fun trip. I think they're holed up at a farmhouse somewhere on Bingham Line, north of Essex junction. Connie followed some of the members of the Kentauran Foundation there, but I haven't heard from her since nine o'clock. I'm on my way there now."

He hung up, wondering if he should call Robillard's office number and leave a message, which would automatically page him, but he was running short of time. After a quick detour to the men's room to clean and bandage his lacerated wrists, he went down to the car, where he opened the glove compartment and took out a GPS unit and suction-cup mounting bracket. It took him a minute to find Bingham Line and set a point two miles along it as his destination. He then mounted the GPS on the dash, plugged the power cord into the cigarette lighter, and tapped the GO button on the screen. The GPS showed an estimated arrival time of 3:05 a.m. Nearly two hours. He could improve on that by ignoring speed limits, but if he pushed it too hard he risked being pulled over by the police, and it would take too long to convince them it was a legitimate emergency.

The GPS guided him out Main to I-89, north to Route 15, east through Essex Junction to Essex Center at the junction of Route 289. Just past Essex Center, he was instructed to turn left on to Old Coach Road and proceed 2.3 miles, then to turn left again on to Bingham Road and proceed another 2.7 miles deeper into the boondocks. Most of Bingham Road was unpaved, icy and largely un-lit, except for the occasional farmstead.

About two and a half miles along Bingham Road the pleasant female voice of the GPS said, "In two hundred and fifty yards turn left on to Bingham Line." Loomis slowed, watching for the turnoff—the GPS was accurate to only about fifty feet. He hadn't seen any other cars since leaving Route 15, but just before coming to the turnoff he saw lights flickering through the trees on his left. A moment later a car came fishtailing wildly on to Bingham Road and blew by like a bat out of hell, barely under control and so close that the Outback shuddered in the slipstream.

It was Kellerman's silver Lexus. As it roared past, the Outback's headlights briefly illuminated Harriet Olsen's face, eyes wide with surprise—or fear. Loomis couldn't see who was driving, but his money was on Quentin Parker.

He turned on to Bingham Line, and the GPS instructed him to drive two miles to his final destination. Bingham Line was rougher and narrower and even darker. A mile and a half along the road Loomis saw lights through leafless trees and scattered pines and cedars. He killed the Outback's lights, turned off the GPS, and slowed to a crawl, creeping along until he came to moonlit field of frosted stubble on the left, dark woods on the right. The lights were coming from a farmyard at the far end of the field. Fifty yards from the farmhouse Loomis pulled as far off the road as he could and stopped. The dashboard clock read 2:48 a.m.

Locking the car, he zipped up his jacket, settled the backpack over his shoulders, and set out with the Maglite. He didn't turn it on, though: the thin clouds had moved out, and the nearly full moon was high and almost bright enough to read by. He kept to the shadows, moving as quietly as possible.

Nearing the farmhouse, he moved farther into the woods and worked his way through the trees, leaves and twigs crunching and snapping underfoot, until he was directly across the road from the house. His heart thudded at the sudden beat of big wings—he'd disturbed an owl. He crouched in the shelter of a copse of trees and, after a second or two of waffling, shrugged out of the backpack and dug out the Glock. Clipping the holster to his belt in the small of his back, he put the pack back on and secured the chest and hip straps. The backpack gently pressed the flat bulk of the holstered pistol into his spine.

The farmhouse was about forty feet back from the road, flanked by two leafless oaks and some scattered plantings of juniper and cedar. It was a square, two-story white clapboard house with dormer windows and decorative shutters. An extension had been added to the back, likely for a new kitchen and utility room. A downstairs light was on in the front of the house, but he couldn't see any activity behind the drawn curtains. If Kellerman and the others were home, he supposed they were in bed.

Behind and to the left of the house was a barn, a pair of bright floodlights mounted near the peak of the gambrel roof, illuminating the yard. There were two other outbuildings, a sagging, tin-roofed equipment shed about the size of a three-car garage, and a relatively new Quonset hut. The Quonset also had a light mounted above a sliding, hanger-style door. There was a smaller people-door set into the sliding door. There were no vehicles in the yard that Loomis could see, but the yard lights partly illuminated some kind of vehicle in the equipment shed.

The house and outbuildings were surrounded by open fields of frosty stubble, silvery in the moonlight. From where he was, Loomis couldn't get closer without exposing himself to view from the house, so he backtracked along the road until he came to a shallow curve. He was still within sight of the house, but a tall spruce tree on the far side of the road masked the moon, casting an impenetrable black shadow across the road. Crouching, he scrambled through the dry ditch, dashed across the road through the deep shadow, and dropped into the ditch on the other side, fortunately also dry. He crawled out of the ditch and, keeping low, ran into the stubbly field until the Quonset hut was between him and the house.

He stood and walked toward the hut.

The vehicle in the equipment shed turned out to be the rusting and dilapidated carcass of an ancient, wheelless tractor, next to an even rustier piece of farm equipment with offset wheels and half a dozen pinwheel-like sets of curved metal spines, half of which were missing, broken or bent. Wriggling into the barn through the gap in a warped back door, Loomis explored by the light filtering through the windows and gaps in the boards. The interior smelled of dust, mouldering hay and dried manure, but he didn't find anything but broken hay bales, various tools and pieces of farm equipment, and a stack of flattened cardboard cartons.

The yard lights made it impossible to get to the Quonset hut without exposing himself to anyone watching from the house, so he just walked to the people door in the middle of the sliding door and, feeling like a jacklighted deer, grasped the handle, twisted, and stepped inside.

At first, as he played the beam of the flashlight around, he thought the Quonset hut was empty, but then the beam glinted off the windows of a vehicle. It was Belle Ryerson's Toyota Yaris. The keys were in the ignition. There was no sign of Belle, Connie or her car, or the Kentauran Foundation school bus, but tire marks on the dusty concrete floor indicated that something, the bus or a truck, had recently been parked in the hut.

Exiting the Quonset, he ran across the yard to the back door of the farmhouse. Holster relocated to his hip, he tried the door and was relieved to find that it was not locked. Cautiously, he crept into a utility room. A faint light shone though the windows of the door to the kitchen. The light came from a nightlight plugged into an electrical outlet over the kitchen counter. He tried the door, but it was locked.

He took the roll of duct tape from his backpack. Ripping off short strips as quietly as he could, he pressed a layer of tape over the window pane nearest the lock. Muffling the sound with the hem of his jacket, he rapped the taped pane with the butt of the Maglite. The glass cracked on the third blow. Tapping with the Maglite, he broke the glass around the perimeter of the pane, then carefully peeled the tape away, taking the shards with it. Most of them, anyway. One small piece fell to the kitchen floor, making a loud *tink* in the silence. Wiggling the remaining shards from edges of the frame, he reached through and unlocked the door. Leaving the Glock in its holster, he went through the kitchen to a short hallway, past a dining room on the right and a bathroom on the left, into the front room.

Thaddeus Kellerman lay face down on the floor, in the pool of light cast by a table lamp.

Kellerman moaned as Loomis eased him on to his back and pressed his fingers against his carotid artery. Although Loomis's first aid expertise was rudimentary, Kellerman's pulse seemed fast and thready. There were marks on the side of his neck, like the bite of a vampire with electric teeth. The old man whimpered, and his eyes fluttered open. He tried to sit up.

"Take it easy, doc," Loomis said.

"What—?" Kellerman struggled to focus. He closed his eyes, then opened them again. "Harriet?"

Loomis shrugged out of his backpack and found a water bottle. He opened it and placed it in Kellerman's hands, but he didn't seem to know what to do with it. Loomis guided it to his mouth. Like an infant placed to the breast, Kellerman responded to the touch of the bottle to his lips and drank. It revived him somewhat.

He choked, coughed, took another sip of water, and tried again to speak. "Who are you? Where am I? Where's Harriet?"

"It's Hack Loomis," Loomis said. "You're in the farmhouse. Harriet's gone. I'll be right back. Will you be okay?"

Kellerman looked at him blankly, then nodded.

Loomis quickly checked the rest of the house, but found no one else. When he returned to the living room, Kellerman had managed to get himself up on to the sofa. He was slumped against the cushions, eyes closed, snoring softly. Loomis went through the kitchen into the utility room, intending to retrieve his car. There was a triple light switch on the wall beside door to the kitchen. He flipped them all on. The lights in the utility room went on, as did an outside light over the door. As he made his way to the door, he wondered idly what the third switch was for—or who bothered with a carpet in a utility room, even if it was old, worn and lumpy.

He froze at a muffled shout.

"Hey!" The shout was accompanied by thumping that seemed to come from under the floor. "Let me out of here, goddamn you!" He felt more thumping through the carpet beneath the soles of his boots. "I need to use the bathroom."

It was a woman's voice. Not Connie's, though. He flipped the carpet aside, revealing a trap door secured by a large sliding bolt next to the recessed flip-up handle. The bolt, which accounted for the lump in the carpet, seemed to have been recently installed. He slid the bolt and lifted the trap door.

Belle Ryerson looked up at him, standing midway up a steep flight of stairs.

31

"Mr. Loomis," Belle said, as Loomis took her hand and helped her out of the cellar, gasping at the stink of urine, unwashed human, and rotting banana peel that came with her. "What are you doing here?"

"Looking for you," he said, closing the trap door against the smell, surreptitiously wiping his hand on his jeans.

"Me? Why?"

"Connie asked me to help her find you when you didn't show up for your appointment with her on Saturday. Your sister is worried about you, too. What happened, Belle? How did you end up here?"

"I was trying to help a friend of mine find her brother and his wife and two kids," she said. "He sold his house, cashed in all their savings, and gave the money to a weird UFO cult. I was supposed to meet her in town on Saturday, but she sent me a text to meet her here instead. When I got here, a nasty little man named Quentin Parker knocked me out with some kind of electric stun gun thing, and I woke up in that cellar. How long—? How long has it been?"

"It's Friday morning," Loomis said. "You've been missing six days."

"Six days?" she said. "God, no wonder it feels like forever. I guess I smell pretty ripe right now, too."

"Have you been down there the whole time?"

"Yes," she said. "Although they let me use the bathroom once or twice a day. Which reminds me, I really need to use it now ..."

"Oh, sure," Loomis said. "Sorry."

While she was in the half-bath off the kitchen, Loomis checked on Kellerman. He was still snoring on the sofa, but he did not look good. Loomis returned to the kitchen when Belle came out of the bathroom.

"I feel a bit better," she said. "Even if my clothes smell like a gas station restroom." She paused, then said, "Mr. Loomis, do you know what happened to my friend? Her name is Maya Thomas."

He'd been dreading that question. "There's no easy way to tell you this, Belle," he said. "I'm afraid she's dead."

"No," Belle said, tears welling in her eyes. "How? What happened?"

"Her body was found Tuesday morning in Burlington Bay," Loomis said. He didn't think it necessary to provide the details of her death. "She'd been in the water over a week."

"Oh, god," Belle said.

"The police found one of my business cards on her body. Did you give it to her?"

She nodded. "She wanted to hire a private investigator to find her brother," she said. Tears rolled down her cheeks. "She didn't send me that text, did she? She was already dead by then, wasn't she? Someone else sent it, using her phone?"

"I'm afraid so," Loomis said.

"Why—?" She swallowed dryly. "Why didn't they just kill me, too?"

"Maybe Dr. Kellerman wouldn't let them," Loomis said. "He evidently wanted you to join the exodus."

"Yes, I know." She looked around the kitchen. "Do you think there's anything here to eat?"

He dug a couple of cereal bars out of his backpack and handed them to her, along with the other water bottle. She chomped a bar down, then drank most of the water.

"They've been feeding me nothing but peanut butter sandwiches, bananas and water. I used to love peanut butter and bananas." She peeled the other cereal bar, took a bite, and washed it down with the rest of the water. "How did you find me?"

"Connie followed the cult's bus here last night."

"Is she here now?"

"No. I think she followed the bus to where Kellerman's people are gathering. They called it the 'staging area.' Do you know where that is?"

She shook her head. "I overheard them talking about something like that. I don't know where it is, but I don't

309

think it's very far from here."

"Who else besides Quentin Parker knew you were stashed in that cellar? Did Kellerman know? Or Dave Ledbetter? Harriet Olsen?"

"I don't know," she said. "The only other people I ever saw were a woman with lots of muscles and her husband."

"Ginny and Hubert Gasche," Loomis said.

"Where is Dr. Kellerman now?"

"In the other room."

Chewing on the cereal bar, she followed him into the living room. Kellerman was slumped on the sofa. His colour was bad, and his breathing was shallow and irregular.

"Is he all right?"

"I don't know," Loomis said. "He's been stunned and maybe dosed with something. He's pretty confused." Loomis gently shook him awake. "Dr. Kellerman, how're you doing?"

Kellerman blinked and struggled to sit up. "Harriet?"

"No, doc. It's me again. Hack Loomis. Belle Ryerson is here, too."

Kellerman grasped Loomis's arms and tried to stand. "I have to talk to Harriet." He fell back. "Harriet," he cried out. "Harriet."

"Take it easy," Loomis said to him, hand on his shoulder. "Harriet's not here. No one's here. It looks like Harriet and her pals stunned you and left you here."

"Harriet?" Kellerman said. His voice was weak and the flesh of his face was waxy and grey. He rubbed his chest.

"He's an old man," Belle said. "That stun gun thing could have given him a heart attack. Maybe we should take him to a hospital."

Loomis tried his cellphone, but there was no service. "Dr. Kellerman," he said. "Is there a phone in the house?" Kellerman shook his head. "You're going to have take him to the hospital," Loomis said to Belle. "Your car's in the Quonset hut. The keys are in it."

"What are you going to do?"

"I'll wait here with him while you get the car," he said. "Then I'm going to find Connie."

Belle went out to get her car from the Quonset hut.

"Dr. Kellerman," Loomis said. "Have you seen my partner?"

"What? No. Who?"

"My partner," Loomis said. "Connie Noble. The woman who was at the meeting with me. She may have followed a busload of your space refugees to the staging area."

"May I have some more water," Kellerman said. Loomis placed the water bottle in his hands. He drank. His colour improved a little, and his voice was stronger. "Where's Harriet? I must speak to her."

"Doc," Loomis said. "You must realize by now that Harriet Olsen isn't really in contact with aliens from Alpha Centauri. You were being conned."

Kellerman took a deep, unsteady breath. "You don't understand. My methods are …There are safeguards …"

He shook his head. "No, I don't believe you. She wouldn't lie to me. They must have threatened her. She's ..." His voice trailed off and his eyes wandered out of focus.

"Doc," Loomis said, snapping his fingers. "Concentrate."

Kellerman's gaze wandered back into focus, but his skin was grey and greasy with perspiration.

"That's it," Loomis said. "Stay with me. Where's the staging area?"

Kellerman didn't answer. He didn't seem to even hear the question. His eyes fluttered and his breathing was ragged. He rubbed his chest.

"I—I think I'm having a heart attack," he croaked.

"Belle is going to take you to the hospital," Loomis said. "That's if I let her."

"What do you mean? You wouldn't—"

"Goddamned right I would, if you don't tell me where the staging area is."

Kellerman looked at his hands, small and delicate, patches of thick black hair on the backs of his fingers. He clenched his fists and the muscles of his forearms flexed and knotted, distorting the faded tattoo of the Rod of Asclepius on his right arm.

Belle came into the living room. "Help me get him to the car."

"In a minute," Loomis said. He grasped the old man by his upper arms, shook him back to awareness. "Where is the staging area?"

"It's—" He coughed, swallowed, coughed again. "It's

312

up an old logging road near the end of the Line road. Now, please ..."

Loomis hauled Kellerman to his feet, then he and Belle half carried, half dragged him out to Belle's car.

"Does Dave Ledbetter still have his forty-five?" Loomis asked, strapping the old man into the passenger seat as Belle got behind the wheel.

"No," Kellerman said. "The Rigilians—Guns are forbidden."

"Mr. Loomis," Belle said, starting the engine.

Loomis stood up, shut the car door, and watched Belle drive out of the yard. "Good luck, doc," he muttered, then he collected his backpack, refilled his water bottles in the kitchen, and set out down the road to retrieve the Outback. The night air was richly redolent of dry leaves, frozen earth, and the heavy mustiness of liquefied manure fertilizer. Somewhere a wood fire was burning. In the far distance he heard a strange, high-pitched howl that ended in a series of yips. A coyote? Whatever it was, it sent shivers up his spine. The gibbous moon was low in the western sky, but so bright he almost didn't need the headlights as he drove slowly along Bingham Line road, looking for a turnoff. The dashboard clock read 4:04 a.m. Sunrise was three hours away.

32

Half an hour later Loomis was jouncing along on a narrow, rutted track, through the tunnel of light carved out of the dark woods by the Outback's high beams, grateful he was driving a four-wheel drive vehicle with adequate ground clearance. It had probably been years since the track had been used regularly by anyone but hunters riding ATVs, but sections of it had been repaired more recently, deeper ruts filled in, badly eroded areas paved with two-by-ten timbers, undergrowth hacked back, fallen trees chain-sawed and hauled to the side. Harriet and her pals were going to a lot of trouble to stage their con.

He came to a Y-junction. Stopping, leaving the engine running and lights on, he examined the junction with the flashlight. He didn't have to be a frontier scout to see the vehicle tracks in the frozen mud or the crushed and broken weeds and tree branches along the sides of the narrow track. Some of the tracks looked fairly fresh. All went up the left fork.

Returning to the warmth of the car, he continued up the track. A hundred yards farther along, the track took a sudden dip at a dry creek bed. He got out of the car again and checked the creek bed. There was a ford of sorts across it, a layer of water-smoothed rocks and smaller stones. The vehicle tracks disappeared on the near bank and reappeared on the far bank.

He eased the Outback down the shallow embankment and across the rocky creek bed. On the other side of the creek, the rutted track climbed steadily through a series of switchbacks. He was occasionally able to make two miles per hour, but barely. He could have walked faster.

He'd travelled about a mile and a half when he came across Connie's car. It was jammed into the trees and underbrush beside the track. The right front wheel was badly askew. He was amazed she'd made it as far as she had. There was no sign of her, but the backpack containing the survival kit was missing. Where the hell was she? Had she continued on foot or had she been grabbed?

He manoeuvred the Outback past the Jetta and continued up the track. Ten minutes later, he came to another dry stream bed. The crossing looked too rough, even for the Outback. With their higher clearances, though, Gasche's G-Wagen and Ledbetter's pickup, even the school bus, would have crossed with relative ease. Driving the latter would have been a challenge, but driving skills were likely useful for a movie stuntwoman.

Unwilling to risk a broken axle or punctured oil pan, Loomis worked the Outback into the trees at the edge of the track. It had been more than an hour since he'd left the farmhouse. The moon was low in the western sky. Dawn was still an hour away, sunrise a half-hour after that. Shouldering his backpack, he crossed the dry creek bed and set off up the track. A half-mile beyond Connie's car the flashlight beam glinted off something in the woods. It was the windshield of the G-Wagen, backed a few yards into the trees. Hubert Gasche had made some effort to conceal it with broken branches and pine boughs, but despite its camouflage paint job, it stood out like a wild turkey in a flock of flamingos.

Loomis realized that the smell of wood smoke had been growing stronger for some time.

Chewing a cereal bar, he pressed on. The southeastern sky began to lighten. The track narrowed until it became nothing but a pair of parallel ruts, the dead weeds and leafless seedlings between, and on either side of the ruts, reaching to mid-thigh. He backtracked a few yards until he found another track that angled off to the right. Bare tree branches crowded close on both sides, many bent and broken, hanging by strips of bark. Loomis supposed Gasche hadn't wanted to take his fancy SUV up the narrower track for fear of damaging its finish. Dave Ledbetter evidently hadn't shared the same concern for his truck: it was parked thirty yards up the side track. Through the trees, another thirty yards or so up the hill, Loomis could make out the geometrical lines of a big shed with a corrugated steel roof. Parked next to it were a one-ton U-Haul box truck and a small bus with *The Kentauran Foundation* emblazoned on its side.

He crept as close as he dared to the shed and hunkered in the trees. By the shed was a smaller structure that looked like a mobile construction site office. It stood in the dry weeds on a steel undercarriage, wheelless and rusted. Beyond the shed was a meadow, scattered through which were eight or ten tents in variety of styles and sizes, from tiny two-person mountaineering tents to big six- or eight-person tourist tents, various shades of grey in the waning moonlight. Tarpaulins had been suspended from trees and poles to provide shelter for cooking and eating. Banked campfires smoked in the cold pre-dawn mist.

A light came on in the wheelless trailer, and a moment later the door opened. A man emerged on to the steel porch, carrying an electric lantern, which he hung by the door. He was stocky and powerfully built, barelegged but wearing a knee-length coat and sneakers with no socks. Hubert Gasche. He was holding the handles of retractable leashes attached to the studded collars of a pair of bulldogs. The dogs bounded to the extent the leashes allowed, came up short with a lurch. While Hubert Gasche watched, yawning and scratching, one of the dogs squatted in the weeds while the other lifted its leg on a wheel of the school bus. Gasche then retracted the leashes and dragged the dogs into the trailer, letting the door slam after him. He came out a moment later, unhooked the lantern, and went back inside.

Loomis retreated into the woods and worked his way around toward the meadow. As the sky continued to brighten, colours began to appear, and the early birds began to stir from their tents, stretching, breath smoking as they blew on their hands. The men went a few yards into the woods, unzipped and urinated against the trees, while the women, most with blankets or sleeping bags draped over their shoulders, crossed the frosty meadow to a portable privy. Some escorted children bundled up against the cold. Loomis wondered how much sleep they'd gotten. December was not the best time of year to be camping out.

Loomis recognized Dr. Spender as he emerged from one of the tents, looking like a blue Michelin Man in a puffy high-tech parka. The woods crowded close to the campsites at the edge of the clearing, but the leafless trees and undergrowth did not afford much cover. Loomis made his way through the trees toward Spender's campsite. After emptying his bladder against a tree, Spender pumped up the fuel tank of a Coleman camp stove and lit it with a butane barbecue lighter. He filled an old-fashioned enamelled coffee pot from a five-gallon collapsible container on the end of a folding camp table and put it on the stove to boil. He took a two-pound plastic canister of Folger's coffee from a bin under the table. He stood by the stove as the water heated, warming his hands by the stuttering flame.

"Dr. Spender?" Loomis said, crouched fifteen feet away at the edge of the woods.

"Huh?" Spender's head popped up. "Who—?" He stepped away from the camp stove towards the woods.

"Just stay where you are," Loomis said. "Watch your pot boil."

"What are you doing here?" Spender asked, returning

to his place by the stove, but still warily watching Loomis.

"I'm looking for my partner," Loomis said, keeping his voice low. "Tall, dirty-blonde, forty-ish. She followed your bus up here last night, but her car broke down about halfway up."

"I haven't seen anyone besides members of our group," Spender said, glancing around at the other would-be colonists as they pumped up stoves and stirred campfires to life. "Are you sure she's here?"

"Not a hundred percent," Loomis said. Someone was frying bacon. It smelled wonderful. "What's in the big shed?"

"Supplies," Spender said. "Construction materials, food, that sort of thing."

"Right. Besides Hubert Gasche and his dogs, who else is in the trailer?"

"Mrs. Gasche. She drove the bus. Dave and Betsy Ledbetter, too, on account of Bets' arthritis. And Colonel Maynard."

"No one else?"

"No. Dr. Kellerman and Quentin Parker are supposed to join us later today."

"Don't count on it," Loomis said.

"What do you mean? Why not?"

"Someone, probably Parker, zapped Kellerman with a stun gun of some kind and left him at the farmhouse. He had a heart attack. He's lucky we found him when we did. Belle Ryerson took him to the hospital. I don't know if he made it."

"Belle Ryerson? Wasn't that the woman you were looking for?"

"Yeah. She was locked in the cellar under the utility room."

Spender shook his head as though he were trying to shake off flies. "Why would Mr. Parker hurt Dr. Kellerman?"

"I suppose Kellerman finally twigged to the scam. I hate to break it to you this way, Dr. Spender, but you and your friends are being taken for a ride—and not in an alien spaceship. It's a hustle. Harriet Olsen somehow convinced Dr. Kellerman she was an alien emissary. Quentin Parker is in on it, too, along with Hubert and Ginny Gasche. I don't know about Dave and Betsy Ledbetter or the colonel."

"I don't believe you." His voice lacked conviction. "Why should I believe you?"

"No reason at all," Loomis said. "Nevertheless, it's true."

There was movement in Spender's tent and a moment later a woman emerged, small and sturdy and dressed in a matching puffy blue parka. Mrs. Dr. Spender, Loomis presumed. From her expression, she was not a happy camper.

"Who are you talking to?" she said to her husband.

"Him," Spender said, pointing to Loomis, hunkered in the woods.

"Mrs. Spender," Loomis said. "My name's Hack Loomis. I'm a private investigator."

"Is it true?" she said to her husband. "What he said?

It's a hoax?"

"No," Spender said. "It's not. It can't be."

"I'm afraid it is," Loomis said from the trees.

"I *knew* it," she said, rounding on her husband.

"Margie, please."

"You goddamned fool." She hit him, a right jab just below the sternum that sank almost to her elbow in his puffy coat. The blow knocked him on to his backside, gasping for breath. "More fool me, though," she ranted, "for letting you talk me into this. How could I be so fucking stupid?" She stormed ten paces into the meadow, then stormed back again. "Shit-shit-shit."

The other would-be colonists started to notice the ruckus. A man came over from the adjacent campsite as Spender was picking himself up off the ground.

"Bill, what's going on?" he asked.

Loomis faded into the woods.

"It's all a lie. A hoax," Margie Spender said.

"What is?" the man asked.

"This, you idiot," she said, gesturing toward the tents arrayed along the edge of the clearing. "The whole fucking alien thing. It's a goddamn con-job."

"How do you know that?" the man asked. "Bill? How does she know that?"

Loomis didn't hear the rest of the exchange—he was working his way back through the woods toward the rear of the big shed, keeping out of sight of the trailer—but he imagined there was at least one divorce lawyer in town who could look forward to some new business.

33

In the pearly morning light, Loomis reconnoitered the equipment shed. There was a sliding barn-type door at the each end, and four windows along each side, which had been boarded over with plywood, scabrous and grey with age. Loomis crept to the door at the rear of the shed. It was padlocked on the outside. The hasp and lock were rusty, and the wood of the door and door frame was old and dry. He took the Leatherman out of his backpack and selected the razor-sharp scalloped blade. Working quickly but quietly, he dug around the base of the hasp. It wasn't long before he was able to wiggle the old screws free.

He opened the door a crack, cringing at the screech of the rusted track, and peered into darkness. He opened the door further, until he could squirm through, left it open behind him. The air inside the shed was dry and musty, overlaid by the familiar resinous scent of raw plywood and new lumber. In the dim light that filtered through the gaps around the edges of the boarded up windows, he could see a large rectangular shape covered by a tarpaulin. Turning the Maglite on low, he lifted the edge of the tarp, revealing stacks of plywood and lumber. Window dressing. After all, the refugees would need construction materials when they reached their new planet.

He turned off the flashlight, waited a few seconds for his eyes to readjust, then worked his way quietly around the stacks of plywood. Pale light leaked around the edges of the door at the front of the shed. On the floor, next to the plywood, he could make out six or seven five-gallon plastic pails—paint, he guessed—an equal number of cardboard shipping cartons, and a squadron of big, floppy-eared rabbits. Closer examination revealed the rabbits to be Lowe's shopping bags, tied closed and each containing a five-pound box of construction nails. More window dressing. He pried open the lid of one of the cardboard cartons and played the low beam of the flashlight over the contents. The carton was filled with dozens of pouches of freeze-dried camp rations: chili con carne, beef stroganoff, rice pilaf, scrambled eggs, blueberry pancakes. Yum.

Loomis exited the shed the same way he'd entered. Where the hell was Connie? He thought about going back to her car and tracking her from there. He didn't have much faith in his tracking skills, but his only other option was to talk to Dave Ledbetter and his pals. He decided to check out Ledbetter's pickup, the bus and the U-Haul first, though, in case Connie was stashed in one of them.

Margie Spender was angrier than a swarm of hornets

when she hammered on the door of the portable office and confronted Dave Ledbetter, demanding the return of their money and the keys to the Kentauran Foundation bus. Accompanying her were two other women and a man—not her husband—all equally unhappy. Ledbetter tried to reassure them that everything was under control and that they should go back to their tents and be patient, that they'd be leaving for the landing site soon, probably that very day. It was then that the Gasches' bulldogs made a dash for freedom through the open door. Loomis was barely fifteen yards down the track from the shed, not halfway to Ledbetter's pickup, when he heard Hubert Gasche shouting.

"Ernie. Bert. Bad dogs."

Loomis turned as the dogs bounded playfully toward him. He drew the Glock. Hubert Gasche stopped twenty feet away.

"Just stay where you are," Loomis said, the pistol pointed at the ground halfway between him and Hubert Gasche, acutely aware that he'd never aimed a gun at anything other than a paper target, let alone fired one.

"Sure, okay, whatever you say," Hubert Gasche said, holding out his hands.

Loomis came close to shooting him then, but realized in time that Gasche wasn't holding a weapon, just the taped-together handles of the retractable leashes.

"Here, you dogs. Ernie. Bert. Come. Bad dogs." The dogs waddled back to their master and he squatted to attach the leashes to their collars.

324

Dave Ledbetter emerged from the office, bulky in a khaki parka, carrying a pump-action shotgun under his arm. James Maynard came out behind him, wearing a navy blue parka. He didn't appear to be armed, but he had his hands in his coat pockets. Margie Spender stared wide-eyed at Ledbetter's shotgun. The other two women and the man backed away toward the meadow. Ginny Gasche and Betsy Ledbetter watched from the door of the office. Ginny Gasche was baring her teeth in a tight, feral smile.

"What the hell?" Dave Ledbetter said. He and Maynard stopped beside and slightly behind Hubert Gasche. Ledbetter's big, bald head gleamed in the morning sunshine. Maynard's expression was dark with anger.

"Hey, Dave," Loomis said. "Colonel Maynard. Top of the morning to you both. Where's your forty-five, Dave?"

"Lock box in the truck," he said. "Charley told Harriet no guns, but—" He shrugged. "I found this old scattergun in Thaddeus's house. That a Glock? Nice, but how about you put it away."

"I don't think so," Loomis said. He did lower it a little, though.

"I'm glad to see you're okay," Ledbetter said, looking as though he meant it.

"No thanks to Parker's stun gun," Loomis said. "What did you shoot me up with?"

"That was Parker, too. Ketamine. His aunt's a large animal vet. I guess I don't have to ask what you're doing here, Mr. Loomis, but if you're looking for Belle Ryerson, feel free to look around. She's not here."

"I know," Loomis said. "I found her. I'm looking for my partner."

"Your partner?" Ledbetter said. "You mean Mrs. Loomis?"

Loomis didn't bother to correct him. "She followed the bus last night, but her car broke down about halfway up. You're telling me you haven't seen her?"

"No," Ledbetter said, shaking his head. "We haven't seen her." He glanced at Maynard, who shook his head.

Loomis looked at Hubert Gasche. According to Connie's message, Ginny Gasche had dropped her husband off at home, before proceeding to the farm. So Gasche would have been behind Connie on the old logging road when her car broke down.

Loomis took a step toward him and his dogs and pointed the Glock at him. Gasche stiffened. The dogs milled about his feet in confusion. Loomis took another step, his gun pointed at Gasche's chest. He stopped a dozen feet away, then lowered the Glock, aiming at the dogs, slipping his finger inside the trigger guard.

"Where is she?"

"I dunno what y're talking about," Gasche said, too stupid to lie convincingly. "Where's who?"

Loomis squeezed off a shot. The report was shockingly loud in the early morning quiet. Grass, leaves, and frozen mud erupted two feet from the dogs. With guttural howls, they bolted, jerking the handles of their leashes out of Gasche's hand. They ran under the trailer, but their joined leashes tangled in the wheelless undercarriage, jerking them to a stop. They cowered beneath the trailer, whining piteously.

"I'm pretty sure I can still hit them from here," Loomis said. He elevated the muzzle. "Or I could shoot you. Doesn't much matter to me either way. Where is she?"

"I dunno," Gasche said. "I found the car and looked around, but didn't see no one. I guess she hid out somewhere. She ain't going nowhere in that car," he added with a shrug.

"You'd better hope she's all right," Loomis said.

"I didn't do nothing to her," Gasche said.

"Mr. Loomis," Colonel James Maynard said.

"Colonel," Loomis said, glancing at Maynard. He looked worried about something.

"When you were at Dr. Kellerman's farmhouse, did you see Dr. Kellerman?"

Oh, shit, Loomis thought. He looked at Dave Ledbetter. "I've got some bad news for you, Dave. Kellerman had a heart attack."

"No," Ledbetter said, as if punched in the gut.

"My guess," Loomis said, "is that Parker zapped him with whatever he zapped me with. He and Harriet took off in Kellerman's car."

"Goddamn," Ledbetter said. He looked at Bets. She stood on the steel porch of the trailer, eyes filling with tears. She and her husband regarded each other a moment longer, then he turned back to Loomis. His pale eyes were wet. "Is he going to be all right?"

"I don't know," Loomis said. "Belle Ryerson took him to the hospital. Sorry, Dave."

"Yeah," Ledbetter said. The life seemed to have gone out of him. Then he looked at Loomis. "Hang on. Belle Ryerson took him to the hospital? Where'd you find her?"

"You don't know?"

"No," Ledbetter said.

It was clear from Maynard's stony expression, however, that he did. Obviously, so did Hubert Gasche.

"She was locked in the cellar of Kellerman's farmhouse," Loomis said. "She'd been there since last Saturday."

"Eh? How's that?" Ledbetter seemed genuinely surprised. "What the hell was she doing there?"

"Ask him," Loomis said, gesturing with his pistol toward Hubert Gasche.

"How would I know?" Gasche said.

"Well, somebody better tell me what the fuck is going on," Ledbetter said, glaring at Hubert Gasche.

"I don't gotta tell you shit, old man," Gasche said.

Ledbetter's face clouded with anger. "Think again," he said, bringing the shotgun to bear and jacking a shell into the chamber.

"Okay, okay," Gasche said. "Take it easy."

"Talk," Ledbetter said, gesturing with the shotgun for emphasis. "Why was she in that cellar?"

"She showed up last Saturday," Gasche said. "Quentin stang her with that shock stick thing o' his and tol' me an' Ginny to stash her in the cellar."

"What the hell for, for Christ's sake?"

"Ask Parker," Hubert Gasche said.

"I'm asking you, you dumb fuck." Ledbetter was nearly apoplectic, face red with anger. He seemed dangerously close to pulling the trigger. Bets had disappeared into the trailer.

"I can tell you," Loomis said. "She was trying to help a friend find her brother and his family." He gestured toward the would-be space travellers watching from the edge of the meadow. "They bought a ticket on Charley's spaceship. Someone, Parker probably, lured Belle to the farmhouse with a text message sent from her friend's cellphone. Problem is, her friend had been dead for a week or more."

Ledbetter looked stunned. Loomis slipped off his backpack and tossed it to the ground at Ledbetter's feet.

"You'll find some cable-tie handcuffs in there," Loomis said. He gestured with the Glock toward Hubert Gasche and his wife, who was trying to untangle the dogs' leashes from the trailer undercarriage. "Cuff Hubert and Ginny to the undercarriage of the trailer."

"What the fuck for?" Gasche said. Ginny Gasche glared at Loomis, eyes glittering with malevolence.

"I'm making a citizen's arrest for the murder of Maya Thomas," Loomis said. He looked at Ledbetter. "Once I've found Connie, you can help us escort them to my car."

"It wasn't us," Gasche said, glancing toward his wife. "That was Parker, too. She was pokin' around Kellerman's house. He jabbed her with his shock stick, then shot her full of horse dope an' made us take her out into the lake an' dump her."

"Made you!" Dave Ledbetter said. "Made you, for Christ's sake!"

"Someone hit her," Loomis said. "Hard enough to cause her to bleed into her brain. That's what killed her. Not the shock, drugging, or drowning."

"Jesus Christ," Ledbetter said. "I don't believe this. Jesus Christ." He picked up Loomis's backpack. Holding the shotgun in the crook of his arm, he unzipped the backpack, fished around inside, and withdrew two pairs of cable-tie handcuffs. "All right, let's get this done."

"No fuckin' way," Gasche said, turning toward Ginny. "Do something, babe."

"Just stay where you are," Loomis said, pointing the Glock at her. "Dave, why don't you give me the shotgun."

"I'll take it," Maynard said, reaching for the gun.

Before Loomis could stop him, Ledbetter handed the shotgun to Maynard.

"Shit, Dave," Loomis said, as Maynard swung the muzzle of the shotgun toward him.

34

"Drop your gun, Mr. Loomis," Maynard said. "Please don't force me to shoot you. I deeply regret what happened to Miss Ryerson's friend, and Miss Ryerson, but I can't let you jeopardize our mission."

Perspiration pooled in Loomis's armpits and trickled down his ribcage. He shivered with tension, slowly, slowly shifting his aim from Hubert Gasche toward Maynard.

"I don't give a damn about your mission," he said, amazed he was able to keep his voice steady. "Or the Gasches, for that matter. Let the police worry about them. I just want to find my partner."

"Dave," Maynard said. "Relieve Mr. Loomis of his weapon."

"And get between his Glock and that shotgun," Ledbetter said. "Not on your life."

"I'll do it," Hubert Gasche said.

"No," Maynard barked.

Despite the old astronaut's appearance of calm, Loomis sensed that Maynard was precariously close to the edge. He wondered if he shouldn't just shoot the crazy bastard, but looking down the muzzle of a 12-gauge was a daunting deterrent. He had no idea what kind of choke the Remington was fitted with, or what kind of shot the shells were loaded with, but it didn't really matter. At fifteen feet even birdshot would take Loomis's head off. Maybe he could bring the Glock to bear quickly enough to shoot Maynard before he could shoot him. Maybe. Just a few degrees to the left. Don't try for a kill shot. Just hit him. It wouldn't necessarily prevent him from pulling the trigger, but it would ruin his aim. But would it ruin it enough?

"What are you going to do when the aliens don't come, Colonel?" Loomis said instead. "You're an intelligent man. I read your Wikipedia page. Vietnam war hero. Aeronautical engineer. Test pilot. Astronaut. You were relieved when the NASA and Air Force psychologists told you that your abduction from *Challenger* was a hallucination brought on by stress and the effects of weightlessness."

"It wasn't a hallucination," Maynard said, shaking his head. "It was real. It happened."

"Okay," Loomis said, arm aching with the effort of keeping the Glock steady. "Fine. It was real. But this isn't. Harriet Olsen isn't in contact with aliens. She's running a con and Gasche and his wife are in on it with her. So is Parker. I haven't made up my mind about you yet, Dave, but I don't think you are. I think you're as much a victim as Kellerman is, as all these folks are." He glanced toward Margie Spender and the men and women standing with her. "You too, Colonel."

"No," Maynard said, the muzzle of the shotgun wavering.

"Gimme that gun," Hubert Gasche said, reaching for the shotgun. "You let him go, he'll go straight to the cops."

"No," Maynard said, moving a step away from Hubert Gasche.

The momentary distraction allowed Loomis to raise the Glock. Holding it two handed, squinting along the barrel, he lined up the sights between Maynard's eyes.

"I have no intention of letting him go," Maynard said, shotgun levelled at Loomis's chest. "Not yet." He looked a lot calmer than Loomis felt. "I don't want to shoot you, Mr. Loomis."

"Colonel," Dave Ledbetter said, perspiration beading his hairless head, steaming in the cold.

"He isn't giving me a choice, Dave," Maynard said. "We can't let him jeopardize everything we've worked so hard to achieve. The future of the human race is at stake. And if you think I'm bluffing, Mr. Loomis, I've killed men before. A long time ago, in Vietnam, but you never forget. Have you ever even shot anyone, Mr. Loomis?"

"No," Loomis said. "But I'm open to new experiences."

"Dave?" Betsy Ledbetter called from the door of the trailer.

"I'm a good shot, Colonel," Loomis said. It wasn't true, but Maynard wouldn't know that. "If I put a bullet between your eyes, it'll instantly short out all your wiring. You'll be dead before you can pull the trigger, even by reflex."

"It would appear we have a standoff, Mr. Loomis," Maynard said.

"Dave!" Bets called again, with somewhat more urgency.

"Hack," Ledbetter said, ignoring his wife. "The Colonel doesn't want to shoot anyone any more'n you do. Isn't that right, Colonel."

Maynard didn't answer. He was still looking at Loomis down the barrel of the shotgun, but for a moment he seemed to have lost track of what was going on. As Loomis was trying to decide if it might be a good time for him to make a run for it, the old astronaut's eyes swam back into focus.

"Tell you what, Hack," Ledbetter said. "You just put that gun down and we'll find someplace nice and warm for you to wait while we look around for Mrs. Loomis. Once we're finished our business here, you'll both be free to go. Couple of days at most. Then it won't matter what you tell the cops. We'll be gone." He'd recovered his faith.

"Hubert and Ginny will be gone," Loomis said. "Harriet Olsen and Quentin Parker will be gone, too, if they're not already. Along with all the money you folks gave Kellerman's foundation. You'll still be here, Dave. All of you."

"He's nuts," Gasche said. "He don't know what he's taking about."

"What about the money, Dave?" Loomis said. "How

much are we talking about? A lot, I bet. Where is it?"

"We used it to buy supplies."

"The stuff you've got stored in that shed? A few sheets of plywood, a couple of pounds of nails, and some freeze-dried food?"

"We couldn't keep it all here," he said, glancing toward Bill and Margie Spender and the rest of the aspiring colonists. "There's too much. Most of it's stored at the landing site. Pre-fab shelters. Tractors and other farm machinery, too."

"Have you seen it?" Loomis asked.

"Well, no. The Rigilians haven't told us where the landing site is yet."

"So who purchased these supplies? The Rigilians? Him?" He tilted his head toward Hubert Gasche. "Harriet Olsen has the money, doesn't she? Her and Quentin."

"It's got nothing to do with them," Ledbetter said. "It was handled by the foundation's lawyer."

"*Dave,*" Betsy Ledbetter said.

"What is it, Bets?" he said, glancing at his wife. "I'm kinda busy right now."

Out of the corner of his eye Loomis saw Betsy Ledbetter dragging two gigantic suitcases out of the office trailer. He missed an opportunity to shoot Maynard as he, too, glanced quickly to the side. Bets passed through Loomis's field of vision as she lugged the suitcases to the pickup and hefted them one by one over the tailgate into the back of the truck.

"Are you coming, hon?" she said, as she opened the

passenger side door.

"Bets …"

"No, hon. It's time to go.

"But …"

"Thaddeus needs us."

Dave Ledbetter looked at Loomis and Maynard, still pointing guns at each other, then at Bill and Margie Spender and the others, then back at Loomis and Maynard.

"Oh, hell," he said.

Loomis watched as Ledbetter trudged down the track to his truck. He opened the driver's door and climbed behind the wheel. His wife got into the passenger side. A movement to his right caught Loomis's eye. And Maynard's. Hubert Gasche was running toward the woods. Ginny, too, the dogs struggling along behind her.

Something was not right, Loomis thought. Then he remembered that Hubert Gasche was a movie special effects technician.

"Colonel, get down. Dave," he shouted. "Don't—"

He was too late. As Ledbetter started the truck's engine, there was a hard, loud *bang,* and smoke billowed out from beneath the truck. Loomis had barely enough time to hope that the engine had simply backfired or blown a gasket before the doors flew open and the pickup blossomed into a huge orange and red fireball. He started to turn away—

The shockwave hit him like a massive fist of fire.

35

For the second time in less than ten hours, Loomis swam up from the depths of unconsciousness. He was on the ground with no idea how he'd come to be there. His ears rang and the acrid stink of burning plastic and electrical insulation was like acid in the back of his throat. The left side of his face stung fiercely, like a bad sunburn, but there was also a damp coolness across his eyes and brow and cheek. He couldn't see. Then he remembered the explosion. He tried to sit up, but a hand pressed against his shoulder, holding him down.

"Take it easy, Hack," a woman said.

"Connie?" he said, a wave of relief washing through him. "Where have you been?"

"Well, to tell the truth I was asleep in the woods not far from here. The explosion woke me up."

"Jesus, you gave me a scare," Loomis said.

She'd stayed in her car for a while, she explained, after the transaxle broke, bundled up in the old sleeping bag

337

she kept in the car to keep her feet warm during stakeouts. Then she saw the lights of a vehicle coming up the track.

"I thought it might be you," she said, "but I didn't want to chance it."

Grabbing the sleeping bag and the survival kit, which included, among other things, a pair of Mylar "space" blankets, she hid in the woods, from where she watched Hubert Gasche check out her car. When he got back into his truck, she waited a few minutes, then worked her way up the hill on foot until she found the campsite. She watched for a while as the new arrivals set up their tents, then retreated into the woods, found a sheltered spot under some pines, and settled down to wait for dawn, wrapped up and warm in the sleeping bag and the Mylar thermal blankets. She knew Loomis would show up sooner or later.

"I fell asleep around dawn."

"I'm glad you're okay," Loomis said.

"Is he all right," a man said.

"I think so," Connie said.

"I can't see," Loomis said.

"You're burned a bit," the man said. "I put a cold gel-pack on your face. I'll take it off now."

He did and Loomis could see again. The man was William Spender. With Connie's help, Loomis sat up. He ached almost everywhere, as though he'd been given a full body massage with a sack of bowling balls, but everything seemed to work. Still, he needed some help to stand. Down the track a group of men and women was working to prevent the fire from spreading to the dry woods. They were using water buckets, filled from a big tank in the back of the one-ton, wet blankets, and a couple of small fire extinguishers. They weren't bothering with the pickup—what was left of it.

"Dave and Bets?" Loomis said, as another man joined them, peering past Spender's shoulder.

"Dave's got some pretty bad burns on his back," Spender said. "Bets was thrown about twenty feet. Amazingly, she was hardly burned at all, but she's got a broken arm. It was a funny explosion. I mean funny odd. First that bang, then the explosion."

"Hubert Gasche is a former movie special effects tech," Loomis said. "It's fortunate for Dave and Bets that he's a better FX tech than car bomber."

"Why would he want to kill Dave and Bets?" Spender asked.

"I don't know, but they may have been planning to kill all of you, eliminate any witnesses. I wouldn't try starting the bus, if I were you. Or the truck."

"Oh," Spender said, gulping. "Harry," he said to the other man. "Tell them to stay away from the bus and the truck."

Harry hurried away.

"Maynard?" Loomis said.

"He's in the trailer with Dave and Bets," Spender said. "Besides being burned a little, like you, he doesn't appear to be hurt, but he's still unconscious."

"And the Gasches?"

"They took off," Spender said. "They left their dogs, though. The poor things were so freaked out by the explosion they couldn't catch them. Margie managed to calm them down."

"Was anyone else hurt?" Loomis said, gingerly touching the side of his face.

"No. We were all farther away from the explosion. It shook us up, knocked a couple of us down, but no one was hurt. You've got first degree burns, but the gel-pack took the worst of the heat out. There's no blistering so I don't think you'll have any scars. You should probably see a doctor, though."

"Thanks," Loomis said.

Spender reached into his coat pocket and took out the Glock. He handed it to Loomis. Connie had the shotgun.

"You must think we're a bunch of idiots," Spender said, as they started toward the tents.

"You all seem like pretty decent people," Connie said.

"I guess we are," Spender said. "Just stupid."

"If it makes you feel any better," Loomis said, "Dave Ledbetter and Dr. Kellerman were taken in, too. And Colonel Maynard. They aren't stupid." Just a little nuts.

"Thanks," Spender said. "It doesn't much. I'm pretty sure Margie is going to file for divorce. I don't blame her. We took a beating on the house. I can reopen my practice, but ..." He paused, looking back and forth between Loomis and Connie. He said, "What do you think of the chances we might get our money back?"

"Not much," Loomis said.

"Would you be willing to try, for a percentage of whatever you're able to recover? I'm sure I can get the others to agree to it."

Loomis looked at Connie. She shrugged, as if to say "Why not?"

"The police are going to be all over this, you know," Loomis said.

"Still, if you're interested ..."

"Just out of curiosity," Loomis said, "how did you make your payments to the foundation? Dave said you made them through a lawyer."

"That's right," Spender said. "The foundation's lawyer. D. Lincoln McHenry."

The would-be extraterrestrial refugees gathered around. Not counting Dave and Bets and James Maynard, there were an even twenty of them: eight men, eight women, and four children, aged about six to twelve. The expressions on the faces of the adults ranged from anger to embarrassment to fear. The kids just looked confused. As Connie had said, they all looked like decent folks, about as average a group of Americans as you could find. Maybe a little more gullible than most, a little more willing to suspend disbelief, but for the most part theirs was a relatively harmless delusion. For the most part.

"Is there a Thomas family here?" Loomis asked Mrs. Spender.

"Yes," Margie Spender said. "Daniel and Joanne and their two kids. That's them. Sophie, their little girl, isn't feeling too well."

She indicated a couple standing in the middle of the group, almost as if they were hiding. Two young children stood with them. The girl was about six, with blonde hair and large blue eyes. She clung to her mother's thigh, looking pale and sickly. The boy was three or four years older. He had his father's dark good looks and stood close to his sister, protectively, a stern and defiant expression on his face. Daniel Thomas was a spoiled looking man with angry blue eyes and a petulant mouth. His wife was a vaguely pretty woman, mousy, and a few pounds overweight.

"Do you want me to tell them about Maya?" Connie said.

"No," Loomis said, taking the coward's way out. "Let the police handle it."

She talked to them, anyway.

The fire was out, but the carcass of Ledbetter's pickup smoked and stank in the morning chill. Loomis and Connie prepared to take their leave. William Spender, who had taken charge of the unhappy campers, looked at the shotgun as Loomis held it out to him. The bluing was flecked with rust, the stock cracked.

"Be careful with it," Loomis said. "Looks like Dave tried to clean it, but it's pretty old and hasn't been very well maintained. The ammunition's old, too. It might have blown up in Maynard's face if he'd tried to fire it. Use it as a deterrent, if you have to, but fire it only if absolutely necessary."

"A deterrent against whom?" Spender asked.

"Maybe the Gasches will come back for their dogs," Loomis said.

"I don't want it," Spender said, but took it.

"We'll call the police and get some help up here as soon as we can," Loomis said. Both Connie's and Loomis's phones indicated no service, and the colonists hadn't been allowed to keep their cellphones, for security reasons, they'd been told, even though there was no service in the area.

"What about the bus?" Spender asked.

Loomis had looked the bus and the truck over and hadn't been able to find any evidence of explosives, but he said, "I wouldn't take the chance. Wait for the police."

Then Loomis and Connie set out down the narrow track.

"So," Connie said, as they passed the burned-out pick-up. "What do you think? Is Dink McHenry is behind this crazy thing or not?"

"I wouldn't have credited him with the imagination to put something like this together," Loomis said. "Or the balls." He shrugged. "I could be wrong, though. But whether he's the brains behind it or not, I'm sure he's involved. Spender told me he and Margie paid more than three hundred thousand to join the exodus. Dave and Bets probably paid even more. If nineteen adults paid an average of, say, a hundred and fifty thousand each, the scam raked in nearly three million dollars. All that money passing through Dink's hands must have been awfully tempting to a man with financial difficulties. From his perspective, Kellerman and his people are a bunch of flakes who were just flushing their money down the drain. He took a beating when the economy tanked in '08. It was probably pretty easy for him to rationalize using some of it to recoup his loses."

"I don't like him," Connie said. "But I can't believe he'd be involved in kidnapping and murder."

"Maybe you're just not trying hard enough," Loomis said.

They reached the spot where Hubert Gasche had stashed the G-Wagen. It was gone, of course. As they continued down the track, Loomis worried that Gasche might have tried to sabotage the Outback, but when they got to it, everything was in order. They piled in. He had to back up nearly fifty yards before he was able to turn around. Thirty minutes later, they arrived at Kellerman's farmhouse.

36

There were three cars in the farmyard: a Vermont State Police four-by-four, a Burlington PD patrol car, and an unmarked Ford. Loomis pulled into the yard and stopped beside the Ford. Alex Robillard came out of the farmhouse, followed by Vivian Scott and two state troopers. A matched pair of BPD uniformed cops got out of the patrol car.

Loomis climbed stiffly out of the Outback, feeling like an old man. "Hello, Alex," he said, as Connie got out of the car.

Robillard nodded to Loomis. To Connie, he said, "Mrs. Noble. I'm pleased to see you safe and sound."

"Thanks," Connie said.

Loomis turned to the state troopers.

"About two and a half miles up an old logging road, half a mile or so farther down this road, there are twenty-three people—nineteen adults and four kids—who were waiting for a spaceship to come and take them to another planet." The troopers exchanged looks. "Three of them were hurt when a pickup exploded. It had been rigged by a former movie special effects technician named Hubert Gasche, likely with help from his wife. The Gasches are also small-time grifters, specializing in extortion. They fled the scene in a camouflage-coloured Mercedes G-Wagen."

"It passed us heading south on Bingham Road at a high rate of speed," one of the troopers said.

"They may have also rigged a small bus used to transport the cult members up there, and a one-ton truck."

"Okay," the other trooper said. "What's the road like? Must be okay if they got a bus up there."

"There are couple of dry creek beds, but you shouldn't have any trouble getting up there in your four-by-four. Mrs. Gasche is a movie stuntwoman, though, probably a better than average driver, and the bus and the truck have loads of ground clearance. You'll probably need a chopper to take out the injured. One of them is James Maynard, a former astronaut. He was knocked unconscious by the blast and hadn't regained consciousness when we left about forty minutes ago. The other injured are Dave Ledbetter and his wife Betsy. He's burned. She's got a broken arm."

"Any of them armed?"

"Dr. William Spender has an old shotgun Dave Ledbetter found in Dr. Kellerman's house," Loomis said, indicating the farmhouse. "I told him not to try firing it, though."

"Okay," the trooper said. "We may need to speak to you again."

"Sure," Loomis said. He handed the trooper a business card.

The trooper slipped Loomis's card under the clamp of his clipboard, then the two of them climbed into their truck and drove out of the farmyard, turning toward the logging road. The trooper on the passenger side was already on the radio.

"Sounds like you've had an interesting night," Alex Robillard said. He gestured toward Loomis's cheek. "That from the explosion?"

Loomis touched his cheek. It stung. "I was lucky," he said. He quickly filled Robillard in on what had gone down on the mountain.

"These Gasches," Robillard said, when he was done. "They killed Maya Thomas?"

"Quentin Parker stunned her, dosed her with something, probably ketamine, and ordered Gasche and his wife to dump her in the lake."

"What about the blunt force trauma?" Robillard said. "According to the ME, that's what killed her."

"That was Hubert Gasche," Loomis said. "Or possibly his wife: she's pretty well developed. Despite the violence of the blow, it might not have knocked her out, so Parker shocked her. Parker also used the stun gun on Dr. Kellerman. When I got here I found him in the living room. He wasn't in very good shape. I've been on the receiving end of that thing and, believe me, it's a very unpleasant experience. If Kellerman had a heart condition, I imagine it could easily have contributed to a heart attack, especially in a man his age. Belle Ryerson took him to the hospital. She was locked up in a cellar under the utility room. Her car was in the Quonset hut."

"I'm going to need everything you can tell me about the Gasches," Robillard said. "As well as this Quentin Parker and"—he looked at his notes—"Harriet Olsen."

"Olsen and Parker were staying at the Green Mountain Motel near the airport," Loomis said. "Units 42 and 48 respectively. I wouldn't count on them still being there. After zapping Dr. Kellerman, they took off in his car, a silver Lexus." Connie was scribbling on a notepad she'd borrowed from Viv Scott. "Parker was also driving a 1994 Chrysler Neon registered to Jane Smiley, a large animal vet in North Hero. Claims she's his aunt. The Gasches live in the New North End, not far from my place. I don't recall the address. You know what kind of car they drive."

Connie handed the notepad to Robillard. "These are all the plate numbers I can remember. And the Gasches' home address."

"Thanks," Robillard said. He handed the pad to Viv Scott. "Is there anyone else I should know about?"

"I don't think so," Loomis said.

Robillard looked at Connie. "Mrs. Noble?"

"No," she said.

"Okay," Robillard said. "You're both going to have to come to the station to make formal statements, of course, but that can wait till later today or tomorrow. Mrs. Noble, I'm sure you're anxious to get home to your kids."

"I am. Thanks."

"We're also going to need to talk to Belle Ryerson. No doubt she'll want to press charges."

"No doubt," Loomis agreed.

Robillard wasn't quite ready to let them go. "All those people camped out up there waiting for aliens to come and take them to another planet," he said. "I generally try to avoid being judgmental, but that's pretty crazy."

"Any crazier than Tom Cruise or John Travolta believing in the tenets of Scientology?" Loomis said. "Whatever they are. Or the Pope, for that matter, believing in angels and immaculate conception?"

"I'm a Catholic," Robillard said.

"I meant no disrespect."

"Yeah, but it's not the same, is it?"

"Some people might beg to differ."

"They can beg all they want." Robillard shrugged. "Okay, but I don't get it. Why go to all that trouble? Why not just take the money and run?"

"Good question," Loomis said.

"How much are we talking about?"

"Probably around three million, give or take," Loomis said.

"Where is it now?"

"I would guess Parker and Olsen have it," Loomis said.

Robillard didn't ask how the money was paid, and Loomis didn't volunteer the information.

"All right," he said. "Drive carefully. The roads are icy this morning."

When Loomis and Connie were in the car, Connie said, "You didn't tell him about McHenry."

"No," Loomis said.

"Once the police get through interviewing Spender and the others," Connie said, "they'll know he's the foundation's lawyer. They're sure to speak to him."

"We'd better move fast then," Loomis said.

"What do you have in mind?" she asked.

"Me? You're the brains of this outfit."

"You're going to try to get the money back."

"See, no doubt about it. The brains of the outfit. First, though, we need to talk to Belle."

After they'd turned on to Bingham Road and Connie's phone picked up a signal, she called the neighbour who was looking after her kids and spoke briefly to each of them. After that, the car grew quiet. Except for two brief periods of unconsciousness, which didn't count, Loomis hadn't slept in over twenty-four hours. He was so tired he drove straight through a Stop sign in Essex and was almost T-boned by an AmeriGas propane truck. He pulled into the parking lot of a place called Hal's Diner.

Connie sat up. "What's wrong?" she said. She'd been asleep.

"I nearly got us killed," he said.

"Is that all?" She scrubbed her face with the palms of her hands. "I'd offer to drive, but I can barely keep my eyes open."

After two mugs of Hal's coffee, a toasted fried-egg and bacon sandwich, and dousing his face with cold water in the men's room, Loomis managed to get them to Winooski in one piece. By then it was snowing heavily, and the stubbly fields and brown lawns were quickly acquiring a coat of pristine white.

Belle's part of the house was dark, but the lights in Hazel's apartment were warm and inviting in the wintry morning gloom. No sooner had Loomis and Connie mounted the steps to the veranda than the front door opened. Inside, Connie and Belle embraced while Loomis and Hazel stood by. Belle seemed momentarily taken aback by Connie's demonstration of affection, but then she returned her hug, a bit tentatively at first, then more enthusiastically. They simultaneously asked each other if they were all right, simultaneously replied that yes, they were, then laughed together. They separated, and Belle turned to Loomis, eyes glistening, expression turning serious.

"Dr. Kellerman didn't make it," she said. "He was alive when we got to the hospital, but he died in the emergency room."

"I'm sorry to hear that," Loomis said. He wondered if Kellerman's chances of survival would have been better if he hadn't been so rough on him.

"He really wasn't a bad man," Belle said. "Actually, he was quite nice."

"He nearly got you killed," Hazel said sharply. She reached out and placed her hand on her sister's arm. "I'm sorry, Belle."

"It's okay. You're probably right." Belle looked at Loomis. "Your cheek …"

"Just a little burn," Loomis said. He quickly explained.

"Oh, god," Belle said, hand to her mouth, a horrified expression on her face. "That's terrible."

Hazel looked as if nothing about human nature would surprise her.

"Belle," Loomis said. "Did Dink McHenry know you were helping Maya Thomas try to find her brother?"

"Yes," Belle said. "I wanted to take the money out of my trust to make a donation to Dr. Kellerman's foundation." Hazel shook her head, a bemused expression on her face. "But Mr. McHenry refused to let me do it. He said it would be a violation of his fiduciary duty to let me do something so irresponsible."

Loomis and Connie exchanged looks.

"What?" Belle said.

"When we spoke to him about your disappearance, he was pretty adamant that you'd just gone walkabout. Did you know he was the foundation's lawyer?"

"No," Belle said, eyes widening. "I didn't. Is that why he wouldn't let me take any money from my trust account to help Maya? Because he knew it was a fraud?"

"I doubt it," Loomis said. "I suspect it was because he didn't want you to find out that there wasn't any money left in your account."

"Oh, dear," she said, although she seemed less dismayed than Loomis thought she'd be.

"He's had financial problems for some time," Loomis said. "Maybe that's why he got involved in the scheme to defraud Kellerman's people, to pay back the money he's been embezzling from his clients."

"Oh, Belle," Hazel said, distraught. "I'm so sorry."

"Thanks, Haze," she said, touched by her sister's concern. "But there wasn't much left in the account. I followed your example and gradually transferred most of it to the same investment bank you use. I only went to Mr. McHenry because I was going to close my account with him."

"Thank god," Hazel said.

"Do me a favour," Loomis said. "Don't do anything until we've had a chance to see if we can recover the money he and his pals scammed from the Kentauran Foundation. Maybe some of yours, too."

"All right," Belle said.

As Loomis and Connie were about to leave, Hazel surprised him. "Thank you both for bringing my sister back to me." She hugged Connie, then took Loomis's hand, stood on her toes to kiss his undamaged cheek.

"Our pleasure," he said.

It was almost noon by the time they got to Connie's place. While Connie collected Susan and Billy from next door, Loomis secured the Glock in Connie's late husband's gun cabinet, which held Connie's CD collection. The kids were full of questions, of course, which neither Connie nor Loomis was in any condition to answer, but she had to tell them something.

"Sorry, guys," she said. "I didn't mean to worry you. I was tied up with work. I should have called, but there was no service where I was."

"What happened to your face?" Susie asked, looking at Loomis's cheek.

"Just a little burn," he said. "Nothing serious."

"Could we save the questions and answers till later?" Connie said.

"Sure, I guess," Susie said.

"Do we have to go to school now?" Billy asked, always one to have his priorities straight.

"'Fraid so," Connie said.

37

While Connie took a shower, Loomis lay down on her bed, waiting his turn, the stall in the en suite bathroom too small for them to shower together without becoming distracted. He fell asleep almost instantly, waking only when Connie shook him.

He sat up with a groan, rubbing his eyes with the heels of his hands, mindful of his burn. "Argh," he said. "I was dreaming I'd been kidnapped by aliens and Harriet Olsen was performing ghastly experiments on me."

"Lucky you," Connie said. "Take your shower. I'll make some coffee." She left the room.

Loomis swung his legs off the side of the bed, stood—and almost fell on his face. From head to toe he was one massive *ache*. And his left cheek itched ferociously. He scratched—and winced. Stretching and groaning, he hobbled into the bathroom, rubbed condensation off the mirror, and examined his injuries. The left side of his face was the colour of a boiled lobster, but there was no blistering. It stung when he showered, but he didn't think a visit to his doctor was necessary. After his shower, he felt marginally less stiff and sore. In Connie's medicine cabinet he found a little blue jar of Noxzema. Remembering his mother's treatment for sunburn, he gingerly spread some on his cheek. It was as soothing as he recalled, at least temporarily.

"You look like a zombie," Billy said, when Loomis went into the kitchen.

Susie swatted at him, but couldn't suppress a giggle.

Connie smiled. "You put a little too much Noxzema on your burn."

"Oh-h-h," Loomis groaned, theatrically zombie-like, walking stiff-legged to a chair, arms outstretched, mouth twisted. Connie poured him some coffee. He refused anything to eat, Hal's fried egg sandwich a dense lump in the bottom of his stomach.

When they were ready to leave for school, Susie and Billy kissed their mother, then Susie bent and kissed Loomis's undamaged cheek.

"Bye, Dad," she said, then blushed furiously. "Oh, shit—I'm sorry, Ha—Mist—oh, *Mom*."

"It's okay, sweetheart," Connie said, hugging her daughter. Her eyes glistened, too. "It's just a slip of the tongue. Don't worry about it. I'm sure Hack isn't upset. I've called him Sam myself more than once." Usually when they were being intimate or arguing, she didn't add.

"Heck, no," Loomis said. "I'm not upset at all. Nor should you be, honey. It just means your dad is still with

356

you, inside here." He pointed to his own heart. "Mine is."

"Thanks," Connie said, when Susie and Billy had left for school.

"No problem, Veejay," Loomis said.

"Oh, shut up," she said. She sat down with her coffee. "You know, I've called you Sam more than once, but you've never called me Veejay. How come?"

"Self-preservation?" Loomis said.

"You think I'd be angry?"

"I don't know. I didn't want to risk it, though. I like you too much," he added, reaching across the table.

She took his hand. "Me, too," she said. She pulled him to his feet. "Come with me. I've got something better than Noxzema for that burn."

Regrettably, she wasn't speaking figuratively. Taking him to the bathroom, she gently cleaned the Noxzema from his face, then sprayed his cheek with something from the medicine cabinet that stung like the dickens for a second, then alleviated both the pain and the itch.

He'd have to wait for his other itch to be relieved.

"Can I help you?" Glenna Campbell said, regarding Loomis and Connie from the fortress of her reception desk. Her smooth cap of red hair gleamed under the overhead lights, her artificially enhanced lashes casting shadows on her rouged cheeks.

"We're here to see Mr. McHenry," Loomis said.

"I'll see if he's available," she said, picking up her phone.

"That's all right," Loomis said. "We'll surprise him."

"Wait," Glenna said, as Loomis opened the door to the inner offices for Connie.

A matronly middle-aged woman was sitting at Heather-Anne Allen's desk, looking uncomfortable as she tried to ignore the shouting coming from McHenry's office. The blinds were closed, the door was shut, and the voices were muffled, but Loomis was able to make out the phrase "...*not fair*."

"*Fuck fair, you two-timing son of a bitch*," a woman shouted.

Loomis didn't have any trouble recognizing that voice. It had been raised in anger at him often enough. It belonged to his ex-wife.

"Sir?" the woman said, as Loomis stepped closer to the door. Connie edged closer, too.

"*Christ, you're pathetic,*" Veejay ranted.

"*It's not what you think,*" McHenry said. "*She's a client.*"

"*Bullshit! I saw you, you bastard. I followed you to that fucking motel. Jesus, what is it with you, anyway? You can't get within ten feet of a woman without trying to stick your dick into her.*"

"*Oh, that's rich, coming from you,*" McHenry shouted back. "*How many men have you been with since you started sleeping with me? For all I know, you're still fucking your ex-husband.*"

Not if I can help it, Loomis thought, with an involuntary shudder. Connie looked at him with a wry smile.

"*So what if I am?*" Veejay said. "*It's not saying much, but *he's twice the man you are, in bed and out."*

"You're wrong about her."

"Sure I am."

"Look," McHenry said. *"Can we do this later? I'll call you."*

"Don't bother." Veejay's voice was a feral snarl. *"We're done. I hope that crazy bitch gives you an incurable disease."*

Loomis had heard enough. More than enough. He straightened and raised his arm to pound on the door. The door flew open.

"Oh," Veejay said, stepping back, eyes wide. She recovered quickly. "What a pleasant surprise. My favourite ex-husband. We were just talking about you, weren't we, Dink? And Connie. How's the shallow end of the secretarial pool, dear?"

"Way over your head, Veejay," Connie said, with a saccharine smile.

"Hack," McHenry said. He was shrugging into a camelhair overcoat. "What do you want?"

"We need to talk," Loomis said.

"I don't have the time right now." He picked up a big burgundy leather file case.

"Make time," Loomis said.

"Oh, this sounds good," Veejay said. "Can I stay and watch?"

"Take a hike, Veejay," Loomis said. "Go join your mother in the circus."

She glared at him, the reference lost on her, then harrumphed and marched toward the exit.

"The circus?" Connie said.

"I'll explain later," Loomis said.

McHenry tried to squeeze past Loomis and Connie, but Loomis put his hand on McHenry's chest and pushed him back into the office. McHenry glowered as Loomis took the case from his hand and hefted it. There wasn't much, if anything, in it. He put it on McHenry's desk.

"Sir?" said the woman occupying Heather-Anne's desk. "Should I call the police?"

"Don't bother," Loomis said to her. "They'll be here soon enough."

The woman looked at McHenry.

"It's all right, Eileen," he said.

Loomis gestured for Connie to come into the office, then shut the door.

"Where's Heather-Anne?" he asked.

"I had to let her go," McHenry said. "I can't tolerate disloyalty. Now what do you want?"

"We've got some bad news for you," Loomis said.

"Oh?" McHenry said, moving behind his desk, interposing its bulk between Loomis and him. He did not sit, however. "And what's that?"

"We found Belle Ryerson," Loomis said.

"Did you?" McHenry said, feigning indifference as he sat down. "Is she all right?" He flicked a non-existent speck of dust from dark marble desktop.

"She is," Loomis said. "No thanks to you. You knew where she was all along, didn't you?"

"Don't be ridiculous," McHenry said, looking up, but

not quite making eye contact. "Of course I didn't know where she was. Ah, where was she?"

Connie snorted with derision.

"Come off it, Dink," Loomis said, propping a buttock on the corner of McHenry's desk, looking down at him. "You knew Belle was trying to help a friend get her brother and his family out of the clutches of Thaddeus Kellerman's UFO cult."

"I knew nothing of the sort." McHenry squirmed under Loomis's scrutiny, then stood.

Loomis stood, too. "You're denying that she asked for some money from her trust so she could infiltrate Kellerman's cult?"

"She doesn't need my permission to withdraw money from her trust," McHenry said. "She did speak to me, however, about closing out her account with us. I suggested that it might be a good idea not to close it out completely, though, to leave something in it, just in case. The subject of Dr. Kellerman's foundation never came up."

"That's not what Belle says," Connie said.

"Perhaps she misremembers the details of our conversation," McHenry said with a shrug. "She did seem a bit preoccupied at the time."

It was Loomis's turn to snort. "You know, Dink," he said, "I couldn't understand why you were so insistent that Belle had just gone walkabout, that she wasn't really missing. I know now, though. You didn't want her to be found. At least, not until you'd replaced the money you'd embezzled from her and your other clients with the money you and Harriet Olsen scammed from Kellerman's cult members."

"That's an outrageous allegation," McHenry said, puffing up with self-righteous indignation. "I have no idea what you're talking about. I suspect you don't, either."

"Maybe you could clear something up for me," Loomis said. "How did Harriet and her pals find out Belle was helping Maya Thomas look for her brother and his family? You told them, didn't you?"

"That's preposterous. You're out of your mind."

"Possibly," Loomis said. "But you're out of luck. Belle's friend is dead."

"That's unfortunate," McHenry said. "But—"

"She died of a cerebral hemorrhage, the result of a blow to the head, likely inflicted by Hubert Gasche. She might have been saved, though, had Quentin Parker not used a stun gun on her, dosed her with ketamine, and had Gasche and his wife dump her in the lake."

"Are you seriously suggesting I had any knowledge of such a thing?" McHenry said. "I'm sorry for Belle's loss, of course, but I don't know any of these people. I certainly didn't have anything to do with Belle's friend's death—or with Belle's supposed abduction."

Loomis shook his head. "You can't wiggle your way out of this with more lies, Dink. Besides, I've played poker with you, remember. You can't bluff worth a damn."

"You're trying my patience, Hack."

"Here's my problem, Dink. Two people are dead ..."

362

"Two?" McHenry said. He seemed to have trouble swallowing.

"Thaddeus Kellerman is dead."

"Kellerman?" He was shaken, but Loomis didn't think it was from grief. "How?"

"Cardiac arrest," Loomis said. "Brought on by Quentin Parker when he shocked him with a stun gun. Or maybe it was Harriet. She's a cold one. I wouldn't turn my back on her, if I were you."

"As I said, I don't know who you're talking about."

"Of course you do, Dink. We overheard you and Veejay arguing. She saw you and Harriet at the Green Mountain Motel, didn't she?"

"Veejay is delusional," McHenry said.

"There's a lot of that going around," Loomis said. "How is it, Dink, that Belle wasn't aware of your association with Kellerman or the Kentauran Foundation when she came to you for money from her trust? Or that when I asked Heather-Anne Allen about it, she'd never heard of either the Kentauran Foundation or Thaddeus Kellerman?"

"My 'association,' as you put it, with Thaddeus Kellerman and his organization is not really any of your business," McHenry said.

"The police are interviewing William Spender and the other victims of the scam as we speak. And they're going to tell them that they made their payments to the cult through you."

"Contributions to a perfectly legitimate scientific research institute," McHenry said.

"Pull your head out of your ass, Dink. You're the lawyer. You don't need me to tell you that if you're an accessory to the conspiracy to defraud Kellerman and his friends, which led directly to the deaths of Maya Thomas and Thaddeus Kellerman, you're guilty of felony murder. Not to mention the attempted murder of Dave and Betsy Ledbetter."

McHenry paled. "There's no proof I had any knowledge of fraud," he said.

"Yet," Loomis said. "The cops will catch up to Harriet sooner or later, and when they do, she'll roll over on you faster than you can say 'E.T. phone home.' She's a hustler, Dink. She'll always play the angles. It's over. Even if she doesn't rat you out, the police can build a pretty good case against you from the statements of the cult members."

"I've known Thaddeus Kellerman for years," McHenry said. "Ever since I helped him establish his institute nearly thirty years ago. He isn't a client of the firm, though. Neither is his institute."

"But you still represent him?"

"On occasion," McHenry said. "As the need arises."

Such as collecting fares for a seat on Charley's spaceship, Loomis thought. "Christ, don't tell me you're a member of his cult," he said.

"Don't be ridiculous," McHenry said. "Just because I knew him doesn't mean I believe in flying saucers or extraterrestrials. And who am I to judge if Dr. Kellerman and the members of his organization believed that aliens were going help them establish a colony on another …?"

He shut his mouth, realizing too late that he'd said too much.

"So you knew about the refugee scheme," Loomis said. "You had to know it was a con, Dink. You're stupid, but not *that* stupid."

McHenry's face clenched in anger. "This conversation is over," he said, maneuvering around Loomis and Connie and opening the office door.

"I've been offered a finder's fee if I can recover the money," Loomis said.

"Well, good luck with that," McHenry said. "You're going to need it. You sure as hell aren't going to be getting any more business from this firm."

"That's true enough," Loomis said. "This firm isn't going to last much longer." He paused, stroking his chin as he regarded McHenry.

"What?" McHenry said.

"I'm considering the possibility that you're as much a dupe as Kellerman and his people," he said. "Where's the money, Dink? You don't have it, do you? You didn't deposit it into the foundation account, did you? You converted it to cash. Harriet has it now, doesn't she?" Loomis laughed. "You poor dope. What did she tell you? 'Don't waste all that money paying your clients back. Run away with me.' Jesus, Dink, you really are that stupid. Well, you can kiss any part of the money goodbye." He turned to Connie. "C'mon, we're wasting our time here."

Loomis took her arm and hustled her out of the office.

38

"You don't really think Olsen and Parker have the money, do you?" Connie asked as they took the stairs down to the fourth floor.

"Nope. I just wanted Dink to think I did."

"Did he?"

"I think so. I wasn't kidding when I said he was a lousy poker player."

When they got to the office, Loomis took the Glock 19 out of the gun safe; he hadn't had time to clean it, and it still smelled of expended propellant. The safe also contained a smaller, more concealable Glock 26, but Connie shook her head when he asked her if she wanted it. She liked guns even less than he did.

"Do you really think we're going to need them?"

"I sincerely hope not," he said, as he removed the trigger lock from the 19. "But, as someone once said, better to have a gun and not need it than need a gun and not have one."

With more than a little reluctance, she took the pistol, removed the trigger lock and went through the ritual with him, then slipped it into her shoulder bag. They went down to the Outback and sat in the car, watching the entrance to the underground garage as it began to snow again.

"Do you think he's going to meet Harriet Olsen?" Connie asked.

"Yeah, I do," Loomis said. "Poor bastard, caught between Lizzie, Veejay and Harriet Olsen. In a way, I feel sorry for him. Not very, but ..." He shrugged.

"I've lost what respect I may have had for him," Connie said. "But I can't believe he could be so completely, well, bewitched. I mean, Harriet Olsen is an attractive woman, but is she so beautiful and seductive that a man like McHenry will lose whatever good sense he might possess? Blame it on my sheltered upbringing," she added, "but is that what it means to be pussy-whipped?"

"Eh? Not quite," Loomis said. "I understand what you're getting at, but I'm not sure a woman has to be beautiful to pussy-whip a man. She just needs the right man. Then again, maybe all men are susceptible to a woman with the right whip," he added with a grin.

She punched him hard on the meat of his shoulder.

"Ouch! On the other hand," he said, rubbing his shoulder, "maybe McHenry really is pulling Harriet's strings, not the other way around."

Connie made an unladylike sound. "It's much more satisfying to imagine McHenry being whipped rather than doing the whipping."

The garage door lifted, and McHenry's Cadillac emerged. Loomis started the Outback as the Caddy headed west on Bank Street toward the lake. The snow continued to fall as they followed McHenry's car as it turned into the customer parking lot of the former Chittenden Bank, renamed People's United, at the foot of Bank Street. Loomis pulled over and watched in the rearview mirror as McHenry went into the bank carrying the file case. He came out five minutes later, still carrying the case, which seemed considerably heavier, and got into the Caddy.

"Jesus," Connie said. "He's not going to run around with three million dollars in cash in his briefcase, is he?"

"He's desperate," Loomis said. "Desperate men do desperate things. As often as not, those desperate things are also stupid things."

"If he's going to run, why not just wire the money somewhere?"

"A offshore wire transfer that big would set off all kinds of alarms at the NSA," Loomis said.

McHenry turned right on to College then right again on to Battery, and headed north. McHenry lived in the north end. Was he going home? Loomis wondered, keeping well back as the Caddy continued past police headquarters. Two and a half miles farther north, when the Caddy turned left on to Shore Road, Loomis had his answer. A few minutes later, McHenry's car turned on to Sterling Place and then into the driveway of his rambling two-story house. Loomis parked a few doors down as McHenry tucked the Caddy into the three-car garage and went into the house.

"Now what?" Connie said.

"Now we wait," he said. "See what happens. And hope the police don't arrive too soon."

"Why don't we just go in and grab it now?"

"Because, technically, McHenry hasn't done anything wrong. He could claim he's just safeguarding the money for the Kentauran Foundation to prevent Olsen or Parker from getting their hands on it."

An hour later, nothing had happened. Half an hour after that, still nothing. They were running out of things to talk about and were having a hard time keeping each other awake. Then, a few minutes before 3 p.m., Loomis's phone buzzed. He didn't recognize the number on the screen.

"Loomis," he said.

"Mr. Loomis," a woman said, but it sounded more like *Nister Loonis*. "It's—it's Harriet Olsen."

"Miss Olsen," Loomis said, looking at Connie, whose eyebrows shot up. "What can I do for you?"

"I need your help." It came out *helt*, as though her mouth were frozen after a visit to the dentist.

"My help?" he said. "With what?"

"Can you cun to Dr. Keller'an's house?"

"Are you all right?" he said. "You sound like you've been punched in the mouth."

"I have," she said, sniffling wetly, as though she were crying. "Can you …?"

"I can," he said. "But if this is some kind of setup, I'm

not going to be very happy with you."

"It's not," she said. "I know you have no reason to trust me, but please, I need your help."

"Are you badly hurt? Do you need medical assistance?" he asked. Connie's lips compressed into a thin line.

"No," Olsen said.

"Because the police can get there a lot faster than I can."

"No," she said, pleading. "No police. Please."

"I'll be there as soon as I can."

"Thank you," she said, almost sobbing with gratitude that he hoped was genuine.

Loomis closed his phone to disconnect the call, then flipped it open again.

"You're not going, are you?" Connie said.

"Someone's beaten her up," Loomis said, keying a number into the phone.

"So you're going to ride to her rescue," Connie said. "For god's sake, call the police. It's got to be some kind of trick."

"I'll be careful," he said, ignoring Connie's scowl. "Phil. It's Hack. I need a favour."

Loomis left Connie with the Outback and walked the half mile to Leddy Park, where he waited in the entrance to the arena as the gloom deepened and snow accumulated on the cars in the parking lot. He'd been waiting about ten minutes when Phil Jefferson pulled up in a bright yellow four-by-four pickup, perched high atop off-road suspension and knobby tires. Loomis regarded it with horror.

"What the hell is this?"

"My new toy," Jefferson said. "Ain't she beautiful?"

"I thought you'd bring a company car."

"There wasn't one available," Jefferson said. "You might as well drive." Jefferson slid over into the passenger seat as Loomis climbed into the truck. "You can drop me off at the office."

"Sure," Loomis said. "I might even slow down."

After dropping Jefferson off, Loomis headed south. On the freshly snow-slicked roads the truck's knobby off-road tires had about as much traction as a skate blade. Twenty harrowing minutes later, he rolled slowly along South Cove Crescent, past the entrance to Cove Lane. Kellerman's car was in the driveway. From the layer of snow that had accumulated on it, Loomis guessed it had been there most of the day. It was starting to get dark, and the porch light was on, but the rest of the house was dark. He continued around the crescent, on the lookout for Parker's aunt's Neon or Gasche's G-Wagen. He saw neither, but that didn't mean they weren't waiting for him in the house.

He circled back to Cove Lane, swung the gaudy yellow truck into Kellerman's driveway. He climbed down from the cab, unzipping his jacket so he could get at the Glock more easily, and walked to the front door. He pressed the doorbell button but did not hear the chimes. He knocked. A moment later Harriet Olsen's voice crackled from the speaker grill.

"Who is it?"

"Loomis," he said.

He heard movement, the sound of something falling, then the door opened a crack.

"Come in," she said from the other side of the door.

"Stand back from the door," Loomis said.

He pushed the door open and peered into the dark vestibule. Olsen's slight figure stood in the dark by the door to the front hall.

"How about some light?" he said.

She reached out and the vestibule light went on.

"Are you alone?" he asked.

"Yes," she said. Her voice was dull and she stood with her head bowed, watching him through wings of dark hair. In her hands she held the crystal vase in which Loomis had found his keys when he'd made his escape from Kellerman's basement.

"Move to the foot of the stairs," he said.

She put the vase on the vestibule table, then retreated and stood by the stairs. Loomis pushed the door open until it banged against the wall. If there was anyone behind it, he or she wasn't much bigger than a broomstick. He stepped into the vestibule, closed and bolted the door behind him. Olsen watched silently through the curtain of her hair. He looked through the doorway into the front hall. The living room was to his left, a dining room to his right.

"Go into the living room," he said.

She shuffled into the living room, where she threw a switch that turned on a pair of matching floor lamps at either end of a grey leather sofa.

"Sit down while I make sure we're alone."

She sat on the edge of the sofa, head bowed, hands in her lap, fingers shredding a wad of tissue. There were dark stains on the front of her pale blue T-shirt. Blood? Tears?

Loomis went through the dining room into the kitchen, opening doors to a pantry, a utility closet, and a powder room, all clear. He opened the door to the basement where he had been imprisoned, found the light switch, and went down the stairs. Fragments of the duct tape that had been used to secure him to the post were still on the floor. There was no one hiding behind the furnace or in the laundry room. He returned to the main floor and went upstairs, checking the three bedrooms and two bathrooms. When he went back to the living room, Olsen was still hunched on the edge of the grey sofa. He placed a straight-backed chair where he could see both her and entrance to the living room and sat down.

She raised her head and looked at him.

"Christ," he said.

Her face was a mess, eyes swollen and beginning to blacken, nostrils caked with drying blood, nose possibly broken, and lower lip split. There was a gash on her forehead just below the hairline, held closed by three narrow strips of clumsily applied surgical tape, and a laceration on her left cheek. The dark stains on her T-shirt were indeed blood.

"Are you all right?"

"All things considered," she said. Tears leaked from

her bruised and swollen eyes. She gathered her hair at the back of her neck and secured it with an elastic hair band. The knuckles of her hands were red and puffy. The older bruises on her wrists were still vivid.

"What happened? Who did this?"

She shook her head, dabbing her eyes with a tissue. There were two gel-packs on the floor. He leaned over and picked them up. Both were warm.

"You need to get to a hospital."

"No, no hospital." Her damaged mouth caused her to slur the P: *hosphital*. She dabbed at her nose with the tissue. It came away bloody.

"If you won't let me take you to the hospital, at least let me take a look at you. Psychiatrists are MDs. There might be a decent first aid kit around."

She nodded. "Upstairs."

She grunted as he helped her to her feet, but managed the stairs on her own. The en suite bathroom of the master bedroom was almost as big as the living room of his trailer and the first aid kit open on the vanity could have equipped a small clinic. Loomis had her sit on toilet seat while he carefully cleaned her face with a soapy washcloth. He opened a bottle of peroxide.

"This might sting," he told her, soaking a cotton ball with peroxide.

"Do it," she said.

He cleaned the cut on her forehead and laceration on her cheek with the peroxide. She didn't react at all. He found some butterfly bandages and replaced the strips of tape she'd used to close the gash on her forehead.

"Am I going to have a scar?"

"It's a clean cut. And close to the hairline. Might even be sexy. Lend you an air of mystery."

"In your line of work, maybe. Not mine."

"I think your nose may be broken," he said.

"You should've seen it before I pushed it back into place," she said.

She winced as he pressed a strip of tape across the bridge of her nose, not sure what the point was, but if they did it on TV, it must be helpful. He dabbed at the crusted blood on her lips with a fresh cotton ball, peroxide fizzing. Mucus dripped from her nose and tears leaked from her eyes, but she did not complain. He admired her toughness and found himself growing angry at whoever had done this to her. He found some extra-strength Advil in the medicine cabinet and gave her three tablets with a glass of water.

"I've done what I can," he said finally. "The cut on your forehead and the inside of your lip could probably use a stitch or two, though."

She stood and examined herself in the mirror, touching her face. "Thanks."

"It's going to be a while before the swelling goes down," he said. He examined her hand. "You may also have a cracked knuckle. You really should have yourself checked over at a hospital."

"I feel a lot better." She plucked at her blood-stained T-shirt. "Do you mind if I change? I have a suitcase in one of the guest rooms."

"After you've changed you can tell me why you asked for my help. I'm pretty sure it wasn't for my first aid skills."

She trudged down the hall to one of the other bedrooms. He waited in the hall while she changed into clean jeans and a fresh T-shirt. She held his arm as they went down the stairs. In the living room, she opened a cabinet and took out a bottle of vodka. She poured a generous amount into a crystal glass and drank half of it down.

"Help yourself," she said.

"I'll pass," he said. "Now, why do you need my help? And what makes you think I'd be the least bit interested in helping you?"

"To answer your second question first," she said, "I can pay you. As soon as you've helped me get the money your friend Lincoln McHenry owes me."

39

"What makes you think Dink McHenry is a friend of mine?" Loomis said.

"Dink?"

"His nickname," Loomis said. "He goes by D. Lincoln McHenry ..."

"Hence Dink," she said. "It suits him. What's the D stand for?"

"Doofus," Loomis said.

"Please," she said, wincing and touching her mouth as she smiled.

"It was McHenry you were talking to on the phone at Kellerman's office, then?"

She nodded.

"You know Dr. Kellerman is dead," Loomis said, dropping it on her with cruel suddenness and watching her reaction.

"Oh, fuck," she said, stricken. Her distress seemed genuine, but her injuries made her harder than ever to read. "I warned him that Thaddeus had a heart condition." She shook her head. "God, poor Thaddeus." She seemed to be struggling for control.

"Why did Parker shock him?"

"He was becoming too insistent that I go with him to the staging area." She lightly touched the gash on her forehead with her fingertips. "I tried to stop Quentin from using that thing on him, but he whacked me it. I let my guard down. Most of this came later."

She downed the rest of the vodka, then started to get up from the sofa. She grimaced with pain and sat down again. Loomis got the bottle and poured another inch into her glass.

"Are you going to help me?" she said.

"I haven't decided yet," he said. "To be honest, I'm not sure I can trust you."

"I don't blame you," she said. She picked up her glass, took a drink, and put it down again.

He wondered if she was trying to play him, gain his sympathy with the poor-little-me routine, but he had the feeling that she was being straight with him. He thought it might be wise, however, to ignore his bullshit detector and assume the worst.

"I'm surprised McHenry had the imagination to concoct such a crazy scheme," he said.

"He didn't," she said. "Not really. He got the idea from me. Well, not me exactly. He actually got it from *Manny the Insignificant*."

"Cut the crap, Harriet," Loomis said, tone hardening.

"Do you want me to help you? Or would you rather I just call the cops, let them have you?"

"I'm sorry," she said. "I normally don't drink much. It's helping with the pain, but it's going to my head. I can't seem to think straight. Do you think I could have a concussion?"

"Do you feel nauseous? Ringing in your ears?"

"No."

"Do you remember the beating?"

"Christ, yes."

"Did you lose consciousness?"

"I slept a bit, before I called you, and woke up with a headache. It's gone now, though."

"I think you're okay," Loomis said. "It wouldn't hurt to have a doctor check you out."

"So you keep saying."

"'*Manny the Insignificant*,'" he prompted her.

She took a breath. "It probably won't come as any surprise," she said, "but Harriet Olsen isn't my real name. It's Deirdre. Deirdre Cowan. I prefer Dee, though."

Loomis recalled the numerous renditions of the letter D in Parker's notebook. It was the kind of thing a schoolboy did when he had a crush on a girl. Loomis had done it himself. Like most of Loomis's early crushes, Parker's was likely unrequited, but at least Loomis had never beaten up any of the girls who hadn't returned his affections.

"I'm not a professional con artist," Dee Cowan said. "Not even a very enthusiastic amateur. Actually, I'm an actress, although except for a couple of small roles on TV,

I've mostly only done commercials. About eight months ago I was broke and had taken a gig with a travelling stage hypnotist who billed himself as *Manny the Magnificent*. We called him *Manny the Insignificant*. Part of Manny's act featured me and two other girls in these awful slutty space-girl outfits. We would circulate through the audience asking for volunteers—men, usually—to go up on stage. Manny would hypnotize them into thinking they'd been taken aboard an alien spaceship and that the girls and I were aliens who wanted to check them out as potential mates. To prove themselves worthy they had to do stupid things, like pretend to lift huge weights, strut around like peacocks on display, or fence with invisible swords.

"Anyway, three months ago, after a show at a convention in Montreal, Lincoln comes back stage and, well, offers me a job. I thought he was just coming on to me. I was desperate to get out of the act, though, so I agreed to have a drink with him. When he told me what he had in mind I thought he was nuts, but the money was good. Fifteen hundred a week, then another twenty thousand after the payoff. Not that I've seen a penny of it, except some expenses. I don't think I really believed he would go through with it, that it was just some scheme to get me to sleep with him, but ..." She shrugged.

"Did you?"

"Sleep with him? Christ, no." She was genuinely aghast at the suggestion. "Not that he didn't try."

"I'd be disappointed if he didn't," Loomis said.

"I had to string him along, though," she said. "It was

pretty awful. He fawned so."

"I'll bet he did. Is that why Parker beat you up? He was jealous of McHenry?"

"I suppose he was, in a way, but that's not why he beat me up. Not this time, anyway."

"What do you mean, 'not this time.' How long have you known him?"

"Most of my life," she said. "He's my stepbrother."

"Your stepbrother?" Loomis said, surprised.

"Yeah, but he's always had this sick thing for me. Usually I can handle it, but I thought this time he was going to kill me. I'm pretty tough, though, and"—she held up her battered hands—"learned early to give as good as Quentin gave."

"So why did he beat you up?"

"Lincoln's plan was to use the money from the scam to pay back what he'd embezzled from his clients, but Quentin wanted me to convince him to keep the money and run away with me. Then we'd take it from him. When I wouldn't go along with it, Quentin lost it."

"Why wouldn't you go along with it?" Loomis asked.

"Well, for one thing," she said, "Quentin was never very good at sharing. And I'd probably have had to sleep with Lincoln. Mainly, though, it was because I was afraid Quentin was going to kill him. I didn't want anything to do with that."

"Who brought him into the scam?"

"To create the Harriet Olsen character Lincoln needed someone who knew about UFOs and alien abductions.

Quentin's been reading about that stuff for years. I didn't really want him involved, but Lincoln was in a hurry to get started."

"You know that Quentin and the Gasches killed Maya Thomas, don't you?"

She shook her head. "I told you before, I don't know anyone by that name. Who was she?" She turned pale as Loomis explained. "Please believe me, Mr. Loomis, I don't know anything about that."

Against his better judgment he thought she was telling the truth.

"Hubert Gasche also tried to kill Dave and Betsy Ledbetter by blowing up their truck at the staging area campsite."

"Oh, Jesus," she said. She took a drink. "You said 'tried.'"

"They survived. They're hurt but alive."

"I'm glad to hear that." He'd have to take her word for it, Loomis thought. "Is that how you got those burns on your face?"

"Yes," he said, touching his cheek. "You called them steroid addled morons. How did they get involved? They aren't the kind of people McHenry normally hangs out with."

"Mrs. Gasche is a member of Thaddeus's cult. She actually believes in UFOs and alien abductions. She was at the meeting where Thaddeus introduced 'Harriet Olsen.' Later on, she took me aside told me she knew I was hustling Thaddeus and wanted in on it."

Takes one to know one, Loomis thought.

"She's a scary person," Dee Cowan said. "When I told her to get lost, she grabbed me in a way that hurt so bad I almost threw up. Lincoln thought she and her husband might be useful, though." Tears formed in her eyes and she dabbed at them with the wad of tissue. "I'm really sorry about—well, a lot. Lincoln—"

"Please stop calling him that," Loomis said. "It's just too creepy. Call him Dink, like everyone else."

"I'll try."

"How did you get Kellerman to believe you were an abduction victim?"

"It was easy," Dee Cowan said. "On the surface he seemed quite normal, even rational—he was by no means stupid—but he was very eager, almost desperate, to believe me—and in Charley. I realize it may not be worth much at this point, but I wouldn't have gotten involved if I'd known how, well, out of control things were going to get."

"You're right," Loomis said. "It isn't worth much. Especially to Dr. Kellerman and Maya Thomas. And what about Belle Ryerson? Did you know she was locked up in the cellar of Kellerman's farmhouse?"

"Not till last night," she said. "Is she all right?"

"Yes," Loomis said. "Do you have any idea why Gasche would try to kill Dave and Bets? Were they planning to kill all Kellerman's people?"

"God, no. At least, I don't think so. I guess he got tired of Dave treating him like the moron he is. Or maybe it was Ginny. Dave told her once she should be institutional-ized. He's one of the reasons things were taking so long."

"Ledbetter? How so?"

"We had to play him very carefully. He may come across as sort of dull and stupid, but he's not."

"But he believed aliens were going to take him to an-other planet."

"I don't think he did," she said. "Not really. He want-ed to, and may have partly convinced himself that he did, but I think he only believed it because Thaddeus did. And Bets. Thaddeus had been treating her for years, trying to recover memories of her own abduction." She shook her head. "Memories that don't exist."

"So Dave only pretended to believe you were in con-tact with Charley out of regard for Kellerman and Bets?"

"I'm pretty sure he thought 'Harriet Olsen' was com-pletely delusional, that she really believed she'd been taken to Charley's spaceship, and, well, I think he liked her. Me. He probably thought Thaddeus was delusional, too, but he loved that old man. If it hadn't been for hav-ing to convince Dave it wasn't a scam, that Harriet Olsen was a true believer, Lincoln—McHenry—wouldn't have bothered with the staging area. He'd have just grabbed the money and run."

And probably gotten away, Loomis thought. "Speak-ing of which," he said, "where's the money now?"

"McHenry kept it in a safe deposit box at his bank."

"How much?"

"I'm not sure. About two and a half million, I think."

"And Quentin? Where's he?"

"I don't know. Or care."

Loomis thought for a moment, then stood. "Come on."

"Where are we going?" she said, as he helped her to her feet.

"We're going to get the foundation members' money back."

"What about the money McHenry owes me?"

"I wouldn't count on it," Loomis said, as he helped her into her coat. "But if you're straight with me I might cut you on a small percentage of the finder's fee."

She held his arm as they went out to Phil Jefferson's truck. It was still snowing and seemed colder than when he'd arrived, but the wind had died down. "Tell me something," Loomis said, when they were in the truck heading north toward town.

"If I can," she said.

"Don't let this go to your head, but you're an extremely attractive woman."

Dee Cowan's laugh was bitter and self-mocking. "Being attractive isn't something I can take any credit for, is it?" she said. "At seventy my grandmother is still turning the heads of men half her age. Thanks for not putting it in the past tense, though."

"You'll heal," Loomis said. "But wouldn't it have made more sense to have cast someone more, well, geeky and awkward to play Harriet Olsen?" Someone more like Belle Ryerson, he thought. Or Hazel. "That you are so attractive was one of the reasons we were suspicious of you from the beginning."

"I wanted to make myself look frumpy—not that difficult—but McHenry said he wanted me to look as attractive as possible. I'm not sure why. I guess he thought I would have to seduce Thaddeus."

Hmm, Loomis thought. "Did you?" he said.

"Seduce him? Yes, I suppose I did. I didn't sleep with him, though." She smiled, winced, and dabbed at her lip with a tissue. "I told McHenry that Thaddeus wasn't interested, but he was. A lot. Both were pretty persistent, but I know how to handle myself. Thaddeus was particularly suggestible. After a while, I could put him into a light trance with just a couple of words and by touching him behind the left ear."

"You're a hypnotist?" Loomis said.

"I picked up some of the basics during my time with Manny," she said.

"Is it that easy?"

"Not always."

"I'm relieved to hear that," Loomis said.

They were about halfway to McHenry's house when Loomis's phone buzzed. He dug it out of his pocket and glanced at the screen. Connie. He flipped the phone open, driving with one hand.

"What's up?" he asked.

"You'd better get back here quick," she said. "Quentin Parker and Ginny and Hubert Gasche showed up a minute ago. McHenry didn't want to let them in, but they threatened him with a black cylindrical thing."

"Sit tight," Loomis said. "We're fifteen minutes away."

"We?" he heard Connie say, as he flipped the phone closed.

"What's wrong?" Deirdre Cowan asked, clutching the dash as Loomis accelerated and Jefferson's ridiculous truck fishtailed on the knobby tires.

"Your stepbrother and the Gasches are at McHenry's," he said.

"They're after the money."

"No kidding."

"They'll kill him if he doesn't give it to them. Maybe even if he does."

"Then you'd better hope we get there in time," Loomis said, finally figuring out how to shift the truck into four-wheel-drive. It helped, but not a lot.

40

Loomis parked the truck behind the Outback, then escorted Dee Cowan to the car and got into the back seat with her.

"Connie, meet Deirdre Cowan, aka Harriet Olsen. Dee, my partner, Connie Noble."

"God, who did that to you?" Connie said.

"My stepbrother," Dee Cowan said.

"Quentin Parker," Loomis explained. "Has anyone else joined the party?"

"No," Connie said. "What are we going to do?"

"I thought I'd crash it."

"Maybe we should just call the police. They can throw a net over the lot of them and sort it out later."

"What about me?" Dee Cowan said.

"You," Connie, spearing her with a look, "could probably cut a deal by testifying."

Cowan didn't appear to like the idea.

A red Ford Mustang went past and pulled into

McHenry's driveway. It stopped in front of the garage and Lizzie McHenry got out.

"Hack, you've got to stop her," Connie said. "She'll walk right into the middle of that nest of snakes."

Loomis was already out of the car. He ran over to Lizzie McHenry. She spun, startled, eyes wide with alarm. "Hack? What's wrong?"

"Your husband has company."

She looked toward the Outback. Connie and Dee Cowan stared back at them. "Do you have my husband under surveillance?"

"You could say that," Loomis said. "You don't want to go in right now. The people with your husband are co-conspirators with him in a swindle he's been perpetrating on the Kentauran Foundation."

"That's a very serious allegation."

"Do you know what the Kentauran Foundation is?"

"I believe it's a charitable organization of some kind."

"I suppose you could call it that," Loomis said. The wind was picking up again, whipping the snow into their eyes and adding a significant chill factor to the already sub-freezing temperature. "Why don't you wait in the car?" he said.

"Where are you going?"

"I'm going to join the party," he said.

"I'll come with you," she said.

"I don't think so," he said.

He gripped her arm above the elbow and walked her to the Outback, where she joined Dee Cowan in the back seat. Lizzie glared at him as he held out his hand. "Give me your keys," he said. When she hesitated, he leaned into the car and reached for her purse.

"All right," she said. She took her keys out of her purse and handed them to him. The key ring had a fob similar to an automobile remote. A green LED glowed.

"Does the alarm beep when the door is opened?" he asked her.

"No," Lizzie said. "Not unless it's armed." She pointed to the key fob. "The LED would be red if it were."

"Sit tight," he told Connie. "And lock the doors."

He shut the door. The deadbolts engaged with a thud.

Loomis jogged through the blowing snow to the front door. He peered through the narrow window beside the door. The inner vestibule door was closed. He let himself in with Lizzie's key. Wind-driven snow swirled around him and into the vestibule. He shut the outer door. After shucking his coat, he opened the inner door a crack. Unholstering the Glock, hoping he wasn't going to need it, he listened for a moment, hearing nothing, before slipping through into the hall.

Silently, leaving wet footprints on the creamy broadloom, he crossed the hall to the living room and stood with his back against the wall outside the entrance. He snatched a look around the edge of the entranceway. The living room was unoccupied, but there was movement through open double doors at the far end of the room. The room beyond looked like a library, or perhaps McHenry's den. Taking a breath, Loomis cat-footed the length of the living room and pressed his back against the wall beside the door to the den, Glock pointed at the floor.

"*What about him?*" he heard Hubert Gasche say.

"*Screw him,*" Quentin Parker said. "*We got what we came for.*"

"*Sayonara, asshole,*" Ginny Gasche said.

There was a sharp, electrical snap and the smell of ozone, following by a grunt and a series of hard thumps. Ginny Gasche laughed, a harsh cackle that made the hair on the back of Loomis's neck stand on end.

Hubert Gasche came out of the library first, Ginny close on his heels. She had the 15-inch black cylinder, a shock baton, in her right hand. In their haste neither saw Loomis. Then Parker came out, carrying McHenry's big file case in his arms, hugging it to his chest. Loomis stepped up behind him, clamping his left hand on to his shoulder and shoving the muzzle of the Glock hard against the back of his pudgy neck.

"Freeze," he said.

"Huh?" Parker said. He started to turn as Hubert and Ginny Gasche spun around.

"I said *freeze*, you moron," Loomis said, tightening his grip on Parker's shoulder and pushing the Glock harder into the soft flesh of his neck.

Parker froze. Loomis moved the muzzle of the gun just enough to aim it past Parker's ear at Hubert and Ginny Gasche. They stopped in their tracks.

"Drop that thing," Loomis said to Ginny, tilting the muzzle of the Glock in the direction of the shock baton in Ginny's hand.

She hesitated, teeth bared, eyes glittering, evaluating her chances.

"Go for it," Loomis said. "I'd enjoy shooting you."

With a snarl, she dropped the baton. Loomis reached around Parker and wrapped his fingers around the handle of the case.

"I'll take that," he said.

He pulled the heavy case out of Parker's arms, then put the muzzle of the Glock against the back of Parker's skull and pushed. Parker stumbled toward Hubert and Ginny Gasche.

"All right," Loomis said, waving the Glock toward the front door. "Off you go. Happy holidays. Don't drink and drive."

Parker stared, goggle-eyed and confused. His left eye was swollen and beginning to blacken. He also had a nasty contusion on his jaw, which probably accounted for his stepsister's fractured knuckle.

"You're letting us go?" Parker said. The Gasches glared at Loomis with an almost palpable malevolence.

"It's either that or shoot you," Loomis said. He didn't have much confidence in his ability to control Parker and the Gasches without handcuffs, or even with them. "I hate the paperwork and bullets are expensive, but if you'd rather …"

"C'mon, man," Parker said, taking a step toward Loomis. "There's more'n two million bucks in that case. Plenty to go around."

"Take another step," Loomis said, "and I will shoot you, screw the paperwork."

Parker stopped. Ginny Gasche's face tightened as she positioned herself behind Parker. Loomis could almost read her mind.

"At this range," he said, "a slug from this gun will go through Quentin like he's made of paper. It'll be the size of a Canadian dollar when it hits you."

Parker paled. Ginny backed off, face ugly with anger.

"Go," Loomis said. "While you've got the chance."

Then things started to go to hell in a hurry.

Loomis saw Hubert Gasche's eyes widen a fraction of a second before he heard the soft footfalls behind him. He stepped to his right as Dink McHenry staggered out of the library, waving a stubby chrome revolver. Quentin Parker backpedalled in panic, colliding with Ginny Gasche as she bent to pick up the shock baton. Momentum carried McHenry forward. Ginny tried to push Parker out of the way as she extended the shock baton toward McHenry, but Parker's soft bulk resisted. She had to step around him to get to McHenry. McHenry convulsed as the electrodes of the baton touched his chest. His revolver went off with a deafening bang in the confines of the room. Parker screamed as blood erupted from his thigh.

Hubert Gasche jumped at Loomis with surprising speed. Loomis hammered the grip of the Glock on to the top of Gasche's head. His baseball cap offered little protection and, with a grunt, Gasche dropped, eyes rolling up into his head.

Ginny kicked at Loomis. He dodged, but her foot connected with his elbow. His arm went numb, and the Glock spun away. Tossing the file case aside, he backed up as she came at him with the baton. He parried a jab with his right arm, the impact sending sparks of pain shooting to his fingertips. Stepping inside Ginny's reach, he set aside a lifetime of conditioning and threw a hard left jab at her nose. She ducked to one side and his knuckles glanced off her cheek. She danced away from him, grinning, and adopted an absurd martial arts stance, holding the baton over her head, tip angled down, like a movie Samurai swordsman. Left arm extended, keening like Bruce Lee, she skipped toward him, then spun and kicked.

Loomis arched his back. Ginny's kick missed his head by inches. He twisted to his right as she came at him with the baton, swinging it down like a sword. She missed him again and bounced away. The painful tingling in his right arm was subsiding. Ginny jabbed at him with the baton. He chopped at her wrist, getting lucky and hitting a nerve. She dropped the baton. Shrieking, she spun and tried to kick him in the head again.

Her movements were oddly slow, off target, as if she were afraid to actually hit him. No, not him, he realized. Her stunt partner. Movie fights were choreographed, like dance routines, filmed in segments from multiple angles, so that near misses looked like hits, particularly when the sound effects were added. She looked scary, with her fierce expression and daunting physique, but she wasn't a real fighter.

Nevertheless, she was strong and motivated, and it

would be foolish to underestimate her. When she came at him again, he held his ground, turning and hunching to take what should have been an otherwise debilitating kick, high on his shoulder. Unaccustomed to contact, she wobbled off balance. He stepped up and jabbed stiffened fingers into her solar plexus. She huffed and sagged but did not fall. He slammed the heel of his right hand against the side of her head. She staggered and went down on to her hands and knees.

"Stay down," he said.

"Eat me," she snarled, popping to her feet.

She had his Glock in her hand.

He dived to his right as the gun went off with a crack, rolled as it cracked again, blowing a wad of foam out of the sofa. He knew his luck wouldn't hold, as another shot barked, that sooner or later she would nail him, but he kept rolling and twisting. Then there was a shot from a different gun. He rolled to his feet, hand clamped to the grip of the shock baton.

Connie stood inside the entrance to the living room, holding her Glock 26 in both hands, by the book, arms extended and stance wide for maximum stability. The pistol barked and plaster exploded from the wall behind Ginny. Ignoring Loomis, Ginny pointed Loomis's Glock at Connie, holding it one-handed, on its side, TV gangbanger style, and fired twice. The first shot blew a fist-sized chunk out of the edge of the entranceway two feet to Connie's left. He didn't see where the second shot went.

Connie fired. The bullet snapped through the fabric

of Ginny's jacket at the point of her shoulder, spattering blood on the wall behind her. Ginny staggered, then steadied herself and took aim, holding the gun properly, in both hands, clearly trying for a body shot.

Loomis stabbed her behind the ear with the baton. The electrodes crackled, and her back arched. The pistol went off, the bullet impacting the ceiling, raining down plaster on Connie's head. Rigid as a statue, Ginny toppled. Blood spattered across the pale carpet as her head hit the corner of a marble-topped coffee table with a sickening smack. Flipping on to her back, she continued to convulse, Loomis's Glock clutched in her fist. Loomis kicked at it, but her grip was relentless. He stamped on her wrist, pinning her hand to the floor. It took most of his weight to hold her as she seized, chewing her tongue, bloody froth on her lips.

He knelt on her arm and wrenched the gun from her locked fingers. Her eyes were rolled up, only the whites showing, as she bucked, head thudding against the carpet.

"She's having a seizure," Connie said. "Turn her on her side."

Loomis rolled Ginny on to her side. Her body was like marble, and she jerked uncontrollably, arms rigid, jaw working, bloody saliva spilling from her mouth on to the carpet.

"Should we put something between her teeth?"

"No," Connie said, shaking her head. "Just keep her on her side so she doesn't choke on her saliva." She took out her phone as she knelt beside Ginny, free hand on her shoulder.

There was nothing more Loomis could do for Ginny,

so he turned his attention to the others. Parker sat on floor, back against the sofa. He was deathly pale, eyes wide with fear and pain. His hands were clamped to his thigh, blood oozing through his fingers and dripped on to the carpet.

"Help me," he said, a plaintive squeak.

The wound was in the outer thigh, midway between his hip and his knee. The entry wound and bigger exit wound seemed to be only two inches apart, nowhere near the femoral artery.

"You'll be okay," Loomis said, handing him a small cushion from the sofa. "Press this against the wounds as hard as you can."

McHenry lay on his back, eyes wide and staring at the ceiling, a spreading halo of blood surrounding his head. Half his lower jaw was gone. So, it appeared, was most of the back of his head. He'd taken one of the bullets intended for Loomis.

Loomis stood as Connie finished her 911 call and closed her phone.

"I thought I told you to stay in the car."

"You did," she said, kneeling by Ginny as she continued to spasm. "You're welcome anyway."

The file case was on the floor near the door to the library. Parker watched as Loomis opened it. It was filled with banded stacks of one-hundred-dollar bills, ten thousand dollars to a stack. Two million dollars would be two hundred stacks. No wonder it was heavy. He closed it.

Ginny's convulsions were subsiding, but her colour was not good, and blood welled from a deep, wedge-shaped dent in her left temple. Loomis turned at the sound of a gasp. Lizzie McHenry stood in the entrance to the living room, staring at the body of her husband, her face a mask of horror. Loomis went to her, led her unresisting out of the room and into the kitchen. He put the file case on the kitchen table.

"He's d-dead, isn't he?" Lizzie said, blinking and repeatedly pursing her lips.

"Yes," he said. "I'm sorry."

She took a small silver pill case from her purse. "Would you g-get me a glass of water, p-please?" she said, opening the case and taking out a small white pill. He did, and she took the pill.

Connie came into the kitchen. She was pale and her eyes were haunted.

"Ginny's dead," she said.

Shit, Loomis thought, a heaviness in his chest. "Hubert?"

"He took off, I guess," Connie said.

"She told me to w-wait outside," Lizzie McHenry said, looking at Connie. "Then a man ran out of the house. He almost knocked me down. He drove away in an ugly yellow truck."

Phil Jefferson wouldn't be happy, but Loomis didn't think it would take the police long to track Gasche down.

"What did you do with Dee Cowan?" he said to Connie.

"I cuffed her to the ringbolt on the floor of your car," she said. "She's probably trying to chew her arm off."

ONE
WEEK
LATER

41

Winter wouldn't officially begin for another ten days, but you wouldn't know it from the weather. It had snowed on and off—mainly on—for most of the week, and Loomis had had to break a trail between his trailer and the plastic-wrapped, unfinished shell of his house. He'd spent most of the week working on the electrical system. It wasn't difficult work, but it required a degree of concentration that he'd hoped would keep him from thinking too much. It hadn't. He'd frequently found himself with the power drill in his hands, a hole half drilled in a stud, with no idea how long he'd been standing there, thoughts drifting, mind's eye filled with the faces of the dead, among them those of his father and brother.

"Was it Mark Twain who said being shot at greatly focuses the mind?" Connie had said in the car as they drove to her place after the police had finished with them.

"Samuel Johnson said that the prospect of being hanged had the same effect," Loomis had said. "Maybe

Twain stole it. He wasn't above such things."

Whether Twain had stolen it or not, Loomis agreed: being shot at did indeed focus one's mind, particularly on not getting shot. Loomis also agreed with Winston Churchill, who'd said that nothing in life was so exhilarating as being shot at without result. He was just so fucking *thrilled* to be alive. Still, he could live without being shot at.

All things considered, he'd rather make beer.

He knocked off work when it started to get dark, locked up his tools, and trudged along the path through the snow to the trailer. On Sunday, Connie's sister had come up from New York to look after the kids, while Connie took some time to visit her parents in Florida. She was due back later that evening. Loomis and she had spoken every day. Being shot at had focused her mind on the kind of future she wanted for herself and her kids, and almost losing Loomis had made her realize who she wanted to build that future with. She hadn't changed her mind about not wanting to be a private investigator.

Almost losing Connie had focused Loomis's mind as well.

On Monday, Alex Robillard had called. Hubert Gasche had been apprehended attempting to cross into Canada in Phil Jefferson's truck, he'd told Loomis, and Deirdre Cowan had cut a deal with the state's attorney to avoid hard time for felony manslaughter in return for her testimony against Gasche and her stepbrother. Dave Ledbetter was doing well, Bets, too, but James Maynard had lapsed into a vegetative state due to a cerebral hemorrhage and was not expected to recover.

As Loomis opened the door of the trailer, a bright yellow Mazda 3 turned into the drive and stopped beside the Outback. Heather-Anne Allen got out, wearing her red cap and black coat.

"Hello," he said. "What are you doing in this neck of the woods?"

"You live in a trailer," she said, an expression of disbelief on her face. "Doesn't it get kind of cold?"

"It can," he said. He invited her inside.

"How's Connie?" she said, shedding her coat. "God, what an ordeal."

"She's doing okay. She's pretty resilient."

"And you?" Heather-Anne asked.

"I'm okay, too," he said. Just a little haunted. "How about you? I understand you've been reinstated. How's the firm getting on without Dink?"

"As you can imagine, he left us with a god-awful mess. I don't know what we'd do without Belle. Which brings me to the purpose of my visit. Have you got a few minutes?"

"A few," he said. "As soon as I get cleaned up I'm heading to the airport to pick up Connie. She's been visiting her parents in Florida."

"I have a proposition for you," Heather-Anne said. "I may be in a position to offer you a job. Mr. Proctor has come out of retirement to rebuild the firm and has offered me a senior associate position."

"You're a lawyer?"

"As a matter of fact," she said, "I am. I've passed the bar, anyway. I just haven't bothered to do anything about it."

"What did you have in mind?" Loomis said, knowing what his answer would be.

"How would you like to be a fulltime investigator for the firm? It would be a salaried position with all the usual benefits."

"It's kind of you to offer …"

"But …?"

"Connie and I are going into the beer business," he said.

When Heather-Anne had gone, Loomis grabbed a quick shower, dressed, then locked up and went out to the car. He glanced at the *For Sale* sign nailed to a tree at the end of the driveway. He'd already had a couple of nibbles. Then he got into the Outback, backed out on to the street, and headed for the airport.

ACKNOWLEDGEMENTS

A number of people contributed to make this book better. Alan Annand read an early version and, as usual, made many helpful suggestions. So did Marc Cassini. A special thanks to the late Marybelle Singer (1921 – 2012), long-time director of the Alburgh Public Library in Alburgh, Vermont, for her encouragement and support. Anyone interested in how people come to believe they've been abducted by aliens should read the fascinating book *Abducted: How People Come To Believe They Were Kidnapped by Aliens*, by Susan A. Clancy, PhD., Harvard University Press (2005). Thanks, too, to Linda Leith and all the good folks at Linda Leith Publishing. Finally, it goes without saying—but I'll say it anyway—that this book could not have been written without the love and support of Pamela Hilliard, who abducted my heart.